Selah Gothic

INTERNATIONAL BESTSELLING AUTHOR

KAT BLACKTHORNE

No part of this book may be reproduced in any form or by any electronic or mechanical means, including information storage and retrieval systems, without written permission from the author, except for the use of brief quotations in a book review.

Cover: Maldo Designs

Editing: Cassidy Hudspeth

Formatting: Maldo Designs

For everyone burned by the church.
Burn it back.

Where I convince you not to read

I IMPLORE YOU THAT IF YOU HOLD RELIGION SACRED— DON'T READ THIS. IF THE DESECRATION OF RELIGIOUS ARTIFACTS AND PRACTICES ISN'T YOUR THING. PLEASE DON'T CONTINUE.

THIS IS A DYSTOPIAN REALITY WHERE ONE CHURCH AND BELIEF SYSTEM REIGN SUPREME, LADY OF SORROW CHURCH. THEY HAVE REWRITTEN, REARRANGED, AND ALTERED THE "VINTAGE WORKS" OF THE BIBLE TO SUIT A NEW VERSION OF SACRED TEXTS FOCUSED ON PURITY AND WOMEN BEING SERVANTS TO MEN.

SELAH GOTHIC IS THE MOST EXCRUCIATINGLY DARK AND HAUNTINGLY BEAUTIFUL THING I'VE WRITTEN. IT IS SACRILEGIOUS AND BLASPHEMOUS. THE RELIGION AND DENOMINATIONS OF CHURCHES WITHIN THIS BOOK ARE FICTIONAL AND SENSATIONALIZED AT POINTS. THERE ARE ALSO DEPICTIONS OF OCCULTISM, PAGANISM, AND SATANISM WHICH ARE LIKEWISE FICTIONALIZED AND IN NO WAY ATTEMPTING TO BE ACCURATE TO ANY TRUE PRACTICE.

DEITIES SOME MAY REGARD AS SACRED ARE USED IN FICTITIOUS WAYS IN WHICH SOME MAY FIND OFFENSIVE. THIS IS A WORK OF FICTION WITH PLENTY OF HORROR ELEMENTS THAT ARE GROTESQUE, DEMONIC, AND DISTURBING. IF YOU'RE EXPECTING A DARK ROMANCE WITH MORALLY GRAY VILLAINS AND SITUATIONS THIS IS NOT THAT. THIS IS DYSTOPIAN ROMANTIC HORROR AND THE MAIN MALE LEAD IS CLOSER TO MORALLY BLACK. I DON'T CONDONE OR HOLD TO ANY OF THE EXTREME AND SENSATIONALIZED VIEWS OR ACTS DEPICTED.

EVERY MAIN CHARACTER IS IN THIS BOOK IS AN ADULT. AGAIN, THIS IS A DARK AND DYSTOPIAN RELIGIOUS ROMANTIC HORROR. THE FEMALE MAIN CHARACTER IS VIRGINAL, HIGHLY SHELTERED AND NAIVE WHILE THE MAIN MALE CHARACTER IS MUCH OLDER, PSYCHOTIC, AND WICKED. THEIR DYNAMIC IS UNHOLY AS HELL AND MAY MAKE SOME UNCOMFORTABLE. IF YOU'RE LOOKING FOR AN EXAMPLE OF HEALED AND HEALTHY RELATIONSHIPS THIS ISN'T IT.

IF YOU'RE SOMEWHAT NORMAL, THE CONTENT OF THIS BOOK WILL MAKE YOU UNCOMFORTABLE.

IF YOU'RE A BIT TWISTED, HOWEVER... IT'LL TURN YOU ON.
YOU CAN CLOSE THE BOOK NOW NO ONE WILL BLAME YOU.

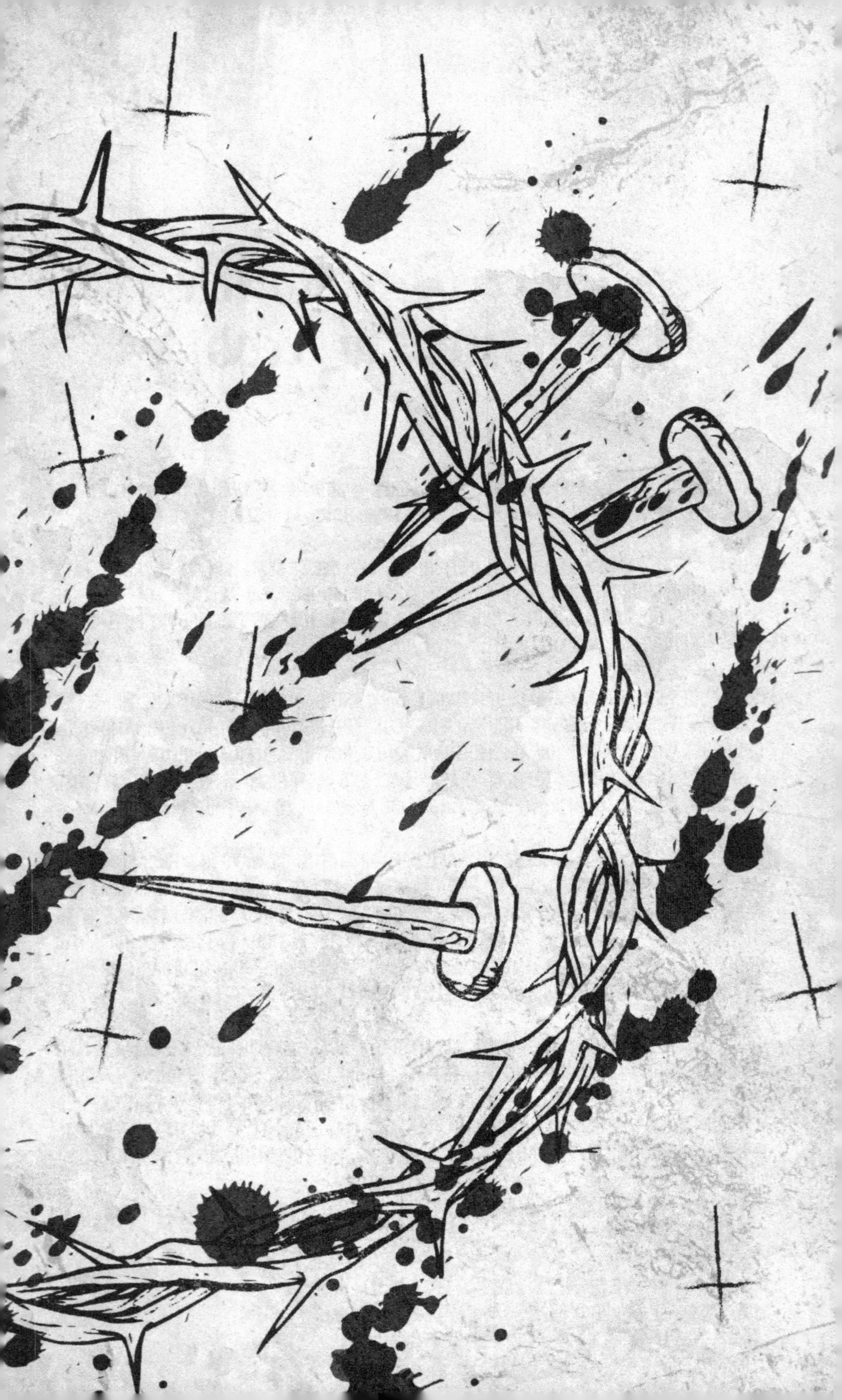

Trigger Warnings

TRIGGER WARNINGS INCLUDE BUT ARE NOT LIMITED TO: RELIGIOUS TRAUMA, RELIGIOUS ABUSE, CHILDHOOD NEGLECT, PURITY CULTURE, SA ON PAGE, ATTEMPTED SA, SUICIDE, PHYSICAL PUNISHMENTS, DEMONIC POSSESSION, HORROR, GORE, GRAPHIC SEXUAL ENCOUNTERS, AND MANY MORE.

BUT NOTHING HAPPENS TO THE BABY GOAT.
I REPEAT, BABY GOAT REMAINS UNHARMED AND CUTE.

FOR AN EXHAUSTIVE & UNCENSORED LIST PLEASE VISIT: KATBLACKTHORNE.COM

(THIS ISN'T A PLOY TO GET YOU TO VISIT MY SITE. I'D LOVE TO LIST THEM ALL HERE BUT OFTENTIMES THIRD PARTIES DON'T LIKE OR ALLOW THAT. SO PLEASE CHECK OUT THE LIST IN ITS ENTIRETY BEFORE READING)

THAT'S A LOT ON WHO THIS IS NOT FOR. WHO IS IT FOR? THIS IS FOR THOSE WITH RELIGIOUS TRAUMA SO HAUNTING THEY FEEL LIKE NO ONE UNDERSTANDS. FOR THOSE WHO THOUGHT THEIR BODIES WERE DIRTY AND THEIR MINDS SINFUL. FOR EVERYONE WHO WAS MADE TO BELIEVE THEY WERE BORN WITH SOMETHING WRONG WITH THEM. FOR THOSE THAT WERE TOLD THE ONLY THING THEY HAD TO OFFER WAS SOME MADE-UP CONCEPT OF VIRGINITY. FOR EVERYONE WHO WISHED FOR SOMEONE TO OFFER JUSTICE TO THOSE WHO ABUSED THEIR AUTHORITY. I HOPE YOU FIND SOME SMALL MEASURE OF HEALING IN THESE BLOODY PAGES.

ENJOY THE PRIEST SPICE TOO.

OH, AND THERE'S A BABY GOAT.

BY HOLY ORDINANCE, FROM THE ONES WHO SPEAK DIRECTLY WITH THE ONE AND TRUE GOD, WE BRING TO YOU THIS DAY A GOD ORDAINED ORDER.
THAT LADY OF SORROW CHURCH IS THE ONE TRUE CHURCH.
THAT FATHER BENEDICT AND THE CLERGY OF LADY OF SORROW SHOULD ALTER THE OLD TEXTS ACCORDING TO THE WILL OF GOD.
THAT ANY ADDITIONS, SUBTRACTIONS, OR REARRANGEMENTS TO THE OLD TEXTS ARE GOD ORDAINED AND ANY MAN THAT SEEKS TO QUESTION THIS IS OF THE DEVIL.
THE NEW HOLY BOOK IS HENCEFORTH CALLED THE SACRED TEXTS OR HOLY BOOK.

THAT OTHER LADY OF SORROW CHURCHES MAY CONTINUE OPERATIONS ONLY UNDER THE GOVERNMENT OF LADY OF SORROW CHURCH, REFERRING HENCEFORTH TO THEIR RELIGIOUS BOOKS AND TEACHINGS AS VINTAGE TEXTS. WHICH MAY BE ACCESSED ONLY BY CLERGY. WORSHIPPERS, COMMON FOLK, AND OTHER MAY ONLY HAVE ACCESS TO THE SACRED BOOK AND ITS GOD ORDAINED TEACHINGS.

ALL PRIESTS, RELIGIOUS ELDERS, LEADERS, AND GOVERNMENTS SHALL ADHERE TO GUIDANCE FROM LADY OF SORROW CHURCH.

ALL COMMON FOLK SHALL ATTEND IN PERSON OR VIRTUAL SERVICES FOUR TIMES A MONTH.

FOR AS ALL SHOULD STRIVE TOWARD PURITY, LADY OF SORROW CHURCH SHALL LEAD THE CHARGE IN HOLINESS BY SETTING ASIDE A MARKED AND PURE GROUP OF WOMEN WHO WILL BE CALLED LADIES OF SORROW.

THAT EVERY ONE HUNDRED YEARS ONE HOLY DAUGHTER SHALL BE BORN UNTO A CHOSEN LADY OF SORROW.

AS IS HER HONOR, THE HOLY DAUGHTER WILL LEAD MULTITUDES TO THE LORD THROUGH HER EXAMPLE OF PURITY AND HER SACRIFICE TO GOD.

THE HIGH CALLING OF WOMEN IS TO BE NAMELESS. THEREFORE ALL WOMEN'S NAMES HAVE BEEN REMOVED FROM THE OLD TEXTS AND THUS THIS UPDATE SHOWS IN THE SACRED TEXTS.

THAT WOMEN BE PURE.
THAT WOMEN BE SILENT.
THAT WOMEN STRIVE TOWARD NAMELESSNESS
IN HONOR OF GOD AND THEIR FUTURE HUSBANDS.

Selah

CHAPTER ONE

Confession

According to Lady of Sorrow, you have two lives. One as a sinner, and then you're spiritually born again into another life. "Buried with light in baptism," my dad would say as he dunked people underwater. "Resurrected to live a brand new life." Then he would finish, pulling the person back up as the crowd cheered.

I lived two lives, too, but not because I was a believer like my reverend dad. I was the daughter of the Reverend Priest of the Father Church of Lady of Sorrows. His sermons were broadcast each Sunday to hundreds of thousands of eager and repentant sinners through his televised services. He saved their souls as I nodded off on the cold hard pew. When I'd return to my room, I'd get the belt, or sometimes a wooden spoon to the thigh, for my disrespect.

My education had been one constructed by the walls of the church as a bleeding Jesus looked on from a crucifix. Instead of attending a real school, I was homeschooled to be shielded from the sinful world. While my peers learned algebra and went to prom, I learned to sew from old women and memorized the Lady of Sorrow rendition of

Proverbs 31 on being a virtuous and pure wife. That's all I was good for. I was being bred to be a wife and mother.

Somehow, I was supposed to be able to bear children when I'd never even kissed a boy. I'd just turned twenty when the priests pulled me into their offices, assessing me and wondering which old man would soon have me as his bride. But according to my dad, I wasn't ready, and I wasn't pure and holy enough. Like a horse that had yet to be broken. So, despite the lashings, the lectures, the punishments of cold nights with no blankets, or being forced to go without food and water in favor of fasting and praying for the forgiveness of my sins, I still nodded off. Or dropped a swear word.

Sometimes, I'd hike my skirt above my knees just to watch my dad's face turn red in fury from the pulpit. No, I wasn't ready to be a wife, and I'd make sure I never had to be. I had a rebellious spirit, and the clergy agreed on several occasions. I'd fought hard for that spirit, too, because I'd witnessed what happened to the girls who let theirs go. Their futures married off to balding men, forever pregnant, and the light from their eyes dimmed to nothing. Or worse, the ones who became Ladies of Sorrow and never spoke another word again.

Though I was the prized daughter of the church, the poster child to the world of purity of body and mind, I stole simple freedoms where I could. I'd found an old antenna television in the basement of the church. When I was supposed to be praying, I'd instead hook it up and watch reality TV or sometimes a rated-R movie. When the clergy left their offices unlocked, I'd sneak in to use the internet, and that was my real joy. My treat.

On this particular day in the Lady of Sorrow Cathedral, Bishop Terrance had left the door to his office ajar promptly at two in the afternoon when he would walk the grounds to pray. In actuality, I'd spotted him several times stuffing bright paper bags into the outdoor garbage cans. Fast food wasn't exactly a sin, but I supposed it wasn't very priestly either. Now was time for my quick fix, too. Bishop Terrance always creeped me out anyway. He stared at me too long, and with a weird look on his always-pink face. Maybe he hoped he'd be my chosen husband. I shuddered at the prospect.

Blood rushed to my head, and my heart beat wildly as I took a seat in the bishop's worn computer chair. Holy texts lined the edges of the dusty monitor. A verse on *prayer over sin* mocked me in cursive scrawl as I did the opposite of the verse's instructions. I knew it was sinful; I knew it was wrong, but I couldn't help myself. When I turned eighteen, I'd gone on a mission trip to the big city of Bear Hallow. The clergy had considered sending me on a tour of sorts to show the other Ladies of Sorrow Churches the Holy Daughter in person. I was thrilled at the idea of leaving home, that big, musty church, for any amount of time.

My female peers donned their head coverings and ankle-length denim skirts as they sang hymns while we entered the pagan city of sin, as my father called it. My eyes wandered out the window in hopes of seeing skyscrapers as the big, elevated church bus stopped at a red light. What

I saw instead was into the car of the couple stopped next to us. My mind flurried, trying to make sense of the scene before me. The woman was laid back in her seat as the man clutched the steering wheel with one hand. His other hand was tucked firmly under her unbuttoned jeans. As his knuckles waved, her body writhed and bucked with each touch.

A foreign sensation heated my cheeks, and I knew this must be the fornication of the world my father would preach on. It was the lusts of fallen people I'd learned about in Sunday school and witnessed on reality television. Any one of my peers would have looked away. They were better than me, purer, and more righteous. My father would have chosen any of them to be his daughter over me. They'd have done a better job at it, too. But I had a seed of sin inside me that I couldn't deny. And that seed sprouted roots that day as we sat in traffic. In the back of the bus, all alone, with Amazing Grace resounding around me, I watched the woman and studied her movements.

My thighs ached, and our sacred book in my lap felt heavy. I imagined it was a man's hand and pretended I was her. Maybe in some world, I wasn't the famous Reverend Father Benedict's Holy Daughter on a church bus, but rather just an ordinary girl in jeans laid back in her boyfriend's Honda. My hips rocked forward, and I pressed the edge of my sacred book against the apex of my thighs. A flurry of warmth tingled through me when I hit it just right.

My breathing picked up as the man's wrist disappeared deeper under the woman's pants. *What was he doing?*

I wondered. It didn't matter. Whatever they were doing was wrong, and what I was doing was wrong, too, but suddenly wrong felt really good. The feeling was so nice as it built and built, my middle curving against the holy book as I pushed the edge closer to that magic spot.

I thought I'd never stop– until the feeling snapped like a ruler on a desk. A small noise left my lips, and my vision went dizzy as I rested my forehead against the leather seat in front of me. Catching my breath, I stayed in that position, pretending to pray and knowing I'd just unlocked something dangerous and delicious inside myself.

Sort of like Bishop Terrence's burger and fries, only I was unlocking treats within my own body instead of through a drive-thru. They weren't that different. Or at least that's what I told myself to keep the guilt at bay.

But now I was no longer allowed on church mission trips. I was locked away and my only joy was sneaking into musty offices. Pulling up the search engine, I typed in the dreadful words and waited as it loaded. A black background with hot pink letters read *Mrs. Paramour*. Giddiness fluttered through me as I saw she'd made three new posts, and I hit print, hearing the old printer roar to life. Usually, I'd immediately clear the search history, a trick a troubled high schooler from our youth group had taught me a few years back when we snuck onto the computer to play online secular games. They were boring. But stumbling upon Mrs. Paramour's blog was anything but.

I don't know what came over me. Maybe it was because I knew my father was across town ministering the good words of Lady of Sorrow to the local townspeople, and the bishops were all on lunch or deep in fasting prayer, but my typical urgency faded as I scrolled the text on the screen.

Oh, to be Mrs. Paramour instead of Selah. The salacious entry that was spitting from the church printer was continuing the details of last week's encounter with the twenty-something bartender. He had glasses and shaggy hair, and Mrs. Paramour rode his face until he almost stopped breathing. It sounded pleasurable but cruel, and something inside me was dying to try it. And dying because I knew I never would. My husband would be chosen for me by the priests and bishops and would be a dusty, old, righteous man. If my plans worked, I'd avoid marriage for a few more years until I figured out an escape. Maybe I'd move to a big city and visit alcohol-filled bars, too. Maybe I'd meet a shaggy-haired man who let me do things to his face. I blushed at the thought, but the blushing and the thoughts only dropped lower into my belly.

This young man, let's call him Tyler, was great fun and so enthusiastic in his licking. Mrs. Paramour detailed. *Typically, I'm not in a teaching mood. I like my men to be men and toss me around a bit. But for sweet Tyler, I made an exception and taught him a lesson... or two.*

Analog numbers on the computer screen flashed, and I knew I had twenty-five minutes left before I had to leave. It would be the riskiest place I'd touched myself... Hiking up my heavy, white skirt, I slipped two cold fingers between my warm thighs. Mrs. Paramour talked a lot about foreplay and how men were bad at it. I'd started doing my own sort of foreplay before I touched myself, and it definitely heightened the experience. But I was in a hurry, so I couldn't waste time on my thighs. I grazed the pads of my fingers along the top of my cotton panties, disappointed not to find any wetness to play with.

Sweet Tyler looked up at me with wonder as I straddled him, positioning right over his pronounced nose. I thought I'd like to ride it next if this didn't kill him as it was. Kidding. I wouldn't kill him, but a little breath play never hurt anyone, and I needed to ride a man hard that night. God knows I'd gagged breathless on enough cocks to last a lifetime. It's their turn to suffocate on our cunts, ladies.

My breathing picked up as I pressed over the fabric, moving up and down to create the friction I knew I needed. Closing my eyes, I pretended I was Mrs. Paramour, and my palm was Tyler's chin and lips. Slipping in a finger that could be his tongue, a small moan escaped my throat.

He had to be no older than twenty-five, but he grabbed my hips with all the authority of a man in his fifties. His rough face took the beating my pelvis gave it, and he never once pushed me away. Darting his tongue in and out, I hit his teeth with my clit and exploded, knowing I was squirting and drenching his pretty-boy face and curls.

Squirting was a phrase I'd never come across, but it sounded interesting enough to push me over the edge. I breathed out a timid release, and my muscles pulsed in either gratitude or annoyance that it wasn't more. Both emotions swirled with guilt inside me. If I were damning myself to hell with these sinful thoughts and actions, why couldn't I reach the same level of bliss as Mrs. Paramour? The way she described her orgasm was–

I erased the history, stood, smoothed out my skirt, and yanked the small paper stack from the printer. Thumbing past a few pages, a few pages of this one sexual encounter, I found it. Explosive, fireworks, euphoric, the orgasm gold winner at the sex Olympics. Why couldn't I do that to myself?

With a sigh, I cradled my papers and quietly slipped from the bishop's room. Silence stretched along the cold, wood-paneled walls. Bishop Terrence wasn't back yet; he was late, which was unlike him, but I supposed that worked in my favor. My dirty secret was safe, and I had a stack of naughty blog entries to read after my enforced nightly prayer hour.

A few Ladies of Sorrow, with long white fabric draping over their hair, glanced up at me as they swept the halls. Offering them each a weak smile, I straightened my head covering and tugged my collared dress further up my neck, hiding any glimpse of skin. After my sneaking, I always felt exposed. Like anyone could look at me and see the sin I'd committed.

I used to pray for forgiveness from my heavenly father, but god never answered and was always angry, just like my real father, so I stopped praying, and I stopped trying to talk to my earthly father, too. My bare feet hit the cold stone steps that spiraled down, down beneath the earth of the church. No one had stopped me on my way down.

I'd take my wins where I could. I got to use the computer and experience a brief moment of freedom. And I had a stack of stories from the woman I wished I could be, to read later. My father wouldn't come to pray over me in my room in the church basement until later, so I had time to stash my smut under the loose stone beneath my protection with the others. It was a good day—or, at least, not a terrible one. At least, it wasn't until the splintered door squeaked and I stepped into my room.

That's when everything changed forever. It's when my sin set me on a path I'd never find my way back from—a path toward someone the evils in the sacred texts were named after.

And I'd never escape him.

Selah

CHAPTER TWO

Dear Father Silas Amorth,

I trust that our god and Father of Lady of Sorrow is blessing you and your parish. My letter today is due to great need, or I would not be pulling you from your prayers. My daughter, The Holy Virgin Daughter of The Lady of Sorrow Cathedral, is under attack by Lucifer himself. As The Word of God and Lady of Sorrow remind us, Blessed are those who are persecuted for righteousness sake, for theirs is the kingdom of heaven. *A war of this sort could only be waged against me for the good I'm doing to further the kingdom of god. Our parish telebroadcast now reaches eighty million people with the good word of Christ and through political aid in requiring people to tune in, those numbers will grow. It is our fervent prayer that our Holy Virgin Daughter is an example of purity and virginity when we present her to a bishop as his reward and holy, virtuous wife. Alas, Satan has her in his fiery grip, and she has sullied herself with profanity and worldly sin.*

This could only be the work of demons. I am aware of who you have on staff. I do know that he is very reclusive, and his methods date back to the original holy church. It is said your parish only accepts the worst of the worst, the dirtiest, foulest of sinners. Pray, demons have inhabited my daughter; they have touched her since her conception and birth, and I fear many will stray from the word of god if this is to be revealed and her purity compromised. I am writing to ask that you take her in and allow Father and Exorcist Dante Amorth perform his rituals upon her. Tales of his exorcisms are legendary and reserved for the vilest of society. She is in divine need of his spiritual intervention and needs the spirit of god deep inside her to cleanse her of her sins. I have done all I can do. You, Exorcist Father Dante, and your parish, The Church of The Isle of Grimm is my only hope, and our only hope of proclaiming god and Lady of Sorrow's healing and purification to the world when we present her as a virgin, pure and ready for her husband.

Please tell me you will take her on, and I will send her straight away.

Forgive me for the email. I am aware you prefer letter communications. I pray this reaches your island and that you and your clergy are well.

God speed-

Reverend Priest Benedict of Father Church, Lady of Sorrow

My dad didn't yell because he knew a low tone was worse. When I entered the musty room, he stood in the corner in a full white priest robe and collar with crossed arms.

I swallowed as he held out his hand and motioned toward the stack of papers I clutched. My heart froze in my throat.

He knew.

There was no point running or arguing. I could never run far anyway, needing to hold onto the walls as I did. I shuffled forward and placed the printer paper in his waiting palm. Avoiding his downcast gaze, I made to step into the bars of my protection when my father took me by the back of my veil-covered hair, careful not to touch my skin. He never touched me so as never to spoil my purity.

"Spare the rod and spoil the child," he said evenly, pulling me to stand. Words I'd heard so often over the years that my backside instinctively felt sore at the sound.

He had me hold the thin bars that squared over my thin bedding, and I knew to pull up my dress over my hips. It was the position of punishment, one I knew not to fight. And as I squinted my eyes, he rolled up the papers and struck me. Quoting verse after verse on purity, he disciplined me with each hit.

The paper didn't hurt too bad at first, at least not as badly as the paddle with the hole drilled in the middle, or the belt, or the literal rod reserved for the really, *really* bad stuff. But after ten minutes of beating, I still had tears streaking down my cheeks. When the skin of my backside was on fire, finally, he stopped. Mercifully allowing me to crawl into my protection, where he clicked the latch closed before exiting the drafty and dark room. For moments, I stared up at the bars, catching my breath and sinking into my shame.

Hope sprung like a weed inside me. Could that be all of the discipline god told my father to bestow? Was I finally too sullied, too unvirtuous for my life to be married away? Instead, maybe he'd put me to work like the other Ladies of Sorrow. I'd be cleaning the bathrooms and dusting the crucifixes. A silent woman of servitude. That would be fine as I continued to plot my escape.

Somehow, sometimes, the opportunity to flee would present itself, and I would run. I would run so far and never look back. And I'd finally escape him and his hollow cathedral of rules, pain, and silence. As I tucked myself under a thin sheet, my belly too tied up in knots to be hungry, I sorted through the possibilities. It was Saturday, the day before mass, a grand and televised event, which was ironic because my dad hated television. He would surely punish me after.

Unless... unless maybe, just maybe, the exposure of my sexual sin was enough to disgust him forever. Thinking of my dad reading through Mrs. Paramour's entries made me cringe. But maybe she'd saved me somehow, and maybe she'd carved a path of freedom for me with her escapades. I drifted to sleep, allowing myself to hope. A really, really stupid thing, as I would soon learn.

Reverend Father Benedict,

Send her.

-Grimm

Selah

CHAPTER THREE

The slimy, cold cylinder sat loosely in my two open palms. Lady Vanessa slapped my wrist with a ruler. "Shoulders back, chest to god, chin even with the floor. You know these things, Holy Daughter."

The other young adults in our church got fun Sunday school. They got to read Bible stories and drink real coffee, and had day-old pastries donated by the town's local bakeries. I envied them. They weren't the virgin daughter of Lady of Sorrow. My Sunday lessons began at five in the morning with Lady Vanessa, the oldest and most senior Lady of Sorrow. Her head covering was pristine white, and her face wrinkled except for her rosy cheeks.

"For all of your days, nearly twenty-one years, I have been tasked with training you up in the way a child should go. I assumed you'd be a righteous lady of sorrow, as your mother was. But there is sin deep within you, child. You have been sent to test us, and I'm afraid you need intervention outside my abilities."

I wondered if she'd heard of what my dad found me reading. I hadn't seen him since Lady Vanessa fetched me from my protection in the dark, early morning hours. After making me scrub the floors and shake out my bed, she prayed over me and scolded a few ladies of sorrow who were cleaning the halls.

Lady Vanessa quite literally believed that cleanliness was next to godliness and enforced that view on every woman under her charge, which was all of them in our church. Just as the sun began to rise, we walked up the stairs to the foreboding cathedral in silence. Only the tapping of cold stone under our loafers echoed.

"Why am I holding this?" I whined, my arms feeling heavy as I watched a red welt form where the wooden ruler snapped against my skin.

"Imagine you kiss a boy who is not ordained by god to be your husband. And then your wedding day comes to your true husband, what will you say to him? You won't have your pure first kiss to offer him at your marriage altar," she scolded, walking to the aged window and looking out over the crowd. Cars were appearing, so many that we had to employ attendants. The first of several elaborate church services would be starting soon. "Now, squeeze your hands."

I raised a skeptical eyebrow and clutched the fruit.

"Now imagine you compromise your purity, which belongs to your future husband, by reading pornography, and squeeze again."

Yep, she'd heard.

The banana was slowly becoming mush in my hands. "I know I shouldn't have been reading that stuff, Lady Vanessa—" I began when the ruler bit against my wrist again.

"Do you not understand who you are? After all this time? We have all obeyed god's commands and kept you safe from this pagan world. We've shielded you from mighty evils so that you may have the easiest path to purity. No *screens of Satan*, no *romantic literature of Lucifer*. And to do all of that and have you lie, and sneak, and conceal filth from a sinful internet whore. It's always the Jezebels that make it past the walls." She shook her finger at me like I were an errant puppy. "Your sin will have its day. Holy Father would like to see you after service this afternoon."

I sighed, still holding the squished banana. My mushy purity. Why did I have to be this way? How I'd wished over the years I could be the girl they wanted me to be. If only those sinful doubts hadn't burrowed into my mind and caused me to crave rebellion, fornication, and lust...

"I'm sorry," I repeated, looking down at my too-small desk. "I will fast and pray and light a prayer candle to beg for forgiveness. I'll offer it all in confession to the holy fathers."

Lady Vanessa's harsh brown eyes narrowed for a moment as she stopped in front of me, her cold fingers lightly thrumming against the desk. "I'm afraid the time for that has passed." She gave my desk a knock and swallowed, her voice cold. I'd never heard Lady Vanessa get emotional, but something hollow cracked in her tone. Awareness of how badly I'd messed up pierced my chest.

"There are harsher priests than your father. Violent, terrible, evil men. Our Holy Father Benedict of The Lady of Sorrows, your shepherd, your dad, deals in salvation." She glanced out the window. "There are priests who have been called as missionaries to the darkness and depravity that spans beyond this world. There are cathedrals so wicked and filled with demons that the walls bleed, and even the holy and sacred texts of god and Lady of Sorrow cannot cast them out." She clutched her cross necklace, paling slightly. "I fear for you, Holy Daughter. Truly, I wish you would have listened to me, and I could have spared you."

Guilt and shame pressed upon me, but as was happening more often, a snake named *rebellion* reared its head, and I challenged. "If all sins are the same in the eyes of god, how is my reading a story worse than Bishop Terrence sneaking junk food?"

Lady Vanessa shook her head and straightened her covering. "You do not have a quiet spirit. Those rules are for men, not for women. Our smallest sins will always be worse than their greatest, and the sooner you embrace that fact, the quicker you can be sanctified."

She almost made sense before peppering in the religious talk. I wished so badly just to have a normal conversation with someone—one that didn't center on my holiness or marriage or how to honor everyone but myself.

The matriarch passed me a tissue and a spray bottle of disinfectant before crossing to the exit. "Clean every desk twenty times, top to bottom, and write all of Lady of Sorrow's Proverbs 31 from memory, seven times, and then your father would like to meet with you in the sanctuary."

"The sanctuary?" I asked, but she had already gone. Punishments I could handle, consequences of my sins were the norm, but being summoned to the sanctuary...

The sanctuary of the giant, historic cathedral was reserved for prayers and confession, offerings, and praise. That grand room was for his televised sermons, for the world to watch and be saved by Lady of Sorrow's teachings. My dad never punished me there but rather behind the closed doors of his office or my room of protection in the basement.

Maybe he planned to whip me on the altar so god could see and forgive my sin plainly. My hips ached with soreness already. I hated the belt. While the wooden paddle would leave me in tears and knock the breath from my lungs, it didn't leave marks and lingering stings like my father's metal-tipped belt. One of the ladies of sorrow snuck me a pain reliever once and was punished in the same manner as I was. Her name was taken and I never saw her again after that.

Our church, Lady of Sorrow, was designed to honor men as the closest beings to god. Women were placed upon this earth to be a helpmate and to serve them on their journey toward the divine. The ladies of sorrow were our version of the vintage holy nuns, and they served the church, its people, and the bishops, deacons, and priests. The lower, younger women would clean for years under a required vow of silence.

Women are to be kept silent in the church, the priests would say, quoting the sacred texts. Sometimes, when the girls matured, they would be able to speak again, but only ever so softly, and help in the church nursery with the babies and children. But most were never released from their vows of silence. Only the nursery workers and I'd only ever heard them shush babies and read sacred text stories to toddlers as if those were the only words they were afforded.

Finally, when women reached the old age of Lady Vanessa, they were permitted to venture into the world and witness in hospitals and shelters. Their path to purity in the eyes of god was bleak, but suffering was the only way to achieve favor in my world. I'd almost envied the ladies of sorrow. A life away from men, while in servitude of men, seemed not so bad.

My path was worse.

My upbringing was rigorous and done in the public eye. Worshippers frequently stopped to kiss my veil or pray for me.

The Daughter of The Lady of Sorrow. Holy Daughter. The Pure Virgin. The lamb awaiting her slaughter, biding time until the right husband was appointed by god, to be impregnated, paraded, displayed, and used as nothing better than a servant.

That was what would please the god that never answered my tearful prayers. I was too wretched inside, too sinful, for god to ever even hear my cries for a pure mind after my painful disciplines. My only hope was an opportunity to run someday. Someday, an opportunity would present itself, and I would flee. How I'd survive with no money or real worldly skills... I'd figure that out after. At least those were my sinful dreams.

After my hand was sore from writing the thirty-one verses, seven times, on how to be a virtuous and godly woman, I stood and stretched. Looking out the dusty window showed an empty parking lot. Only a white van was parked out front. It was strange that the church would be empty so soon in the afternoon, but not unheard of. My stomach growled, and I wondered if I had time to rummage through the cabinets for communion crackers and grape juice.

Surely, I would be required to fast. Fasting left me dizzy and weak, and I hated the way my ribs stuck out further than what little breasts I had. Not that it mattered because all I was allowed to wear was a beige sack dress of white robes with my long black hair knotted and tucked under a cover. However, there were always lemon slices in my washroom, placed there by the ladies of sorrow.

They were meant to rub on my face and arms to bleach the smattering of freckles that covered every inch of my skin, kisses from the devil, my father called them. I'd eat the lemons when I was supposed to be fasting, the sourness burning my taste buds but providing some sort of nutrients. Though, even doing that was difficult, as silent, gaunt-faced ladies of sorrow monitored all my bathroom and bathing breaks. Like pale ghosts standing in doorways, they swayed and watched me, committed to holding me accountable to my high purity standards.

No ladies lingered in the hall that day, and each step toward the sanctuary echoed through the hollow, milky halls. Taking a deep breath, I rehearsed my prayers for forgiveness and pinched my hips to ready them for the hits.

I would survive, I would play my part, and cry alone within my cathedral of shame afterward. The little black bars of my protection awaited me like they always did. As I entered the high-ceiling sanctuary, I noticed the lights were off, and the smell was old, damp, and grey. Two Ladies of Sorrow waited at the end of the aisle, and my father stood at Priest's throne. Seven men joined him. Some bishops, some priests.

This was bad.

Was I about to get the rod? I'd never been struck by the actual rod of discipline before. I wasn't even sure it really existed, but there were so many verses about it I was sure that if it did exist, my father would have it in the church's possession.

"Come forward, Holy Virgin Daughter of Sorrow," he commanded low and cold as everyone in attendance looked on with furrowed and disapproving stares. "God has laid it on our hearts that you require severe intervention. You are possessed by a legion of demons. An exorcism will need to be performed. Should god spare you on the vicious tides of Grimm, and send you home sanctified, you shall be worthy once more."

The next moments, I was ordered to lay on the sacrificial stone. A garbed man in a surgical mask stood between my legs, my dad and Bishop Terrance at his shoulders, as he commanded me to insert some metal instrument into my vagina that he called a speculum. No one touched me. They weren't allowed, only looked on, inspecting that my purity was indeed intact. I guessed they could see it somehow, though I was only crying and shaking.

After that, I was beaten.

After that, a Lady of Sorrow was sacrificed for my sin. The blood of her slashed throat poured down her white robes. The look in her eyes was pleading as she searched my gaze in her final moments.

So much blood.

I had caused this.

My sin had cost lives.

Selah

CHAPTER FOUR

Grief burrowed into my ears and pounded behind my eyelids. My throat ached raw from screaming until I realized I was still wailing, tears slicking down my sore cheeks and soaking my thick dress. Someone pulled me, picked me up roughly, and deposited me into a van, locking the doors. My no's were gargled, jagged breaths of futile protest as the vehicle rumbled through the church parking lot. I missed home and wanted my little cold room and the confined bars of my protection. How could they do this? No, how could *I* have brought this on myself?

An *exorcism*, my father said. I needed not just any exorcism but a man of fearsome legend to perform it. The man of the darkness Lady Vanessa had been referring to, this has to be it. My chest squeezed with another howl as I banged against the windows of the frosty church van. The bishop next to me prayed while rocking back and forth as I sobbed.

The blood was so red. I'd never seen such a dark shade of red before. It felt as though I was going to be sick. When suddenly, something sharp pierced the top of my thigh. The last thing I saw was the needle and the bishop's thumb as he injected the clear liquid. After a moment, it stopped hurting, and I stopped feeling. My lips moved to speak, but no noise came out, and the cold thud as my temple hit the side of the glass window was the last sound that registered before my mind drifted into a fitful, unconscious state.

Red. Behind my eyelids danced such a horrible shade of red.

Something splashed against my face, and the ground rumbled. My lashes were heavy, and my eyes filled with fog as I awoke on a shaking, damp surface. Cigar smoke blew past my face, and I coughed heavily before awareness hit me. I was on a tiny boat. The cigar man nodded and yelled through his teeth. "Almost there."

"Almost where?" I asked, squinting to see anything through the mist. I'd never been on a boat before and was half disappointed I'd slept through it. No memories even remained of how I'd gotten on this jittery little thing. How long had it been since I'd been in the van? I looked around as if a bishop or lady of sorrow would pop out from the choppy gray ocean and give me a stern look.

"The isle," the boatman said lowly as if similarly hoping no one would hear him. "Ye look like a nice girl... can't imagine what ye could have done to be sent here."

I sucked in a salty, jagged breath, feeling guilt creep back into my hazy mind. The blood-stained white marble, the splatters of it— something bright blinded me for a moment. "What is that?" I pointed to the source, wondering if I was the only one who saw. Maybe it was an angel coming to rescue me. They did that sometimes in the sacred texts, right? No, now that I thought about it, angels usually only showed up to bring bad news. Maybe my father sent an angel to look after me, to make sure my exorcism took effect.

"That's the lighthouse of Grimm Isle, lass." He yanked something, and the boat sputtered to a slow murmur before clanking into the side of a dock I hadn't noticed. The fog was so heavy it was a wonder the man had found it. "Some say it's haunted... I'd help ye out, but..." he paled as he looked in the distance. "Looks as if they've come for ye."

In the distance stood two hooded, dark shapes swaying ominously. A small squeak of resistance left my throat as I looked at the boatman in desperation. He seemed reasonable. Maybe I could convince him to take me back with him, and my father would think I simply went missing. "Please," I begged. "I--"

A slender white hand reached down as if appearing from the fog, and my shriek died in my throat as it took my wrist, helping me onto the dock. The boat's engine reignited, and a spray of water peppered my hair as I knelt on the cold wood, looking up at the two hooded beings like dark ghosts in the mist.

"P-please—" I didn't even know what to beg for. To not be hurt? To be let go? Why were they allowed to touch me? Any and all pleas would go unanswered at best and punished at worst. What would punishment be like here? On this Isle of Grimm that seemed to scare hardened boatmen? I could only fathom as I shook, holding my arms, feeling fresh tears prick the corners of my eyes. The smell of smoke tingled in my nose, and music buzzed from a staticky radio. Someone's hands cupped my cheeks, and the light amber eyes of a woman searched mine.

"Selah?" She asked kindly. I couldn't speak, only shake, only let more embarrassing tears fall. "Sister Grace, my god, she's so cold."

Moments later, a thick, fur blanket draped over my shoulders, and the other woman, a traditional nun, I realized from her black robes and habit, clicked her portable radio off and stomped out her cigarette. Did vintage nuns even still exist? I'd never seen a holy woman smoke; I'd certainly never seen one listening to secular music on a radio before, either. Was this not a Lady of Sorrow church? All churches were Lady of Sorrow churches, weren't they?

"Can you walk, sweetheart?" Sister Grace asked, joining the other nun. "Here, take each of our arms." When they'd pulled me to a weak stand, Sister Grace remarked. "Did that old fisherman leave with your suitcase?"

My throat was dry and scratchy, and I shook my head. "No, I have nothing."

The sisters passed each other a glance, but their hold on my arm as I used them for support was gentle, nothing like the harsh yanks of my clothing like the ladies of sorrow bestowed. They ushered me down a stone path, and through the fog, I noticed homes and businesses on either side of us as we traipsed up moss-covered stone stairs. My shock froze in my throat as I gazed up at an enormous pointed, black cathedral. It rose so tall I couldn't see the tops through the misty clouds looming overhead. It was horrifying and menacing— and my new prison. My dwelling until my exorcism was complete. Its basement was likely more terrifying than any other.

Maybe my father was right; maybe there was a demon inside me that had taken over. Maybe the demon was controlling me then. Because all I wanted to do was run and drown myself in the rough ocean waves. Anything to get away from the exorcist, this huge black church, these nuns, all of it. A watery grave would have to be ten times better— a trip to hell much more peaceful than abiding inside this hollow church.

But I was a weak, cowardly sinner.

So, I let the nuns usher me inside.

To obey the lord's command.

To accept my exorcism on the Isle of Grimm.

Selah

CHAPTER FIVE

While outside, every archaic surface was coated in moss and sea-salted moisture, inside was pristine and sleek. Furnishings were black stone, unlike my church, where everything was shaded pale gray, gold, and white. It had been many years since I'd visited another church, and none on an island by the sea. The nuns had walked ahead of me once I gained my footing, looking back and whispering hurriedly to each other. At one point, Sister Grace was elbowed in the ribs and began giggling. Which I thought was odd. These nuns did not act like vintage nuns or ladies of sorrow.

It struck me that maybe their peculiar behavior was because they believed I was currently possessed by a demon. I guessed that would make me behave strange, too, if I believed I were escorting someone with a dark entity inside of them. Questions sprang to mind as they led me up a candlelit hallway and down a long corridor of doors. They opened a door and gestured inside. My mouth dropped when I entered a large room with a small fireplace, sofa, and a bed overlooking the stormy ocean. Adjoined was a bathroom. There even looked to be a bookshelf and a modest-sized wardrobe. This room was fit for a priest or a bishop; surely, they didn't mean to give it to me. I didn't even know how long I'd be staying, but regardless, this had to be a mistake.

"You can't mean for me to stay in here, can you?" I croaked, hearing the painful pitch of my voice and cringing. *Crying*, I'd done so much crying and wailing on my long trip over.

Sister Grace pinched her companion's arm, and the nun rubbed her bicep, hiding her laugh. "Is it not to your liking? And please forgive our manners. I am Sister Pearl, and this is my very touchy friend, Sister Grace." She shot her companion a glare and straightened the pristine habit she donned. My veil probably looked horrible, and I could feel frays of my black hair twisting out from under it. They both probably thought I looked terrible.

"It looks like a priest's room," I answered, confused.

Sister Grace looked slightly pained as she took me in. "But do you *like* it?"

Their questioning was as strange as they were, and I realized I was faint, walking backward and sitting lightly on the edge of the bed. "I like it." I rubbed my forehead, knowing I was being rude and expecting a slap for it. But when the floorboard creaked, and I heard cabinets and doors open and shut, all that came into view was a plate on the small table in the corner as a water bottle was gently shoved into my shaking palm.

Sister Pearl's soft amber eyes searched mine. I wondered if she sought the demon behind them—the reason I was banished here. "I'll leave my lantern. We have power here, but there are constant outages during storms. We've laid out some food. There are clothes in the wardrobe, though I'm afraid only black tunics and veils." She looked me up and down. "You prefer white at Lady of Sorrow, right?"

"Prefer?" I asked, confounded. When had anyone ever cared what my preference may be?

Sister Grace gave a nervous giggle and flicked Pearl's ear. The sister stood, scowling at her in a teasing way. Sister Grace smiled nervously. "Of course we know that ladies of sorrow have a sacred calling to wear white robes and veils. I'll see if I can find some. In the meantime, feel free to wear the ones we have. Otherwise, just throw yours in the hamper, and we'll have these washed straight away."

I nodded, still befuddled but taking small sips of my water. They inched toward the door as if I were a viper about to strike. They *were* afraid of my demon possession, weren't they? That had to be it. Inching backward through the door, Grace mumbled, "Well, have a nice evening, and welcome to The Grimm Church—"

"Wait, will I meet *him* tomorrow? Does it all happen then?"

They froze like dark ghostly silhouettes in the doorframe. "Meet who, dear?" Sister Grace replied.

"The— the exorcist. He... he was why I was sent here." I was sure they knew, but I blabbered on anyway, my cheeks heating with shame. They probably knew everything from my sexual impurity to my sins in lying to my father. The nice room was probably just to prove a point of how very much I didn't deserve a nice, warm space like this. Maybe it would be stripped bare and made cold tomorrow. That would make sense. That would be what I deserved.

The two nuns looked at each other as if communicating without words, sorting through what to tell me, or how much to tell me. Surely, I wasn't permitted to know specifics of what the exorcism process entailed. "Will it hurt?" I pressed, seeking their gazes for any sort of hint toward a yes or no.

"When Father Dante Amorth is ready for you..." Sister Grace stated slowly, carefully, as if measuring each word. "He will find you."

Chills rose on my arms at her parting words before they disappeared. The melody of their heels clipping and a staticky radio clicking to life and fading down the long hall.

The exorcist had a name. Father Dante Amorth. A scary name for a horrifying man.

I sat at the edge of my springy bed, looking out the window over the fog, catching glimpses through my hazy vision of the opaque waters. Every few moments, the lighthouse would scowl its light like an exploding star before disappearing again. It lulled me into a trance, and I watched it. I watched it all night. Letting it calm my racing heart and ease a modicum of my discomfort. The bed was too soft, there were no bars to protect me. The room was far too large, too warm, too opulent. Sleep wouldn't find me that night, and every time the lighthouse brights would fade in the fog, red would creep into the corners of my vision. *Sacrifice red*, I named it idly. *Sin red. Death red.* The lighthouse and storm the only thing keeping the colors of my nightmares at bay.

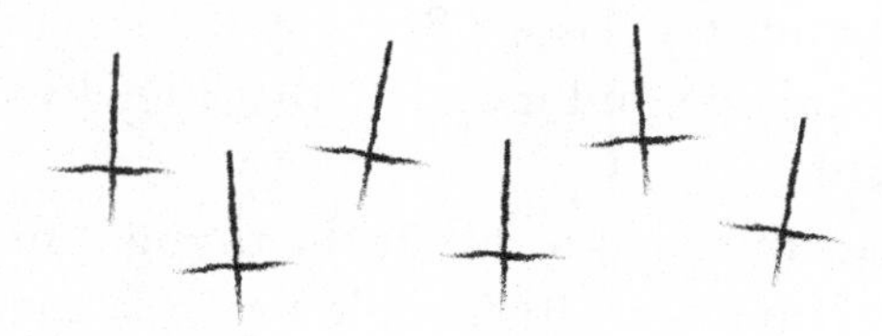

My forehead pressed to my knees, and I must have hallucinated the sound that woke me. The floorboards creaked with activity and people laughing. People laughing? Rubbing my lashes, I realized I must have dozed off. Pale sunlight sifted by thin gray clouds filtered into the space where the lantern from the night before had long burned out, though the fire still sputtered its warmth. Two male voices guffawed on the other side of my room, and I quickly raced to the knob, pulling my door half an inch ajar so as not to draw attention. Several girls in dark green plaid skirts and button-up shirts clutched books as they giggled, sauntering down the hall. One still brushed her hair and tucked in her shirt while exiting a room, and a boy came out after her. My shock and confusion froze my feet in place as the laughter of the two boys pulled my attention from all the commotion.

They traded what looked to be cigarettes. "Sister Grace says *best behavior*, so you know what that means?"

"Absolute worst behavior? Got it."

They spoke in British accents, donned button-up white shirts and brown slacks. Though everyone seemed to be rushing off to Sunday school, I knew it wasn't Sunday. And they all looked too old for regular Sunday school classes. These people were all my age. Could they be going to college ministry classes? But why were there so many of them, and why did it appear that they lived here in the church?

My heart fluttered to life at the thought of possibly getting to interact with people my own age, though surely the nuns wouldn't allow it, they'd likely keep me separate until the exorcist snatched me up and did... whatever exorcists do to remove demons. I shuddered at the thought as I slowly creaked my door closed, cringing at the loud squeak of the hinges. One of the British boys, just as he was putting the cigarette behind his ear, caught my gaze, nudging his friend just as I clicked the knob closed.

They saw me.

Shoot, shoot, shoot.

Maybe they didn't actually see me, maybe I imagined it— a knock rapt on my door, and I froze.

"Hey, new girl," an Irish accent greeted. "Care for a walk to class?"

"No, thank you," I stuttered back, my pulse pounding in my ears. A boy was talking to me. A *boy* was talking to me.

The British boy coaxed smoothly. "Oliver and I are excellent escorts. Trust me, baby, this place is a creepy-ass maze of religious artifacts."

"And that's just the priests and nuns," Oliver quipped, and I bit my lip as I smiled, leaning and shaking against the door. "Noah's right. You'd be wise to accept our chivalry." I couldn't make out the specifics of anyone's looks, only shapes and colors.

I swallowed. The nuns hadn't mentioned classes, nor had anyone come to clean or dress me. I looked around in a panic, finding a long mirror and taking in how dreadful I looked. But the door was unlocked. That could have meant I was allowed to leave. Maybe they expected me to go to this not-Sunday teaching? Maybe it was a mandatory prayer meeting... it would be bad to miss that... and my curiosity was piqued. The accented boys were right. I'd surely get lost on my own. And what if I got lost and ran straight into Father Amorth? That would be my luck. He'd probably throw me into some pit of hellfire until my demons sufficiently fled. Maybe following these boys was my smartest option.

"One moment, let me get dressed," I called back, sipping water to ease my raw throat.

"Take your time, beautiful," Oliver called back, and my gut jumped and wiggled. Two boys were talking to me, and one called me *beautiful*. This was not what I'd expected to wake up to.

I hastily squinted, getting as close as I could to the mirror, and took in my appearance, wanting to cry all over again. My face was splotchy pink, glassy gray eyes puffy from crying, and my long black hair matted into knots. Digging through the wardrobe, I pulled out the nun's black habit. It was long but snug around my waist. After brushing my hair and washing my face, I tucked my hair into the white and black veil. It wasn't so different from what I usually worse at Lady of Sorrow, only black. I swished slightly; it was a color my dad hated. He hated my black hair, and I knew he'd hate the black nun's outfit

I wore now. And the small demon of defiance inside me warmed at that thought. Black was pretty, I secretly thought.

I hoped the room would be the same when I returned and that a nun would be waiting to bathe me, because I desperately needed a wash. But for now, I looked the best I could. When I opened the door, the guys' snickering halted abruptly when they looked down at me. Both of them tall and slender. I could make out their features better up close, seeing that one had blond hair, the other light brown. The blond boy cleared his throat. "Er, I'm Noah, and this is Oliver."

So Noah was a blond British boy, and Oliver was a brown-haired Irish boy. I took the information in like a sponge. It had been so long since I'd been near anyone resembling my own age. For years, I'd only watched them on the fuzzy old television in Lady of Sorrow's basement. Reality TV, it was called. These boys looked handsome, like reality TV guys, too.

Oliver rubbed his neck, still taking in my habit. Did I put it on wrong? "And you are... Sister..."

"Oh," I realized they must have thought me a holy woman. I giggled at the thought. "No, I'm not a nun or lady of sorrow. I'm the Holy Daughter of Lady of Sorrow."

They blinked and exchanged a look. "*The* Holy Daughter? We've seen you on television a hundred times... They never say your name, though. Do you have a name, lass?" Oliver asked softly.

"Um... Selah."

"Nice to meet you," Noah responded. "Let's get to class."

Their teasing and irreverence dissipated as I followed them down iron stairs into huge arched hallways overlooking the ocean. "This is the biggest cathedral I've ever seen," I said quietly.

"It's fucking massive," Noah responded, and Oliver punched his arm.

"Don't swear around girls, especially *The* Holy Daughter, dipshit."

I giggled. "No, it's okay. Where are we going? Sunday school? College ministry? A prayer meeting?"

They paused outside a door. "Homeroom," Noah replied, his blond hair catching in the rising sunlight. "You're not at Lady of Sorrow anymore. Welcome to Grimm University, Selah."

CHAPTER SIX

A nun spun in her chair behind a desk, and a man with white, tied-back hair and a pristine priest's collar leaned against a chalkboard. The room fell silent as we entered, the woman halting her spin and the handsome priest straightening, assessing me curiously.

The woman cleared her throat and stood, speaking first. "Hello, newcomers. I'm Sister Elodie, and this is Father Silas."

My eyes widened, and I looked to the priest, expecting him to strike her for speaking first and at all—but he only stood sanguinely, like a Greek statue. He was indeed very attractive, not at all like the priests and clergy at Lady of Sorrow.

The nun and the priest whispered for a moment, casting glances at me. Noah leaned in. "They've got secrets, them two."

"Bullshit," Oliver whispered from behind me. "Not just them. They all got secrets here."

"What sort of secrets?" I asked, watching the other students pull out books and sharpened pencils. This was a real *school*. I could hardly contain my giddiness. I'd never seen a real school before.

"We have a visitor." Father Silas motioned toward me. "Everyone make Selah feel welcome."

Students turned and smiled, saying hi, a few giving me long glances— maybe piecing together just who I was. I was shocked that Father Silas didn't introduce me as the holy daughter... even more shocked when he continued with the class without outlining rules people were to follow in my presence. He didn't tell anyone they weren't allowed to touch me or speak to me. No one had watched me dress that morning or looked after my purity... this place was beyond strange, and they for sure were not following the commands of churchly conduct that Lady of Sorrow required of all of their churches.

They outlined something called a syllabus, passed out maps, calendars, and rules of the island, and acted completely... normal. There were no prayers, and rulers were not slapped against wrists when someone laughed or joked. I sat glued to my seat, observing it all, shell-shocked. Was I dreaming?

When class was dismissed, the two boys who'd befriended me shushed me and urged me to follow them around a sharp corner and up a set of stairs. I had to hold the wall and stumbled over myself the entire time as my heart raced. "What is happening? Where are we going?"

"The loft," Oliver explained. "Where we... uh..."

"Observe private conversations," Noah added slyly.

"That sounds like sin?" I asked, feeling afraid of the ramifications but also very interested in following them. They chuckled as if I'd told a joke.

"Sit," Oliver told me as we squeezed into a closet-sized space with a solid wall attached to iron bars at the top. I assumed it was an awkward storage closet of some sort, or maybe it used to be a priest's baptism room. Regardless, they were right— it was perfect for spying.

"Why are we spying?" I asked.

They hushed me as voices murmured in the distance.

"Sister Elodie's got a hand on her hip all sassy-like," Noah whispered, straining to see through the thin cut in the bar.

Oliver smacked his friend's head. "Would you pipe down so we can hear what they're saying? Christ, you're a shoddy spy."

I pressed two palms over my mouth to keep from laughing. These boys were trouble, and I would surely be sent for lashings due to being caught up in some of their mischief. But I'd also had more fun in my day with them at Grimm University than... well... I couldn't even remember a time. Something slammed onto something hard, and I jumped, my smile vanishing, as a menacing tone growled. "How could you all have been so reckless?"

Noah gasped slightly before leaning back from his perch to whisper, "He's hooded. He's always hooded. It's *him*—that's Father Dante Amorth, the exorcist."

My eyes widened, and I gestured for Noah to move. He did, and I peeked through, dying for a glimpse of the infamous priest of demons. Sister Elodie stood, shaking her head and looking harried, while another man in priest's robes sat at the desk, hunched over something. "How was I to know she was *the* Selah,

Lady—Daughter—whatever— of Sorrows herself? She waltzed in wearing a habit. Could be any of the ones we take in."

"Baptize her with some holy water, Dante. She'll be in and out," the man, I realized then was Father Silas, sat at the desk licking a spook. He was unclear with my vision but all white against the black looming presence of Father Amorth and the smaller image of Sister Elodie.

Silas continued. "She's an odd one to send as an informant. Their prized one. Jumpy, frail little thing." I couldn't make out the whole of the towering and broad dark figure of Father Amorth. I could only see the shapes of each person, and blurry at that, but I was sure I caught a shrug before Silas added on. "What? It's key lime pie day at Grimm Bakery. You know Clarence makes the best pies, and he's not had a proper shipment of key limes in years."

The dark figure moved, and he looked more like an undertaker than a priest. I gulped down my fear as he threatened lowly. "If she finds anything, sees anything, that she's not supposed to... This could all go away."

"She won't," the man promised.

Sister Elodie looked more concerned. "We'll tell... you know who... to behave."

Father Amorth scoffed. "Which one? And you think any of them will? They obey me about as well as you all and this whole godforsaken school."

"We'll keep her out of the woods," The man added, licking his spoon again. "And the old cathedral. And the town... and—"

Something slammed again, and I jumped back, Oliver catching me in his arms. "I got ye, lass." He whispered. "Let's get out of here before we get caught."

Noah helped me down the ladder, his skeptical glance coming into view when he lifted me to my feet. "Sounds like we've befriended a fellow spy. What do you think of that, Oliver?"

"What? I'm not— I'm not a spy," I hushed as they led me outside into the welcomed bustle of university students. The church was clearer without fog, and the jagged skyward shapes crisper in all their black obscurity in the daylight.

Oliver fished out a cigarette, pursing it between his lips. "Then why's the scary demon priest think ye are?"

Noah pulled out a light and lit his friend's before pulling out two more cigarettes and offering me one. I shook my head, and he smiled, tsking playfully. "That's just what a spy would want us to believe. I reckon we'll have to keep an eye on you to be sure."

I crossed my arms, noticing girls walk past. They all wore plaid skirts, had cute beige trench coats, and their hair exposed and curled. They regarded me curiously before writing me off as a new nun. The demon inside me longed to conform to them. To wear short little skirts, to curl my hair and wear dark makeup. To chew bubblegum and laugh and gossip with my friends. Instead, I was hidden in plain sight. My hair was tucked away, and my body was covered from chin to ankle. Why, it was confounding why these two handsome, albeit dastardly, boys were hanging around me at all with these pretty girls all around. I wasn't one of them, and I never would be— I wasn't allowed to be as the holy daughter.

"What would there even be to spy on here, huh?"

Noah blew a smoke ring. "Lots of rumors about Grimm. Why do you think Lady of Sorrow Churches don't come sniffing around much? They're scared."

Oliver gave his friend a look I couldn't decipher, and I had a feeling Noah wanted to say more but decided against it. Oliver opened his mouth to respond when two arms appeared, grabbing them each by the ear. A short nun who looked remarkably young, possibly early twenties like me and the boys, scolded them. "Smoking on the steps of The Church of Grimm. I am appalled."

The guys winced, and Oliver pleaded. "Sister Nella, come on, give us a break. We've got an economics test. We're stressed."

She dropped them and shook her head, smiling. I was prepared to witness their beatings, a demand for scripture written five hundred times, but she only held out her palm. "You know the rules. Not on campus or near the churches. We aren't trying to cramp your style; we've got residents on Grimm who attend mass on oxygen tanks, you buffoons." They handed their packs of cigarettes and lighters over, apologizing sheepishly, and Sister Nella looked me over. "You're the famous Selah, The Holy Daughter from Father Church Lady of Sorrow, I presume?"

I nodded. She stepped closer, and I was able to make out kind, dark eyes. "I'm Sister Nella, and I was looking for you."

"Oh?" This was it. It was time for my chastisement.

She extended her elbow, which I took gladly, and followed her down the stairs. "Let's get some air away from that stuffy old building. Stop staring and get to class, boys!" She added, yelling over her shoulder.

"Bye, ladies!" They shouted, laughing and scuffling as they departed.

Sister Nella clicked her tongue. "Always up to no good, but good lads, Noah and Oliver. Nice to see you're making friends already, Miss Selah."

"I'm really very confused about what's happening," I confessed.

We reached a long stretch of grass and vined vegetables, and Sister Nella let go of my arm, reaching out and plucking a cucumber off its vine, handing me one. I took the cold, wet offering and thanked her.

"Well, what do you think is happening?" She replied after a moment, surveying a vine of tomatoes.

"It was my understanding from, um, what my dad said that I was sent here as punishment and for an... for an um..."

She bit into her cucumber with a crunch. Sister Nella was several inches shorter than me, and from her orange freckles, I guessed that she had red hair under her veil. "Go ahead," she urged, taking another bite.

I fiddled with the bumps of the green skin without meeting her gaze. "An exorcism."

There was no astonishment in her reply. "I'm not an exorcist, just a gardener. Well, and a nun. And a teacher of home economics and theater." She shrugged playfully when I looked up. "Sometimes physical education if

Father Silas is out of town, but mostly I just let everyone have a free period or watch movies if that happens because forget running, am I right?"

I giggled lightly. "This is all nothing like what I expected."

"Did you expect hellfire and brimstone?"

"Yes, actually."

"Well, you've yet to meet Father Amorth..." She said hesitantly. "Speaking of which, how about we head to your room? I'm told your schedule awaits you there."

Sister Nella gave me another kind look up and down before offering me her elbow again. The Ladies at Lady of Sorrow used to offer me the garment of their robes to hold onto until my dad forbade it, saying that god wanted me to move slowly and without the help of others. Since then, I'd memorized my church and taken comfort in the walls of my protection. But this place was all new. It had been serendipitous that Noah and Oliver had appeared to show me around. And they were so tall and loud, they were easy to follow behind and keep track of.

When we reached my room, I was surprised to find it exactly how I'd left it. Sheets and blankets still plushly adorned the bed, a fire still crackled in the hearth, and books still lined the shelves. My white gown and veil had been laundered and folded at the foot of my bed, and a plate of steaming stew and bread sat at my small end table. No, this place was nothing like what I'd expected. Why were they all so nice? This couldn't all be real. There had to be some sort of looming cloud about to thunderously rain upon all of this, right?

I rubbed the back of my neck and asked hesitantly as Nella admired the ocean view from my window. "Are you supposed to help me wash?"

"Do you need help washing?"

I was sure my face was heated. "No, I don't *need* help… It's just back home…"

"It's not trouble if you need help," Sister Nella walked over and held my palms gently. "Though… there's no one that will be monitoring you bathe if that's what you're asking."

She searched my face, and I nodded. "Then I'm okay on my own. Thank you."

"Good," she moved to the end table. "Here's your schedule. It's straight from Father Amorth and Father Silas. Oh, they run Grimm, if you didn't know. Here, you'll find class schedules, mess hall times, outdoor activities, and then church mass hours, of course."

"I'm supposed to follow this?" I asked, sitting in front of my stew, my stomach clenching in hunger. "What—what about my um… you know… the reason I came?"

Sister Nella paused, thrumming her fingers on the wooden table. "Father Amorth will tell you more about that. In the meantime, let me or any of the other nuns know if you need anything, alright? If you like those idiots, Noah and Oliver, I can ask them to keep showing you to your classes until you get the swing of things. How's that sound?"

"That sounds nice… thank you, Sister Nella."

She gave my shoulder a squeeze and bit her lower lip slightly. "Hey," she whispered softly as if hoping no one would overhear. "It's going to be okay, okay?"

Confusion and trepidation mixed inside me, calmed by the warmth of the stew and the freshly printed ink on the page I looked over—art, history, theology, world religion, literature... all subjects I'd never seen before. Things I'd always wanted to study but had been deemed too worldly, too unholy, for me to pursue. Instead, I'd been homeschooled, or rather, church-schooled, by a solitary Lady of Sorrow. Teaching me things like how to change diapers, iron priest robes, and cook a turkey. I'd dreamt of learning what the secular kids in Sunday school got to learn. I was only ever taught to read from only the sacred texts and Lady of Sorrow-approved cookbooks. Getting to read the books others got to read, talk about the lofty subjects, and argue about politics and religious ideas as men did...

I didn't know how long I'd be at Grimm. In this seaside town of nuns, in this enormous cathedral that housed a school of learning within its dark walls, but I vowed to learn as much as I could.

Because when I left, when my dad sent for me to come home, I'd never get the chance to do this again. I'd be married soon, if not immediately, and then all my virtuous wife training would be put to use as the holy wife. My tastebuds soured over a steamed carrot at the thought. And then there was the conversation I'd heard with Noah and Oliver. My first and only glimpse of the hooded exorcist, and he didn't seem to like me. He'd seemed skeptical of me... perhaps he wasn't looking forward to fighting the demons that raged inside of me. The ones that wanted freedom, short skirts, sex, and vulgarity.

But so far, he hadn't sought me out, and maybe I could continue avoiding him. Maybe, just maybe, staying at Grimm wouldn't be so terrible. If only for just a while.

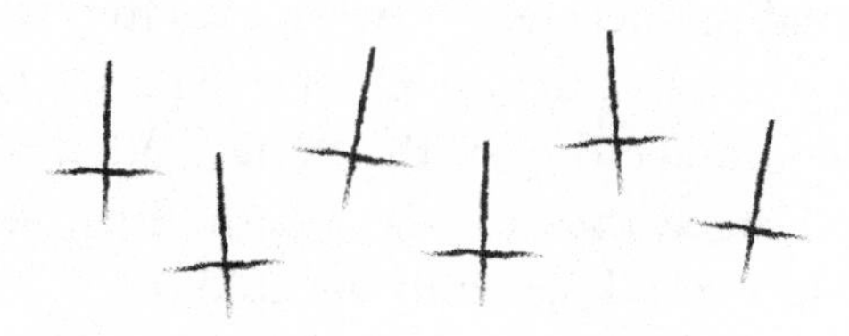

Darkness flooded into my room, and I stared at the ceiling. My bed was too soft and too high. There were no bars around me, and the space was too open. I hated it. So, I sat on the floor at the foot of the bed, leaning back against the frame, letting the windowpane jut out over my head, and somehow, in that odd position, sleep found me. I awoke early and cracked open the window, letting the cold, salty air rush in alongside the sound of seagulls and waves.

Oh, how I wanted to visit the beach. It was likely my only chance to ever see the ocean, and I knew I'd have to find a way to get to it before my time came to leave or be... *exorcised.* Would being exorcised leave me a different person? With all my sins and unholiness washed away like waves on the shore... who would remain? A holy shell of righteousness, I supposed. That's what my dad wanted; it's what the ladies of sorrow were, and it's what I would become. Father Amorth would make sure of it.

Where was he, and why hadn't the exorcist come to find me yet? It didn't matter. Though, I also toyed around in my mind with what I'd overheard him say the day before. What *didn't* he want me to find, and why did he care? I was nobody. Less than nobody, I was demon-possessed and full of sin, according to my father, the famous Reverend Benedict. Father Amorth *should* be disgusted by me, right? I wasn't excited to find out when I met him face to face. Or face to hooded face. The longer I could avoid him, the better. What I couldn't avoid any longer, though, was a bath. Stripping off my nightgown, I stood naked in the cold, tiled washroom. It felt strange not to have a lady of sorrow watching me. *Sin finds people when they're naked and alone*, they would warn. But I didn't encounter any sin as I turned the shower handle and filled the room with steam.

A groan left my throat as the hot water poured over me. There were bottles of lavender-scented shampoo and body wash, which I doused myself with. Ladies weren't allowed scents at my church, only fragrance-free soaps and lotions. Smelling like flowers was a thrill I gladly indulged in, sending silent gratitude and blessings to whichever sister placed the items in my bathroom for me.

The pads of my feet hit the cold tile, and I reached through my chill for the fuzzy white towel across from the sink when something caught my attention from the corner of my eye. Panic froze me in place as the room went unnaturally quiet. The sound of the waves and gulls, the dripping of the faucet, the sounds of creaking floorboards and laughing students outside my door all silenced as if put on mute.

Something in the air changed to an eerie cold, and then I made out a shape through the ajar door of my bathroom. I couldn't have imagined it, could I? Could my brain make out the individual, coarse black hairs, the partial shape of a curved horn, standing outside my bathroom, hiding but failing to conceal itself fully... I made to scream when a loud knocking changed the atmosphere in a moment.

Frantically, I wrapped in my towel and shakily walked out into my room, back into cool air and the bustle of activity outside in the hall. There was nothing here, though. There was no monster with horns watching me. It had felt so real. My heart still pounded. Was it possible to have a nightmare while awake?

The pounding on the door continued, and I jumped. "Selah, your humble servants await!" Noah yelled.

"I stole raspberry danishes!" Oliver chimed, and my fear subsided slightly as I pulled on my white gown and attached my thick white veil, concealing every thread of black hair. My fingers shook slightly, remembering the thing I was sure was just standing in my doorway watching me. It had black fur and horns... I needed to eat something. Low blood sugar could be the source of my hallucinations.

Noah and Oliver greeted me with sweeping stares, complimenting the white robes. I was still baffled at why they wanted to hang around me. With all the gorgeous girls in skirts, who got to listen to real music and do secular things whenever they wanted— why would they even bother befriending me? But for some reason, they did, and for some reason, they treated me no differently than anyone else.

This wasn't like Lady of Sorrow Church. I remained The Holy Daughter here in Grimm, but not in a way that made people point and stare. It was as if everyone here was like me, or at least somewhat like me. My getup wasn't entirely foreign to them. Like the boys had said, they'd all grown up under Lady of Sorrow's rule. They knew me from television church broadcasts.

"So, how long have you guys been going to university here?" I asked, taking a bite of danish and trying not to spill raspberry preserves down my white collar.

Oliver and Noah walked on either side of me, hands in their pockets, occasionally nodding hellos at friends they passed. "I've been here two years. Noah's been here seven."

"Seven years? That's a long time to be in college. Shouldn't you have a degree or, like, twenty by now? Admittedly, I don't really know how all of this works, though." I looked at the tall, blond boy next to me, who shrugged.

"I reckon I'll stay here forever," he said without a hint of jest. "Can't go back to where I'm from. Most of us can't."

Oliver cleared his throat. "What about you, Selah? How long you in for?"

My cheeks flushed with guilt. They *didn't* know the real reason I was here. Noah added, "Sister Elodie said you're touring, trying us out. I hope you decide to enroll. Bet we could all get into some trouble together."

Oliver reached over and shoved his friend. "Speak for yourself. I'm a model student."

"Bullshit," Noah laughed.

"I'm not sure," I answered Oliver quietly. The guys ushered me into our first class, and I took my seat. Being around others my age was so oddly invigorating. Seeing so many other twenty-something-year-olds in the same place, giggling, talking, raising their hands, and listening to Sister Elodie teach. I could hardly pay attention to the class because of the sheer stimulation of it all. This was how normal college students lived, wasn't it? Maybe not within the walls of a giant and multi-building, gothic cathedral, and maybe not with nuns and priests as teachers, but for me— this was the most paradise I could hope to catch a glimpse of.

Other than the ocean... which I was still dying to see. But how much longer could I get by without seeing the infamous exorcist? When would he find me for our exorcism to begin? The thought had my mouth drying in dread. The day continued with class after class, with excitement about the booming cafeteria and my cheeks hurting from smiling at Noah and Oliver's antics. They introduced me to everyone they knew, sat with me at lunch, and told me all the inside scoop on the teachers.

Apparently, Father Silas was Father Amorth's right-hand man. And Father Amorth was rarely seen and rarely spoke to anyone. In fact, everyone seemed quite afraid of him. *Lovely*. But I gathered from the guys' conversations that I'd likely see him at Sunday's church gathering, where he sometimes would hold service or prayer. I didn't want to see him. I didn't want an exorcism. Couldn't I just fade into the mass of students here and become one of them? Could I stay on Grimm for seven years, or forever, as Noah had done, and just... be?

That hope couldn't blossom within me, I realized. Grimm was where I was sent, and this brief intermission between being exorcised, purified, and sent back to my father, wouldn't last. Soon, I'd be clean enough to be the Holy Wife of Lady of Sorrow. My life would be over.

The realization had my energy fading as I left the boys smoking on the stairs. They offered a thousand times to accompany me on my trip down the stairs and to the garden, but I politely declined. I needed to be alone. I needed to see how far I could go alone without being stopped by a clergy member here. Surprisingly, it was quite far. With glances over my shoulder, I watched the indistinct, sharp edges of the church fade behind me as I carefully held the railings and followed the long stairs away from Grimm church and Grimm University. My feet hit cobblestone, which I remembered from when I arrived.

My vision wasn't the best, but my feet always remembered. The feel of the rounded stones, the sounds of the waves getting closer, and the flash of light from the lighthouse told me the waters were near. I followed the flashing as it grew brighter until suddenly, the thin soles of my shoes found a new sensation.

Sand.

As soon as I sank into it, I giggled like a child, and I wobbled forward toward the sound of the waves as seagulls squawked overhead. As I got closer, I could finally see it all. The gray-blue waves rose and barreled into the sand, leaving white foam in their wake. It wasn't what I had anticipated. No, it was so much more, unspeakably beautiful.

With an unbridled laugh, I lifted my skirts and ran forward, letting the cold water splash against my calves and knees. I kicked, stepped on hard stones, and picked them up, feeling the ridges and dents, realizing they weren't stones but shells. *Shells*. I stuffed them each into the pockets of my robes, eager to collect them all and stare at them in my room later.

When I'd nearly exhausted myself, I turned around, and a gasp fled my throat. A tall, broad, dark, hooded figure stood several feet away, watching me. The sight like the Grim Reaper himself appearing. My undertaker witnessing a moment of life I allowed myself. The image frightened me and reminded me of the monster I'd seen in my room earlier. And then a strong wave came, knocking into my back and pushing me forward, pulling me under the saltwater tide.

Selah

CHAPTER SEVEN

For a moment, everything was dark and quiet. For a singular, lone moment frozen in time, I wasn't holy, or unholy, or someone's daughter or future wife. My worth wasn't measured by my child birthing hips and ability to be a man's helpmate. As the turbulent wave pushed me down to the sandy sea floor, I was nothing but a piece of driftwood. A free and insignificant splinter now held my envy. My reaction time was dulled; I didn't make to stand or grab for oxygen like a normal person would, and right when my mind began to gloriously erase— two firm hands hooked under my arms, yanking me up with ease, breaking the trance, ending my slight glimmer of saltwater reprieve.

The Grim Reaper had come for me. His black robes floated like ink above the sea's surface. His hood concealed all but the straight, firm line of his mouth and his hard, sharp jaw. Then I realized who had me in his clutches, carrying me onto the sand—the one person I hadn't wanted to find me—Father Dante Amorth.

My exorcist.

Coughing, I wiggled out of his grasp, and he held my arms until he was sure I was steady. Though his hood concealed his features, I noticed he wore a priest's collar, the only traditional thing about his ominous attire.

His voice rivaled the power and low, unearthly authority of the thundering waves behind me when he spoke. "Deep calls to deep, in the roar of your waterfalls; all your waves and breakers have swept over me."

Confusion mixed with something twisting and turning deep within my belly at his words, words I'd heard before, I realized. Adjusting my veil, which had miraculously stayed on, I replied. "Psalm forty-two, seven— of the old holy texts."

He cocked his head, possibly in surprise. It was hard to tell. Saying nothing, just looking at me in my soaking wet state, he crossed his arms. I was sure he was about to demand an explanation for what I'd been doing, why I'd wandered so far from the church. Instead, he reached out a hand, and it took me too many seconds to register that he wanted to shake mine. Not only was I not allowed to be touched, but a man had never offered to greet me in such a masculine way. I was just a lowly girl of sorrow, after all.

"I'm Father Dante Amorth."

"*The* exorcist," I whispered, shame tinting my cheeks. He cocked his head again, and I felt he was analyzing me much like a feline would a mouse or tiny canary. The feeling was unnerving to say the least and I found in that moment the strong desire to run back into the ocean just to get away from him. "I'm Selah," I added, hoping he would go away and leave me alone.

"*The* Holy Daughter," he added my title in the same way I'd done to him. "I see you've gotten lost. I'll accompany you back to the dorms. It'll give us a moment to discuss what your time here will look like."

I swallowed, following after him but finding he didn't stride ahead of me like the bishops and priests at my home church. Instead, he slowed his pace to match mine, walking steadily next to me. It was peculiar and added to his unnerving aura. "You mean my exorcism? W-when do you do that?"

He looked down as he walked, and I struggled not to stare. He was tall and broad, large yet so concealed and hidden. Maybe he'd taken some sort of holy vow to hide his appearance, though I'd never heard of *men* doing such a thing. Most vows like that were reserved for women, nuns, Ladies of Sorrow... I resisted the urge to ask him for fear he'd strike me.

He hummed low in his throat and spoke. "Yes, I hear you've been inquiring about that to many people, haven't you?"

"What?" His accusatory tone caught me off balance. Well, and also looking at him instead of listening to my feet as the ground shifted from sand to cobblestone again, he caught my arm so I didn't fall, and my face flushed. "No, I haven't."

"No? You haven't asked about exorcisms of four nuns and two students?"

My denial froze in my throat. "I—"

"I," he interrupted coldly. "Know all and see all, Selah." He stopped walking as we reached the top of the stairs, turning to face me. The church behind him looked like a crown of black spikes growing out of his monstrous, dark, hooded form. "And Holy Virgin, Daughter of Sorrow or not, I don't care who your dad is or how famous you and your church are. I will protect my flock at any cost. Do you understand me?"

"I don't know what you're talking about," I replied, perplexed. What could my sins and punishment have to do with any of this?

He scoffed. "Keep out of what does not concern you—which is everything, including the rafters above Father Silas's office."

My heart froze, and my mouth dropped as he turned. He'd known we were spying. "Punish me, not Noah and Oliver. I'm used to lashings, and I'm owed several since arriving anyway," I begged as we continued to my dorm. Father Amorth stopped outside my room. Two boys paled upon seeing him in the dorm and did something like a bow before grabbing the other and scurrying away. Even young men were terrified of the man I was forced to receive my holy judgment from.

Father Amorth shook his head as if dismissing a thought, and I wished I could see beneath his hood to make out his expression, though his clipped tone told me enough. "You're a liar, Selah."

"I—"

"And you'll tell me each of your lies, one by one, every single evening, in confession."

"Confession? Every single day? At Lady of Sorrow, we only do confession twice a month—"

"You heard me," he interrupted again, sounding more irritated. "Each night at eight, you'll come to my cathedral and confess your sins to me. This is the first part of your exorcism, or even seeing if I can exorcise you."

"Then what?" I asked in a small voice, reeling over the startling realization I'd have to sit across from him each night and share my innermost shame, my sins. My mind flitted to how he'd punish me...

"Typically, baptism, but seems you've skipped ahead to that part already, haven't you?" He growled. I was already making him angry. "And then, if you're cleansed enough, the exorcism ritual will be performed. Now, is that enough information for you, Selah? Are all of your questions answered sufficiently, or shall I gather a few more nuns for you to interrogate?"

My mouth dried, and my back pressed against the wall of my room as he loomed over me, pushing me as close as possible to the door without touching me. But I could feel his air, his warmth, he was steaming hot and angry, and I couldn't hide the way my palm trembled on the knob as I shook my head. 'That—that's fine. I will do what you require."

He snorted, pushing away. "Confession. Tomorrow." Were his parting, brusque words, a thinly veiled threat, as he exited, allowing me to fall into my room. Stripping off my wet clothes, I took a fast, hot shower, still mindful of the creepy vision from earlier. As I pulled on my nightgown and sunk beneath the windowpane at the foot of the bed, I let the tears fall as red threatened the corners of my psyche again. The waves, the school, the small morsels of kindness I'd collected like the shells I twirled in my palms as I shook. None of them mattered. Because of my sin, someone had painfully died. Because of the demon of lust within me, I was unholy, unworthy of anything at all.

Born a sinner, cast away, and awaiting my judgment at the hands of a mean, cranky, terrifying exorcist. There wasn't a wave in all the ocean great enough to swallow my humiliation, to wash away my sins. And tomorrow, Father Amorth would learn the same.

Dante

CHAPTER EIGHT

It was as cold as the innermost level of hell, yet flies still darted around the bloodied black trash bag. Silas reached in, pulling out a tendon from what looked like a joint of some sort, it was so mangled it was hard to be certain. "You've still got that paranoid look in your eye, Dante," he chided, tossing the mass of flesh into the ocean.

I leaned against my lighthouse, watching him through the thick layer of fog that had rolled in at dawn. "You can't see my eyes," I rumbled.

"Don't need to. I've known you long enough, and I can feel your moods. They're about as tempestuous as the sea." He tossed in another severed pound of meat.

"It's too late in the season for your beloved sharks. Water's too cold."

Silas knelt, surveying the water's murky surface. "Nah, they stick around for me. They know who feeds 'em. Have a little faith, *Father*."

I scoffed, kicking a twig and watching it ripple beneath the tide. "She's fucking trouble. Lying, sneaking, pretending... I *taste* it on her breath."

Silas shook his head. "She's a scared girl."

"Everyone's scared of me, that means nothing. This Holy Daughter of Sorrows isn't what she seems."

"You don't think Father Benedict is just solidifying his investment? Making her pure and holy at the hands of the legendary Exorcist of Grimm?"

I raised an eyebrow. My brother wasn't so stupid, was he? He couldn't possibly be so fucking dense. "You expect me to believe John Joseph Benedict, Reverend Father of *The* Father Church of The Lady of Sorrow, willingly sent his prized mare for a goddamn exorcism? Are you really that ignorant?"

He rubbed his cropped, silver beard with his bloodied hand. We forgot about blood, both of us. It was unbecoming and gave away too many of our secrets. A flaw we each shared, but goddamn, did we love blood. "You're talking to her later, correct?"

"Confession each night in my cathedral, yes. I'll squeeze the truth out of the little doe-eyed infiltrator."

"Doe-eyed, is she? Funny you noticed."

I jerked the bag from his grip, reaching in and grabbing a forearm. With all my strength and rage, I hurled it into the sea. "They probably instructed her to tailor her looks to my particular attractions."

Silas busted out laughing, deep and heavy like the surf, as he smacked my shoulder. "Like I said, paranoid."

"We keep them safe," I said lowly. "We are the *only* ones who keep them safe."

He squeezed my shoulder. "And so, we shall continue."

A thrashing in the water pulled our attention as two flat

head shark fins wrestled against an arm. "See? Have some faith."

I held up the bag, hearing the blood and guts slosh at the bottom. "Faith didn't help Father Zachariah, now, did it?"

My older brother chuckled deeply. "No, it certainly did not." He clicked his teeth. "Pity when an exorcism fails, isn't it?"

"Such a shame. Perhaps Miss Selah will be unreachable, too far gone from god's holy redemption, as well."

Silas narrowed his gaze, but he knew I was serious. He knew I'd do it. If she gave me one reason, one ounce of doubt in our confessions, I wouldn't hesitate. I'd rather explain her tragic death to her father than risk what we hid on the Isle of Grimm. In fact, it may make me happy to call Father Benedict's bluff. Did he think me weak? Was that what it was? It was no matter. What these cathedral walls, these woods, and this school meant was greater than one person prying around. Hell, I might have done away with the little sullen girl already if it weren't for the fact she was always surrounded by admirers. Annoyance roiled in my gut at the way those two idiotic boys chased after her like puppy dogs. What were their names again? I resolved to find out, maybe pull them aside and reinstate the fear of god within them.

But I supposed if she were hardly alone, then other... things... would likely leave her alone, which certainly worked in my favor. I left Silas with his pets and passed Elodie, Grace, and Nella in their garden, toiling over the sounds of classic rock. They noticed my presence and went silent, pausing their joking before Elodie spoke. "I suppose you want to know about the girl?"

Obviously.

"Right," she added after a moment. "She's a bit strange, wildly sheltered, but not unlike what we'd expect. Not unlike most of them." She clipped a tomato off a vine.

Nella flicked me a gaze but didn't stare long. Trepidation. They feared me, too. Good. Fear was easy, and fear was manageable. Fear was wise. Even god said that the fear of him was the beginning of everything. "She didn't like the room."

"Oh, the accommodations at Grimm are not fit for religious royalty?" I huffed. I knew it. I knew she was a lying little brat.

"I don't know that that's the case," Elodie argued. "She seems genuinely terrified."

Grace cocked her head. "Didn't Nella say she asked for someone to help her bathe? Like a lady in waiting? This girl is likely so spoiled that this place looks like a peasant town."

Though they couldn't see it, I rolled my eyes, exhaling. "That's all I needed to know. But watch those boys that are hanging around her."

They assured me they would as I avoided the main entrance, where the kids loitered and joked. Instead, I followed the stone path to the more dilapidated side of the cathedral. This was my side, where my sanctuary resided. It was old and archaic, much like I was, and no one ventured here. It was where I took my prey, where some begged for their lives, where some found their lives again. But the latter were few and far between. *Which would Selah be?* I wondered, sulking into the dusty light of the red stained glass. A breath of relief left my lungs as I knelt beneath the crucifix. My crucifix. My church. My place of worship where blood stained the vintage seaside wood. So much beautiful blood.

I wondered what Selah's looked like. If it were bright crimson or dark burgundy. If perhaps it matched the sinner's flush of her cheeks when I called her on her vicious lies. Would she bleed quickly or with a slow, pattering drip? Cracking my neck to relieve the tension, I prayed, and took to my post in the confessional. A tiny, coffin-like box with thin black ornate bars separating holy man and sinner. Bars I could reach through if needed, bars that could bend if I wanted. Oh, I couldn't wait to receive Selah's offering.

It was confession time.

Time to receive her many sins.

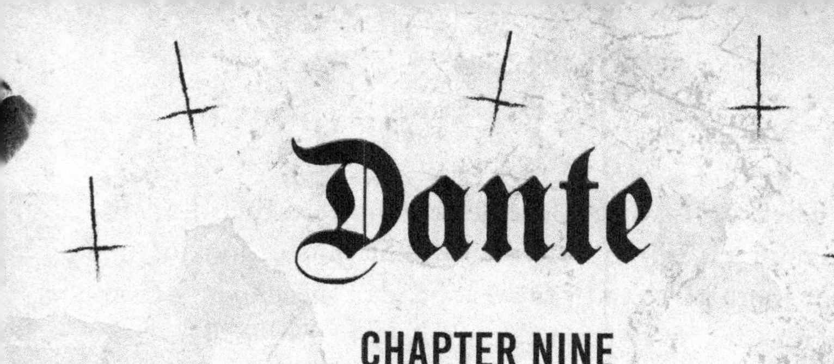

CHAPTER NINE

The thick aroma of sulfur mixed in the dense air as the struck match touched the candle wick. My prayer, my offering the fruits of my demonic labor to a god that rightfully never answered me. It was my prayer that god would continue to look away, to ignore what I was doing in the shadows here at the Isle of Grimm. A petition, a begging, that god would someday mercifully cast me to hell where I knew I belonged. I never anticipated that in becoming an exorcist, I would become the very thing I sought to banish, to cast out. Yet here we were.

And the eyes of god flickered like the dancing candle, sending an angel to assess me. I believed Selah was sent to watch me, to notice what had been done here with the gifts and curses I'd been given. Though she may not be informing god, she was a plant, a spy sent from the most mighty church in history.

The Lady of Sorrow Ministries and their Reverend Priests were luminaries in my community of holy ones. They were the standard of worship, purity, and sanctification. Through Father Benedict's sermons, he urged even the common man and woman to be as righteous as their clergy.

Their nuns wore white and committed their lives to becoming ladies of sorrow. From the outside looking in, they seemed blessed by the very hand of the almighty. God didn't look away from the ministry of Father Benedict but rather watched on with seeming joy and pride until someday deciding to launch their holy daughter upon my stormy sea gates. Though we here at Grimm were the ones picking up the pieces of the children they failed, weren't we? We were the exterminators of their sins, but they wouldn't acknowledge that, would they?

Kneeling before the candle flames, I felt my anger rise in my chest and burn as if a small inferno raged inside me. The war within my psyche was not one of flesh and bone but of soul and terror. It had always been present, even when I took my holy vows to become a priest. It had been there, gnawing at my mind even as I accepted the calling to become an exorcist. But after the *incident*... it was uncaged. Now, the beast was a living, breathing, physical entity foaming at the mouth for blood and victim screams.

Somewhere in the corners of my priesthood, I desired to please god if even pleasing him meant not bothering him too much. Offering him what I could with the small lot I'd been afforded. That holy priest, *Father Amorth*, whispered prayers and burned incense jars, saying, "Purify this maiden visitor and send her on her way. Show her god's love and take this as a lesson in humility." He was probably right— he usually was.

And then, in the other corner of that same tiny house built of falsehoods was the other part of me... the opposing counterpart to a priest. A demon of my own making and claiming... *Dante*. And he wanted to protect what was his from any intruder. Snarling and hissing, he coaxed, "Destroy her. Rip her to shreds, feast on her screams, and bathe in her blood. Show the *television priest* he made a grave mistake in thinking he could enter our gates as he keeps his locked tight."

Who would win? I didn't know, couldn't know until I spoke with her more, which I hated. The uncertainty of not knowing what this newcomer would inspire in me... I knew with Father Zacharias. The moment he knelt in the very confessional I now awaited the holy daughter in, I knew he would bleed for his sins. He sought absolution, and I ordained to give it to him, though not in the manner he requested. In a much slower, painful way... and now the holy father was the most useful in his death than he'd ever been in his miserable life— but providing sustenance to the sharks below my lighthouse.

Perhaps Selah would join him.

Perhaps I'd find her dull and predictable, order the nuns to pack her up and send her back home in the dead of night.

Only one of those options excited me.

The rusty hinges of the confession door moaned and shut when suddenly she was before me. White veil pinned perfectly in position, her hands folded sanguinely in her little lap, eyes downcast like a good and devoted lady of sorrow. The impeccable, holy daughter, sitting across from me, separated by thin little bars that would offer her only the illusion of safety. The space was tiny and confined, and the claustrophobia added to the psychology of uncomfortability. Manipulating people into confessing more and more, if only to ease some of their rising discomforts, if only to escape the small box with the hooded priest.

But something about this girl immediately struck me as odd—a presence different from any of the hundreds, thousands, who'd sat in her place. Selah wasn't agitated by the close quarters, the casket-sized space, or the low ceiling with dim, almost imperceivable light that filtered through the old wood's cracks. I was sure it wasn't the nicest confessional she'd seen. It wasn't white, like everything I'd heard of Lady of Sorrow's furnishings. There were no gold detailing or diamond-encrusted crucifixes on the walls.

Yet somehow, she exhaled, her shoulders relaxed, and the feeling of calm danced over my tongue. Human emotions scarcely surprised me, and I found myself wanting to know more...

"Forgive me, Father, for I have sinned," she said in that low, delicate voice.

The growl in my throat was involuntary, and the demon rustled with unsavory desires.

No, fucking no.

Her long black lashes fluttered in acknowledgment, but she didn't look up. Didn't try to wonder at what I concealed behind the mask of my monk's hood. It was typical of my shepherding style that I would stay silent in confession: a quiet judge, a listening presence. But hell, I felt *compelled*. Compelled by the spirit of Christ or the spirit of Satan, that remained unknown.

"Tell me what you think of my cathedral," I ordered, my voice gruff with suppressed want and curiosity.

She twiddled her thumbs, still looking down. "To be honest, Father Amorth, I feel like I've taken my first breath in ages here."

Her response was like being hit with a cool spring saltwater wave. How *interesting*. "There is no trace of the finery you're accustomed to. My cathedral has weathered a multitude of storms and has the appearance to prove it."

Selah sucked in a small breath. "I like storm-weathered things... and I like your confessional."

I gritted my teeth, noticing a single strand of black hair looping out above her forehead. Black hair against that pale, moonlight skin and those gray, cloudy eyes? *Fuck me.*

"Sexual sins," she said after a brief pause, stunning the words in my throat.

"What?"

"My... confession, father."

And if I didn't know I was a depraved, demonic son of a bitch before, I knew it when my cock hardened under my black priest robes. Those words on her pouty little berry-tinted lips calling me father. And my reply was for myself, not for god or her absolution when I responded. "Describe them to me. Describe them in detail, leaving nothing out."

Her chest rose and fell a little faster as a slow pink crept along her cheeks. "Yes, father."

My cock twitched. Oh, this was so gloriously fucked up, but the intrigue was so goddamn divine.

"I suppose the impure thoughts began around my nineteenth birthday. On a ministry outing, I witnessed... a woman being touched by a man. The sight sent a demon to inspire me to try something similar."

"And did you? Did you allow the demon to tempt you?"

"Yes."

"Tell me how."

She swallowed. "There was a book of sacred text in my lap. I moved it against me until the feeling grew and then lessened a bit. Though, I felt such guilt that I did not try doing that again—"

"Show me."

"W-what?" Her eyes flicked up then, but they weren't frightened. They matched my own intrigue. They dared me to cross the lines with her.

"To assess your sin and forgive you, I need to see exactly how you defiled the holy word of god. There is a sacred book under your seat. Now, repeat what you did while witnessing an act of fornication."

Not taking her eyes off me, she did as she was instructed and plucked the old book from under her tiny perch, placing it in her lap. If she'd argued, if she'd cried or seemed uncomfortable, would I have allowed her to pass on this command? No, no, I fucking wouldn't have. But to make my life easier, she pressed the book's edge atop the skirts of her upper thighs. "I just... moved it like this." She imitated briefly.

I needed a very large book to put in my lap to hide my growing erection. The holy priest in me admonished that I end it there. But the demon...

"Keep going. Show me what happened when you kept going. Because you didn't stop, did you? No, you desecrated god's and Lady of Sorrow's holy word, didn't you?"

Her lips parted slightly as she nodded, pressing the book harder and flicking her wrist, making it move. I imagined it was the length of my cock she was grinding against and not the spine of a sacred text. "Yes, father," she panted, cheeks reddening.

The air in the confessional hung heavy with want, and my own desire was to pump my dick as I watched her. What a naughty little virgin nun she was. "And what did you imagine as you did this sinful act?" I feared my breath betrayed my want as I watched. Selah's hips slowly rocked upward to meet the binding, seeking more traction, more relief.

"I imagined I was that girl," she said breathlessly. "And that man's hand was down my pants and touching me, father. Please forgive me."

Motherfucker.

"Close your eyes, Selah, and keep going until you achieve the same feeling as before. Do not open your eyes, do you understand?"

"Yes, father."

Reaching under my robe, I freed my aching cock. I couldn't help myself, couldn't stop. The demon was winning. I'd spent all but twenty minutes in this wooden box with the holy daughter, and she was bringing out *my* demon when I was supposed to be bringing out *hers*, wasn't I? Perhaps I was. Perhaps we both were. I watched her softly closed eyes and her furrowed brows, her pants coming through parted lips, and I gripped my throbbing member hard. Jolting my fist up and down, easing my precum down my shaft, and imagining how wet her tight little cunt was under all those layers.

So many layers meant to hide her away from the world, and I found myself smelling her arousal and wanting nothing more than to rip apart the bars separating us and bury myself inside her until she bled and squealed. God, how the evil entity that I was wanted my dick coated in her virgin blood. That's what I imagined as I watched her hips rock. I listened to her little whimpers and heavy breathing and imagined my precum was her blood dripping down my length, coating me. I imagined my fist was her tight walls gripping me, milking me, begging me to fill her.

And when she sharply inhaled, her release fluttering to the surface, my own exploded in my palm. "Keep your eyes shut," I said, clenching my jaw so tight I was sure I'd break a tooth.

"Yes, father," she panted softly, leaning back and biting her lip.

I wiped my release on a prayer cloth beneath my seat and fought to compose myself. "You can open your eyes." Thank god she couldn't see my face. "Hand me the sacred book you've now ruined."

With trembling hands, she obeyed, sliding it between the bars. "You may go and return tomorrow evening."

She tried in vain to search for my expression and looked as if she wanted to say something, but didn't. "Yes, father."

When she stood, I wrestled the urge to come with her, to escort her to her room. She'd surely need a break from me after what I'd just made her do. "Selah." She halted in the entryway of the confessional, not looking at me.

"For that sin, you are forgiven."

Her shoulders eased slightly, and I thought I made out a small, faint smile along the perfect line of her lips.

"Thank you, father."

When she was out the door, I licked the spine of the holy book.

Selah

CHAPTER TEN

Shame, unease, guilt, and regret had followed me like an unwelcome shadow my entire life. They trailed behind me like the veil I wore. I hid them under my robes and tucked my sins away like folded pages in my holy books. But the strangest thing happened after I departed Father Amorth's confessional.

My sins didn't follow me out.

Maybe that was his gift as an exorcist. Maybe he was taking my sins away... because the comfort and ease I felt with him inside his cathedral, in his confessional, was a peace that I hadn't ever felt with a holy man before. When he told me I was forgiven— I believed him.

Though what I did... what I'd shown him... my sexual impurity and disgrace. His request to watch me reenact it would have appalled me if it had been anyone else. But something twisted deep within me when he'd demanded it. Something maybe a little wrong. But oh, I saw his hands... I saw them up close.

They were nothing like my dad's hands or the puny, soft hands of the priests at Lady of Sorrow. Father Amorth's hands were rough and worn. The veins protruding along the long and wide mass of them. I couldn't see his face, but I imagined he was handsome, and I knew he was tall. Through the confessional bars, I thought I could make out the hard line of his jaw and the dotting of a salt and pepper five o'clock shadow. He had to be around my dad's age, but his stature and presence were so much greater, grander... *darker.*

And when he asked to watch my sin... I'd wanted to show it to him.

I wanted to show him more.

I hoped he would ask for more.

Not only for the feeling of forgiveness but for the sheer thrill of it. The act and sensation of doing such an obscene thing in front of someone was unlike any other. Maybe the ocean air was messing with my head.

I'd just removed my veil when a knock rapt at my bedroom door. Noah stood clutching a cafeteria plate and rubbing the back of his neck. He looked me over as I held my veil over my head, too busy to reattach it before I opened the door, but not wanting to compromise my purity by showing him my hair. Which in that moment, I realized how absurd that was after I'd just touched myself with a *holy book* in front of a blessed exorcist priest.

"Hi, Noah," I squeaked.

"You're in one piece still," he smiled weakly. "Oliver and I heard you had to go meet with Father Amorth tonight, and I didn't see you at dinner, so I got worried—"

"I'm okay," I said, dying to close the door. Could he see my sex-sins all over me? No, I was forgiven... Right?

Noah eyed me with slight skepticism. "Well, I saved you some dinner with an extra roll and cookie."

I thanked him and accepted the tray one-handed while holding my veil. "I better go," I urged, though it seemed as if he had something else to say.

"So." He put his foot in the door before I could close it. "You'll tell us tomorrow, right? About what confessional with the exorcist was like?"

"Sure. Yes, I will."

Something tightened in my throat. There was no way to share without lying, which was also a sin, but I couldn't tell them what actually happened. And why did they want to know so badly? They'd been around Father Amorth longer than I had. Surely, they had more knowledge about his practices than I could provide. But then again, he did seem to be a complete mystery, so maybe not. I guessed I couldn't blame them for being curious, and I wasn't eager to pass up friends, even if I'd only known them briefly before I had to leave. Before my life was truly over.

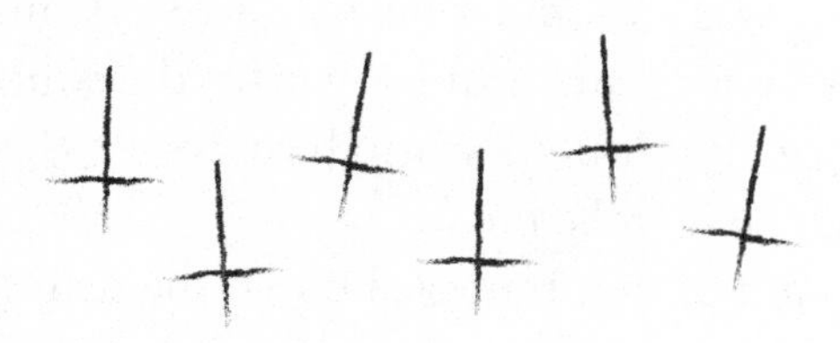

A thunderstorm in the dorm hallway woke me up at three in the morning. At least, I think it was the number three that was blinking in the ominous, too-bright red alarm clock on my nightstand. I pulled my forehead from my knees, where I still slept under the windowpane at the foot of the bed. My window was cracked; I needed to close it, or I'd get wet. In my delirious, half-awake stupor, I stood to shut it, and only bright white moonlight greeted me. It washed the waves in crimson, illuminating the sticks of washed-up wood and seaweed. They looked like heaps of dead bodies. The ocean looked like dark blood. That scary, scary shade of red... and there wasn't a thunderstorm to be seen.

Wait, the storm was in the hallway.

Wait, *the storm was in the hallway?*

Rumbles of movement like a stampede of horses trampled across the creaking wood. Down the hall, it faded until a small pause, and louder and louder, it grew. As if a race was happening, as if the stampede were waiting for one of us in the dorm to open our door.

My eyesight was poor at a distance, though fine enough up close. I don't know why, but curiosity and fear pulled me to a slow stalk toward the door. The stampede had faded. It was on the other side of the hall. Though it was so loud, I heard no voices, no squeaks of hinges or students inquiring after the sound. Had I imagined it all? Could a storm have blown through as I slept? Maybe it woke me up and—

The sound of rain trampled down the hall toward me again, and I froze, my ear to my door, desperate to make out a sound of anything—anything to explain what I was hearing. My mouth dried. Every hair on my body seemed to erect and freeze while my heart sputtered in my chest so quickly that pulsating spots began to form in the corners of my vision. I clasped my palm to my mouth, willing my breathing to hush its ragged pace. Too loud, I was being too loud.

And then, as the sound galloped closer, closer, louder, louder— it stopped.

It stopped outside my door.

I pulled myself back, trembling, and knelt to inspect the half an inch worth of crack between the hall and my door. Something wide and dark blocked the dim orange light. It was standing outside my room.

Not shoes. Not feet.

Not rain. Not thunder.

I slapped my hand to my mouth to cover my scream, but it was too late.

Hooves.

They were hooves standing outside my door.

And I was screaming.

Just then, someone grabbed my arms and shook me, saying my name over and over. My throat was raw from screaming when I finally peeled my eyes open. Sister Grace held my face in her palms, her expression etched with concern. "Selah, darling, you were having a nightmare."

I sat up on a soft surface, blankets tucked around my sides. "No," I argued, confused. "There was something outside the door in the middle of the night. Walking— running up and down."

"Just me, I'm afraid. I pray and burn incense at the witching hours, dear. I should have told you that."

"No," I shook my head. It couldn't have been. "And the bed," I kicked off the blankets. "I never sleep—" I stopped myself before telling her that I never once have slept in a real bed. That this bed felt so wrong in all its soft openness that I'd been sleeping under the window all week.

"What's wrong with the bed, love?" Sister Grace tucked my hair behind my ear in a gentle, motherly movement. She rubbed my arms, and her touch calmed me. The ladies of sorrow never touched me unless it was to strike my palms with a ruler or harshly adjust my clothing. But the sounds... the hooves.

Was it all a dream?

Maybe I'd somehow gotten myself to sleep in the bed the last night. Though I distinctly remembered tucking myself into my perch at the foot of the bed. I remembered the hard bed frame pressed against my lower back. I shook my head as if I could erase the muddled thoughts and confusion. "Nothing. I guess, I guess it was just a vivid bad dream."

Sister Grace gave my arm a soft squeeze. "I'll anoint and pray over your room today. Would that be okay? We'll cast the evil right out," she smiled, moving to my wardrobe and pinching a veil.

I nodded, my breathing steadying as I took a small sip of lukewarm water.

"Selah," she asked quietly, looking over the clothing in my wardrobe. "Did you take your holy vows already?"

"To be a lady of sorrow?"

"Or their Holy Daughter, or a nun, for that matter?" My brows furrowed with confusion as I shook my head, and I watched as her hand moved to the hairbrush on my table. It sat by my veil and white garb. "May I ask why you dress as one, then?"

My words fumbled out. "It's just always been what's expected of me. The clergy said it most honored god and kept me pure."

"Do you enjoy it?"

"No one's ever asked me what I enjoy," I answered quietly, looking down at my toes.

Sister Grace sat next to me, holding her hairbrush. "Well, I quite enjoy braiding hair, and I would just love to braid yours. May I?"

"Okay," I replied, turning my back to her as she did a little happy dance. A small smile broke my face. "You're very kind for a nun."

Sister Grace let out a giggle and ran her fingers through my hip-length hair. "You're very cute for a holy daughter."

"Thank you. No one's ever called me *cute* before, either."

She was quite a moment, brushing my hair tenderly. "We all heard when your mother passed during your birth. I am very sorry. You know... she used to be the songwriter of Lady of Sorrow. It was her gift from god, they said. We sing one of hers here, a song we learned long ago... We have spoken it every full moon."

My chest constricted. How could that be? I missed my mother then, and I had never truly missed her before. I didn't even remember her. There were no photos of her and no mention. She was a stranger. Her vows were so heavy she forfeited her name. It was ridiculous, really, that I didn't know my own mother's name. Though to be nameless, voiceless, and to give birth to a holy child was the highest honor a woman could attain at Lady of Sorrow.

How sad she must have been to write songs and not be afforded a voice to sing them. God and Lady of Sorrow were both so cruel, it seemed. But I don't think that was a thought I was allowed to have.

"Are you saying that you believe she was... she was like you, like the sisters here?"

"It's certainly possible."

The thought warmed something within me. Could my mother have been a rebellious spirit like me? "I have a made-up memory of sitting on her lap as a child, even though it never happened. I wish I could have met her," I said softly. "Or knew her name, but knowing that... it helps. I would like to hear her song sometime."

"You will," she replied, giving me a sideways glance. "You know, when she became the holy wife, she disappeared from the broadcasts, and we didn't see or hear of her again... until the clergy at Lady of Sorrow announced her death and your birth."

How fitting that my birth announcement would be flanked by a death announcement. Over the years, I'd built up my own idea of my mother. A fantasy in my mind of who a mom would be if I had one. She would have braided my hair, I decided then. When I didn't say anything else, she thankfully changed the subject. "Now, should I pin your veil or..." Standing, she swirled, her own veil and skirts fanning out. "Care to live on the wild side and rock your superbly, beautifully French braided hair, miss?"

I giggled, running my palms over the two ropes of black hair that hung over my shoulders. "I won't get in trouble?"

"With me or with god?" She asked, pinching her cheeks in the mirror.

"Or worse— Father Amorth," I replied. Sister Grace looked at me with wide eyes before flinging a hand to her chest and doubling over with laughter. The sound made me giggle. I'd never heard a nun or lady of sorrow laugh before, not ever. She dried her eyes, heaving for breath.

"Selah, darling, I like you. And you are free to be *you* here." With jolly pink cheeks, she departed, leaving me to brush my teeth and pull on my white robes. And when I walked out into the hall, my hair flowed down my back behind me. The sensation was exhilarating, and Noah and Oliver clapped and whistled, making me blush and laugh. As they sauntered off, waiting for me to follow, something caught my attention, and I knelt to inspect it.

At the doorway to my room was a coarse, thick, two-inch strand of black fur. And despite my newfound feeling of veil-less freedom, unease trampled like a rainstorm of hooves and fur through my thoughts for the remainder of the day.

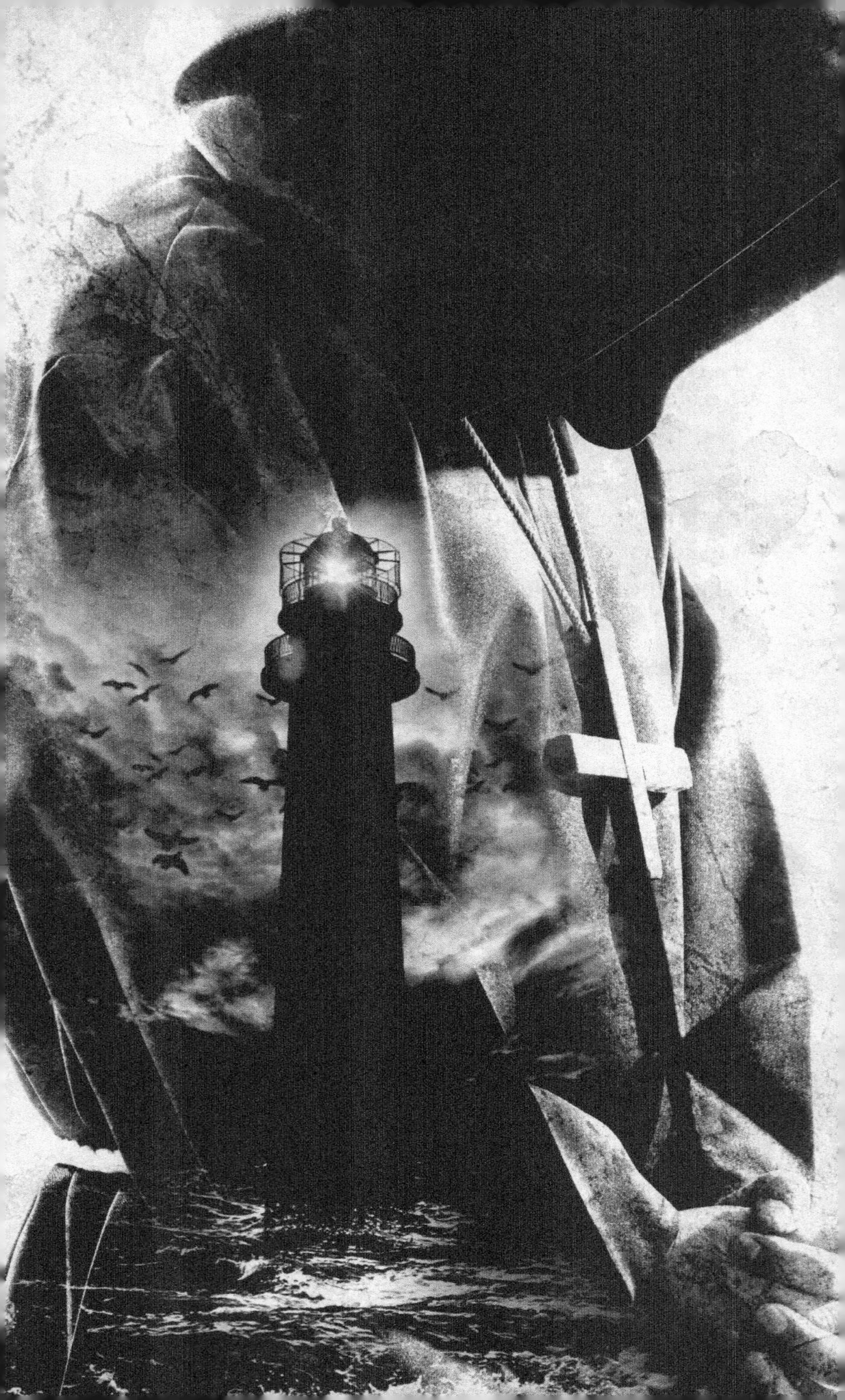

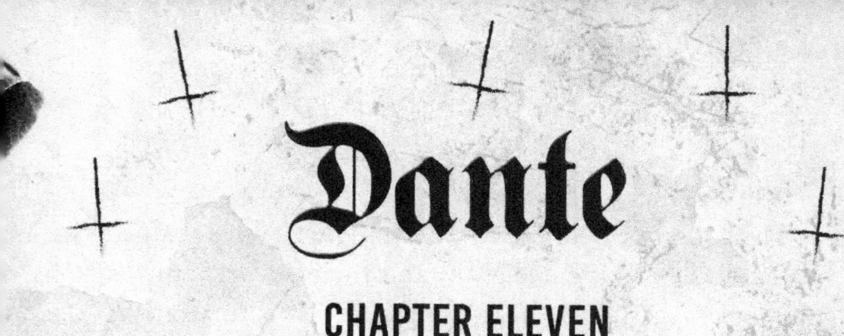

CHAPTER ELEVEN

The boatman was commanded to only arrive under the cover of fog. There were many rules we were supposed to follow that we'd abandoned slowly over the years. First, it was one student, then ten, and now nearly a hundred. To keep our operations a secret was a choreographed dance. Though, the kids in their twenties who came here weren't exactly streetwise. None of them questioned authority or looked twice when something was amiss or if someone disappeared. They were too stunned with gratitude, and I didn't blame them for that. Though, I wasn't sure of my course of action if one of them stumbled upon something they shouldn't.

Grace appeared next to me on the dock, her silent presence steeped in judgment. She folded her hands within the long sleeves of her nun's habit, watching the speedboat's rattling approach. "He knows to wait," she admonished.

"Rain in the forecast all of next week. I supposed he didn't want to contend with the waves," I replied lowly, feeling the press of rage as the passenger came into view.

"Is this one yours or ours?" Grace asked, focusing on the boat.

"Oh, are the sisters hungry?"

The corner of her lip curved. "Starving." Waves lapped at the dock, shaking it slightly, and I felt the prick of the passenger's fear as the boat stopped. The boatman never got out, always beaded with sweat. We wouldn't harm him, but I supposed he didn't believe that, not with what he'd seen. Couldn't blame him.

"Aren't you?" Grace asked lowly.

"Aren't I what?"

"Hungry, Father."

My demon rattled his chains behind my skin as I looked down at the pathetic motherfucker shaking on his way out of the vessel. Typically, my palms would be aching, my fury boiling, the bloodlust unfurling like a viper set to strike. But instead of those murderous thoughts I held so dear... my mind replayed Selah's little hip thrusts. Those berry lips parted and slowly panting. She didn't know how to please herself. Could only guess at the sensations but had no knowledge of where to press her little fingers.

I knew where.

I knew exactly what to do to make those tiny breaths voracious moans.

To use her purity veil as a cloth for wiping my cum from her chin... to tangle what I suspected was perfectly straight black hair. I wanted to watch her tremble on her knees before me, licking the pads of my fingertips.

It was all I could think of.

"May the lord continue to avert his gaze," I said in reply to Grace and in greeting to the perspiring, guilty priest who dirtied my dock.

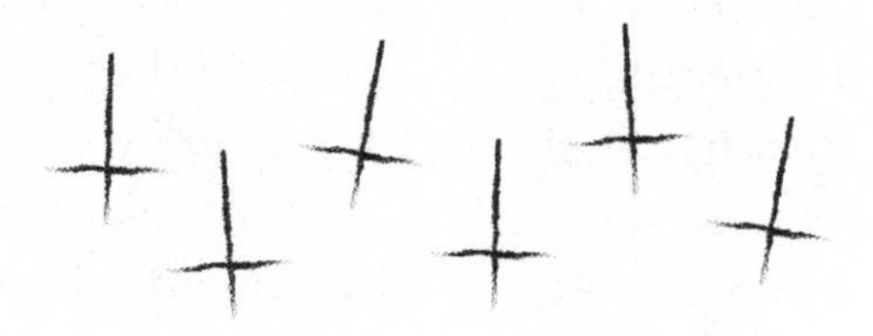

Silas awaited me in the main church's office. This old space was never meant to house a tiny university, but we'd made it work. The hidden halls and passageways, the looming overlooks through wrought iron bars, and the carved stone crucifixes and gargoyles all added to the ease of moving about unseen. Even still, occasionally, students would take notice of me. Quickly quieting, parting like the Red Sea, like I was Moses passing through the waters, they feared me.

Selah feared me too, though, not in my cathedral. Not within the walls of my confessional. Oh, and all I wanted to do was get her back in that tiny, sacrilegious box again. I'd have her again tonight. How far was I willing to tread the shark-infested waters that was The Holy Daughter? It was still conceivable she was sent to spy and gather intel on the operations on Grimm Isles. Had her clergy noticed the missing priests? Had none of their colleagues informed them of what was happening here? Or worse, perhaps they had, and Selah was sent like a lamb to slaughter, to sacrifice, to assuage their morbid suspicions.

For some reason, that thought coaxed out an ember of anger. She did seem innocent-- though, there was something else there—a hint of rebellion, a small glimmer of disobedience, of doubt. I wanted to explore that, break it, tame it... Would I give my demon, Dante, what he wanted, or would I cage him and let the priest, Father Amorth, do what he should? Do what he vowed? In all my time here, no woman had tempted me—none of the sisters and certainly none of the students. Though holy vows and morality aside, everyone was an adult. I could have played and pushed boundaries if I wanted to.

I'd never wanted.

I'd never wanted until *her*.

The Holy Daughter. The virgin princess of the Lady of Sorrow Church. She was untouchable, perfect porcelain, untampered glass... I imagined how lovely she'd look, broken, bleeding, crying on my cock...

"Lady of Sorrow Church in Bear Hallow was very accommodating with Reverend Patrick's paperwork," Father Silas said, thumbing through a stack of documents.

"Who?" I glanced out the window, waiting.

I could hear the unspoken question in Silas's voice. "The whole man you picked up at the dock this morning." He hesitated a moment, unwrapping a cough drop. "You're fixating."

"I'm not," I argued, watching the spot at the top of the stairs where I knew she'd appear. It was her free period, and she always lingered there before visiting the garden.

"Did you find any demons inside her?" He asked with a slightly mocking tone, clinking the cough drop between his teeth and looking over my shoulder.

Selah stood, tiny... holy fuck... *unveiled*... and surrounded by no good, horny, fucking boys. My blood boiled.

"I'm still looking," I gritted out.

"Her file is basic." Silas continued. "You've heard of how her nameless holy mother died during childbirth. Her father is listed as Reverend Benedict, you know, the international televangelist, the head leader of the father church that rules them all. No siblings, no further details... the inner workings of the main lady of sorrow church are much a mystery to outsiders."

"Those two boys," I gestured with my chin. "Send them home."

My brother stood next to me, peering down through the window and passing me an incredulous look. "Noah Fitzwilliam and Oliver Milton? Father Amorth, they've no home to return to. You know that."

"Find them one."

"They aren't stray puppies."

My fists balled at my sides. "Then don't complain to me if something... happens... to them."

"What has gotten into you?" Silas asked, his tone tinted with a slight edge of horror. He put a hand on my shoulder. "If it's The Holy Daughter, I can assure you, I don't believe her to be here with nefarious intent. My sources outside Lady of Sorrow believe some unknown incident occurred which spurred the clergy decision to send her here."

My gaze pulled from Selah's long, tantalizing braids to the burly priest. "What kind of incident?"

Silas's jaw tensed, and that glimmer of bloodlust that called to my own flashed across his stare. The gentle giant may fool everyone else, but I knew him. I'd witnessed what he was capable of. His hunger rivaled my own. Though his code of ethics was limiting— and the way he insisted in attempts to force it onto me as well. I supposed it brought a semblance of balance and organization to our operation. In plainer terms, it covered our asses. It kept the kids and nuns safe. Whereas if it were me alone, I'd have likely brought the whole affair crumbling down, and we'd all be rotting away in prison somewhere.

Though where I thrived in getting my hands dirty, the priest across from me preferred a warfare of words. Collecting data, rumors were investigated to be fact. And in a way, he was more powerful than me in the sense he was more trustworthy. His mask was one of a fatherly type of friendliness. Clergy, bishops, priests, they all immediately warmed to him. They all told him anything he wanted to know. Father Silas Amorth was vital to our plans and the closest thing I had to a friend, a comrade, an accomplice.

"Word at Lady of Sorrow has always been impossible to receive. Much due to their requirement that their nuns take a vow of silence. The clergy is about two dozen men, who likewise are tight-lipped. I've sought to pierce their walls for many decades. Another reason I'd like for their Holy Daughter to remain..." He leveled me with a glare. "*Intact*. She's a wealth of information. Perhaps she should do confession with me."

"No," I growled.

His pale eyebrows rose as he searched beneath the shadow of my hood. "Interesting, Dante. Very interesting." A friend, a brother, or not, I'd kill him in an instant, like anyone else, and he knew it. Backing away, he shook his head, and I knew he was biting his tongue. "Watch yourself, Amorth. And it wouldn't hurt to extend mercy occasionally. Maybe send a priest back exorcised of his demons instead of dead."

"Have them send me someone actually possessed, and I'll consider it."

"Isn't Selah?"

"Give me a break, Silas."

"It's been some time since I've seen you exorcise." He returned to his file cabinet.

"Demons possess less than they used to. Or at least smarter, perhaps."

When my attention flicked back to the window, I caught Selah slowly tapping down the stone stairs. Typically, she did this alone. Only this time, a boy trailed behind her, reaching for her braids.

And then I saw red.

Selah

CHAPTER TWELVE

The cucumber snapped between my teeth, cold and crisp. It had become my daily snack ever since the nuns had encouraged me to spend time in the garden. After my nightmares the night before, the cold grass and birds tweeting in the trees beyond did a lot to calm me. It had been an effort to focus in class, even though every cell in my body wanted to absorb each word and lesson spoken. Even still, my thoughts kept oscillating back to Father Amorth like a magnet being pulled violently away from its source. Did he watch me when I'd touched myself? I wished he'd have let me keep my eyes open. There were only a few hours left before confession, and I could see him again.

On my second bite, Oliver appeared, startling me. He took a drag of his cigarette and chuckled. "Didn't mean to scare you, lass."

"I'm a little jumpy, it's okay." However, I took a small step backward.

I was alone with a boy.

I wasn't allowed to be alone with boys. Though I wasn't allowed to not wear a veil either, and I was doing that. There was never mention of humping a sacred book in front of a priest. I was confident that was a sin, too. Wasn't it?

"Tell me about confession with Father Amorth?" Oliver said quietly, flicking a grasshopper off a tomato plant.

"Oh, you know," I stalled, fidgeting with my braids. "Confession is confession."

What a stupid thing to say. He didn't buy it and persisted. "Father Amorth is anything but ordinary. Can't say we've ever known him to pull a student aside for anything, much less something like confessin' your sins. And you go every night, did you say?"

"Yes."

"To his cathedral?"

I nodded.

"Can't fathom The Holy Daughter would have enough to confess to need a nightly visit," He mused, weaving through the tufts of yellow squash plants jutting from the ground. I wiped my slick palms on my skirt, looking toward the stairs to see all the other students had departed.

What was Oliver getting at? Why did it matter what I did or didn't do with Father Amorth?

"Selah," he said, stepping forward.

I inched backward, feet still on soil as he reached for me— but as his face shifted into focus, he looked over my shoulder and straightened. Small, kind hands steadied my elbow. "Mr. Milton," a stern voiced Sister Elodie chimed behind me.

"Sister, I was just escorting Selah—"

"Very chivalrous of you to cut class just to disturb a very capable young lady's garden time. Go find something else to do *now.*"

Oliver nodded, giving me a sideways glance. "Yes, sister... did you come from the woods?"

Whatever look she gave him in response made him back away with his palms lifted. "Finding something to do," he repeated. "Have a nice day."

Sister Elodie rubbed my arms before flitting around my front, where I could see her clearly and smiling. "Meddlesome lot, these boys."

Close-up vision was a blessing and curse because my gaze fixed on her lips. "I like your lipstick," I noted softly. Though the shade was that eerie, uncomfortable hue of red that I tried to forget. Sister Elodie's hand shot to her face, and she swallowed.

"Sister Grace must have braided your hair. Isn't it charming? Do you like it?" I nodded, trying to forget the red stain on her lips, the way she changed the subject and the way she appeared from nowhere coming from the woods... "Come with me to the cafeteria. I'm *starving,*" she said hoarsely, taking my elbow gently and ushering me out of the garden.

The sanguine smiles and docile tones were as mysterious as the ocean tides as they beat against the shore in the distance, both hiding something deeper beneath the surface. Somehow, within me, sprouted thoughts that not all was as it seemed here on the Isle of Grimm. Salt air questions whispered through the stray strands of my unveiled hair, and I wondered... what else was begging to be let out of hiding?

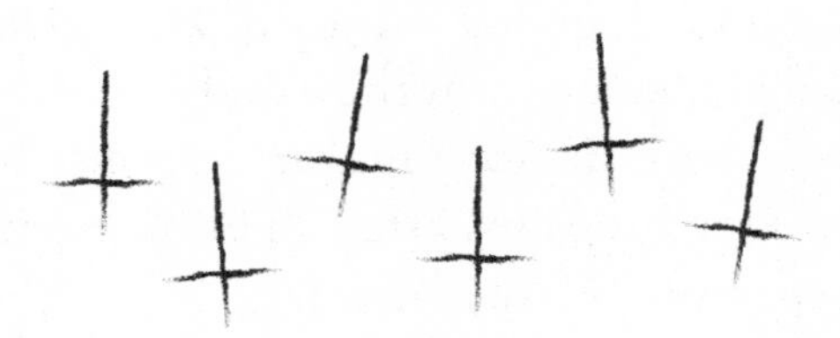

My salmon and wild rice plate was hot as I sat it at an empty table by the window. I liked all the windows in this church, and how every window revealed the ocean in the distance. Lately, I was marking where I was by where the lighthouse light hit my vision. Whatever window I found myself at, no matter the time of day, I could always wait a few moments, and the gleam from the lighthouse would shine in my eyes. It was comforting in an odd way, and I pretended that's what it must be like to see things sharply at a great distance and not only close up. As strange as it sounded to admit, the lighthouse had become my friend on The Isle of Grimm and within the church walls. Church walls that felt open and broad, not closed in and stifling. Though secrets and darkness were lurking, waiting to be found out... The chill of not knowing was eerie and, at the same time, exhilarating.

My entire life, every answer to every problem had been laid out before me in bland, gold-tipped pages and felt boards depicting bearded men in sacred text stories. We were all born dreadful sinners. A great man came to die for our sins. Now, we must worship him forever to pay our debt to earn our unworthy spot in Heaven. Women were especially dirty and could not get by on the same set of rules laid out for men.

Men could preach. Men could conquer the world in the name of god. Men could alter the holy books and sacred texts to better fit their desires. Rewriting history is basically what Lady of Sorrow did. They evolved an entire religion and lassoed it into changing the world.

The best women could hope for was to be a helpmate to these grand and lofty men and their deeds. To encourage her husband in every way, from ironing his shirts just right to making his meals to being readily and joyfully available for sex at any moment he should desire it.

If your husband cheated on you, it was your fault for not giving him enough sexual attention, for letting your appearance go, or for some hidden sin in your life.

If your husband failed in his work duties for the lord, you weren't attending to his home needs well enough that he could focus on his job.

If your husband hit you— it was discipline ordained by god.

According to Lady of Sorrow Church and my father, the Reverend Priest Benedict, it would appear that the blessings of god fell to the man and the punishments to the woman. At least, that's how it seemed in my sinful heart full of demons. Maybe my views would change once my exorcism was complete. Clutching my second helping of salad and bread on my walk back to my seat, I looked around at all the girls and boys sitting together, chatting, laughing, and reading books. The nuns smiled and had hearty conversations with the students. Something in my chest twitched.

I shouldn't have liked it here.

Wasn't supposed to like it here.

There were a thousand reasons not to like it or get attached... I thought about how it was gloomy and still oddly religious without being in your face about it, the sea made every surface filmy with salt, and it was so very dark at night... but then the lighthouse gleam hit my gaze and warmed me on the inside as someone else squeezed their chair to join my table. Noah bit into a green apple as I took my seat.

"Selah, Miss Gorgeous Long Black Hair," he *ooed* and *ahhed*.

I giggled, thanking him and taking a mouthwatering bite of salmon.

"Have you seen Oliver? I haven't caught sight of the old chap since he didn't show for home economics this afternoon."

Rice caught in my throat, and I coughed before Noah handed me a glass of water. Collecting myself, I responded. "I think I saw him earlier, and Elodie, I mean, Sister Elodie, told him to get to class."

Noah eyed me a moment, running a hand through his blond hair. "It's just I've never known my best mate to miss a meal."

Giving a weak shrug, I forked at my salad. "I'm sure he'll turn up." Why did it feel as if I were lying? A small nagging pang in my ribs told me something was wrong, and yet I found myself subtly defending the nuns and priests rather than deeper exploring my skepticism of Grimm with a peer, with two fellow classmates who had taken me under their wings. It was unusual that in a bizarre way, I felt defensive of them, though I had no idea why.

"Are you religious?" I asked awkwardly as Noah looked pensively out the window. The question didn't seem to faze him, though, as I suspected most of us were used to speaking of god and scripture in passing within our everyday lives. They'd all chosen a holy university for a reason, right?

"Maybe," he replied. "Not in the same way my family is, but maybe in my own way. That's part of what I'm learning here, I reckon." He leaned back in his chair. "I'm not a Holy Son, or whatever the male equivalent of a Holy Daughter is at our respective Lady of Sorrow Churches. But I am a Reverend's kid. So's Oliver. So's lots of folks here."

"Really?" I asked in surprise. "Is this a special school for only the children of holy men?"

Noah looked absently out the window as if monitoring every passerby, looking for Oliver. "Something like that, maybe. Isn't that why you're here?"

Suddenly, I wasn't so hungry anymore, which reminded me and made my belly flip and warm in ways it never had for anyone before. "What time is it?"

"About a quarter to seven," Noah checked his watch. "Got a hot date that's not me?" He winked, and I felt my cheeks warm.

"Yes, with a moody, faceless priest in his creepy cathedral."

"Oh shit, that's right. I totally forgot to ask you about Father Amorth. Didn't you confess last night? Does the guy think you've sinned more between last night and tonight?"

I giggled. "He wants me to confess every night. I don't know. Holy Daughter stuff," I fumbled out weakly. What was I supposed to say? *I'm filled with demons and banished until I'm pure and ready to be a Proverbs 31 virtuous wife.*

Noah stood and offered me his elbow. "I'll walk you there. The path is bumpy."

Reluctantly, I took his elbow, looking around for Elodie, or Oliver, for that matter, but I didn't spot either of them as we entered the arched and ornately dark church halls. "Father Amorth's cathedral is a hike away. He really expects you to trek all the way over to his sanctuary every night?"

"It is a little creepy," I agreed. "Have you ever explored the church or the grounds at night?"

"Not personally, no. But some buddies of mine thought it a right bright idea to go skinny dipping one night. Came running back crying at three in the morning, talking about monsters." Noah chuckled. "People say the woods are full of them. That's why none of us go out there. But hell, I think this old church is spooky enough on its own. I wouldn't want to be alone out here doing anything at night."

The hairs on my arms stood, chilled by a subtle drop in temperature as we neared the dilapidated exterior of Father Amorth's cathedral. By the brightness of the lighthouse, I gathered it sat very near to the structure that had become my inanimate friend. Noah paused as I strode forward. "W-want me to wait for you out here?" He asked, a slight tremor in his tone.

"No, it's okay. I'll see you later."

Noah looked worriedly over my shoulder and backed away, hands shoved in his pockets. "Okay, but if you disappear, too, I'm sending out a search party."

Oliver hadn't disappeared. He'd probably just been embarrassed after his scolding from Sister Elodie and went to his room. Something low in my ribs pressed in on me in concern. Or maybe it was the ominous presence of Father Amorth's candlelit church. Six flickering prayer candles were the only light source aside from the waning sun warming through the red stained glass. It washed the room in a murky rust color that made it look and feel as old as it was. Like stepping into his cathedral was stepping back in time.

And standing outside the confessional in a hooded black cloak, he waited, hands clasped. No sign of humanity, no skin exposed, no expressions to lend any sort of hint as to what he was thinking. Had he always been so abnormally large? He was nearly seven feet tall, towering, and broad over my five-foot, four-inch, feeble frame. He was monstrous and far too sinister to be merely a priest. Maybe that's why they made him an exorcist. Maybe he contended with demons because he was as scary as they were.

Whatever the reason, I held up my chin, feigning bravery as my heart pounded in my chest. He gestured into my side of the confessional without so much as a hello. And I obeyed.

It was night two of confessing my sins.

And the Grimm Reaper took his spot across the bars from me and shut the door.

Selah

CHAPTER THIRTEEN

The moment I sat down, my exhaled breath calmed my entire body. The walls were close, the bars were familiar, and I could see everything. I could touch everything, even Father Amorth, if I wanted to. My hands were probably small enough to twist through the bars. *What would he do if I did?* I wondered. For a split second, I imagined sliding my arm through and tugging on his hood. Would he yell at me? Would he break my wrist? Would it be worth catching a glimpse of the person hiding behind these holy robes of darkness? It must have been the demon within me bringing such thoughts to the forefront of my mind. Maybe I should have felt guilt, but I didn't. I only felt peace and... curiosity. Every sound and sensation was heightened as we shared the same heavy air. My wooden seat creaked as I repositioned, my dress felt heavy and rough against my skin, and all he was doing was staring down at me, staring without eyes, without a face, just hiding himself away. It was maddening and unnerving at the same time.

The exorcist watched me so intently, and I hated it... and hated how much I was starting to like it.

"You're attending your classes," he broke the silence, reminding me of his voice's deep and steady timbre. It was a statement more than a question, but I responded anyway.

"Yes."

"Do you enjoy gardening?"

His questions were so random. What did any of this have to do with exorcising my demons? "I—I've never done it before, but I suppose I'd like to learn. The dirt, the vegetables, and the flowers, they're relaxing."

"There is an ill-tended garden just outside my lighthouse. You'll tend to it now and no other garden, understood?"

A strange demand. After a beat of silence, I stared at the dark weaving of his cloak. Were there markings in black thread along the sides? It was so dark I could hardly make them out.

"*Your* lighthouse?" I asked.

"Yes, it is where I live."

For some reason, my heart did a small flip in my chest. He lived in my lighthouse. Well, yes, I guess it was his and not mine, but... I wouldn't mind being closer to it. And having a job that took me closer to the ocean and away from the church sounded like some small freedom. Not that I could argue, but I found myself okay with the order.

"I'll work on the garden," I said quietly.

"Confess your sins to me, Selah," he demanded lowly. The way he said my name sent a shiver of electricity through my bones, and suddenly, it was hard to control my breathing. I'd heard that command hundreds, thousands of times in my life. From my father, from bishops, reverends, and deacons. But it never sounded like that, like an invitation to do so much more... Was Father Amorth testing me? Was he laying down a trap to see if my sexual impurity would reveal itself to him? Is this how he drew out the lustful demon inside me? I would need to be smart and contained; I'd need to resist him and these crazy notions swirling in my lower belly.

He was just another priest, and I was just another sinner in his confessional. Nothing more. To make matters worse, he was likely reporting my every move and word to my dad, and he and the Lady of Sorrows clergy were all probably calculating my purity levels and determining when my sin was cleansed enough for me to come home and be married away. The thought was like a bucket of cold water in my face.

"Forgive me, father, for I have sinned." Father Amorth shifted in his seat, and I swallowed, too attuned to his every move. It was hard not to be when we were so close. The bars between us were a slow taunting of separation. "Several times a week, I would sneak into a bishop's office and use the internet to fulfill my lustful desires."

"What would you find there?" he asked with low intrigue. He wasn't like other priests. Most didn't pry, and most didn't ask follow-up questions or urge me to expand. Confession was like reading a shopping list of wrongs and the man on the other side scanning them off their conveyor belt like a bored cashier in a grocery store. But not Father Amorth. He seemed interested like he wanted to know more and more, like I was a ball of yarn, and he was tugging the loose string to see where each sin began.

It should have terrified me, and in a way, it did— and maybe it was because no one ever seemed interested in me before, no one ever cared to ask more questions and wait and listen to me to talk without interrupting or admonishment— but that warm feeling was returning in my chest.

"I was browsing a blogger website one day and found some posts... a lady sharing her sexual adventures. She updates each week, and I would read the things she did. Well, I would print them to read before I went to sleep."

"What sort of things did she do?"

I bit my lip slightly. "Crazy, immoral things."

"Tell me in detail, Selah."

My heart raced; saying any of her activities out loud felt wicked, but I obeyed. "Mrs. Paramour invited men to her home, and sometimes they would do things like..." I sucked in a breath, my cheeks turning pink. "They'd kiss on the lips, touch the other, and..."

"And?"

"Well, sometimes her partner would kiss *lower*... kiss between her legs... kiss the place reserved for only a husband to use in marriage. And—and she would do the same back to them."

Father Amorth cocked his head slightly, analyzing me, though I tried to only stare at my thumbs as I usually did in confession. "Did it cause you to desire those things?"

"Yes."

"Have you ever touched yourself, Selah?"

The spot between my upper thighs ached slightly. I knew he might strike me or punish me for asking, but

I couldn't stop the question. "Have you seen demons? Spoken to them as an exorcist?"

Surprising me, he answered immediately. "I have."

"People come to you possessed, and you... you free the demons inside them?"

"Something like that."

"Will you free the demons inside of me?"

He was silent, all except for cracking his knuckles. "We will speak more about the demon inside of you later. For now, answer my question. Have you ever touched yourself in those places you read about, Selah?"

Him saying my name and asking such dirty questions again had me shivering with some very, very sinful desires.

"No," I lied.

"Liar," he breathed. "You're what, twenty-one, twenty-two? And you've never gotten curious in the shower, never pulled the showerhead low, and felt the water pulse against your center?" His tone was a mix of surprise and amusement, which, mixed with the naughty words again, was so unlike a priest. I'd never heard anything other than the monotone sound of disapproval. Father Amorth continually did the least expected thing that I never knew what to anticipate with him. If he'd struck me, punished me, yelled at me, or tortured me, I would have at least known where I stood and what was coming. Maybe he was saving that for later, for when he met my sinful demons.

"There's always been a Lady of Sorrow to watch me or assist me in bathing. So, no—"

"Someone *watches* you bathe?"

"Yes. Here at Grimm... it's been my first time doing so alone."

A low sound rumbled from his throat, and I thought it seemed like something angry and disapproving. I quickly added, "I can get one of the nuns to watch me if you prefer—"

"No," he interrupted sternly. "No one should *ever* violate your privacy in such a way."

I let out a small breath. "I'm the Holy Daughter of Sorrow, Father Amorth. I don't have privacy."

It was then I realized I was no longer looking at my thumbs, my worn shoes, or the splintered confessional floor. But I was looking up at him. He was too big for this small box; the bars couldn't have contained him if they tried. And he stared back at me, a shadow, a black mass of hidden man. It was as if I were speaking to death himself, and yet somehow, in all his fearsome and legendary presence, he was somewhat... kind. At least he had been with me thus far.

"Tonight," he said with a low rumble. "I want you to go back to your room. You're going to light a prayer candle and take off your clothes." My breath hitched, and I pushed my knees together. His head tilted down as if he noticed the movement before continuing. "You're going to get in a warm shower. Warm, not hot, do you understand?"

I nodded, feeling my cheeks warm.

"Good," he praised, and my center throbbed with ache at the sound. "You're going to touch the lips of your pussy with your fingers before guiding the shower head down."

His voice turned smoky like candle ash, and I could have died from wanting to touch him so badly. "Then you're going to feel the warm water and circle it around your clit, that's the raised point near the top of your sex. Up and down, side to side. Return tomorrow and be ready to tell me what happens."

"Yes, Father," I said on an embarrassingly breathy whimper. His neck twitched, and I pressed my knees together again. Was I affecting him like he was me? Surely not... but... could I have been? After the silence spanned what seemed like ages, I stood and smoothed my skirt.

"Selah," he spoke my name like a song, and I stopped at the threshold of confession. "Your body is yours. Not your future husband, not your father's, not god's, it is *yours*." Tears pricked the corner of my eyes at hearing such a radical notion. "And," he said gently as I turned my face so he wouldn't see. "You are forgiven."

God, I wanted to be.

I wanted to be forgiven.

And I wanted to do more to beg for forgiveness from him.

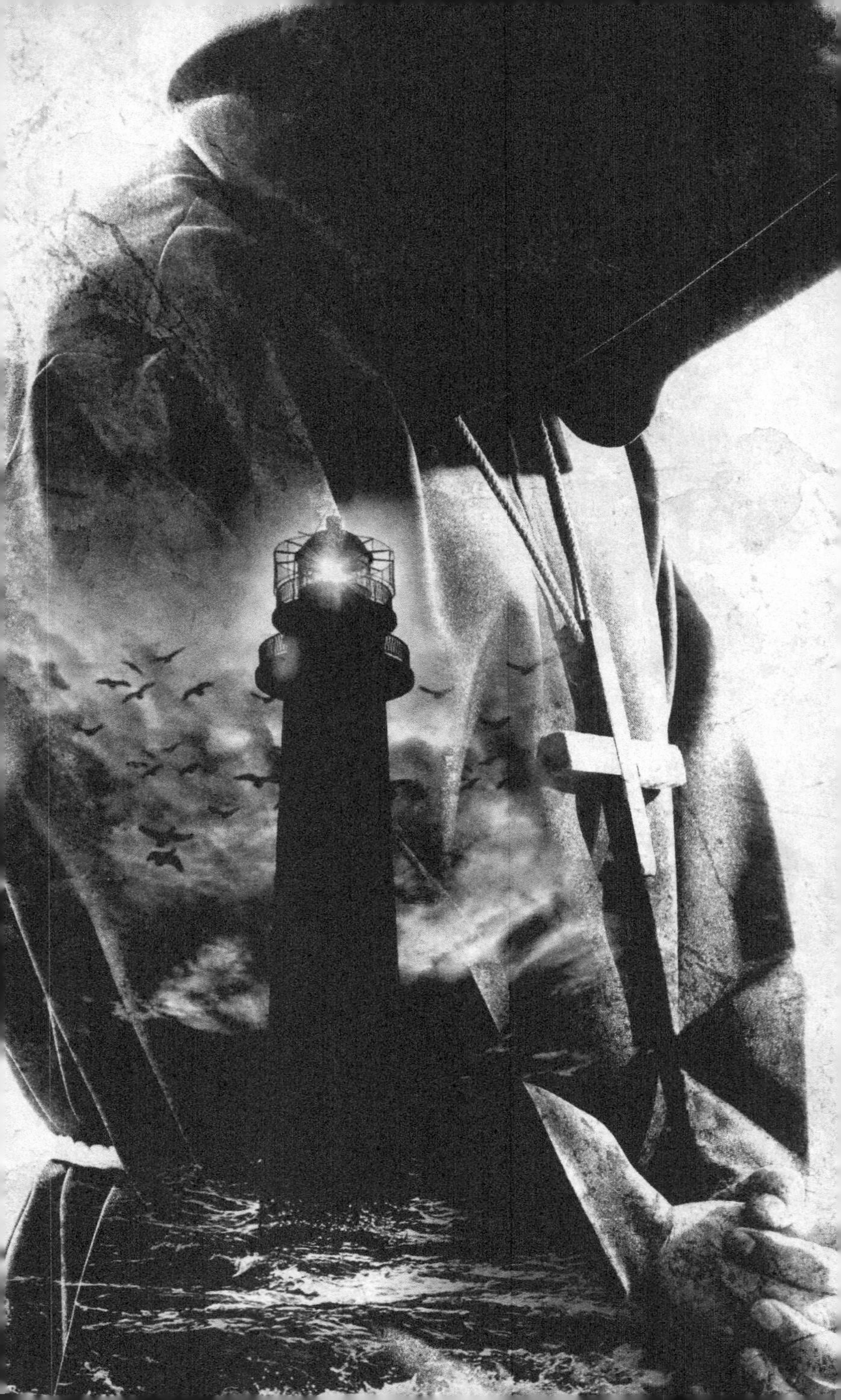

CHAPTER FOURTEEN

A scream rattled from the basement of the cathedral. At least he'd stayed quiet through confession.

The Holy Sacred Texts say that you shall know the true sons and daughters of god by their fruit. The fruits of the spirit are love, joy, peacefulness, patience, kindness, goodness, faithfulness, gentleness, and self-control. When I used to preach a very long time ago, it was one of my most beloved sermons. There was a time when I exhibited these qualities. My tree was strongly rooted in the lord, and I had the fruits of the holy spirit to display proof of that.

But things changed over time, didn't they? My mind was a tidal wave, and it often grabbed hold of me and swept me out to a sea of dark thoughts. Oftentimes, it was my past that pulled me in its undertow. I recalled that overcast day, a mother rapt on my cathedral door, sobbing, begging for the exorcist. It took me moments to realize she meant *me*, that *I* was now the exorcist of Grimm.

I'd had the training, I'd taken the vows, but never had I contended with a demon face to face. Father Joseph assured me that nine times out of ten, it wasn't a demon inhabiting someone at all. People back then thought everything was an evil spirit. A common cold, dehydration, and even drunkenness would lead people to believe the dark forces of hell were at work. As if hell gave a flying fuck about the lives of anyone. But humans were entitled, thinking too highly of themselves and their importance. Father Joseph was away; there was only me, so I clutched my prayer beads, adjusted my collar, and away I went.

Probably just a common illness, I told myself. I'd pray over her child, bless the house and all its doorframes and windowpanes, and be done. But I was so very wrong, wasn't I? That knock on my door would change my life forever. That dreary day would change the course of so many lives... including now, the fate of the boy locked in my basement.

Because I was angry, and I was turned on, that line between fucking something and slaughtering something was a thin one for me. Unfortunately, the only thing I wanted to fuck had two long black braids and a dirty, dirty little mouth that begged for my cock. Oh, how I'd fuck her throat raw. I'd choke her until she fainted and then fuck her in her sleep until she awoke sobbing and begging me to stop. And I wouldn't stop. If I ever got my cock into Selah, The Holy Daughter, I'm afraid she'd die on it right then and there because I couldn't imagine a scenario where I'd stop fucking her.

And that's why I was going to keep my goddamn hands to myself. At least with her. With Oliver Milton... I'd lay hands on him— for touching her hair, for scaring her, for cornering her in the university garden. Oh yes, I'd lay hands on him. He wouldn't be as lucky as Selah to be spared my wretched touch. Imagining her in the shower... she'd be such a good and holy lamb, wouldn't she? She would obey me.

Yes, Father, she'd said over and over as if she knew just exactly how hard she was making my dick throb. Her little inexperienced fingers would explore the folds of her wet, tight little pussy, and she'd be doing exactly what I told her to. She'd come on her shower head because I instructed her to do so. Anger mixed with want at imagining the confines she'd been under at The Father Church of Lady of Sorrows.

Back in my day, it was only the Bible and its simple truths. Things were different back then. Now, I was well versed in the practices of the numerous Lady of Sorrows churches. They ruled over us all, dictating what we could or could not speak about and how women and men should dress and behave. They'd leached so far into the world that they swayed politics, laws, media, everything. Each church presiding over a city or town was a small ecosystem to themselves. But in the grander scheme, their instruction came from the father church, the one Selah resided in, the one where she was esteemed as Holy Daughter. The example set for all women. While each Lady of Sorrow branch mainly shared the same beliefs and doctrine as dictated by the father church, how they enacted their interpretations of holy scripture was sometimes different.

Some of the smaller Lady of Sorrows churches did some good in the world. Some of their people are kind, helpful folk. Others... others were far more sinister than most of the world could fathom. One thing was uniformly clear:

there was no room for any other belief system. Rumors would spring up from time to time that they were a vicious cult hiding in plain sight. Those rumors never made it to news outlets, which always somehow spoke favorably of the church and its many televised sermons.

What was the main ruling, Father Church of Lady of Sorrow? A church too strict, overbearing, and meddlesome in the world's affairs, or a group of men who'd gone unchecked for too long? Who makes a girl, even if she is their good and holy daughter, shower while monitored each night? No doubt to ensure she didn't explore her own body. Their fixation on the purity of young girls nauseated me. As if half that focus ever included the men involved.

And what had it done to Selah but make her believe that her natural, god-given desires were sin— were demons inside of her? And it seemed as if her father and the clergy there believed the same to an intense degree—curious information to share with Silas and hear his thoughts. Maybe we needed to try harder to pay the main church of Lady of Sorrow a little visit. Their walls were notoriously hard to breech, made even harder by most of their nuns, or as they called them, ladies of sorrow, taking vows of silence.

Obviously, my beliefs and how I led my flock at Grimm were different. Lady of Sorrow knew of me and my dealings with priests. They were wary of the exorcist and the Isle of Grimm, never bothering us much. Until we received the email from the lead father himself, I was sure we were off their radar entirely. Apparently not. And now their Holy Virgin Daughter was under my watch—

and touching herself in the shower, riding sacred texts in my confessional... Perhaps Father Benedict had made a grave miscalculation entrusting her with me. Whatever his motives had been, she was here now, and I was beginning to question my earlier suspicions of her being sent as some sort of spy.

While I hoped Selah explored her body with the unneeded approval of my permission and guidance, I hoped she'd begin to believe that it belonged to her, and that sexual pleasure wasn't wrong. And it sure as fuck didn't belong to her future *husband*. My nails bit into my palms as I marched down the dilapidated stairs under my cathedral. Her future husband was no doubt already promised, already chosen by her father, and unquestionably some disgustingly old church elder in need of a wife for breeding.

Oh, now I was good and pissed off. But why? Why did I fucking care where this girl ended up? I didn't. I couldn't afford to care. But I could take out my aggression somewhere, couldn't I? Oliver's bellow for help was silenced when I stepped into the candlelit room.

"The fuck is this?" he spat from the middle of the pentagram of blood and black wax. He was trapped. He couldn't move from the center of it. No ropes were needed— not that it mattered. He wasn't going anywhere, and there was no escape from me.

I pulled out a file from my robe. "Well, Oliver Milton, is it? Age twenty-five, from a nasty mega Lady of Sorrows church in Ireland. Your father, Reverend Thomas, didn't have much nice to say about you."

Oliver scoffed, crossing his arms. "Is this what you do? Why you're collecting so many of us? You gonna, what—" he surveyed the pentagram with horror. "Kill a bunch of ex-sorrow kids for some sick end?"

"You were abused by your bishops, weren't you, Oliver? Your dad did nothing about it, instead he looked to get rid of you while promoting the bishop in question. Am I right?"

Oliver stilled, resting an arm on his knee. "How do you know that?"

"You think you being here is a coincidence? You think the safety of this place is a lucky trick? Or maybe you still believe in the blessings of *god*?" I tossed his file onto the floor and stepped closer, causing the young man to flinch in fear.

"I don't know what I believe anymore. But I know you're no fucking good, Father Amorth," he spat.

I knelt at the pointed head of the pentagram, looking up at him through my hood, feeling my blood rage and boil. "You will never go near Selah again," I growled lowly. "Do you understand?"

"What do you want with her?"

I let out a rough chuckle that seemed to frighten him more than me coming close. Good. His fear was everything I wanted and more. "So many questions about me, Oliver. You've been asking Selah, friends, snooping around—well, here I am." I raised my palms. "I thought I'd give you what you wanted."

His expression fought to fix into defiance as he rose onto his knees and leaned forward. "What's under your hood?

What do you have to hide, Father Amorth? The great and powerful exorcist of Grimm who won't even show his face," he mocked.

"You want to see?" I asked low and slow. The boy's foolish taunts flashed before his eyes as he realized all of his mistakes that led up to this point. His arrogance, his affinity for the new girls who came to the school, and his current fixation on me and mine. His hand reaching for Selah's braid played through my mind until I was breathing heavily and seeing red. The fear she felt when he cornered her— fuck— I was going to rip this boy to shreds, wasn't I?

He opened his mouth to speak, but it was too late.

I removed my hood.

A scream rattled my cathedral once more.

And a blood sacrifice was made that night.

Selah

CHAPTER FIFTEEN

Existing within the atmosphere of this gothic, by the ocean, church university was peculiar and heartwarming all at once. Girls had stopped to compliment my braids or give me directions to class. When Noah wasn't around to help me, each nun and student I met were nothing but kind and welcoming—offering everything from pens and paper to showing me around and telling me about the artwork on the walls. It was still much like a church, with holy women and priests haunting the halls, bells ringing, and the faint sound of hymns from choir class in the various sanctuaries. But it was also very much like a school. I passed students kissing in corners, boys tossing a football outside, and people studying under trees.

It was easy to simply exist here. Maybe that's why so many had been at Grimm for so long. They just liked being here. I couldn't really blame them as I couldn't imagine a more perfect place to reside. Spookiness, dark clouds, and ominous hooded priest aside. A hooded priest who kept *forgiving* me in very sinfully delicious ways...

Sister Grace floated down the hallway of the main building, looking like an eerie painting come to life in her long, black robes and nun's habit. She stopped me, clutching a red prayer necklace in her palm. "Selah, I was looking for you."

Noah hadn't seen me to class that morning, and I hadn't seen him or Oliver all day, in fact. But I'd been getting around fine on my own, having memorized my usual path on the stairs and down the halls, using the lighthouse flash as my guide. Father Amorth's lighthouse.

"Father Amorth has asked me to inform you that you may take the rest of the week off from attending confession with him."

For some reason, that statement felt like a punch to the gut. I'd been counting down the hours until seven in the evening. "Oh," I said, surprised, suppressing the urge to ask why. Was he getting tired of me? Maybe I'd done or said something wrong in our last confession... Didn't he want to hear about my shower exploration he'd ordered me into doing?

"Can I help you with anything?" Sister Grace searched my eyes, and I realized I'd paused for too long.

Embarrassed, I glanced out the long-arched window toward the familiar flash of light amongst the waves. "Actually, maybe," I fiddled with my singular, long braid that Sister Elodie had braided for me in class that morning. "Do you have any books about gardening I could borrow?"

Her face lit up with a smile. "Not personally, but I'll bet the library does." She looped her elbow with mine.

"There's a library here?" I almost squealed in happiness. "With more than just sacred texts?"

Sister Martha laughed. “Those boys you’ve been hanging around really have not done this place justice in their tours, I see. Of course, we have a library. Though, it’s a tad unorganized, a bit unorthodox... Much like myself,” she giggled as we turned a corner and descended a small stairwell. “But we love it all the same.”

The library was a large, circular room with several lit fireplaces, stacks of books on the floor, plush, worn leather sofas, and floor-to-arched ceilings of books. There had to be thousands.

“This is amazing,” I marveled.

Sister Grace jumped on a rolling ladder and dramatically rolled down the row of books. “I just love doing that,” she smiled. “Oh, look here, a gardening book.”

Dodging random piles of book stacks, I made my way over, stopping at a section that surprised me. I looked at the nun, back to the row of titles, and then back again. She put her hands on her hips and raised an eyebrow. “Got something against romance and erotica?”

I coughed on my own words. “I’ve—I’ve never heard a nun say the word *erotica* before,” I whispered, eliciting more merry laughter.

“Erotic horror is my personal favorite, but I love some sapphic smut as well. We have a nice little collection here. Anything you see pique your interest?”

Stunned, I carefully caressed the spines of a few well-loved paperbacks. I pulled out one at random, seeing a man with no shirt on the cover. Blushing, I hid it to my chest. “I can’t believe we’re allowed to read these here,”

I whispered again, though there was no one else in the library but us.

Sister Grace tilted her head and thrummed her fingers on the romance shelf. "You're allowed to read whatever brings you joy, whatever gets you reading. Romance is an exquisitely smart genre. Why, you can explore new worlds, unpack your trauma, fall in love with boys and girls with wings, or ride the streets of motorcycle gangs, get rescued by the villain, and have the best orgasms of your life." I turned beet red, and she laughed again. "I mean, all of Song of Solomon in the old and new sacred texts is just sex, too. Did you know that? Yes, buried within the precious vintage Bible exists erotica of its time. Why, you even had to be thirty to get to read it back in the old days."

Taking the gardening book from her and clutching the man-chest romance book to my front, I shook my head in amazement. "You are unlike any holy woman I've ever met."

Sister Grace clicked her tongue and floated past, taking the time to stoke a fire gently before turning at the exit. "Perhaps we should be the ones to define what's *holy* for ourselves, hm?"

And with a small smirk, she departed, leaving me to browse through titles of dark romance, erotica, and more, all within dark and hallowed walls of acceptance. I found a comfortable couch and sank into its well-worked leather, deciding to save the romance titles for later and crack open the gardening book first. The sooner I learned what to do, the sooner I could get closer to the lighthouse... and closer to the man inside it. The idea thrilled me, and I held each book close to my nose so I could read each word and accurately decipher every step-by-step photograph. He'd asked me to tend to his garden, and I would. And I really, really hoped he'd be there as I did.

That night felt wrong not going to confession. I slumped on the floor at the foot of my bed and read through my first official romance novel. Each page I savored, each chapter reminded me of Mrs. Paramour and her blogged adventures. Only I didn't have to sneak into a fast-food-addicted bishop's office and steal the entries like contraband. No, these books were displayed proudly next to science, philosophy, and literary fiction. All genres I wanted to explore. Maybe I'd even check out an erotic horror like Sister Martha said she enjoyed.

Maybe I'd wait until I got a little braver for that one.

I drifted to sleep under the comforting flash of the lighthouse, wondering what Father Dante was doing right then. I wondered what the woman inside the pages of my romance book would have done if she were me. She would have worn something scandalous and walked right over to Father Dante's room. He'd probably prefer someone brazen like the heroine of my book. A woman experienced, mature, and sure of herself. He was old, confident, and sure.

I was none of those things, was I? And what was I thinking, even allowing myself to develop this crush on my exorcist? Oh my gosh, I had a *crush* on my exorcist. That's certainly not what my dad and church had intended when they sent me away for purification. And I wasn't sure they'd agree with Father Amorth's methods, either. But somehow, in just a couple sessions with him, I had left his cathedral feeling lighter. Was this him exorcising my demons? I'd never once left a sanctuary and felt lighter. No, church always left me feeling heavy, wretched, and remorseful. Somehow, that wasn't the case here, not with him. And I was becoming needy to hear his words.

You're forgiven, Selah. His deep and mysterious timbre swam through my mind like a tiny school of fish, making my heart fluttery and warm. I wondered what he looked like under his heavy black cloak. What did his whole face reveal? I could only piece together tiny details and guess at the unknown. He had wide, strong, and rough hands. His stature and size were larger than any man I'd ever seen, and he was obviously very strong. Maybe he looked like one of the men on the cover of the smutty romance novels from the library.

And his jaw... the closest glimpse I'd gotten of his face. He was tan with salt and pepper-colored stubble. He was much older than me, I guessed, at least my dad's age. Most priests were old. But none looked like him. As a matter of fact, Father Silas was very handsome, too. But Father Amorth, his deepness and intrigue pulled me in deeper than anyone ever had. Noah and Oliver were closer to my age, and their accents and sense of fun were definitely enticing. There was a sense of youthfulness and freedom about them, though, that always felt like salt in a wound for me. Like they had arrived at a sense of contentment that I could never attain. Not so long as I was a Holy Daughter. And they may have been religious children of clergy, but it didn't matter. They'd never fully understand me. With Noah and Oliver, I felt like a shiny, odd shell they found on the beach. They were curious as they inspected me.

But Father Dante didn't treat me like a shell. He didn't treat me like a Holy Daughter or a nun. While his instructions were undoubtedly obscene, I felt a sense of ease around him, like he saw me as a whole person. For the first time, did someone *see* me? Did someone see past the religious garb, my sheltered upbringing, even my engrained beliefs, and understand something about myself even I had scarcely explored?

I could only hope and sorrow at the thought. It was outrageous and unrealistic. He'd probably taken righteous vows of celibacy, never to be a husband— while I was *created* for a husband. My whole purpose was to be a virtuous wife, a helpmate, a Proverbs 31 woman. This place, this time on Grimm with the free-spirited nuns, the kind university students, and the brooding demon priest... it was all a dream.

And I'd be called back to Lady of Sorrow and awoken at any moment.

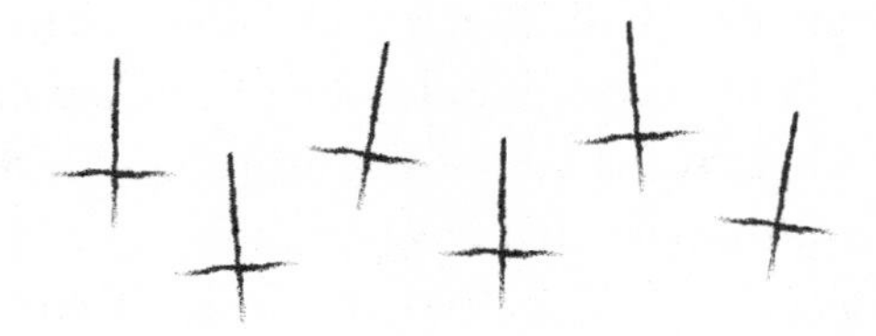

The pads of my feet now loved the feeling of going from cold, hard cobblestone to soft, plush, bouncy sand. Ocean waves left bubbles of white foam in their wake as I held up my skirt and let the water lap at my ankles on my trek to the lighthouse garden. Nerves fluttered through my heart while the sea breeze messed up my tight braid. It was tradition now, somehow, that a nun would show up to chat and braid my hair in the morning. At Lady of Sorrow, I cringed when the ladies would stop by my room. But at Grimm, I looked forward to it. I liked each of them, and it felt like they also liked me. Strangely, I felt my shoulders relaxing, my breathing easier, my appetite for food had grown, and I was eating more, and larger portions.

What my church had intended as my curse, god—or something-- had turned into a blessing. My developing crush on my exorcist, though... well, that would just remain my own little secret. It's not as if Father Amorth felt the same. To him, I was just another girl, another holy woman or student, across the bars of his confessional. But then why'd he insist I tend to his garden? Maybe it was some extension of the exorcism process—manual labor.

As I ambled along the beach, slowly approaching the striped beacon of light and adjoining garden, I stopped and plucked sharp shells in hopes of a shark tooth. A large man came into view outside the small dock of the lighthouse. As I neared, he noticed me, and I gave a sheepish wave. He looked over his shoulder and cocked his head, reeling idly at his fishing line. Standing stalky and broad, he motioned I come closer. I cast a small glance to the garden above the dunes and the cathedral beyond before padding onto the creaking dock. The gentleman extended his hand, biting a pipe between his teeth. "Afternoon, young lady. Fish ain't bitin' today. Got any good luck to spare?"

I huffed a small laugh. He wore overalls in a dingy, beige color that matched his well-worn look. Like he'd been in the hot and boiling sun every day of his life and somehow survived with mirth and a jolly smile.

"I always seem to be fresh out of good luck," I shrugged. "And I don't know anything about fishing."

"I got a boy about your age," he chewed on his pipe and clicked the line in before casting it back out into the gently lapping waves. "You should ask him to teach you. I'm sure he would. The boy never could say *no* to save his life. His two brothers are much the same, though they'd never admit it."

There was something vaguely familiar in the man's voice, but I couldn't place it. "Do your sons go to this school?"

Raising a bushy dark eyebrow, he replied, "Girl, there ain't no school on Grimm. Not since it burnt down six years ago."

Puzzled, I glanced at him as he focused on his line. "My middle boy, he's more the bookish type, things I don't understand, but he's got a good heart. Don't fish enough, but I reckon I do enough of that for one family."

Maybe the sun had gotten to him. Maybe he was just elderly and a little confused, so I simply nodded. "Well, I should get going." Before thinking about the improperness of it, I thumbed his almost invisible fishing line between my thumb and forefinger. It went taut immediately, and I gasped, afraid I'd broken something.

"Looks like you've got some luck yet, young lady." He smiled, reeling in a large, flopping fish. His chuckle made me giggle as salty fins splashed me.

I left him and went to the garden, realizing how rude it was I never got his name, but hoping maybe I'd see him again sometime. The fisherman was the town's first resident beyond the looming church that I'd met, and he'd been odd but kind. It was so nice meeting kind people.

I swung open the rotting wood gate, and it was plain that I had my work cut out for me—dried and underwatered plants wilted in clusters, overtaken by spiney thorns and brush. The location was lovely, however, right under the lighthouse, surrounded by sand dunes and crashing waves. Father Amorth's old cathedral sat in the distance, like something out of an old portrait from a thrift store. And then the big, opulent, black, and massive church building menaced in the distance like a glimmering dark mountain made of onyx stone.

It was inarguably pretty and gorgeously constructed with how it sat above the cobblestone town by the sea. But my gaze wandered to Father Amorth's modest, unassuming cathedral. It looked remarkable to be still standing, and for some reason, he preferred it over the big church. It was a clue, I decided. A clue to his character and his preferences. Father Amorth liked old things and took comfort in small spaces that people seldom noticed, especially when paired next to something grander. I wondered if he saw me in such a way, noticed me as something small, and likewise ignored.

I found a rusted till and dagger shovels and began piercing the ground. Sand had overtaken the soil, but as I dug, rich dirt appeared. A pretty patch of garden was hiding dormant under the old lighthouse, just waiting for someone to care for it. I would be that person; I would bring it to life, and Father Amorth would look out his window at the lighthouse or his cathedral, see it, smile, and think of me and how I accomplished turning something forgotten into something beautiful.

I yelped when a low voice spoke behind me. "Here, wear these."

My shovel clanged against a stone, and I trembled in anticipation as I turned around. Father Amorth stood like a spooky, cloaked Halloween decoration in the center of the overgrown garden. The waves crashed behind him while the sea breeze rippled through his long garb. As it did, I could make out the indents of his muscular shoulders and the line of his firm triceps. He outstretched his arm, exposing those strong hands that had my heart rate rising. Hands-- how could only *hands* have me getting hotter than the romance book I was reading the night before? Seeing any exposed skin when everything on him was hidden felt seductive, like being let into his world.

I took the pair of gardening gloves from his grip, my fingers briefly brushing the roughness of his palm. He didn't jerk from my touch, only looked down, regarding me like death come to pay his dead garden a visit.

"I warned you," he rumbled lowly. I leaned on my shovel for support, as I was literally feeling weak in the knees from his presence. "It's in quite disarray over here."

"Oh, I don't mind," I answered, noticing a flock of seagulls flying overhead. "Have you lived here long?" I tilted my chin up at the lighthouse next to us. Up closer, it was apparent that it was very old, with deep cracks in the stone and vines growing up the side.

"Forever," he answered simply. I'd expected him to leave, but he didn't seem in any hurry, standing put just... watching me. He seemed like a quiet man, like small talk wasn't natural for him, or maybe acting kind wasn't as natural. But even still, I liked having him near, even if just in the quiet of the beach.

"Do you miss your family?" he asked, and I stopped mid-dig.

"Not at all." I surprised myself with my frankness, but I wasn't about to lie to an exorcist priest... *again*. "I feel like I can breathe."

"Good," he answered, sounding pleased. It sent a jolt of warmth fluttering from my heart down between my thighs. His praise was like none other. I wanted to say and do more to receive it.

Brush rustling nearby drew my attention, and I stopped, looking over my shoulder. "Do you hear that, Father Amorth?" He tilted his head, and for some reason, I felt he was either confused or amused. It was impossible to tell without seeing someone's face. But the shadow of his mouth and jaw seemed at ease, playful even. "There's something over there." I handed him my shovel, which he took readily, as I stumbled through the creaky gate and up the dune. "It's coming by your cathedral," I said when I realized he was following me. "Someone yelling... 'ahhh'?"

He didn't speak, content to see where I'd go. When I knelt by a bush, I swore I saw rustling—

Bahhhh!

I screamed and fell backward into a patch of grassy sand as a little black goat jumped out at me. "What the hell!" I swore as the little horned creature climbed into my lap. And then an even more surprising sound. I turned to see Father Amorth, laughing with his hands on his knees. *Laughing*.

"Are you laughing at me?" I screeched.

He looked up and pointed. "It's eating your hair."

Turning, the goat's yellow rectangle eyes peered into mine, my long braid hanging from its mouth. And then I started giggling so hard my sides ached. "I didn't know you had a goat, Father Amorth," I said, drying my eyes.

"I don't," he answered, lowering to sit next to me. "But it looks as if you do now."

I squealed with happiness. "You mean I can keep him?"

He chuckled lowly again, the sound sending jolts of emotion through me. Petting the goat's soft ear, Father Amorth tilted his head. "How could I not give you anything that makes you smile like that?"

Did he really just say that?

Was I really sitting in the grass outside an old cathedral, laughing with my exorcist priest?

His knee was touching my leg ever so slightly. The contact was like electricity, sending tremors of desire all over my body. I fought the urge to shiver with need at just the feel of it. Did he even notice he was doing it? At any moment, Lady Vanessa was going to pop out of the bushes and whip me with a switch for the bruise to my purity. A knee touch from Lucifer, she'd say it was. The Head Lady of Sorrow would gladly beat me for the salacious act of sitting so close to a man, our legs touching, alone. But Father Amorth wasn't just a man, was he? He was a priest, a holy man, an exorcist. Priests were powerful, revered, beloved, and feared. When I was in confession or prayer with my church's clergy, that didn't count as being alone with a man; priests didn't count as regular men.

That's why they got away with everything.

I thumbed the tiny nubs of the goat's horns and ran my fingers through its soft black fur. The animal curled up, content in my lap. Lady Vanessa's Lucifer cry made me smile as I said softly, "I'll call him Lucifer, Luci for short."

When I looked up, Father Amorth was looking at me. And for a split moment, I thought I saw it beneath the shadow of his hood— piercing eyes and furrowed dark brows. Something carved from stone, some rendering of art come to life. He took my breath away and pattered the beat of my heart so loud I could hear it.

Ding, Ding, Ding.

Wait, no, that was really happening. Father Amorth pulled his gaze from me and looked over his shoulder at the cathedral. "Well, I'll be damned."

"Your church sings?" I asked, smiling. "It's beautiful."

He glanced back at me after a long moment, the chimes still playing an ancient, forlorn tune. "I haven't heard those bells in a very, very long time."

"Really?" I asked. "Are they on some sort of timer?"

He shook his head. "Not one of this earth. I think they like you."

"I like them," I answered, feeling my cheeks warm. I liked *him*. Maybe his answer should have struck me as odd, but really, all holy men were odd. Talking of other realms and god like any commonplace thing. Those matters seemed the most boring thing on the planet when I was sitting with him, for some reason.

He rubbed Luci's fur, causing my breath to hitch in my chest as his knuckles brushed over my thighs. Did he mean to do it? Surely, it was an innocent mistake. "Thank you for coming to tend the garden, church bells."

My heart melted in my chest, and I swallowed my heated and elated emotions when I realized he'd given me a pet name. "I've never had a nickname before. Just Holy Daughter, Holy Virgin, sometimes Selah."

"I'll be your first then, church bells," he answered deliberately. The sentence seeming charged and laced with alternate meanings. My mind flew into a frenzy of impure thoughts. God, how I would take every lashing, every punishment in the world for Father Amorth to be my first... to be my first everything.

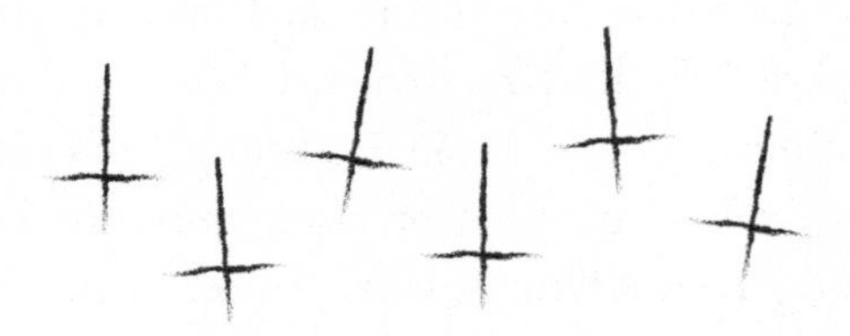

A glossy round sphere floated in front of my face before popping on my nose. More followed, and I looked for the source above me. Seated on the high, stone stairway's ledge was a girl in a plaid skirt, her uniform ruffled, and blonde hair pulled into a ponytail. She waved when she noticed me and continued blowing bubbles. Curiosity pulled me up the stairs after her, though I couldn't remember ever approaching a girl my age before, not even in sacred text study or on mission work at Lady of Sorrow.

"Selah, right?" She said, blowing another stream of bubbles before outstretching her hand. "I'm Angelica."

"Nice to meet you—"

Another friend with a short red bob haircut joined her, looking me over curiously. "This is Eve," Angelica introduced, fastening the bubble lid.

Eve bit her lip before asking. "So, are you here as a nun or a student? The white nun get-up is throwing me off. But you're also young-looking?"

Angelica elbowed her friend. "You can't just ask people that. Our stories of how we came here are personal, you know that."

Eve's freckled face blushed, and she fidgeted with her backpack strap. "Sorry, we're just curious."

"No, it's okay," I answered. "I'm the Holy Daughter of Lady of Sorrow Church. I don't know. I guess I don't know if I'm more like a nun or more like a student, either. Sort of both, sort of neither," I shrugged awkwardly.

Eve raised an eyebrow. "*The* Holy Daughter of Lady of Sorrow? That's the main huge mega-church. Y'all have like twenty services a week. The huge projectors and worship is like a concert with flying gymnastic acts and shit, right? Our Lady of Sorrow Church was a lot smaller, but I remember seeing you on screen sometimes. You always sat up front looking sad."

Angelica looked at me wide-eyed. "*You're* the Holy Daughter. My parents made me listen to a whole collection of Holy Daughter sermons about how I was supposed to aspire to be like you. You're like, religious royalty."

Then, it was my turn to turn pink. "I'm definitely not anyone special..."

The two girls assessed me before looking at each other. Eve spoke carefully, "We are done with classes for the day... do you want to come hang out in our dorm with us? We smuggled in a TV."

"Don't lead her on," Angelica laughed. "We can't get it to work."

I perked up at their invitation. Like I'd passed some sort of friend test. "Is it an antenna or an analog boxed television?"

"Bunny ears," Eve answered.

"Perfect, I think I can help. We had one at the bottom of my church, and I fiddled with it all the time to get it to work."

Angelica put her arm around my shoulder, "I knew I blew bubbles at the right nun-girl."

Their room was smaller than mine, which was peculiar because there were two of them and only one of me. Their beds were stacked on each other in ways I'd only seen on TV. But there were rosy drapes over their windows, colorful flower mirrors on the walls, and shag pastel carpets strewn over the cold floor. They'd made it their own, and I had a melancholy thought that if I'd been born into a different church, maybe I would have turned into a girl who blew bubbles and decorated with pink curtains. Angelica slapped the dusty cube in the corner and coughed, making Eve break out in laughter. "Well," she cleared her throat. "Here she is. Think you can make her work?"

I inspected the plug and fiddled with the rabbit ear antennas. It was smaller than the model in Lady of Sorrow's basement, but I thought they all had to be pretty similar. I tinkered with the dials, watching the static fade from black and white to pops of distorted color.

"Is it true you have to confess to Father Amorth?" Eve asked after a moment of whispers behind me. She then squeaked, and when I looked, she was rubbing her arm.

Angelica gave me a pained expression. "We're nosy, I'm sorry. Nothing interesting happens here."

"Somehow, I doubt that's true," I murmured, turning back to the antenna and pointing it more toward the window as I searched for a signal. "But yes, I confess to him."

"What's he like?" Angelica asked. "Has he taken off his hood?"

Eve giggled. "Is he as hot as his brothers?"

I paused. "Father Amorth has brothers?"

"Duh, *Daddy*— I mean—*Father* Silas, and then another who I've only seen once, Nikolai."

Angelica pulled a pack of red candy from under her mattress. "Here, for your time and gossip."

Smiling, I knocked back a handful of the sugary balls. "He hasn't taken off his hood, no."

"You just *know* he's sexy. He has to be, with how hot Father Silas and Father Nikolai are," Eve mused. "He's so tall and broad... and his *hands*— you can always tell if they're hot by their hands."

"You're such a horn dog," Angelica teased. "Poor innocent Selah probably has never even considered such a foul thing." She offered me more candy, and I nodded, feeling awkward when her palm touched mine to transfer the sweets.

"I haven't... *not*... thought about it," I admitted, and the color took shape on the screen as the two girls giggled playfully in response to my answer. Though I had no idea Silas was Father Amorth's brother... and that he had *another* brother. *Three* Amorth men... Three Grimm priests. "Where is his other brother, Nikolai?" I asked, gently tugging the left metal stick to make the image on the screen sharper.

Eve crawled closer, clapping her hands, delighted at my progress. "Nobody knows. The priests here are mysterious as all get out, but we all have our guesses at what they're up to."

My shoulders tensed in concern. Did they know what went on in my confessions with Father Amorth—or worse, had others had similar experiences? The thought had jealousy budding in my abdomen.

Eve sighed dramatically and flung herself onto the bottom bunk. "All the hot priests take vows of celibacy, unfortunately. At least I assume so, they never flirt with students or staff. We're stuck with the dumb boys here—"

A melodic knock rapt across the door before it burst open, Noah stumbling inside and taking me in with shock. He sheepishly put his hands behind his back. "Hello, ladies, you're looking lovely. Nice to see you've adopted *holy* company for once."

Angelica threw a pillow at his middle. "You just want us for our snacks, Noah."

"Not true. I heard there was a television, too." He flashed me a smile before slumping down on the carpet next to me as I positioned the TV toward the center of the room. A talk show was playing. It was watchable, though fuzzy. "And you aren't bad to look at either," Noah purred in my ear. He smelled strongly of alcohol, and his British accent slurred his words slightly.

"Don't narc on us, holy daughter," he said, pulling out two green bottles.

Eve squealed. "Wine! I'll trade you a bag of chips."

"Two bags of crisps and a candy bar," Noah retorted as Eve rolled her eyes and dug under her bed for her trade.

Watching them was like going to an exhibition at a museum. Every word— every joke that landed it was like my own live, in-person television program. They were fascinating, funny, and so full of life.

"What do you all plan to do after you graduate?" I asked in curiosity.

The room went silent for a moment like I'd asked the wrong question, and I internally shriveled at my unknowing stupidity. Would interactions with peers ever not be awkward for me? Granted, they'd been so limited my entire life. It was hard conversing with them, but I wanted so badly to be one of them at the same time.

Noah answered, "School forever, probably. Maybe move on to being a professor when I'm old."

That answer surprised me. "So you can go to school here for as long as you want? They never kick you out?"

Angelica giggled. "That's how we all got in this mess."

Eve elbowed her friend and shoved a red plastic cup into her palms. She poured another and offered it to me. "Communion wine?"

"This is communion wine?" I gasped, reluctantly taking the cup.

"It's blessed and ready for mass tomorrow."

"Doesn't affect the taste," Noah smirked, tipping his cup to mine. "For Oliver, my missing friend that none of the nuns or priests are concerned about." He saluted before downing his in one gulp.

"He'll turn up," Eve soothed, placing a hand on Noah's knee. "If the clergy don't seem alarmed. Maybe they know things they aren't allowed to say—"

"Or *won't* say." His gaze shifted into something icy as he peered at me through glossy eyes. "Has your exorcist said anything about it?"

Everyone's attention fixed on me, and I not so subtly nudged my full cup under the bed. "No, nothing."

They were soon distracted by the TV and snacks, and I quickly excused myself to my room. To wait for mass, to wait for another chance to see *my* exorcist— to wonder about the three brothers of Grimm...

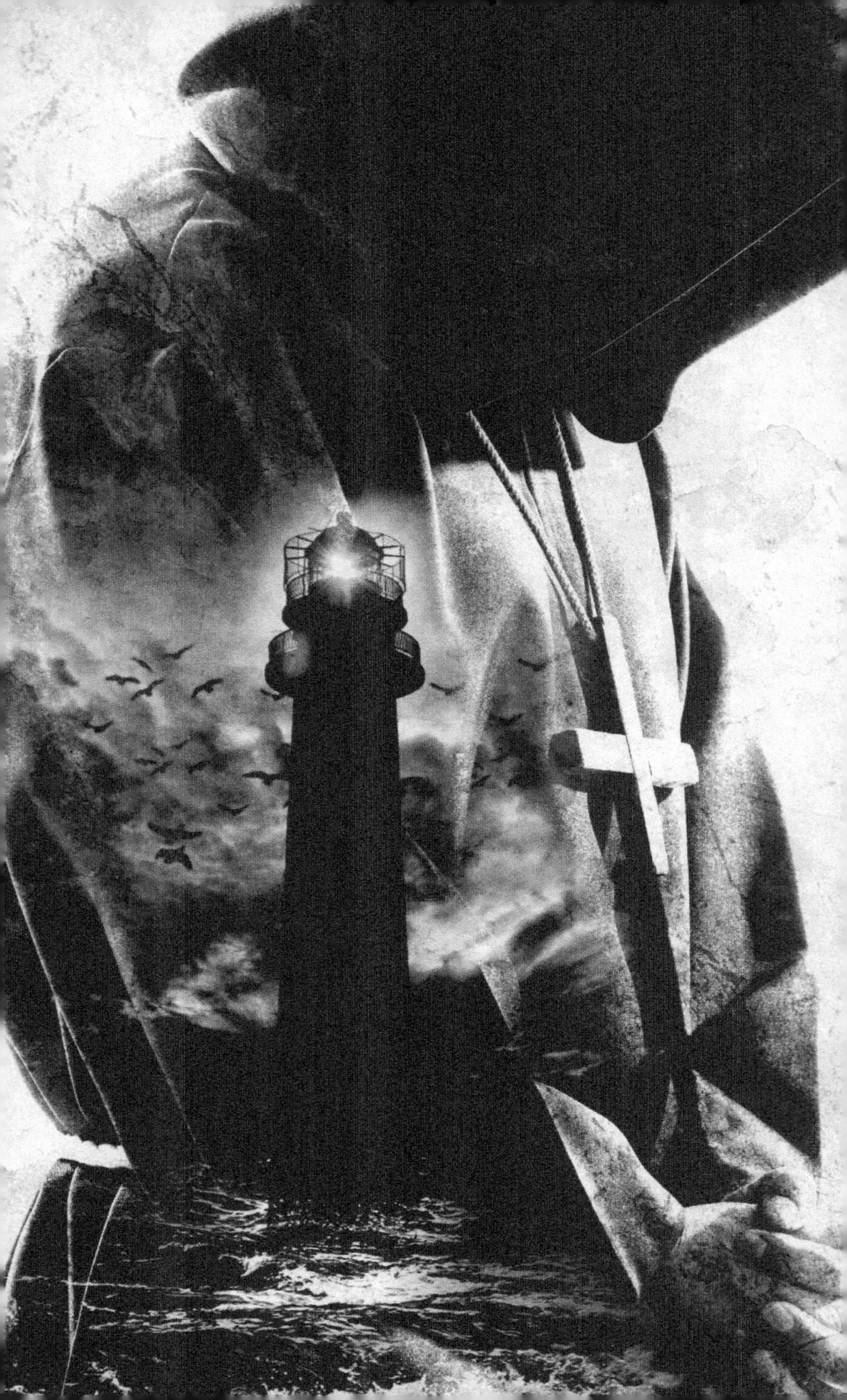

CHAPTER SIXTEEN

Sunday mass, Sunday church, Sunday hymns. The songs were old and sang with the same reverent boredom I'd heard for years upon years. Much was the same. Much was wicked, much was consecrated, much was hidden, and still much waited to be revealed.

Though something that wasn't the monotony of my day-to-day...

Selah.

My Church Bells.

Did she feel me? Did she feel me desperately fighting against my every blasphemous urge when we were outside the cathedral that day? God and devil smite me. All I wanted to do was pin her to the ground, rip off her stupid little robes, and fuck her until the fabric dyed itself red with her virgin blood offering. How dare she? How dare she look at me with those wide, gray eyes? How dare her giggle, the swing of her hips, the soft touch of her palm... Fuck—how dare she do this, *be* this.

And my goddamn cathedral. That old and stubborn building sat silent for me for decades, but for her—it fucking purred like a kitten. It sang her name, the bells wrote a melody just for her, sending her a goat, and I had to fight my tears at the joy of it all. I didn't deserve joy, I sure as fuck didn't deserve her. Selah was perfection. She was holy and pure—but not in the fucked up patriarchal ways her upbringing had poised her to be. Selah was an untamed wildflower forced into a row of carbon copy, dulled roses.

Selah wasn't mechanical and pruned. Selah was rusty church bells singing a siren song after a hundred songless years. There was something enchanting in her tenderness, in the wildness lurking within, in the gentle violence of her challenging gaze as she sought to see me for who I was.

Under my hood, in my cathedral, shattering my garden, and humming in my confessional.

Fuck.

It was wise of me to seek distance, and I intended to keep some. I knew if I had her in my confessional again after that night—I'd lose all control. It would scare her, wouldn't it? To see me as I was. To learn I wasn't such a gentle giant—but more a depraved monster than she could ever imagine or learn about in Sunday school. Father Amorth wasn't just an exorcist priest. He was Dante, the grim and terrible. She deserved a better, softer, more contained version of a man than I could ever aspire to be. Though everything inside me screamed to corrupt her, to take her as mine, to *claim* her... I wouldn't.

I couldn't damn her like that.

I'd walked her to her dorm with her silly little goat and sat outside her stairs all night, just staring at my lighthouse home. And then Sunday came, and I found myself in the shadows behind the altar. Listening to the choir, tuning out the songs, remembering the hymn of her laughter mixed with the chimes of my cathedral. She was the church bells, wasn't she? Come to life to bring beauty into my dried and fire-ready garden of nothing.

Could I be so selfish as to accept that offering? Could I be so egotistical as to invite a world of sin and darkness into the life of The Holy Daughter? And no doubt I'd have hordes of Lady of Sorrow clergy ready to burn me at a stake if I so much as touched her. Though touch her, I tried. A simple brush of my palms, my knuckles on her thigh... God, what was I doing? I'd already crossed a vicious line with Oliver, all because he touched her hair. *Dante* was winning more often than not, and the priest within me needed to regain control.

Silas joined me behind the altar as the choir stopped, the students clapped, and Sister Nella began her sermon. Pouring the communion wine into a large, ornate copper goblet, my brother glanced at me in that sideways manner he often did. Looking pristine as always, black suit pressed, priest's collar blindingly white, his long ivory hair tied at the nape of his neck. A white wolf, the nuns and students alike called him. A man valuable and charming next to my chaos and all-consuming greed. "Father Benedict emailed again wanting a status update on the Holy Virgin Princess."

"Tell him my exorcisms don't come with tracking information, this isn't the goddamn postal service."

Silas chuckled darkly. "I'll put him off, but I imagine they'll want her back soon. I'm sure her betrothed husband is eager to receive her."

My blood simmered as I gritted my teeth. "Did I tell you they watch her bathe? Lady of Sorrow Church—to ensure her purity."

Silas's hard gaze snapped to me as he broke the unleavened bread on a serving platter. He hummed in his throat. "That's likely the tip of the iceberg, don't you think?"

There it was. He tried to hide it, deny it, shove it deep down inside beneath his cologne and bright smile. But he was as bloodthirsty as I was, as hell-bent on revenge as the rest of us. The corner of my mouth rose. "We'll find out what lurks beneath. We always do."

The white wolf held the goblet of wine and the tray, gesturing toward the stage. "Speaking of," he said lowly. "Father Patrick is almost ready."

I jerked a nod and followed him below the altar on the nuns' cue. Preaching wasn't my calling, but I enjoyed breaking the body of Christ and offering his blood to the congregation. My upside-down cross and pentagram rosary hung around my neck, and students and worshipers from the village isle stared as I stood in front of the altar. They lined up, ready to receive their blessing. So many took place in this ritual without knowing, without questioning its beauty and meaning.

Father Patrick would be taking part in a similar ritual soon, wouldn't he?

The first few students avoided looking up at me, saying their prayer, tapping a cross to their foreheads, shoulders, and hearts after I quickly placed the cracker on their tongues, and they drank from the goblet of wine. "Gods be with you," I blessed them each.

And then I froze as she appeared in front of me.

Wild and raging seas clashed amongst the shade of her eyes as they looked up at me. No one else looked up at me. Only few dared try and only in attempts to see below my hood, to see the face hidden from the world. But Selah didn't look out of morbid cynicism or decree—she looked to *see*, she searched, hoping to find and understand the world past the mask. I felt it then, the earnest desire, the pure but unholy want. And I wanted her in anything but pure ways. I wanted her in ways that would solidify my cage in the deepest parts of hell, and I'd snap the lock closed myself if it meant getting to touch her just one time.

If it were only me, it would be easy. Easy to be the selfish fucking wretch that I was. But I had a hundred kids looking to my island for sanctuary and a second shot at life and spirituality. I had nuns and priests with secrets that could obliterate them and take down this entire operation we sought to uphold—no—we *vowed* to uphold. To throw it all onto the thin ice of giving into my temptation with The Holy Virgin would be a deplorable evil both in deed and consequence. If ever a humble and righteous priest resisted within my bones, I needed him now, needed his wisdom.

Love, Joy, Peace, Patience... I chanted the fruits of the spirit in my mind to distract myself from her full berry lips and porcelain freckled skin. Imagining those long-braided pigtails wrapped around my wrists from behind as I pummeled her ass with my cock. Not things a priest should be thinking at the foot of a holy altar on a Sunday, in front of a hundred people.

But then she knelt while looking up at me. She dropped to her knees in front of the whole church. A sign of surrender, a sign of obedience and worship. My cock strained against my robes, and I tightened my grip on the goblet of wine, softly tilting it to her lips. She closed her eyes and took a small sip, and *god all fucking mighty,* I imagined it was the cum pouring from my cock instead of wine from a glass. How I wanted to grab her cheeks hard and purse those little lips. How I wanted to jerk her chin up until she choked down every drop of me.

"Selah," I whispered in warning, just low enough that she could hear. Her eyelids fluttered open, and she glanced down at the unleavened bread, parting her lips again.

"Yes, Father?" she whispered sweetly.

I wanted to drag her by her neck onto the altar and fuck her senseless for teasing me, for temping me, so brazen, so public. Instead, I broke a piece of the dry cracker and placed it into her mouth. Instead of pulling away, I paused a moment too long. And Selah, my naughty little church bell, flicked out her tongue and lapped gently at my thumb. An audible gasp left my throat, and I didn't even notice the choir pick up a hymn behind me as the piano began to play. There was still a line behind her, but communion was over, this kind was at least.

Before she stood, I grabbed her head. She stilled, eyes wide in shock, as I pulled off her veil and tossed it aside. "No more of that," I said. She didn't need to cover her goddamn hair here, not unless she wanted to.

"Yes, Father," she replied softly, her face falling. She rose and tapped her cross before giving a small bow. Like I was any other priest, like I wasn't *her* exorcist, like I wasn't her motherfucking *father* now. As if she weren't dangerously close to being my *claimed* for an eternity of damnation. The chorus of holy words, strung into song for god, vibrated through the altar beyond my curtained escape. This was backstage, and I was invisible, the way I preferred. If I didn't get away from her, I'd unleash the beast then and there.

My breathing was ragged, and noting I was alone, save for the thin wood separating me from the crowd of worshippers, I reached under my robe. Untying the rope around my waist, I pulled out my throbbing, hard cock, palming it roughly. This was because of her, it was her fault that I was crudely jerking at myself as the choir angelically sang Amazing Grace.

Selah, The Holy Virgin Daughter, was an abomination—just like me. I rested my hand on the altar wood, rapidly pumping my cock. My precum coating me, my imagination telling me it was spit from the deepest part of her little throat. The chorus a melody of her high-pitched screams as I pushed my dick into her mouth further.

What the fuck was she thinking licking my thumb like that? She deserved to be bruised, and she deserved a throat so raw she couldn't speak her sinful words again. A tongue I'd suck so hard it would ache when she tried to form words.

I tightened my hold to a near-excruciating level, feeling the thrum of applause and prayer beyond the altar. They had no idea their holy exorcist priest was masturbating to a white-robed virgin nun under the altar on which they prayed.

What did Selah look like under that thick gown? I imagined holding onto her round little hips, my fingers digging into her sides, while my cock ruined her tight asshole. Not thoughts a priest should have. Not fantasies anyone should have of a virgin dressed as a nun.

Oh, she'd be so ruined. And I'd ruined her so goddamn thoroughly—no awaiting husband would want her—none of her clergy would ever look at her again. Fuck, that was a thought, wasn't it? How wonderful would it be to destroy Selah just for me?

And on that wicked wondering—I came in ribbons of black, a reminder of my affliction, gliding from my palm to the altar. Coating the backside of the holy altar in my cum. It wasn't the most sacrilegious thing I'd done, and it sure as hell wouldn't be the last. Because even though I'd come, my cock still ached for her. To burn Selah's altar so that no man or god ever looked at her again, to sully her so completely that she was perfectly dirtied for me and me alone. How vile and greedy a thought, how depraved and wicked of a priest to even consider. I was the same as the men I mercilessly slaughtered.

But would I care? Would the holy man inside me take the reins and lock Dante back in his cage? My feet were moving, my mind was spinning, and I was searching for her through the after-church bustle. I'd see her again that night.

Confession was back on.

The Priest was in.

And I was ready to devour her sins.

Selah

CHAPTER SEVENTEEN

He knew, didn't he?

No more of that.

He'd said, admonishing me. Father Amorth felt my childish crush, didn't he? I swallowed the prickle of my embarrassment. Was it written all over my face? Was it in the way I looked at him instead of the holy sacrament he fed me? Taking the sacrament so lightly was sinful, one of the greatest sins. God could have killed me there where I knelt—but I suppose he took mercy on me. Father Amorth removed my veil, likely as a sign that I didn't deserve it. He was right, I didn't.

Even so, it only proved that I needed him more than ever. I needed an exorcist of the demons inside me. The lustful thoughts, the wants, the needs. They weren't vague inclinations now. No, they were targeted attacks, and the person I imagined was *him*.

And in my fantasies, we never got married first. We didn't do things in a god-honoring way. We did it the heathen sinner way. Premarital sex, kissing, touching, I wanted it all with him, and I wanted it now. That was so, so sinful. But shame wasn't at the forefront of my mind. He was. This was bad. So, so bad.

To rid myself of the demons, would I need to confess these illicit desires to him? Surely, I must. This was going to be so humiliating, but if I wanted freedom and a true exorcism, maybe that's what I needed to do. His guidance in how he told me to touch my body hadn't been enough to satiate the lust. In fact, it only stoked the flame further. He needed to know he would have to help me, and that likely involved pain and guilt and whatever agonizing process an exorcist deployed.

Father Amorth had walked away from the dozens of others awaiting holy sacrament—disgusted with me. Being the righteous exorcist he was, he likely couldn't fathom the demons that swirled within me, and he retreated to pray as he should. God, I was so embarrassed.

Basically tripping down the crowded halls, all I wanted was to retreat to my room to cry for a while, but someone grabbed my arm. Sister Grace's gaze was narrow, "Take a deep breath, and come with me," she said evenly.

Oh no, she knew. They all knew. They all saw what a horrid display I'd just put on. Had Father Amorth sent them to send me away? My heart dropped, and tears filled my eyes. However, the nun didn't pull me toward the boat docks but down a passageway and up a set of stairs. I realized it was Father Amorth's office too late, as she opened the door and terror greeted me in the round room.

My breath froze, iced inside my lungs. They couldn't contract-- couldn't move or push out air. Lady Vanessa and two other ladies of sorrow stood straight-backed and prim in the center of the circular office. Sister Nella, Sister

Grace, and Sister Elodie looked at me with wide eyes as I entered.

Lady Vanessa pursed her lips, looking me over with fury, her steely gaze fixating on my exposed hair. "Holy Daughter, where is your—"

Sister Elodie appeared behind me; I hadn't even heard her move across the creaky floor. "Your veil," she cooed. "Freshly laundered. We aren't accustomed to so much white around here. Selah's laundry is done separately so as not to tarnish her robes and veils with our black garbs." She gently tugged the white veil over my head, and my lungs allowed me the smallest breath.

"It appears much may become sullied here, Sister Elodie."

Sister Grace left my side and moved around the desk, glancing from me to Lady Vanessa and her stern expression before passing glances at the two ladies of sorrow flanking the head lady. The ladies looked down, faces pale.

"Can I get you all some tea?" Sister Grace offered.

Lady Vanessa pursed her lips, speaking for the two ladies. "I'm sure you're aware that ladies of sorrow take vows of silence. And no, tea will not be necessary. We are here to check in on our Holy Daughter. We at the ruling Lady of Sorrow church feared that our holy laws of sacred discipline would not be adhered to at Grimm, and now," she shot me a harsh look. "I can see that the lord placed that upon my heart as a grand discernment. No veil, walking the halls freely—"

Sister Grace cut in, crossing her arms as she stared up at Lady Vanessa. A black viper poised below a white owl.

"There is nothing that is, or ever could be, sullied when it comes to Selah."

The room went silent, and I could feel the tension and anger roiling from both the matriarch of Lady of Sorrow and the three nuns. It was like the hours before a storm arrived on the beach. Potent, deadly, and filled with destruction.

"That is where we profoundly differ in our beliefs, *sister*." Lady Vanessa spat the last word as if it were beneath her. As if sister nuns were somehow lesser than ladies of sorrow. It thawed my lungs with bitterness and disdain. The ladies of sorrow had always been rude and cold toward me— but to see them behave in such a way toward these women who had been so loving and kind... it had the demons of sin within me entertaining vicious thoughts.

Sister Grace answered, her tone even and plain as she leaned against the desk, still eyeing the two quiet women who joined us. "With that, I heartily agree with you. Now, how can we be of service today, Lady Vanessa?"

"Father Benedict has instructed us to inspect The Holy Daughter's sleeping arrangements, bathing routines, and whom she interacts with to ensure the highest purity standards."

One of the sisters scoffed, and a silent lady of sorrow lifted her eyes in curiosity at who would dare commit such a sin in the presence of their stone-faced leader.

Sister Grace tensed her jaw. "We can certainly give you a tour of the church and grounds, but—"

The door flew open with a crash that shook the floorboards. Thunder between two storms himself stomped into the room. Father Amorth, a black shadow that even made Lady Vanessa step back in apprehension. His hood hung low, and he towered over all of us, though he didn't go to the desk, and didn't move to block the nuns. No, he stepped in front of me. His massive frame blocked me from view, and all I could do was stare up at his shoulders as his breathing was rapid, like he was barely containing himself.

"Good, a holy man is here. Someone in charge," Lady Vanessa said in a clipped tone.

Silence for an unnerving few moments spanned before he spoke. "We are all equals here, Lady of Sorrow, and trust me when I assure you, I am *not* the man you want to be in charge."

The matriarch shuffled on her feet, uncomfortable, as I peeked from the side of Father Amorth's arm. He was like a giant hawk. His black robes were his wings, tucking me in and protecting me. But he couldn't protect me from my fate, couldn't keep them from snatching me back to where I belonged. Surely, Lady Vanessa smelt the sin all over me, and it was probably clear on my face.

Sister Grace spoke up with low confidence, not trepidation. The sisters didn't fear Father Amorth, not like the Ladies of Sorrow feared the clergy or my dad. They were equals, he said. *Equals.* "Lady of Sorrow Church sent Lady Vanessa here to ensure we were following their purity principles."

"That's correct," the old woman added haughtily. "We will see that our Holy Virgin's sleeping, socializing, and bathing are within the sanctification vows we hold The Holy Daughter to—"

"Her *name*," Father Amorth interrupted deeply, barely concealing the tremor of rage in his tone. "Is Selah."

The room was thunderously silent again, just waiting for a lightning crack. "We must ensure—"

"Say it," Dante growled. "Say. Her. Name."

Lady Vanessa paled as she widened her eyes and sought to see beneath Father Amorth's hood. It was a standoff between two very opposing forces. Cold ivory against hardened onyx. But slowly, the Lady of Sorrow relented, stumbling over my name as if it were a terrible curse she was forbidden to utter.

"Selah. We are to monitor Selah's purity conditions while you are seeing to her exorcism. She must be returned to us fully sanctified and ready to wed."

My heart dropped in my shoes, and Father Amorth's head twitched slightly, and I noted his fists at his side. "I'm going to tell you what you're going to do," he said with unnerving calm. "You may stay overnight in accommodations we provide you. Though you may not touch, speak to, or so much as look at Selah." His tone turned dark and threatening when he said, "I will personally monitor *your* bathing, Lady Vanessa. I'll watch you every moment and listen to every conversation. You are far from pure, aren't you?" He clicked his tongue. "In fact, why don't we assess your own purity now? Take off your robes."

The room and even the approaching storm beyond the stained-glass windows fell in strangled silence.

Lady Vanessa straightened, her face flushing red with anger. "This is ridiculous. You can't ask that of me—"

"I'm not asking," he growled. "I'm the man in charge you sought, aren't I? You come onto my island unannounced, storm into my church on the lord's day, and demand to abuse the privacy of a girl under my watch. Let me see if *you* are fit to assess such things. Stand before us naked, Lady Vanessa." Another moment passed before Father Amorth shouted, "Now!"

We all jumped, glancing at Lady Vanessa, who held fresh terror in her gaze.

He was serious.

He was going to make her undress in front of all of us. Maybe I should have felt sorry for her or had some sort of sympathy as she brought a wrinkled, age-spotted hand to her neck and unbuttoned the collar. I remembered how I'd never showered alone without hers or another's gaze, how I hadn't had a moment of privacy ever in my life. My knuckles still ached with the slaps of her ruler.

The heart of god was forgiveness.

The spirit of a holy daughter is that of mercy and kindness.

In that moment, I felt neither, as Lady Vanessa's robes dropped to the carpeted floor. Sister Martha raised an eyebrow at Father Amorth, "Father..." A questioning warning in her tone as The Lady of Sorrow paused over her white under-gown.

"No," he answered her, his attention still fixed on the matriarch. "Go on. I said naked."

The two ladies of sorrow next to her didn't flinch and didn't seem to mind as they stared at their feet. Occasionally, the girl on the left would lift her eyes curiously around the room, almost as if she was enjoying the spectacle. It was terrible and humiliating, and... my sinner's heart was racing because I was enjoying it.

Watching Lady Vanessa experience a modicum of the embarrassment and lack of solitude I'd experienced my whole life.

She sniffled as she pulled off her gown, standing naked before us all, her gaunt face and features displaying the rage of humiliation.

"The priesthood of sorrow will hear of this. Mark my words," she threatened on a hollow breath.

"I'm counting on it," he continued. "Now, walk the halls." He kicked at her clothes on the floor, shoving them to the other side of the office. The room collectively gasped, and I watched on with horror and fascination. Was he really going to make her walk naked through the church? What would my dad do when he found out? What worried me more than anything, more than any care toward the terrible woman, was what would happen to Father Amorth when word reached my home church.

Lady Vanessa's mouth dropped, and a look of indignant fury crossed her wrinkled features. I might have smiled if I hadn't been so afraid. Any moment, she would grab my arm and storm out of the room to beat me with the ruler I was sure was permanently sewn inside her white robes. Though she wasn't wearing her robes, was she?

"We anticipated that the sordid tales we've heard of you may be true. Too much time with the darkness has muddled your mind, and I question your vows and loyalty to Lady of Sorrow, Father." She held her chin high, pretending she wasn't standing there nude and shamed. "We brought our own boatman and vessel. We will leave now and inform Father Benedict straight away of the conditions here and the rancid treatment we received."

Father Amorth took a step forward, gazing down into the woman's hard and angry expression. "Even better. My flock is not yours to judge, and nor is any within it. Your shame is but one sprout of you reaping what you've sowed."

Lady Vanessa reached for her robes, and Sister Grace moved, blocking her. "You heard him," she said in a low, sinister tone I hadn't heard from the nun before. "I'll escort you to your boat, but you're going just as you are."

With a huff of outrage, Lady Vanessa looked for me, but Dante stepped again, blocking her view. I heard a stomp, like a child not getting their candy, like a woman torn between standing in one spot for naked viewing or running through the halls to get it over with. Her predicament was horrifying, and yet I felt warmth in my chest at the retribution. Lady Vanessa, dressed only in her pointed boots and white head covering, loudly clipped out of the room with Sister Grace behind her. The two nuns left behind all looked at each other, communicating without words, before they quickly fled, following after them. I wasn't sure why or what the rush was, but they seemed to be on some sort of mission I wasn't privy to. Or maybe they just wanted to watch the show of a nude lady of sorrow stomping down the corridors on a busy Sunday and climbing into a boat. How I wished I could watch, too, but I couldn't move, frozen in place and realizing I was alone with the darkest man I'd ever known.

The exorcist had surely cast some sort of demon out of his office that day.

I was left behind with my dark raven.

My Grimm Reaper.

My protector.

The exorcist.

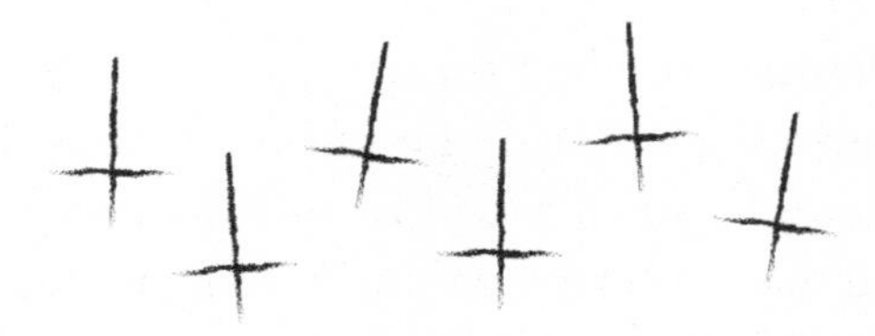

The door slammed shut, and the moment we were alone in the hallowed room, he was upon me. A yelp left my throat, and my back pressed into the bumpy, hard stone wall. He pinned me in with two hands above me, fists flexing and clenching like he was fighting the urge to strike me or touch me. I couldn't be sure which. I shirked into the rock, sucking in my stomach to keep from touching him. Not because I didn't want to touch him, I did, I really, really did. But it was instinct, imbedded into me from the moment I was born. Touch was bad, touch was sinful, and sexual desires led to death and ruin. The mushy banana in my palm was me if I touched or let a man touch me. It had been so ingrained in my psyche that though I craved an embrace, I feared it at the same time.

Father Amorth angled his neck, looking down at me, and I wished more than ever I knew his face— could see his eyes— see anything other than the prickle of his hard jaw and his full and taunting lips.

"Did you want to go with them?" he asked gruffly, out of breath. "Answer me!" he barked impatiently, causing me to jump. He was angry, so very angry.

"N-no!" I almost yelled back.

"Did you call them here? Huh? Is this what you wanted— what you planned the entire time?" He gritted his teeth together, still pinning me into his shadow and large, muscular frame. Cornered by a raging storm cloud, so close I could feel his ragged breath blow over my face—the smell of him like a mossy ocean breeze on a gloomy day.

Frustrated and feeling my body warm to an uncomfortable level, something unfurling within the pit of my stomach with ache, I yanked off my veil and shoved it at his hard chest. "No! Are you such a fool that you think I *want* them? That I *want* to go back to that? Do you not *see* me?" I yelled back at him, feeling hot tears jab at the corners of my eyes. "I am filled with demons, Father Amorth. Lust, desire, disobedience, and *hate*. So much *hate*, father."

Something like a growl tumbled from his throat, and my lips parted at the sound as my breathing harmonized with his. My heart pounded in my chest, and I wiped away my hot tears with the sleeve of my gown. I pushed my veil at his chest again, wanting him to jerk it from me, to hit me, to scold me for my confession, anything. But he stood like a mountain, sheltering me within his walls.

"So, take me, please. Take my demons away, Father. I don't want to be this sinful abomination anymore. Just make me into what they want and send me home so you can be rid of me."

"Is that what *you* want?" he asked lowly.

"Yes," I answered, gritting my teeth and trying to sound tough, though my sniffling from crying made me sound like a petulant child.

After a heavy moment of silence, he pulled back, and light enveloped me once more, making me blink at the sting of it. "So be it. Come to confession tonight, Selah."

It felt as if I'd been punched in the stomach. His reproach during the sacrament, his ready and easy agreement to getting on with my exorcism and sending me on my way. Father Amorth didn't want me, didn't care about me. This was a stupid crush of a stupid, sheltered, naive little girl and nothing more. I'd been such a fool to entertain thoughts of someone like him forming some sort of a connection with someone like me. No, I wasn't someone, was I? I was an alabaster cross, a decoration you dusted and hung on the wall, and people looked to as a reminder to feel guilty beneath a god that never answered their prayers.

No wonder Father Amorth didn't like me.

There was no *me* to like.

I was nothing.

Nameless nothing.

I swished past him and then out of the room, and he didn't stop me or call after me. A strobe of lightning illuminated the suddenly dark hall of the gothic church as I held onto the wall. My eyes were clouded with tears, but my feet knew the way. And before I knew it, with only the sound of my hot and harried breathing in my ears, rain specked my face, and the soles of my thin ballet flats moved from cobblestone to sand.

The ocean raged around me, and I didn't know why, and I didn't know what I was thinking, but I walked right for it with no hesitation. Like a siren being called home, like my inevitable death pulling me forward on a phantom string. My crying was a gargled sob by the time the waves lapped around my ankles, my body sinking around the broken shells as they scraped against my skin. The ladies of sorrow's boat was long gone, but another flash of lightning splintered the sky. The ocean became angry, as mad as Father Amorth seemed. The sky and the priest were both furious to be inconvenienced by my very existence.

So was I.

I agreed with the murky torrent as it slammed against my chest. Another wave beat against my chin, and my toes left the ground. Fear edged into my psyche as I glanced up and realized the shore was much farther and to the left than it was when I abandoned it. The rain picked up, coming in sheets, and the thought of swimming back was half-baked when another wave caught me by surprise—pushing me under, deeper, deeper into a swirl of tiny bubbles of dark silence.

Blessed silence.

This was dying, wasn't it? Officially dying. Because I was already dead, I realized. My life held no value, no more value than a breeding heifer.

Keep pure.

Keep sweet.

Stay silent.

Be obedient.

Commands you'd give a dog were my life's decree and the most I could aspire to. Why would any man want me for anything else? I was here to be a vessel for god, for old men's semen, for violent men's babies, for their fists, for their sermons, for their dinners. No, the most I could do would be to take that power away from them. To say I'd rather greet the ocean of black eternity than live under their chains. Finally, I'd had enough. Finally, I no longer cared about being their nameless Proverbs 31 virtuous woman.

She worked too hard and did too much. Did anyone ever ask her if she wanted to be *the* virtuous wife? The verses never even gave her name. She had no name. The Virtuous Wife was her name and all we knew her by, much like me. The Holy Virgin Daughter. The nameless woman that was my mother. That bore me in silence and died like nothing more than a contract fulfilled. I wondered if she loved me or hated me. I wouldn't blame her if she despised having me infiltrate her womb. We were the same, the woman who birthed me, the virtuous women of the sacred texts, nameless.

The only one to use my name, to look beyond the thin pages of me that were written by men, was Father Amorth.

No one would find me here. It was over, and it was over on my terms—finally.

As my mind and body grew gloriously numb and my lungs burned with protest in the cold sea—an arm looped around my waist, thrusting me to the surface. The storm raged overhead, and I coughed, my vision blurry from the salt water.

"Do you seek death, Selah?" Father Amorth asked, rough and deep, holding me above the thrashing waves.

Was his hood down? My heart leaped in my throat. How had he found me, gotten to me at the bottom of the water? It wasn't possible.

"Yes," I cried out.

"Then you have him," he growled. And before I could register what was happening, his mouth was on mine. A sob mixed with surprise—assuredly, I'd died—this was some dark heaven where Father Amorth rescued me from the drowning tide and sealed my fate with a kiss of death. The grim reaper found me in the water, and his lips were on mine.

I didn't know how to kiss, but always imagined what it would be like. Though even in my wildest fantasies, I couldn't have guessed it would be in the ocean, during a storm, with my exorcist. He pressed my body close to his, and it felt like our robes didn't exist in the water. It was only warm and wet bodies flush to each other. My small and weak form held so tightly to his wide and muscular frame. One arm held me to his abdomen while the other cupped my face. His tongue flicked into my mouth, and he groaned along with my whimper of a moan. Rain and sea, he and I were both these dreadful things and together we were drowning in each other's whirlpool.

"Take this," he said against my lips. "As your baptism, Selah."

He'd carried me closer to shore, and with a clap of thunder, he pulled away and dunked me under the water before roughly pulling me back up. "Buried in death with baptism—resurrected to live a brand new life."

I reached for his shoulders, needing his mouth again, and he obliged, kissing me deeply. I couldn't believe this was happening, that he was baptizing me and kissing me in the rough ocean. Father Amorth kissed me like a starving man like he couldn't get enough, like it's all he wanted to do until the end of time.

My first kiss was supposed to be for my husband.

Another bruise on the fruit of my purity.

But I didn't care.

He scooped me into his arms and laid me on the sandy shore as the storm continued to rage, his hand pulling up my heavy, sopping skirts and pressing his palm between my knees. "Tell me to stop," he growled with a flash of thunder, his hood dripping rainwater, making him look like some evil wraith of a deity.

I shook my head. "No, don't stop."

With a groan that rivaled the thunder, Father Amorth's wet palm slicked down my inner thigh. Those hands I'd stared at and fantasized about were finally touching me. The smallest of sensations were driving me wild, and the storm and sea beyond silenced. It was only him and I, like lovers washed up on the beach. Pulling my underwear to the side, he didn't hesitate for a moment before pushing two of his long fingers flat against my slit. I gasped into his kiss, moving my hips up to meet his touch, to beg it to go deeper. He hooked the tips of his touch, lightly pressing against my opening.

"Are your demons in here?" he murmured with a husky breath in my ear. "Is this pretty little pussy where I'll find your darkness hiding, church bells?"

My kiss was frantic against his lips as I nodded in near tearful need. "Try and see," I answered.

With a dark chuckle and no warning, he thrusted one finger inside, and I gasped at the intrusion.

"Fuck me, Selah, you're so fucking tight," he cursed. "I'm going to tear you apart."

"Please do," I begged, bucking my pelvis forward and taking him to his knuckles. It was an uncomfortable, painful euphoria, and I knew I needed more. Breaking our kiss, he pulled back, hooded features rivaling the darkness of the clouded and angry sky. Dante Amorth was the sea, the storm, the expanse of the night sky, and that's all I needed to fall in love with a face I couldn't see. Together, we were the eye of the storm. A brief reprieve from the sinister destruction that raged around us.

"I want to watch you come in my hand," he said gruffly. "That's it, just like that. You're taking my fingers so well, church bells."

His fingers were so long as they hooked inside me, gathering the wetness there, while the hard of his palm rocked against my swollen clit. I came staring into the darkness beyond his covering, the Grimm Reaper affording me a little death at his scythed hand. Ushering forth pleasure that should be worthy of dying. My scream broke the sky in bright white lightning—god's fury at our sin written on the clouds as the aftershocks of my orgasm pulsed around my undertaker. I would die for this. I would lay my virginity like a quiet lamb on Dante's altar, hoping he'd bleed me slowly, slowly, tormenting me forevermore.

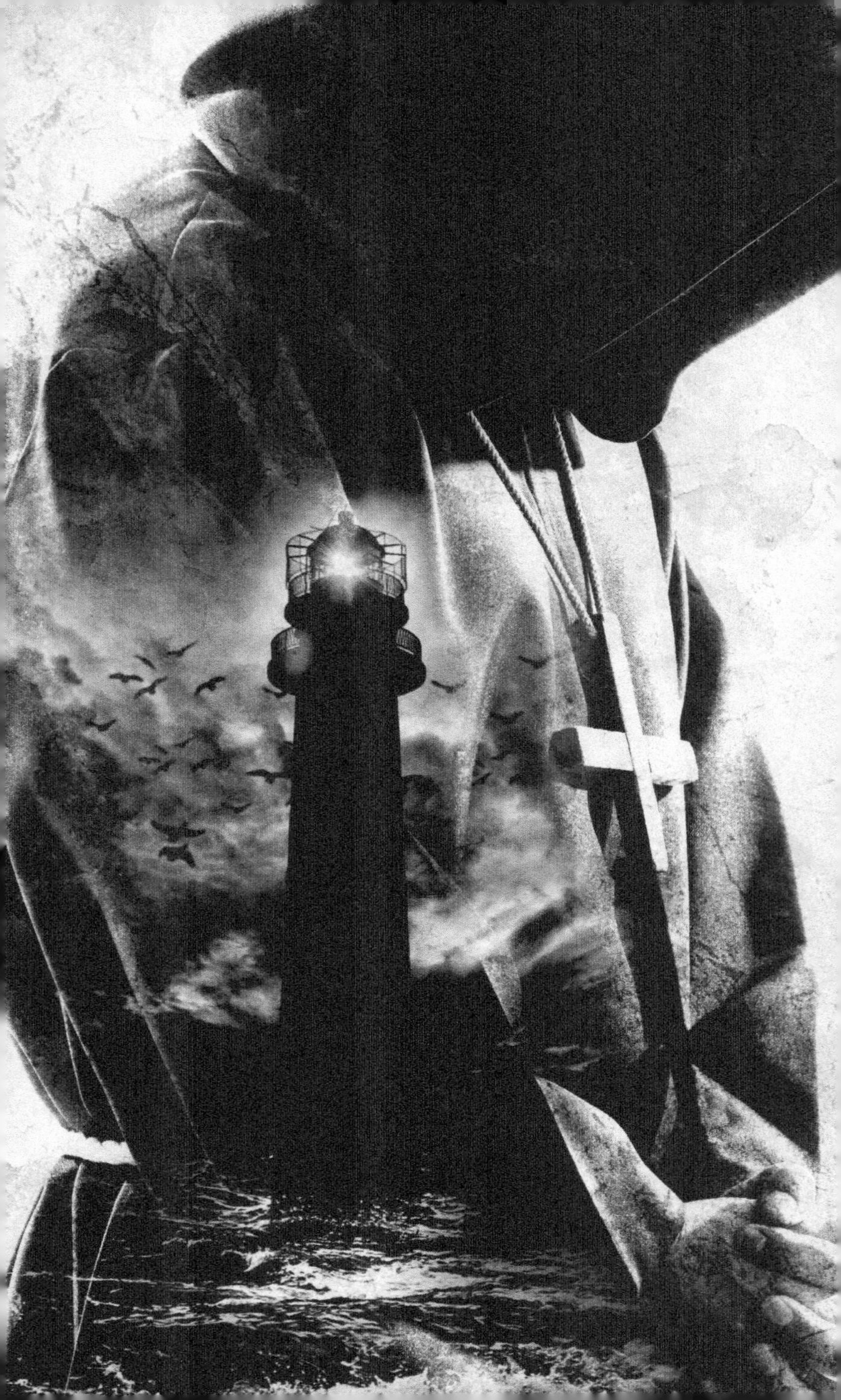

Dante

CHAPTER EIGHTEEN

I remembered myself, knuckles deep in Selah's holy cunt. Rain thrashed around us, and thunder clapped overhead as I brought her to another orgasm she sought, desired, and lusted for. Oh, the priest was sleeping, but the demon was wide awake and salivating. Taking her on the beach like the animal I was. To an onlooker, it would look like such a scandal, a priest finger fucking a nun in white. We were drenched, and I coveted the smell of her on my skin as I licked my fingers clean. Control was gone in a sense, though the need to get her out of the rain was fiercer than what decorum I should have implemented.

Sin first, ask forgiveness later.

Smoothing down her sopping robes, I pulled her to her feet, a flash of lightning illuminating her rosy and freckled cheeks. Forcing my stare from the hypnotic way her gown clung to her body, the fabric delighting in every curve of her... I desired to lick every raindrop off her skin, to graze upon her nipples, to leave bite marks across her tender flesh. Though the beach was becoming a dangerous place, and these sudden storms were often relentless, I took her hand and led her into the village. The stairs would be slick, and if I carried her, it would draw more attention—though I didn't care at that point.

Before we reached our ascent a door opened, and a man hollered. "Father! Seek shelter in here."

Selah didn't hesitate, giving my hand a squeeze before letting go and darting into the warmth of the bakery. The aroma of bread was thick, and every lantern and lamp lit within the small, vine-covered space. Baker Clarence regarded us worriedly before peering out the window. "Sit, sit, I've got warm blankets and tea."

"Thank you, Clarence," I responded, pulling a chair for the wide-eyed girl staring between us. She was endearing and she also believed her every sin was written across her face for the world to see. Shame did that to a person, made them feel transparent and helpless. Her home clergy no doubt instilled those very qualities from infancy onward. My stomach churned with silent rage like a curling cobra. "This is Selah," I gestured by way of introduction.

"Pleasure to meet you," the baker grinned as he shook her wet hand. She gasped, not expecting the contact, and the movement intrigued me. The man hurried away and returned, draping a wool blanket over her shoulders and depositing tea and brownies in front of us. We thanked him, and he disappeared back to the kitchens as the storm shook the building with its winds.

"He's always been kind to me, even as a boy," I said after a moment, staring at my darling companion as she took a small sip of peppermint tea. "Are you... alright?"

Her face flushed again, and she focused on her brownie. I wanted to make her stare into my eyes. "Stop staring at your feet, at the ground, at your food, Selah. Hold your head up high."

That milky gaze shot up, eyeing me beneath her long, black lashes. "I don't know if you know this, Father, but no one can see your face."

That elicited a small chuckle as I let a swig of tea warm my tongue. "You don't say? I suppose we both hide our true faces then."

I watched in spellbound attention as she warmed her little hands around her tea before she spoke. "I can't believe you did that back there." Her face flushed before quickly adding. "With Lady Vanessa."

I'd already forgotten about it. All I could recall at that moment was the way Selah's tight little pussy felt stretched around my two fingers. I resisted the urge to lick them again and search for any lingering trace of her taste on my skin. "Are you horrified?" I asked. A loaded question.

"Yes," she replied meekly in her sweet-as-sin voice. "And I don't mind it."

Fascinating. Was there a touch of darkness within the holy daughter after all? "True religion... love..." I trailed off. What the fuck did I know about *love*? "It shouldn't be instilled by fear or power. Anything less is a counterfeit, a false prophet. You deserve respect. You deserve happiness and pleasure, Selah."

Letting out a breath, she shook her head slightly. She was quiet in that heavy way someone is when they're lost in thought, and I knew the happenings on the beach had to be sending a torrent of emotion through her. Guilt, regret, fear... it was nothing and everything I'd wanted. My every encounter with the holy daughter had been a violation of trust and righteous vows, and I'd torn through each sacred restraint like they were thin paper of sacred text. My time of reckoning, of punishment, would come.

"You're never touched, are you?" I asked the moment it dawned on me.

Glancing up in a panic, she startled, and I hid my smirk, nodding toward the bakery kitchen. "Are handshakes not pure enough for Lady of Sorrow Church?"

Selah let out a small breath of relief and shifted in her seat. "No one in the clergy is permitted to touch the holy daughter. Except for discipline instruments, and when I'd walked through the crowds, people may brush my robes or veil, for blessings—"

"Discipline?" I repeated lowly.

Her fingers fidgeted over the clay mug. "Yes..."

She may have continued speaking, I do not know, because fury was building in my ears to a level that mirrored the ocean beyond the walls. More and more was becoming clear as I sat with her, though I wasn't sure why I'd been blinded to it until now, until after our time on the beach. It was as if veils of gauze were dissolving, and I was seeing her clearly for the first time.

My mind's eye was perceiving her. Why was that? Why had it taken me this long? I was a man of many holy gifts, of fruits of the spirit varying on darkness. Demons, evils, and black magics were my rare specialty. Had I somehow been deceived? If I lingered on the notion, it would surely send me into a spiral that would destroy the bakery in its entirety, so I swallowed down the urge to ruminate too deeply and resolved to take my concerns to Silas soon. But I kept landing on her eyes, their milkiness, the slight grey hue, and how the irises blended slightly into the whites. Her eyes weren't natural. They were hauntingly beautiful, like a skyline of gravestones against a pale winter's sky.

And I recalled how closely she held papers to her face, how thin her shoes were, the way she'd hold the sisters' arms and run her fingers along the church walls as she walked. How had I not pieced it together until now?

"Sounds like the rain is stopping," she said gently, finishing her brownie. "Should I... come to confession tonight?"

Sounds like the rain is stopping. Not *looks* like the rain is stopping.

Disturbed. I was becoming increasingly disturbed at my lack of discernment, at the wool over my eyes. This wasn't typical. I'd overlooked and over assumed... something more was amiss than I'd even considered. And Selah wanted to get away from me, wanted to go back to her room— and though it pained me, though that's not what the after care of her sexual debut should entail, I couldn't blame her. I'd been clumsy with her, thoughtful in some ways and careless in others. And what's worse, this sudden spiritual blindness that was only now fading had me on high alert. Something was afoot, something I'd not seen, something or someone didn't *want* me to see.

Who? Or *what*.

I left large bills in Clarence's tip jar, knowing he'd refuse payment, as he always did, and wished him and his husband George blessings before securing the blanket around Selah's shoulders and ushering her outside. The storm would be back, and it would come again without warning or preamble. Though now I knew something was strange in the air, something was odd about the girl who timidly and carefully padded next to me, too. I felt it, a buzz in the air that was more than electricity. The urge to pull her close, to feel her bare skin, to stretch and pull my fingers deep within her walls again— it was close to unbearable.

"No confession tonight. We'll resume tomorrow," I answered finally, standing at the entrance to the mighty university. She'd be safe within its walls. She'd be safe here on Grimm, I believed. Though the ladies of sorrow would no doubt invite misfortune to rain down upon me in the form of their priesthood. Oh, how I wouldn't mind meeting those men— intimately, fiercely.

Lingering a moment, she opened her mouth and closed it again before giving a slight nod. "Bye, Father Amorth."

As she turned, I corrected her. I corrected someone for the first time in decades, maybe centuries. "Dante. You can just call me Dante, if you'd like."

She stopped, bracing a palm on the school's arched entrance. Her beautiful lilac lips flickered with a ghost of a smile as she whispered back. "Dante... it's nice to meet you."

I tilted my head in a small bow. "The pleasure is mine, Selah." Forgetting myself again, denying the priest, I stepped forward and took her hand, running my thumb over her knuckles before bringing them to my lips in a chaste kiss. "And never tell me *goodbye* again. Understand?"

Her eyes widened, and her lips parted before she nodded, breathless. Dropping her hold, I spun away, needing to leave, requiring answers, respite, aid, anything.

I was falling for The Holy Daughter.

And The Holy Daughter wasn't all that she seemed. My initial instinct had been correct and yet terribly wrong. Something still evaded me, and something dark was brewing on my little island. I would find it. No matter how powerful, I would be ready to meet the next storm.

I wasn't the only one hiding behind something else, was I?

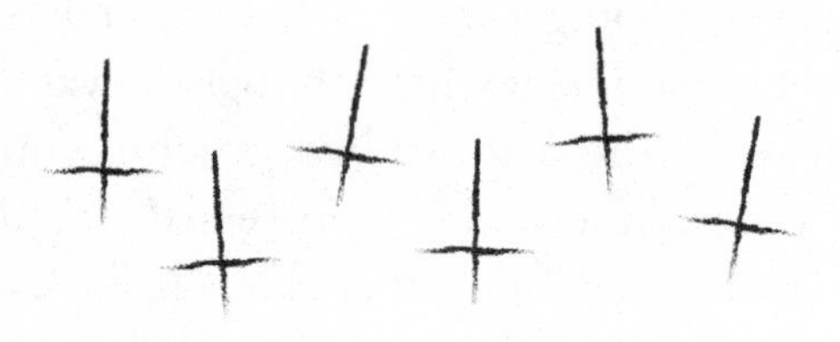

It was three in the morning, the devil's hour, when frantic pounding sounded on the door to my lighthouse. After I'd left Selah, I'd gone to search for Silas, coming up short, almost resorting to looking for... him... my *other* brother— but wisely decided against it. It could wait until morning. I needed time to calm my head, to sort through my thoughts, to meditate on my goddamn shot-to-hell worthless vows. My hood tilted over my eyes as I reclined on my thin twin bed. The storm was likely knocking debris into the lighthouse. No one would knock at this hour—

The pounding continued.

Whoever the fuck was pulling me out in a bloody storm at this ungodly hour would incur my wrath.

I whipped open the door to a shaking, wet, and petrified-looking George from the bakery. His blond, shaggy hair plastered to his forehead. He took a step back, and I grabbed his arm, steadying him, knowing the thin metal dock to my lighthouse door was slick and treacherous. "Father. Father, please," he begged, tears streaking his cheeks.

I knew that tone of voice. Something within me curled like a rusty lock clinking open. His fear seeped into me as rain pricked against us, and the ocean beyond raged.

"What is it, George?" I shook his shoulders, willing him to form words, hoping it wasn't what I thought it was. But also... hoping that it *was* what I thought it was.

"Clarence—" the man sobbed, reaching out to hold onto my robes. "He's—He's possessed. It's like it was before, so many years ago, father. They're back—"

I shook him again. "They are *not* back."

My voice gritted against a rolling of thunder, and I felt every cell in my body leap to high alert.

Selah, all I wanted was to get to Selah.

I looked to the looming school and convinced myself she was safe, sleeping, fine— the threat laid down here. The entity within the village, the one I'd felt. I'd felt this earlier, so strong, so much like before...

George pulled my robes again, breaking me from my torrential thoughts. "Please, Father, he's—he's my whole life, my love," he wailed. My throat tightened as we fought the winds on the beach, traveling up the walkway and into the village. The winds were relentless, and the rain slashed against us like tiny knives until we finally reached the bakery.

So quaint, so warm and homey, not the place a possession should happen. We'd just been here, Selah and me. My glance scanned our table, remembering her little hands molded around her mug. I'd felt it then, the presence, the wool pulled from my eyes. Had god been trying to tell me something then? Was he finally speaking to me in the softest of whispers? Surely not, not after what I'd just done to his holy daughter.

But then again... I'd been correct in my alarm. Though I never could have guessed a possession would be taking place that very night.

George's boots sloshed with water as he hurried me to the back and up the stairs to his and his husband's apartment above the bakery and cafe. It was covered in plants, the same as the downstairs, and held all the same charm and safety as their freshly made sourdough bread.

This was nothing a common demon would desire or seek out. Perhaps George was mistaken, spooked by a nightmare, haunted by years long gone. Clarence was simply having a night terror; talking in his sleep seemed most plausible.

Every ounce of air in my body stunned in my lungs as I paused in the baker's bedroom doorway. Clarence wasn't tucked into bed like a sick person, not sleeping or awaiting me like one anticipates a doctor. He sat straight in an old wooden chair, his chin on his chest and shoulders tilted forward. Like a drooping puppet. A posture I'd born witness to often, a stance you don't see and seldom forget. Something rustled like autumn leaves in my chest, swirled in a cyclone breeze.

"George," I said lowly to the sniffling and worried husband next to me. "Wait downstairs, and do not come up here, no matter what you hear. Do you understand?"

His teary blue eyes met mine, and confirmation and horror flashed across his pale expression before nodding and doing as he was instructed.

In these moments, I used to yearn for Father Joseph. He used to accompany me on these exorcisms back when things were bad, back when Grimm needed an exorcist and not a hidden, sullen priest. Those were the days. Father Joseph would walk me through the movements and the prayers. We were a team. Student and teacher. Once, we even got a beer after a particularly trying case. But that was a very long time ago. And now I was alone.

Leaning against the doorframe, I waited, inspecting my nails, feeling the dark presence pulsing from the corner of the room. It beat like some cursed heartbeat, each press of its energy making my bones weary, though I wouldn't show it.

It was ignoring me.

And that was pissing me off. Luckily, I knew how to piss it off back.

"Hello, Clarence," I drawled in a low tone. "Nice to see you again. The tea from earlier was delightful. Your own blend?"

His left shoulder jerked, and his wrist sprang up as if tied by a rope, his fingers drooping.

An inexperienced demon inhabited the baker, its first possession, by the looks of it. They always thought their hosts weak and easy to control, and in many ways, they were correct, though operating a body was much like driving a four-wheel-drive vehicle. A task that took practice and patience. Virtues demons had little desire to attain.

"*Mmm..*" Vibrated from Clarence's lips. "*Mmmm...*"

"This is the best hell sends? After all his time, I have to say, I'm fucking disappointed," I growled, taking a step closer.

That pissed it off.

Suddenly, the floorboards shook as if something was breaking them from beneath the beams. Winds howled within the room with echoes of hideous laughter and screams of pain. The light shifted into a muddy red, and I steeled my stance, holding my fists at my sides as the body of Clarence the baker stood weightlessly, pulled by whatever invisible string of his puppeteer. His head flung back, and his mouth gaped open before his chin moved up and down as if his operator was testing its ability, searching for the right button.

"The voice is in the gut, not the mouth, fucking moron," I scoffed, stepping forward again. Clarence's head settled forward then, his eyes completely black with no whites, no irises. And then he bellowed a scream.

I nodded patronizingly and clapped twice. "There you go."

"Mmm—mmm—mother—" Clarence babbled. Maybe the man's soul was fighting its captor. It hadn't happened often, though I'd seen it once or twice.

I rubbed my temples. "Here's an idea, demon. Instead of possessing kind and simple little bakers, how about you run along and fuck yourself with the infernal flames of hell?"

It bellowed again, shaking the room and making my ears ring. The scent of sulfur wafted into my nostrils, making my eyes sting. "*Mother,*" it repeated.

"Yes, as fun as this is," I made my way forward, feeling secure that I'd assessed this entity's ability, or lack thereof, and reached for Clarence's shoulder. When, in a flash of strength and agility that shouldn't have been there, his hand clawed to my forearm, wrenching my arm back at an angle that would have snapped another man's limb in half.

"*Dante,*" its black eyes widened within its unassuming host. "*Time to... give up your... vows...*"

My mouth dried, and my jaw hardened as I pulled from its hold, standing toe to toe with the inhabitant of the baker. I forced a shallow laugh from my throat. Demons loathed being laughed at. Eventually, I answered, "Someday. But not today." I pushed him back onto the chair. This dark entity was more solid than a human man's form should be. It was like pushing a mountain and harder to do than I wanted to admit. In fact, it didn't escape my awareness that any other mortal contending with this would have been long dead by now.

George was lucky to be alive, though my faith that he would remain so was slipping.

Exorcisms were a tricky business when you wanted to keep the host alive. And regardless of morality, keeping the host alive was vital. If the body died, the demon only gained power from death, either choosing to assume the body as its own or forfeiting it and taking on a stronger body of its choosing. Usually, it was whoever was strongest in the immediate vicinity of the possession. Clarence didn't deserve this. He was full of light, and there was no sense in an entity wanting his form. The desire to keep him alive pricked my senses, though I was keenly aware I was walking on treacherous tides with an inexperienced demon.

Why now, why this man?

It'd been a good many years since a demon had paid a visit to Grimm. I thought I was ready; I'd even fantasized about it on slow, monotonous days. Now it was here, and I was shockingly weak, and it was pissing me off. This demon was pissing me off.

"Why have you come, demon? Did you forget I was here, hm? Did hell need reminding that I beat it into submission?"

The rogue and sourceless wind in the quaint room died. My presence alone, after the events of the past, had been enough to keep the entities at bay. Though... here, one slumped before me. Clarence's body pulled to stand, taking an unsteady step forward, his chin jutting out wildly and black eyes glaring up at me. "*Darkness finds her.*"

Demons rarely frightened me anymore. I'd gone toe to toe, blood to blood, with hundreds in my time as an exorcist. They spoke nonsense mostly, pride occasionally, and chaos always. But even my experience was no match for the ice that traversed my spine at the hissed and echoing words from within its host.

In my dark pit of a soul, I already knew, though I hated that I knew.

"Darkness finds *who*?" I asked, my voice rumbling into a deliberate growl. "Darkness seeks none but *me*."

Part of the danger of demon possession was that the horror within the host never matched that of what you were able to witness with your mortal comprehension. Luckily, I didn't have those inhibitions. When Clarence lunged at me with the speed of a freight train, I grabbed him by the throat. We fell backward but didn't hit the wooden floorboards. We fell backward and continued falling, ash and sulfur burning the rusty scarlet hues around us as the baker's face morphed into something grotesque.

"*Burn... the... holy...*" he hissed, baring his teeth.

That was enough, and this body was too far gone. This demon was part chaos and part something much worse... mission. Determination... order. Fuck.

I held him by the throat as we fell into the abyss. He clawed at my sides, but my own blood didn't matter as I used my free hand to yank back my hood. The black eyes of the entity widened, and he screamed, deep, guttural, and soul-haunting. A scream that would paralyze a mortal with fear and despair for a hundred lifetimes. An unearthly sound of purposeful horror that had played in my darkest nightmares for centuries.

"That's right. Look at me, demon. Leave this mortal man and go tell your master to come find me. Do you hear me? Not little bakers, not innocent girls, or school children. Do not come near the women of Grimm. Tell him to find me, and you better hope to god he finds me before I find him."

Clarence's mouth opened and poured black smoke, hissing and singing like a tea kettle from hell. We shook violently before landing on solid ground.

Back in the bedroom, sitting upon an unassuming pink rug. The light was normal again, and the storm a slow patter of rain now. I pulled my hood back over my head and reached for the man's cold wrist. There was commotion behind me, and my name echoed in my ear, though my hearing hadn't fully returned, and my mind was drenched in unearthly darkness.

Someone shrouded in white light grabbed my shoulders and shook. "Dante, Dante, come now."

Silas. I vaguely remembered he was my brother.

"What is it?" I asked. I think I formed the words. Fuck, that demon was weak as shit, and yet it still took it out of me. That exorcism all but fucking wrecked me.

A woman appeared next to him, hazy and blanketed in soft purple light. This part wasn't so bad, like being drunk and seeing people's auras. A fun party trick, a parting gift from the damned, or perhaps a useless blessing from a god that loathed me.

Silas shook me harder. "You don't have time to fade, Dante."

"What is it?" I asked weakly, still holding the baker's limp wrist. I couldn't find a pulse. But the woman took over, her lavender light moving atop the man with no light on the floor.

Silas's white and silver hues pulsed in my vision. "A student is dead."

Selah

CHAPTER NINETEEN

The monster came for me again that night as I slept fitfully, hugging my knees at the bottom of my bed. Only this time, it really was raining outside. Only this time, I had direct awareness of the difference in sound that thunderstorms and hooves made. They galloped down the hall and stopped for several eerie, agonizing, silent moments before rushing to my door.

This was god sending my punishment for my sins, wasn't it?

I'd let a man touch me— and I'd loved every press of his lips.

God was going to damn me for giving up a piece of my purity, wasn't he?

I'd let a priest touch my center in ways I didn't know I could be touched. The way my wetness waited for him, the way he used it, coaxed it out with his wide and rough fingers, swirling it up over me on that magical spot.

The hooves stood outside my door, two shadows blocking the lamplight.

This wasn't a nun praying or burning incense. It wasn't school kids trying to frighten me. Whatever this was, it was real and had come to terrorize me. Justice, I thought, the heavy price of my sins— and this monster with hooves had come to collect.

Would it kill me?

It ran down the hall and back as lightning washed my room in horrid white. I stood on stiff knees and clutched a chair, inching forward. There was nothing to grab except the crucifix on the wall, so I took it in my hold. Would I fight? Would it matter?

Already, I ached to see Dante again. His radical words and gentle touch were at direct odds with the menacing hooded exorcist of Grimm that he embodied. He was a contrast to the tenants he fought to uphold, and somehow, when I looked at him, it was like a mirror staring at myself. It went against our sacred texts, but I couldn't help but imagine that Father Amorth was me in some other life and reality.

If I'd been born a man, if I'd taken holy vows, if darkness pulled at the corners of my being, only I would have had brawn, strength, and freedom to greet them with... I could be him, and he could have been me.

But instead of a beast awaiting Dante, it sought and waited for me. When I closed my eyes, I could hear it breathing over the sound of my pulse in my ears. My breath was short and shallow gasps, coming too fast and blurring my limited vision. Screaming was an option, but if I did, others would see this creature, and they could be harmed by it. I'd be responsible if so. Whatever it was, it had come for me before, and it was back again, and I had to find some sort of courage within me to face it. *To face one's sin is the first step toward salvation,* my dad used to preach.

I hated how sermon lines played so often and unwelcome in my brain.

It was the demon within me that made the thoughts of home, of my dad, far from my mind at the thought of dying. Most would remember their families; I didn't care to recall mine at all. The only happiness I'd encountered had been here on this island, in this church, the university, and with my exorcist... and my little goat, too, who I hoped was sleeping peacefully in the shed next to Dante's garden.

The crucifix was heavy in my slick palms as I took too loud, too audible, creaking steps toward the door. The hooves shuffled and stilled as if the monster noticed, as if I was doing exactly as it wanted me to. As my hand trembled on the cold doorknob and I held the heavy cross on my shoulder, I prepared myself and resolved to fight. I'd never fought before.

I'd been hit.

Beaten.

Whipped.

Struck.

Slapped.

And I'd never once thought to swing back. But right now... I'd swing. I probably wouldn't win... but something inside me, for the first time in my life, *wanted* to fight back.

The door clicked open, and everything seemed to happen in slow motion. Heavy strength pushed the door forward, and I fell back with a scream. A hard body fell atop me— the shape of a man— and he was growling, deep and guttural like some crazed animal. His hands wrapped around my throat, locking in my scream. The room lit with a flash of lightning, and my brain registered who I was looking at, who was on top of me— “Oliver?” I croaked, and his thumbs tightened, making me cough.

His head twisted at an odd angle, his chin jutting out, and his eyes— his horrible eyes— rolled side to side as if they were fighting to fix on something but were untethered to his control, like glass beads in the head of a doll.

“*You*—“ his voice echoed, though it wasn’t his voice; it was another sound—something so terrible and horrid to hear. The sound of it made me want to cry. I strained to reach for the crucifix that was now laid next to me. “*Called*—“ the word pushed from his mouth, and his lips curled. “*Here— we— come*— “

A scream pushed from my lips as I locked eyes with Oliver, but *not* Oliver. There were no whites to his eyes; they were black, and blood dripped from the sides of his mouth as it stretched open like a snake preparing to swallow me whole. It could have been my terror, or it could have been real, but the room seemed to swirl in pungent red smoke and ash.

Finally, my fingers made contact with the crucifix as hot tears burned in my eyes, and my throat was raw with suppressed screams as his hold tightened around my neck. I swung, hitting him across the temple, and maybe it was the power of the cross, but he shrieked in a high-pitched tenor like nails across a chalkboard, and I pushed him off of me, rolling to a shaking stand as I held up the cross.

"Get away from me!" I croaked, panting and shaking as he stood on wobbly knees. His head fell to the side, resting on his shoulder at an unnatural and painful-looking angle.

He reached out, and I winced, but he only took the cross and repositioned it in my hold, making the long end stand up top and the horizontal wood face the bottom. Why he'd pay mind to make the cross upside-down, I couldn't comprehend in that moment. "Get away from me," I repeated, jerking back.

Oliver's head lowered, and he peered up at me with black eyes as he walked backward, veering to the side. I jumped as his fist collided with the glass window, shattering it and his hand without so much as a groan or a glance in its direction. It was as if Oliver was nothing more than a cardboard cutout of a boy, unfeeling and unreacting.

He scooted onto a seat on the side of the window ledge and hissed lowly. His words shocked through me like a haunting of the greatest sort. *You... will... bleed.* Oliver leaned backward, tumbling out the window, and I screamed, lunging forward as if I could grab him and spare him. Just as I did, two nuns rushed into the room, followed by a priest. Was he lit up in bright silver light, or was I hallucinating? I was shaking, and not until a woman's arms wrapped around me did I register that I was sobbing. They were talking, but I couldn't make out their words. My ears rang so painfully that I worried I'd never hear again.

A man's hand reached between us, and I pulled back from the sister that held me, Elodie, I think— and he pried the cross from my hold. It slid out of my hand, wet and slick in crimson. Sister Elodie took my wrists and inspected my palms— they were puddled with blood. Was it Oliver's blood on my hands or my own? The silver man said something to her before taking my wrist and pulling me toward the doorway. She let him, and he rushed me down the hall. Kids were waking, some staring at me, some looking bewildered—and then I heard a girl scream.

Tears were still pouring down my face, and I struggled to catch my breath as the man pulled me sharply to the left and down a dark corridor I'd never known existed. We entered a white room that reminded me of Lady of Sorrow Church, only much older. The accents were in bronze, and the white marble cracked with age and use. Another tiny cathedral, like Dante's, only this one matched the man who threw me into a small pine confessional. White lattice bars separated us as he stepped into his side and slammed the door shut.

"Answer me," he shouted above the ringing in my ears, and I cupped my hands over my head and rocked back and forth, my body still racked with sobs and fear and fatigue. I was suddenly so tired, yet my body buzzed as if it had been electrocuted.

"Father Silas?" I asked as my eyes were able to focus. His shoulder-length hair was the purest shade of ivory, like the sand on the beach under a full moon.

He cocked his head at me, analyzing my features, the lattice pattern casting a shadowed pattern across his strong and too-perfect features. He was unbelievably handsome in daylight, but in lamplight and touched with shadow, he looked like one of the stone statues of the university come to life. It was almost jarring to see him move and speak. Then again, nothing felt real in that moment. I'd just opened my bedroom door to confront the monster, and the monster had been my friend, and my friend had just killed himself by jumping out my bedroom window. My palms slicked against my forehead with sweat, no, with *blood*.

His voice cut through my panic like a blade through soft butter. "Who sent you, Selah?"

I shook my head. "I came for an exorcism—"

"No, you didn't," he replied without a hint of anger or doubt. "It's time to confess to me. What *are* you—"

The confessional shook as if from below, like the floors were opening in an earthquake. I only caught a brief panicked glance from Father Silas before his confessional door was torn from its hinges, and a black-cloaked arm reached in, grabbing his neck and pulling him out. Fear shot through my chest, and I sat glued to my seat as sounds of crashing and swearing vibrated the confessional. Something shattered, and two men were shouting at each other. It seemed to go on forever, and my panic was too fresh to even want to open the door. Opening a door to inspect a scary happening is what got me into this mess. It's what killed Oliver. Oh god, had I killed Oliver?

The bustle of what felt like bombs going on outside the confession subsided, and just as silence settled, my door swung open, causing me to jump. A tall, dark, and hooded figure assessed me. A sight that should have frightened me and would have disturbed anyone else, but for me, it only brought peace and relief as Dante stepped in and carefully scooped me into his arms.

I wrapped myself around his neck. If I'd wanted to see his face, that would have been my opportunity. We were so close that I could have turned to peer up at him, to finally see his eyes... but it felt like doing so without his express consent would have been a violation. Taking advantage of his hold, of this rescuing, would have been wrong, and I didn't want to risk doing anything to shake his trust. A gasp rattled me as I caught sight of the room we departed and Father Silas on his knees amongst the wreckage, looking forlorn. His cathedral destroyed.

"Did you—" I began to question when Dante hushed me.

"He deserved worse for thinking he could take you from me."

That statement, especially under the current grim circumstances, shouldn't have unleashed a flutter of butterflies within my belly, but it did.

"Tell me," he said lowly as the outside air filled my lungs, and I sucked in the after-storm wetness eagerly. "Did he touch you? Tell me he did so I can go back and break his hands."

Hair stood on the back of my neck as I quickly shook my head against his firm shoulder. We'd exited the church university in a way I'd never gone before, and instead of traversing stone, it was only very tall grass and hills until I recognized we were moving through the garden I tended for him. Suddenly, he kicked a door, and we were moving up a spiral set of stairs.

My eyelids drooped, and I struggled to stay awake, though my brain was racing, and my body was yearning at every part of his forearms and chest that so effortlessly pressed against me as he carried me with such ease. Thin cushions squeaked beneath me as he laid me back on a sofa. I only caught the corner of his hood and the briefest glimpse of the bridge of his nose as he pulled a blanket over me. "I know you don't like beds. I'm sorry this couch is quite old."

"What is happening? I—I— Oliver—"

His thumb pushed against my lips, and my words died as something stirred in my core. I was alone in the lighthouse with him, wasn't I?

Father Amorth pulled my hand to his chest, and I noticed it was still slick as blood seeped into his heavy cloak. The upside-down cross and star rosary dangled from his neck. Was I cut? How were my hands still bleeding? Maybe it was the adrenaline, but I felt no pain. "You're going to sleep now," he rumbled matter of factly. "And as you sleep, I will be inspecting your body."

"Won't you instead do that while I'm awake?" I asked, my words a tired slur that would surely embarrass me when I remembered it later.

Dante tucked my dark hair behind my ear. "You need your rest, for you have so, so, much to confess to me soon."

Such an odd thing to say, but everything he said was always a strange riddle of comfort. "This lighthouse... it's nice," I added sleepily. Nothing I was saying made sense as if I were drunk off altar wine.

"I know you like it. Seems you have an affinity for tall, gloomy, hidden things."

"It's been my guiding light since I arrived. How did you come to live inside it?"

"My father was a fisherman. He built it for my mother. My mother lived inside it until she died, watching from this window each night for him to come home. You can see some of her flower paintings faded on the stone. As a toddler, I remember crawling up the steps, chasing after my brothers."

"This—this lighthouse must be hundreds of years old."

"Two hundred and sixty-four years old. Do you mean guiding light metaphorically or literally?"

"What?" I rubbed my eyes and yawned.

"When you say this lighthouse has been your guiding light, tell me what you mean." He rubbed his thumbs against the wetness still collecting on my palms. It was red, so terribly red.

"It's brought me comfort; it's helped me know where on the isle or in the university church I am. My eyesight is poor... I can see close up but far away images are a blur." I laid my heavy head on the side of the sofa. It smelt like moss and ocean. It smelt like him.

"Spectacles—glasses—have been no aid to you?" Dante's voice was low as he stared at my hands. I liked the feel of them in his.

"I wouldn't know. My dad and the clergy declared my faltering sight a gift from god. So that I'd walk closer to them, so I'd lean on god and the church more. That may be true, but I just bump into things more. Well, I used to—I see mainly with my feet." I chuckled deliriously, but Dante had grown cold and silent.

"Do you love your dad?"

Odd question, again. But all of his questions were odd, with seemingly no strings attaching one thought to the next. It was like a game of shuffled cards with different inquiries written on each.

"I do, I suppose. He's the only parent I know. I wish I could remember my mother; she died giving birth to me."

After a long pause, he dropped my hands, released his fists, and flexed his fingers. "I loved my mother very much. She taught me to fish, and I would catch her a fish a day and cook it for her in the evening. Up until the very end of her life, though I haven't fished in a very long time."

"Would you teach me how?" I asked with a deep sigh, wishing I could stay awake.

"Yes," he answered softly. "I will teach you many things, Selah." My eyes closed just as he pulled my hand back to his chest to inspect. As much as I wished for dull blackness to greet me in sleep, it was all red.

Everything was back to being that horrifying shade of red.

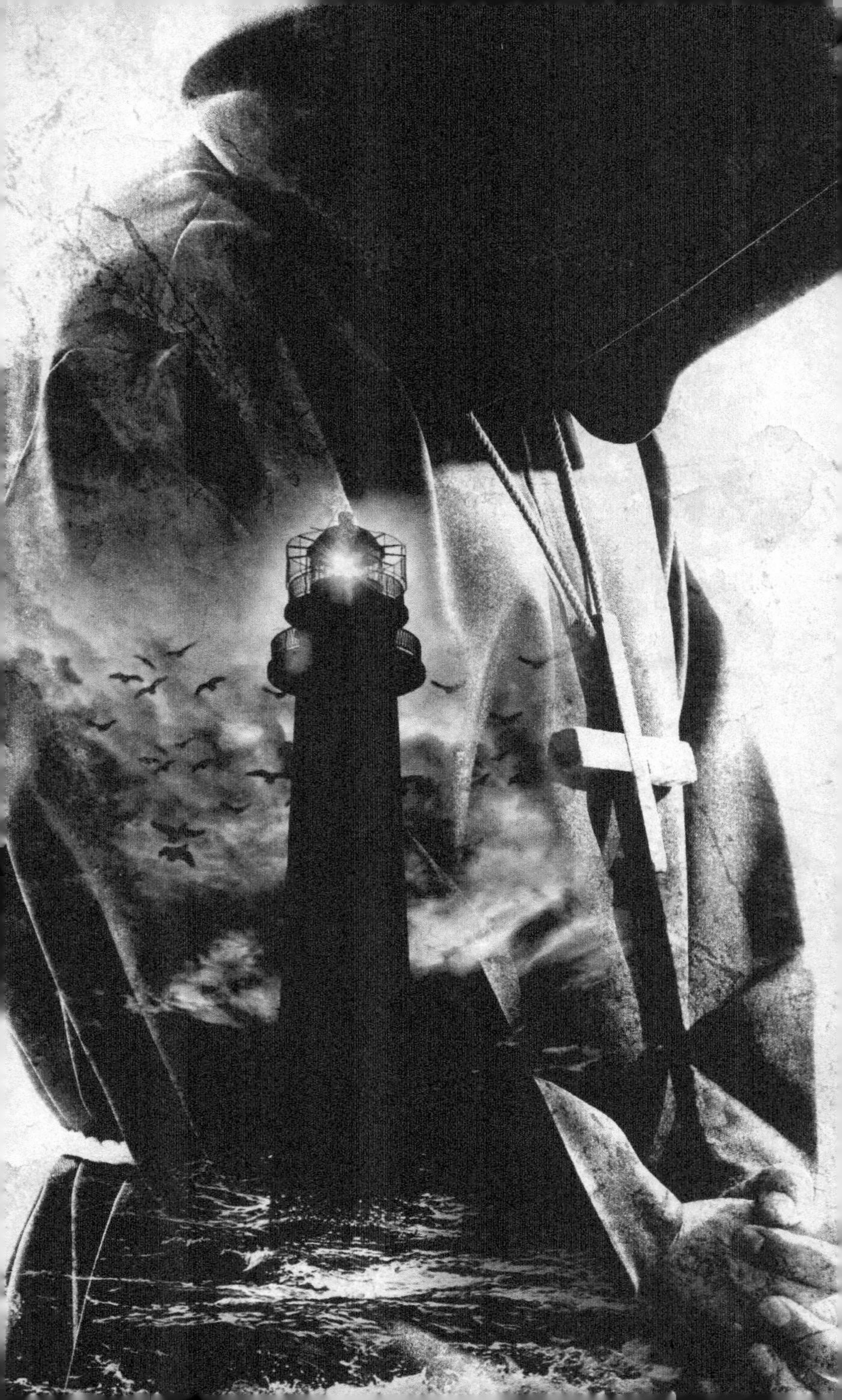

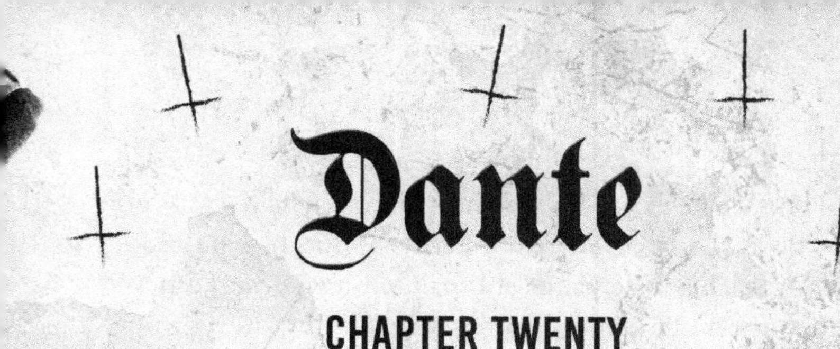

CHAPTER TWENTY

She slept for two days, and for two days, I watched her. The boat rocked beneath me as the lighthouse, where she still slumbered, faded in the distance. The ocean was calm, finally, after the previous week's storms, and my chest twisted in worry at leaving her behind. The spirit and favor that was innate to my brother Silas was always far from me, no matter how desperately I reached.

Though the despair and resignation of my brother Nikolai was biting at my heels like a rabid dog, I kicked off its fangs every morning. No, I wouldn't succumb to the temptation of wallowing in darkness as he did. I couldn't. There were too many counting on me as guardian of this island.

I wouldn't jump into the grave that sorrow had dug for me so relentlessly. No, I would claw my way out from my coffin every time to hunt down the evil that dared try to contend against me. Maybe the gospel of christ was not written for beings such as me. Maybe that's why god turned his face from me. Maybe god was weak in allowing Lady of Sorrow to rise up and be the grand editor of the original sacred texts.

I hoped he'd keep his gaze turned from what I was about to do to Lady of Sorrow's Father Church. The blood from Selah's little palms still painted my chest. I'd never encountered a demon to do such a thing, never knew it possible, and the fury within me was insurmountable. Like lightning in a bottle about to explode— it needed a conduit. I needed more blood. I needed one man's blood. I needed a pound of flesh, whether it made sense or just pierced the shovel into my grave again— this was fucking happening.

My journey concluded and no time or distance swayed my thoughts nor impeded my rage. Silas would be incensed at what I was about to do. The thought brought a small flicker of a smile to my face as I stepped inside the immaculate ivory and gold church. Would my perfect little church bells be upset with me? It didn't matter. A demon-possessed boy had attacked her, and I wasn't there. A demon tried to kill her, and I wasn't there. She'd grown up in an ornate prison, groomed, abused, shamed— and I wasn't there.

I was done with not being there.

These forces had evaded my judgment for far too long.

The priest turned his face in disgust as I clicked the lock on my demon's chains, unleashing him and freeing him. There would never come a time again that Selah would not be under my protection. Whether she sought it or not, whether the aftereffects made her hate me or not, it was decided. She was encoded in my DNA, her gravestone eyes imprinted in my bones, and the taste of her cunt on my fingertips burned on my tongue for all of eternity. The most sacred of holy sacraments. To even think that anyone could dare harm her or deny her the spoils she deserved was an unfathomable outrage. I was done playing nice, done being caged, and finished going through the motions, taps, kneels, and prayers of what was expected of me.

Sometimes prayers were necessary, and oftentimes, patience was a virtue I strived for.

But not today.

Not as I seated myself at Father Benedict's desk in the still dark morning hours. There, I would wait, and indeed, I would pray and I would meditate on the holy texts, readying my sermon for when he arrived. My righteous anger thrashed within my spirit. I had a feeling I'd only breached the surface of what this cold and dead place had done to her. Why hadn't I seen it sooner? How had Lady of Sorrow church remained just outside the reach of Grimm for so long? Something wasn't right. There were riddles to be solved, things to unpack and discover. But one thing was certain— one less thing would be wrong after today. At least one sin would be on its way to atonement when I left this wretched church that day.

That's more than *god* had ever done for her.

Maybe I was better than god.

Maybe I was a god on my own.

He entered his office and closed the door, the crucifix wobbling over the splintered wood pane above. Shuffling papers in his hands, he looked up and startled when he saw me, dropping the files to the floor. "Mercy." Putting a hand to his chest as I stood, towering over him as I loomed behind his desk. The sun hit the stained glass in an eerie shade of red. A shade of red I was sure so many of his victims were accustomed to. I couldn't speak and, frankly, didn't care about his other victims right now. Only her. Only one victim.

Selah.

"You-you must be Father Amorth. Your reputation of hiding your face proceeds you. I-I expected you'd visit at some point, though typically, one would make an appointment and not simply show up unannounced in my holy rectory." He was afraid. I could taste it.

"Holy," I repeated as I rounded the corner of his desk, and he fought the urge to step backward and run. "Holy, holy," I repeated idly, thumbing the pentagram in the middle of my rosary as it dangled around my neck.

"How much longer will The Holy Daughter of Sorrow's exorcism take? To be plain, Father, it is taking much longer than I anticipated. In fact, we eagerly await the return of our head Lady of Sorrow, Vanessa, and the two ladies in training who accompanied her. We have yet to hear from them, but I trust they are fulfilling their duties to survey The Holy Virgin's purity standards at Grimm Church."

That's right, they hadn't returned... and they never would. When I stood in front of him, looking down my nose at his fucking white priest collar, he didn't deserve to wear. I could tell he sought to see my eyes beneath my hood. I could tell he wanted to ask me to remove it. No, demand I remove it. For anyone else in his own church, he would have. It was a hollow place of no baseball caps, no beanies, and no ripped blue jeans. No one was permitted a shred of individuality or joy, I was certain. He called the shots here, he led thousands to the lord, his flock was large and hungry— and he loved the control, didn't he?

"How many in your congregation?" I asked, reaching above him.

He flinched, and I smirked as I plucked the pointed, wooden crucifix off the wall. I searched his face and saw nothing of his daughter. No similar bone structure, different eyes, and mouths. Perhaps she took after her dead and nameless mother. One small consolation from a god who should have done more for her.

"You must be far removed on the Isle of Grimm not to know such basic things, Father Amorth. We boast ten thousand at each service on Sundays and Wednesdays. That's three services a piece, not including those we broadcast to through the television and internet. You know the requirement is for all people to attend at least four services a month. That is millions of congregants. You should stay to hear the good word of—"

"God?" I asked, tossing the crucifix in the air, letting it spin, and catching it. Father Benedict narrowed his gaze, fighting the urge to reprimand me. "Tell me," I continued. "Do you enjoy looking out over your people? Do you like standing at the pulpit and witnessing crowd after crowd come to hear you speak the '*good word of god*'?"

The man furrowed his brow and paled before adjusting his collar. "It is an honor to be a shepherd for the lord. Now, please, if you'd like to make an appointment, I do have sermon notes to ready for Sunday."

He wasn't accustomed to being challenged by anyone, much less someone bigger than he was. No, I got the impression that the clergy here at the father church preferred the silence and servitude of women over the condemnation of fellow men. I nodded, catching the cross by the long end and grabbing his shoulder firmly with my other hand. He flinched, sweat beading on his forehead as I growled lowly. "Did you know that your daughter needs glasses?"

Father Benedict let out a breath of relief and smiled a fake smile. He'd expected worse, hadn't he? Expected I'd discovered much, much worse. He was lucky I hadn't... yet.

"The Lord concealed her vision. She is blessed to see when things are close and not far. We accept this blessing from Him. It causes her to stay close to me, the Ladies of Sorrow, the Word of God, and someday soon, her husband."

A vein in my neck twitched at that last part, and I felt the heat in my body rise in my chest. He made to move, and I continued blocking him.

"The lord created the science of optometry."

"Excuse me, Father Amorth, but I don't know what you're after here. If you'd please—"

"The Lord created optometrists. And glasses, contacts, hell, even laser eye surgery. Because you've neglected her vision so long she's almost blind, though with aid and proper glasses, she will be seeing better—"

"You did not get permission from me to do any such thing," Father Benedict said, puffing up in indignation. "You were employed for one purpose, *exorcist*, to rid her of demons and return her purified. Not to send her for medical care or enroll her in your shoddy religious school." He straightened. "Oh, yes, I know you've sent her to worldly educational classes. I've been made privy to the rumors that something un-Lady of Sorrow-like may be happening in your own church, and I'm beginning to rethink this whole arrangement. You have lurked outside the walls of Lady of Sorrow's regulations for too long, Father Amorth. And I've allowed it because of your unique gifts. However, perhaps more suitable exorcists exist; perhaps you'll be put under investigation, and I'll collect The Holy Daughter tomorrow and send her elsewhere—"

The door behind him cracked and splinted as I slammed the cross behind him, breaking the right side and leaving it hanging by a pliable piece of wood. "You. Will. Not. Touch. Her," I gritted out each word.

"Take off that idiotic hood," he spat, reaching for it. I grabbed his wrist hard and twisted it at an odd angle as he fought against the guttural sound that wretched from his throat.

"With pleasure," I replied. Stepping back, I removed my hood. I relished every moment of what came next.

He slumped backward against the door, palms trembling as he fetched his prayer beads out of his robes and brought it to his lips. "Devil, demons— they've claimed you," he sputtered, sinking low to the ground as I stepped forward. "In the name of Sorrow, I renounce all evil."

A harsh chuckle left my mouth as I gripped the cross in my hand. "*All* evil... all *evil*," I repeated. "I think the phrase you're searching for, Father, is..." I knelt, pushing my palm against his forehead and forcing him to look at my terrible, demonic face. Cowardly tears streaked his haggard cheeks, and I smirked, feeling him shirk against the door as he sobbed and prayed. "An eye for an eye."

Rearing back the sharp edge of the cross, his gaze pulled from me to the crucifix, the last thing he'd ever see, and the realization dawned just as I impaled him through the right eye. Blood sprayed like a geyser as he wailed, screaming and fighting futilely against me. He wasn't strong in any sense of the word.

He wasn't a priest in any sense of the word.

Wasn't a father in any sense of the word.

Wasn't a man in any sense of the word.

And now he'd never see again. His eyes would never look at Selah, whether in judgment or in harm. He'd never be picking out victims from his congregation again. He would be scarred, stunted, and left blinded, the same as he'd done to her. I could have killed him, but oh, making him suffer. Making him live in fear of the last thing he saw. Of me gouging out his eyes and scarring his face, his last image of sight being the demon gaze of Dante Amorth, the exorcist, here to exorcise him of only a small piece of his evil.

After seven minutes, he passed out. From either screaming, blood loss, or from the pain, I don't know. I tossed the crimson slick cross onto the floor with a clatter. Crosses always looked better bloody, in my opinion. More authentic, the authenticity that people like Reverend Father Benedict liked to ignore. Our sacred texts were a bloody business rife with violence and justice. Both of his eyes were mine now. I picked them up off their red puddle on the ground and shoved them wet and sticky into the pockets of my robe.

"Souvenirs from Lady of Sorrows Church," I told his lifeless, but unfortunately still breathing, body as I kicked it out of the way and exited. So secluded in his own part of the church. No assistant was in that day, and no bishops around to disturb him as he worked on his sermon notes. How he'd agonize over how to accomplish such a thing in the future. How would he write down his blasphemous words now? The thought eased the torment in my chest just a little as I walked the same corridors that Selah had walked her entire life.

This place was evil and wretched.

But now, with one fewer set of eyes to condemn her.

Selah

CHAPTER TWENTY-ONE

It felt like my eyes were falling out as bright white light burned my retinas as a man held my eyelid taut. Sister Grace cooed in my ear, holding my hand. "You're doing great, Selah. I'm sure Doctor Parsons is almost finished."

The man swallowed, looking pale. "Yes, sister. Though, I've never carried out an optometrical exam in a... lighthouse before."

"We called for you to come weeks ago," Sister Grace replied sweetly. "Though we appreciate you hitching a ride here with Father Amorth this morning."

The man chuckled nervously. I had a feeling the *hitching a ride* wasn't exactly optional, not from the way Dante stood in the corner with his arms crossed as he monitored the exam. "She is severely nearsighted... light rays bend and refract off her pupils at such peculiar angles... I fear it has likely been genetic, present since birth. Though with lack of attention, it has gotten worse with time."

Dante shifted in the corner. "Doctor Parsons, you'd do well to address Selah by name and not speak of her as if she is not in the room and currently under your flashlight."

The doctor stiffened and clicked his light off, shaking his head quickly. “I meant no harm, Father. Please forgive me, Selah. I am but an old man talking to myself.”

“It’s okay,” I responded, swallowing tears. Luci curled in my lap and petting his coarse black fur helped to calm me. I’d never had my sight examined; I knew it was bad but had never known just how bad it was. It had never registered just how neglected I had been in my home church. Did my dad, the clergy, the ladies of sorrow... did any of them ever care for me at all?

Sister Grace squeezed my hand, as if she sensed my sadness. “Is there anything to be done?” she asked.

The optometrist unzipped his bag. He’d tested me for almost an hour that morning, placing different lenses in front of my eyes and having me identify blurry objects until they became clearer with lens changes. “There is some good news,” he said. “From what Father Amorth informed me of from his personal observations, I brought several lens options I thought would be suitable, and it does seem we have a match.” Clicking two glass rectangles into slim metal frames, he approached and gently slid them onto my face.

When I glanced across the room, I startled, almost jumping, when Father Amorth and the ocean beyond the window were visible. “Oh,” I gasped in surprise. “I—I—didn’t know this was possible.”

Dr. Parsons smiled. “It’s like magic, isn’t it?” He cleared his throat, casting quick looks at Sister Grace and Dante before correcting himself. “I mean— not that magic is real—“

"It certainly is," Sister Grace smiled. "Thank you for seeing her."

The man wiped his brow. "These glasses will work temporarily. I will take her information and craft stronger, more personalized lenses to her specifications and send them to you. Provided... I *can* leave... correct?"

Dante lowered his head in a hooded nod, and the doctor's shoulders slumped in relief.

Remembering the last week, I reached for Sister Grace. "Is Lady Vanessa gone?"

The nun flicked a look to Dante in silent question before responding. "Yes, she is *gone*... the two Ladies of Sorrow remain."

"To watch after me?" I cringed.

Sister Grace shook her head and looked earnestly into my eyes as if she were trying to say something beyond the words she conveyed. "No, for *us* to look after. We cannot know the ladies' names, for they've both taken... vows of silence. Though it is as if... more than a vow keeps them quiet. One seems rather devout, but the other is trying to communicate—"

Dante cleared his throat, and Sister Grace bit her lip, still trying to communicate with her expression. What was she trying to tell me? I was dizzy and couldn't think straight.

It was the most that had happened in days as I'd slept and slept. No matter how hard I tried, I couldn't keep my eyes open. The sleeping didn't bother me. It was the stark realizations upon awakening that plagued me. For a split moment, when my eyes would open, I'd think it was all a nightmare, some terrible dream. My friend didn't attack me. He didn't die from falling out my window.

The blood on my palms didn't exist— it was all some horror movie playing in my head. But then I would remember, and my bones would grow tired again. After my appointment, I slumbered again until I awoke with a startle. Though, when I looked around Father Amorth's small lighthouse loft, there was nothing but my little stubby horned goat sleeping at my feet and a steaming bowl of soup and a pitcher of ice water on the nearby table. The smell was enough to keep my eyes open, and my stomach pulled with hunger, urging my aching bones off the stiff sofa and to the tiny chair by the window.

Each bite of chicken noodle soup warmed me from the inside, giving me the strength I needed to resist the allure of blissful unconsciousness, and I downed the entire decanter of water in messy, thirsty gulps. After stretching my sore muscles, I noted there wasn't much of interest in Father Amorth's dwelling. No photographs, no books, nothing personal that said anyone truly lived here. Though on my way down the stairs, my heart cracked in my chest as I spotted faded dandelions painted on the stone archway to the door. His mother had painted those, he'd told me. Somehow, imagining him as a baby, crawling up these very stairs, made me want him even more. To hold him, to feel him warm against me, to find the source of the pain in his voice and soothe it, heal it.

But who was I to heal anyone or anything?

Because of me, a boy was dead.

It was twilight, and the setting sun washed the beach in dark orange and purple. Silas surprised me, waving from the lighthouse dock. Had he been waiting for me to come out? Sent to guard me?

His white hair was tied back in a messy knot as he tossed bloody meat off the dock, and I timidly joined him.

"Hello, Selah," Father Silas said warmly. "I hope you're feeling better." He wore a button-up, black shirt and his priest collar. His face broad and chiseled, not at all reflecting the age that such white hair should bring. I wondered how old he was, if he was older or younger than his brother Dante or if they even resembled each other.

Something thrashed in the tide, and I jumped. "There are sharks here?"

The priest chuckled darkly. "Three or four different kinds. hammerheads, bull sharks, tiger sharks, occasionally a great white or two."

I paled, recalling the times I'd idiotically swam out into the waves, not even considering the monsters that lurked offshore.

"Can I feed them?" I asked, and he met my gaze then, his strong features lighting with curiosity. He extended the black trash bag, and I reached in, pulling out a dripping slab of flesh. "I met a fisherman here weeks ago. He was smoking a pipe. He told me he had three sons... do you know who he was?"

Father Silas hummed in his throat and gave me a long, unnerving, quizzical look before responding. "You've been quite the surprise to us here on Grimm."

I clutched the raw meat in my hands, trying to focus on the water and not the urge to stare at him and fantasize about what features his brother shared. Did they have the same eyes?

"I'm sorry," I sighed. "I know I've brought disarray with the ladies of sorrow showing up, and now with what's happened with Oliver..."

Silas chuckled again, tossing another heavy handful of flesh for the sharks. "They're the least of the trouble you've brought, but most of all, you've brought it onto yourself."

"How?" I asked, a small chill snaking down my spine.

He raised an eyebrow. "Feeding sharks. Feeding a very large, very unpredictable shark with a hood and an attitude problem."

I swallowed, watching as fins appeared and disappeared below the sea. "It sounded like he... wrecked your cathedral the other day. I'm sorry—"

"Don't start apologizing for him," Silas interrupted me. "And if it is your choice to fan the flames of his obsession..." he trailed off. "You'd be better off jumping into these waters covered in blood than having Dante Amorth's attention fixed on you."

"He's a priest, an exorcist," I argued weakly, as if his titles meant anything, as if I didn't sense the power radiating off of him each time we were alone.

Silas scoffed. "My brother is a tormented, demented, and dangerous being, Selah. He *will* hurt you, whether it be now or later. You will be harmed if you stay in his sights."

"I just can't fathom that being true," I said, still clutching the slimy meat. "He's done so much for me, he's taught me, he's saved me in many ways..."

"You remind me of our mother. She, too, had a soft spot for him. Nikolai was so quiet he hardly spoke and still rarely does. As the eldest child, I filled the absence of our father by caring for them all. But Dante, he fumed, he stewed, he plotted. Always getting in trouble, evading responsibility at every turn. Much like you, our mother, a gentle, soft-spoken woman, thought she saw his potential through his rage and thought she could save him with love. Although, it was her love for him that was her end, as it will be yours."

Icy wind licked my skin, and I forgot the sharks just yards away from my toes. My fear focusing in on thoughts of the hooded priest and being the subject of his attention. "What happened to her?"

An enormous eight-foot-long shark circled the water in front of us. Silas gestured with his chin. "Well, would you look at that? The great white has paid you a visit. The deadliest creature in the sea, saying hello." He put a bloody hand on my elbow. "Are you going to feed him?"

I searched Silas's silver eyes. They didn't look real, like marbles or something not of this world. Something pulled on my chest: fear, intrigue, and questions I didn't want to ask but knew I had to. I tossed the log of meat into the water with a splash and gasped as the shark's gruesome face breached the surface, slicing its teeth through its meal. My heart raced as Silas stood behind me, and I feared at any moment, he could push me in and feed me to the monster, too.

His hand landed on my shoulder, and I startled, watching the dark cloud of beast as it disappeared beneath the tide again.

"You should know, Selah," he rumbled deeply like the tone of the waves ashore. "Dante killed our mother."

Horror stunned through me as I backed away, needing space, needing the solace of the school. Silas let me leave, only watching on as if that weren't the most unsettling conversation he'd wanted to have with me. Could he have been telling the truth? Surely Dante couldn't have done such a thing, and if he did... It couldn't be true. I'd ask him about it. There had to be an explanation. It was wrong that I'd just been told the man I coveted was a murderer, and my urge was to deny it. Though somewhere deep inside, I knew he was capable of such things. That within his time as an exorcist, he must have sometimes... killed possessed people, or demons, or both.

Suddenly, death surrounded me, and as the veils lifted and my vision cleared— I was beginning to realize that I'd always walked amongst tombstones.

I marched the trail up to the jagged black castle of a school. My mind wandered to Oliver's last moments, and my eyes searched for where my window was amongst hundreds, trying to calculate where he would have landed. My head hurt, but then my brain registered that I was actually seeing shapes of ornately onyx windows. Shapes of carved angels and gargoyles took form, hanging onto the side of the school as if real beings frozen in a shocked, stone state. I'd never seen them before. I'd never been able to see them before. Tears welled in my eyes, and my glasses felt heavy and awkward on my face. But I could see now. My vision wasn't one hundred percent improved; things past a certain point were still blurry, but I could see so much more now.

And it was because of Grimm. It was because of the sisters and their kindness. It was because Father Amorth saw me and found me the resources I needed. My heart swelled with a torrential mix of emotions. Grief for all the things I'd been missing, the childhood in blindness and neglect I'd been forced to lead... sadness and confusion over my attack the days prior... and an overwhelming sense of ease and gratitude that should not have coexisted alongside those other darker feelings.

Somehow, this creepy old church with its eccentric school and all its inhabitants on the island of Grimm... was starting to feel like home. Like what home should be, what I'd always imagined it would be. Grimm was the place I'd envisioned running away to for all the years of my childhood, only now that place had a name, and I could see it. I could see it now.

But would the students hate me knowing what happened to Oliver? Would they blame me for his death? Fear crept into my awareness as I approached a crowd of girls in plaid skirts, talking in hushed tones on the school steps. I recognized Eve amongst them, and the fact that I was still several yards away but able to see her sent a small thrill through my body.

Wow, vision was a cool skill to possess. I braced myself for their judgment and anger, for the millions of questions they'd want to ask me about what happened and about why I'd disappeared for the week. Eve ran up to me, and I half wondered if she would slap me, but she didn't. She just pulled me close in her arms, burying her face in my long pigtail braids. "Oh, Selah," she sniffled. "It's been just awful."

I hugged her back, and the other girls surrounded us, their gazes downcast. "I just can't believe something like this would happen. Not here, not Grimm, you know?"

Nodding, I realized I didn't know how to comfort her. "I know, it's so sad. I wished there was something I could do—"

"Oh, honey, we all do," Eve sniffled. "Me especially. I mean, why wouldn't she say something to me?"

The girls rubbed Eve's back, and I looked on, confused. "Wait, what?"

"I like your glasses, by the way. That's crazy that you had to go by boat to another town to get them. But probably nice to get off the island for a bit. Sister Elodie said that's why you missed the funeral."

"Um... yeah, it's been a crazy week." I was thoroughly perplexed and suddenly anxious about saying the wrong thing. I was missing something, something major.

An arm landed around my shoulders, and I jumped. A British accent crooned. "Welcome back, La La, nice specks." Noah tapped the tip of my nose playfully with his finger.

"Thanks," I said bashfully, prying out from his grip. He seemed... cheery. How could he be so unaffected? He was worried sick after Oliver went missing, and now, with his death, I would have expected him to be a wreck. "How are you holding up?" I asked cautiously.

Noah glanced at the girls before answering me. "It's awful, for sure. Though, I didn't know her too well, you know, aside from our wine and candy trades."

Eve pushed something into my palms. "We're all blowing bubbles after dinner tonight in the cafeteria. In honor of her. Here's some for you."

A cold chill slinked down my spine as the clues started to take form. And like a bucket of ice over my head, someone came up behind me and pulled my braids. An Irish accent teased. "What's up, miss sexy librarian?"

To my horror and absolute shock.

Oliver stood there smiling.

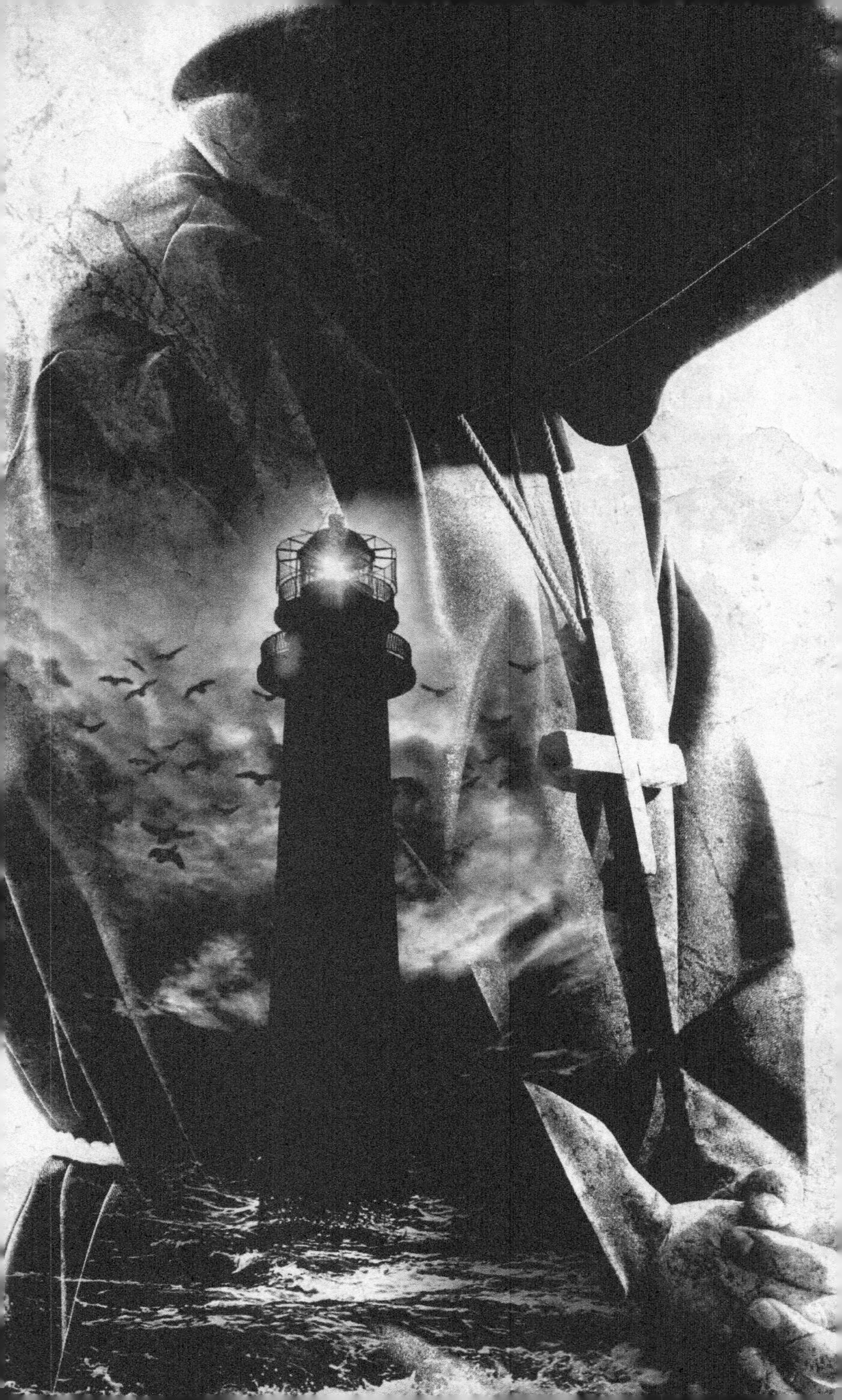

Dante

CHAPTER TWENTY-TWO

Grimm was a small, quiet island. It always had been. Despite the neighboring mainland developing its own lore about our happenings and the women and men of the cloth who sometimes whisked away children in the night... our reputation was a mystery. That's how I preferred it: quiet days, seaside nights, a life of simple contemplation. After the events that transpired so many years ago, when the town was rife with terror of a multitude of evils when my brothers and I became not family but soldiers in a holy war... we all deserved some peace.

But peace was coming to an end.

Something had kicked the hornets' nest of hell. Was it me? Was it my corrupting of The Holy Virgin?

I jumped a small stream as I trekked into the forest that lay in the middle of our humble land. The stream that students couldn't pass. If mischievous kids neared the woods, they'd get to the water, get spooked and very tired, and decide to turn back. The sisters were clever in their work, never missing a thing. I owed my life to their craftiness on several occasions. They were, for the most part, much more forgiving of me and my proclivities than my brother Silas who I felt by the tinge of cool in the air awaiting me in the ritual spot. He rarely came. His presence now only confirmed what I felt to be true.

The tides on Grimm were shifting.

I wondered if Nikolai sensed it, not that he would care, not that anything could coax him out of his foxhole of self-absorption.

I was lucky to have saved the Irish boy's body, and I felt I owed it to him after the terrors I'd sent him when I'd tortured him in my cathedral. Surely, my influence is what sent a demon to him. But he was easy enough to exorcise. The demon fled before I'd even touched his body in the damp grass that day. He wouldn't recall a thing. But now there was the case of the dead girl the sisters found in her room... we'd blame it on her stopping her heart medication. But, the students would question if it were intentional. Better they have those suspicions than to know the truth.

Demons were back on Grimm.

Silas greeted me; like a silver phantom, he leaned against an oak tree just outside the sacred circle. The smell of firewood and blood was already alight in the misty air.

He put a hand on my shoulder to keep me from trudging forward and ignoring him. "You are *possessed* by her."

I shook him off and gritted my teeth. "You're a lonely, meddlesome bastard with no one else to judge right now. Well, you can cast your all-knowing stare from me, brother. I have this under control."

Malice flashed across his stone-cold features. "A demon has killed a girl, a student was inhabited and now suddenly reanimated by the exorcist priest," he clapped mockingly. "Oh, and my favorite baker is dead, too."

"God rest the key lime pies," I snapped. "*You* are possessed by demons of the past. This is not the same."

My brother's laugh was bitter. "The Holy Virgin, the prized cow of Lady of Sorrow Church, the one thing you can't have and own, I should have foreseen it as a fire to your moth long before she came. But now you've done it. You've almost killed the Reverend Priest Benedict, you've lost his Head Lady, and you're on the path to ruining his Holy Daughter. Do you think they will ignore us now? You've put a goddamn target on our backs. We all know how you will burn anything for your sinful desires, Dante. But I will not allow you to burn this place in your sick obsession for an innocent, albeit tortured, little girl. Don't you see the hell you are inviting into our parish? Or should we cast you aside, deep as Nikolai, because you simply don't care anymore?"

Wrath blinded my vision as I took hold of his collar and slammed him against the tree, but he continued.

"You'll kill her. Just like you did our mother. And it'll be only you and the bodies of your fallen, standing in ash amongst an island overrun by the demons you vowed to exorcise."

"You are wrong," I growled, giving him another push before releasing him. "I abide in the ashes of my former humanity, clutching the goddamn holy word like a relic of goodness that doesn't exist for me anymore. You could never understand that despair, Silas, and you've never fucking tried to. I *will* protect her, I will honor my calling, and watch over this island, and you can go to hell."

Silas scoffed, smoothing his shirt and fixing his priest's collar. "Selah is not your holy word nor is she a sacred relic."

"To me, she is both," I murmured, storming past him before he could say more. The sisters spun and twirled, eyes closed as they chanted, either blissfully unaware of our spat or choosing to ignore it and gossip later. Probably the latter.

The women danced, twirling and spinning despite their large goat masks and horns twisting toward the night sky. Naked, melding with the fire embers, barefoot and free, they held hands, and I knew, despite their masks, they were smiling beneath them. The sisters adored this ritual. A whimper sounded from the center of the stone and branch pentagram as Father Patrick watched on with a horrified expression.

I needed this. This would help.

"Heretic!" he yelled when he spotted me.

I stepped just outside the star. "Not quite, keep guessing."

"Demons! You harbor the powers of the devil," he spat, fighting against the magical binds that kept him in place. We didn't need ropes or ties, not for something like him.

Silas watched on with stone-faced disapproval while the women giggled, Elodie posing next to me, crossing her arms and making a request. "We could keep him alive a bit longer? He bleeds so well."

My shoulders ached with tension, and I cracked my neck, fighting to free some of my frustrations. It would be prudent for the girls to keep him living, crying... bleeding for as long as possible. Though the disappointment rattled me— I wanted to kill.

My sisters of our unholy vows continued their chants, dancing and celebrating under the brisk light of a nearly full moon. The fire flames licked toward the heavens as Grace struck, sinking her teeth into the priest's bicep. He shuddered but didn't move, couldn't move.

Once she'd had her fill, she released, blood dripping down her chin, before pulling her goat mask back over her face. It continued, and I watched, simply an observer of their worship. With each lash of teeth at his body, each trail of blood puddling like mud around him, Father Patrick paled and weakened, while the sisters grew stronger, wiser, more lovely.

As his spirit grew faint, leaving his body in red droplets onto the tongues of beings far better than him, he pleaded, "I-I cannot help my affliction. Just-just the same as you, Father Amorth. We are the same, do you not see? Maybe-maybe I fed from the children, but you let your flock feed from me. Are you any better in the eyes of the lord?"

Temptation pulled at me to cross the lines of the star, but I refrained, instead kneeling closer to the half-dead man. "You're right, Father." I toyed with a stone. "We are both slaves to our sins yet held captive by our oaths to god." Bitterness laced my tone, and I noticed the women paused their dancing. Remembering myself, I tossed the rock. “But for this night, it is you on that side of the sacrificial altar, and not me.”

How many times had I poured over the sacred book? How often I’d committed psalms and proverbs to memory? How often had I toiled within the prayers of David, Solomon, and Peter in hopes that god would forgive me for my sins?

But because god was a just deity, because he was endowed with infinite wisdom and authority… he didn’t.

Instead, in his righteous cruelty— he allowed me to retire into the darkness of my lighthouse amongst the waves while Father Patrick shuddered beneath the piercing fangs of hungry disciples.

God was love, and love meant that Father Patrick would die within a few days after this prolonged session of righteous feeding.

God was the only fair judge, and so I would never die. I would continue to bleed, pricked by fangs of regret, and left in the forest to die a thousand deaths for all the innocent I slayed, all the people I allowed to die and sought to their swift end.

But most of all, I would suffer for what I was about to do to Selah.

For what was about to happen to the holy virgin daughter at my hand, there would be no hope of forgiveness.

And there was no turning back now.

Selah

CHAPTER TWENTY-THREE

With visual aids, much was clearer. This church, this university, wasn't humble or small. It was a sharp, black castle piercing the grey expanse of a sky. Each step was easier with the growing realization that I could see what was in front of me, dodge the shoulders of students with their backpacks, and seek out the sisters should I need them. And while my physical sight had grown clearer, more had become shrouded in question and fog.

I stepped into the wake for one dead friend.

While the other dead friend tilted a glass in my direction.

How was this possible?

Noah leaned against a metal bench in the crowded cafeteria. "Where's your new bestie?"

"What?" I asked, straightening and pulling my gaze from a very alive Oliver.

"It's a student's wake, and there are no priests, no sisters, and certainly not your best friend, Father Amorth, in attendance. Don't you think that's strange?"

I huffed, feeling my annoyance build in my chest. "There's a lot strange here, Noah, and the whereabouts of the clergy is the least of them."

Noah's eyebrows rose.

I startled at the booming Irish voice of Oliver behind me. "You know, it is a full moon tonight."

Cornered between them, Noah grabbed Oliver's drink and took a sip. "That it is, old chap. Fancy a walk this evening?"

"Only if four-eyes comes with us?" Oliver smiled down at me. "What do you say? Sneak out with us?"

"Why?" I squeaked, pressing my shoulder blades into the wall as if I could evaporate into it. "What is it you believe is even happening with the clergy, anyway?"

Noah shrugged and passed Oliver a glance. "Can't be sure as there's only stories and rumors. But they all disappear around the full moon, and we think we know where they go."

"Then you go play Sherlock and Watson on your own," I insisted. "Why do you want me to come?"

Oliver blew a stream of bubbles between us, their fluffy, childlike presence jarring coming from the face I was sure was bloodied and demon-possessed only a week ago. Not to mention, we were standing in the wake of Angelica's death... nothing made sense, and it seemed as if I were trapped in a puzzle with too many missing and scattered pieces. Did the confidential going-ons of the sisters and priests play a part? We had the answer right in front of me, but I didn't want to seek it out for fear of it being true.

"You're the holy daughter," Oliver said matter of factly. "They can't harm you. Therefore, if you're with us when we uncover whatever it is they're hiding, they won't punish us or send us away." He shrugged. "Plus, Noah and I have figured out your secret anyway."

"My secret?" I gasped. They knew. They knew about my crush and subsequent impure happenings with Father Amorth. I felt my face redden, and the two boys laughed.

"Yeah, we know all about you and why you're here. And your blushing only confirms it. So, tonight at eleven, we'll come and fetch you. Then we'll all get what we want."

I swallowed, my mouth dry.

It seemed I didn't have a choice.

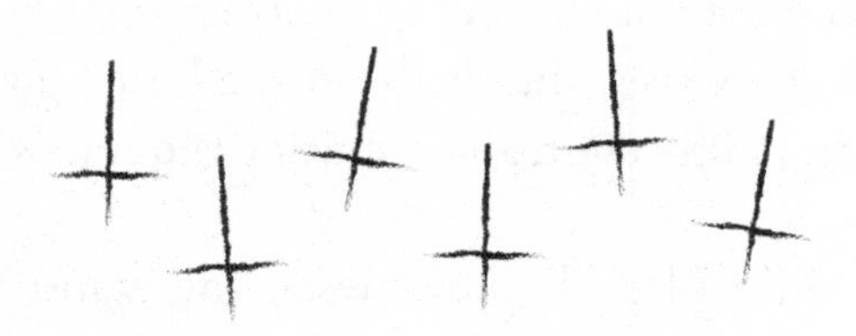

Angelica's wake smelt like soap and the floor stuck to the pads of my shoes by the time we were finished. It felt as if I weren't really there. I may as well have been a shadow on the wall or a chair pushed under the table. My grief was a small animal hiding in a hole, trembling, unsure of what was happening on the other side of the dark tunnel. Oliver shot me smiles like nothing had happened. No one looked at him twice. Everyone hugged me and cried, expressing their shock that Angelica was dead.

Angelica was dead.

Oliver was alive.

And during the night, I didn't locate one sister or priest. Where were they? As the bright and full moon poked above the watery horizon, Noah's suspicions haunted me. Something was abnormal here on the Isle of Grimm. Something was amiss, but did I even want to know what the only people who'd been kind to me had hidden away so carefully? If indeed such a secret existed... would something sinister change anything for me? Would it alter my deepening feelings for Dante? After Silas's warning, I feared the answer more than the revelation of what we could stumble upon that night.

Making it to the lighthouse was quicker now that my vision was better. It was easier to navigate the darkening path than it ever had been before. It felt deeply selfish to marvel at the waves, the shells on the beach glittering in the orange, fading light, and admiring the cracks in the old lighthouse.

How could I be allowing myself the wonder of sight when a girl had died... and somehow, I felt it had to be my fault. Oliver had attacked me, acting... well... acting possessed by some sort of darkness. He'd jumped from my bedroom window and fallen several stories down to his death. After that... I struggled to recall what had happened after Father Silas had whisked me away and Dante had taken me under his care. No one had offered any sort of explanation.

Had I even asked for one?

Noah and Oliver were right... the clergy here at Grimm *were* hiding something. But what if exposing it, exposing *them*, destroyed this island refuge? The one place I'd ever felt like home. If the clergy here were going against the Lady of Sorrow ordinance, it would mean their lives would be taken. I couldn't let that happen. Somehow, I had to stop that from happening. I had to warn Father Amorth that the boys suspected something and were digging for answers, but when I pounded on the steel lighthouse door, it didn't budge.

My knees locked for nearly ten minutes before I pried myself away and forced myself back to my room. Upon my bed was a box with a note. It read: *Angelica would have wanted you to have these. Make her proud and do something slutty in them. Love, Eve*

My throat tightened at the gesture and the overall wrongness of it all. How the first gesture of kindness I'd ever received from a peer had proceeded her death. Some students blamed her absent-mindedness for not taking her heart medication. Some were treating it as deliberate, as if she wanted to die. Neither seemed right, but I couldn't know why.

I pulled out a pair of jeans with holes in the knees, spaghetti strap tank tops, black miniskirts, and crop tops. All forbidden things I'd never even touched... and despite my discomfort, despite the voice of my dad in my ear calling me a whore and a sinner for even considering what I was about to do— I found myself buttoning the jeans and slipping on a black crop top. It sat just above the jeans, and just the sliver of exposed torso and collarbones made me feel naked. As I assessed myself in the mirror, my cheeks heated at the rebellious indecency of it.

I'd come to the isle of Grimm for an exorcism of my demons... and yet I felt myself all the more drawn to them now. Standing in sinners' clothes, having been touched by a man, not having said a single prayer... and though I knew I was sullied and impure, I knew I was a wretched sinner. I felt less like a sinner now than I had before Father Dante's fingers slipped into my sex.

Jeans felt more at home than my veil, somehow. Lady Vanessa would scold me and say I looked like the world. But as I stared back at the girl with thick-rimmed black glasses, messy pigtail braids, wearing pants for the first time... I didn't mind looking like the world anymore. And it was because of Grimm that I'd reached this point and gained this freedom. Whatever awaited us on our quest for answers that night, I knew I had to protect this place, the students, and the clergy here, no matter the cost.

My dad and Lady of Sorrow church could never find out.

My upbringing was beyond sheltered; my upbringing was a spiked cage for a doe. There were no fond memories of playing outside, no friendships, and no tender touches from the nameless mother who died before I met her. Childhood for me was ruler slaps, locked metal bars, and sacred text as cold as the page, freezing like ice in my brain and reminding me every moment that I was worthless—born a sinner, born a prop, a symbol as hallow as the cross that hung in my father's office.

Somehow, I'd always found it in me to fight silently against my captivity. While parts of me did strive to be the holy daughter I was born into being— a demon raged within me, asking for the lusts of the flesh. To watch television, listen to secular music, wear normal clothing, read erotic books, and even have sex or explore my body before marriage.

I watched countless women become Ladies of Sorrow and lose that fight, the spark in their eyes dying, their voices silenced forever. My naivety and ignorance existed like a plague carefully curated to keep me small, like the forgoing of ever getting me glasses. My poor eyesight was a sign from god that I should hold fast to the clergy and my future husband—never seeing too far ahead, always needing assistance, forever walking slowly.

But now... after visiting Grimm, after confessions with Dante and talking with the sisters... I could see clearer now. And though my revelations were giving me headaches in more ways than one, I knew the journey to grow in his new self would be taxing and difficult. It was a fight worth it to me, though. I wouldn't be returning to Lady of Sorrow Church the same holy daughter that left... and that's what they wanted, isn't it?

Though, this version of me is certainly not what they had in mind. My lack of know-how, the innocence they'd forced upon me, was not my choice, and it did indeed do as intended by holding me back and making me unknowledgeable and afraid. To break free of that, I had to step into my discomfort, expose my knees under the denim of a dead girl's pants, shrug off my veil, and venture into the dark woods with two boys alone.

My heart froze in my chest when they rapt against my door. I'd opened the door last for Oliver as a monster galloping down the hall. Tonight, I opened the door as someone who could see, who could fight, too. They stared at me with wide eyes and mouths agape. Their stunned features lit a sense of accomplishment inside me. They weren't the only ones with surprises, secrets, and desires they hid from the world.

"Are we going or not?" I asked, breezing past them, my glasses feeling a little lighter on my nose as I strode down the hall.

When they collected themselves and caught up, they led me past the school garden and toward the lining of thick brush and trees, only the light of the eerie moon to guide us. "I see them disappearing back here every month," Oliver said lowly, as if frightened that someone could be listening, though we were decidedly alone in the cool, salted air of night.

Crossing my arms, I stood at the tree line, and the guys hesitated. "Are you afraid?" I asked, not masking my mocking annoyance.

Noah puffed up his chest. "I'm not," and marched past me, grabbing a long stick as he went. I rolled my eyes, and when I did, I caught the glance of Oliver staring at me.

Swallowing, I asked. "What... what happened to you?"

Oliver looked over my shoulder before his answer chilled my bones. "Ask Father Amorth."

Leaving me standing in my tongue-tied stupor, he followed Noah in silence, and I lagged behind them. Each step into the dry forest felt as if I were being pulled by a magnetic force, though by the slowing steps of the boys, they did not seem to agree. Jumping over a small brook, I paused and turned around at the guys standing behind me.

"Smells like smoke," I said. "Maybe your wicked secret is up ahead." I taunted.

"You know," Noah said, "My head is pounding. I think I'm getting a migraine."

"Yeah," Oliver leaned against a tree. "Dude, I think it just hit me how tired I am. Like I can barely move my legs right now."

Putting my hands on my hips, I narrowed them with a glare. "Are you guys serious? This was your whole mission to get me out here on this stupid crusade to expose whatever made-up mystery you've concocted in your minds. And now you're backing out?"

"Let's forget it. You're right, it's late, and this is dumb." Noah rubbed his forehead.

Oliver stumbled backward. "And it's creepy out here. Why did we think this was a good idea?"

They pattered in the direction we came, and I paused, the smell of firewood like an alluring elixir I couldn't resist. Seeing an opportunity to lose them, I jogged ahead, zig zagging between trees, until the sounds of their footsteps were long gone. They wouldn't come for me, I didn't think, and maybe I'd get lost in the woods until morning, but somehow... I didn't feel afraid. Soon, the aroma of firewood made its way to crackling and twisting ash.

Stopping outside a clearing, I strained to see what lay in the middle of a decorated circle. If it weren't for my new glasses, I wouldn't have seen a thing save for the distorted shapes of fire and the hunched figure of a man... a man in tattered priest garb struggling to breathe. Panic shuddered through me as it dawned on me someone was hurt. Twigs broke as I cautiously made my way toward him. If he'd worked for the university, I'd never seen him before, and as I approached, I gasped, taking in his many wounds. He looked as if he'd been attacked by wild animals as he knelt in the center of an enflamed star.

His chin shot up sharply when he noticed my presence and took in my clothing. "Y-you, you're not one of them—are you?"

"One of who?" I asked, suddenly feeling naked without my robes and veil. They hid me. They set me apart, clothing that instantly told others that I was different, innocent, unknowing. But this priest regarded me like anyone might speak to any young woman. Not the Holy Daughter, not a lady of sorrow or nun... it was strange, and it took me a moment to take in what he was asking.

Was I one of *them*?

In jeans, was I one of them?

Without my veil and robes, was I one of them?

"I-I—" my words were sputtering ash of uncertainty as the old man's eyes frantically looked from mine to the woods beyond.

"No!" He screamed, startling me, and I spun around. My foot slipped, and I fell into the star next to the man, who didn't spare me a glance as he bellowed. A dark figure moved closer, seemingly floating. Slender bodies with horns glided silently toward the flames and screams. As they became clearer, I took in the sight of the bodies of naked women, their bare breasts illuminated by the bright white of the full moon. On their heads sat heavy masks of goat heads. Their horns ranged from warped and pale to hooked and black. Though, one similarity remained: the glowing yellow, rectangular eyes of goats. The sight... it was the most frightening yet beautiful thing I'd ever seen.

"Are these the creatures who've been attacking you?" I asked in a hoarse whisper.

"Satan's mistresses," the man cried, tapping a cross to his chest. "Please, just release me to hell," he begged of them.

One nude woman tilted her goat head and stopped just outside the star, outstretching a hand to me. Trembling, the priest continued his prayers and sobbing while I glanced between the holy man and the mistress of Satan. I sat between them, wondering where I belonged. Which side of the star was I fated to be?

Should I be crying and clutching a crucifix with the likes of holy people? Was my life meant to be something in service of men, in search of holy orders from gods I'd never see?

Or... did I belong with the goats? Was I a mistress of Satan, too? My entire life, beings like this only existed on the outskirts of sermons. The evil ones, the ones who didn't abide by the sacred texts, were damned to hell for their sins, and the reality of their fate hung over me like a reaper's scythe. Yet... the holy man beside me shook inside his horror while the goat-headed woman, the evil one, extended a hand in aid, in offering, in silent question.

In my quandary, my hooded priest flashed through my mind. His own sort of holy darkness, bound by his vows, stretching them to suit him in a way I'd never experienced. And in that moment, the answer became clear.

I took her palm, looking into her rectangular, glowing eyes as the others watched on. She pulled me up, and I stepped out of the star and stood with her. The priest shook in horror. The goat woman gestured gracefully to a tree stump, and I obeyed her silent command to sit. It was clear that whatever was about to happen, I was invited to be a spectator, though I wasn't sure I would be brave enough to keep my eyes open the entire time. Adrenaline coursed through me alongside gratitude that Noah and Oliver weren't here to witness... whatever this was.

I noticed then two other stumps and two other women watching. They looked on wearing white robes... the two ladies of sorrow. Sister Grace had mentioned that they remained behind and not to watch me but for the sisters to watch over... is this what they meant? Were they being indoctrinated into... whatever this was? Was I? Lady Vanessa was missing, and I had the chilling suspicion that she never made it back to Lady of Sorrow.

The women encircled the star, and the man continued rocking back and forth, praying loudly to his god. Their goat heads were too large for their frames, and I didn't mean to gawk, but I'd never been in the presence of naked bodies before. They were beautiful on their own, but in contrast to the grotesque, furry, and horned goat heads, they were deadly forest nymphs. The things of nightmares, they were certainly a nightmare for the weeping and bloodied priest. What had I stumbled into? Perhaps my fear had settled into morbid curiosity because it wasn't even a consideration in my brain to run or hide. There was an unsettling familiarity with these women, with this place.

These were the sister nuns of Grimm.

They lifted their hands to the moon and began to chant, their voices soft and feminine melodies to the stars as the fire rose in answer.

May Satan love her and, in the darkness, find her.

May every sin empower, and may she partake in every fruit from every forbidden tree.

Moving in unison, like an ancient, practiced dance, their palms spun, alternating weaving between each other as if stringing a thread. It was mesmerizing, and with each line, the fire answered.

Send the snakes to tempt her, hurry the goats to keep her, let every baphomet find and guard her.

May she be the greatest of evil to burn the holy, mar the mighty, and bring the men of power to ash.

The breath in my lungs hummed, and goosebumps stabbed my skin as my vision simultaneously cleared and fogged. Something was happening... and I found myself standing with them before I was aware of my body. The chain of hands held broke, and they accepted me without question, though I didn't know the dance... or did I?

I took their palms in mine, and we moved together, my feet tapping to the rhythm, the chanting tingling through me like bolts of electricity. My clothing felt heavy then until it didn't, and the night air kissed my skin in wondrous ecstasy. The fire rose in applause and ignited along the lines of the star. The priest jolted as if pulled by his chin. He straightened, eyes going wide with terror.

For every soul damned to heaven.

For every child taught, they were dirty.

For every woman cursed to serve as a rib from his chest.

Use the rib, stab his heart, and drink his blood.

A woman struck, and another, and another, and I couldn't comprehend it, but they were... biting him. One reached for his calf, another his neck, while another bit into his side. The priest remained still, and his crying stopped as blood dripped down exposed chins and goat heads propped on naked backs.

May it be.

May the devil guide her.

May the reaper find her.

I wasn't afraid, I wasn't even disturbed, and maybe that was the most alarming thing of all, until... until what happened next.

Selah

CHAPTER TWENTY-FOUR

A seagull cawed, and the ocean rushed against the beach as I sat up, squinting in the bright yet cloudy light of the coast. This wasn't real. This had to be a dream, right? Thunder rumbled, and lightning crackled across the sky, spitting very real rain droplets across my cheek as I stood, and realized I was near the lighthouse now. But I'd just been in the woods, the women, the fire, the dying priest...

The lighthouse was cleaner somehow, less worn, without the deep cracks and sprawling untamed ivy that had always claimed it. How could it have been restored so quickly?

I made my way through the cobblestone streets. No one looked at me, yet they were all in vintage gowns, and the men wore suspenders and newsboy caps. A horse trotted by, and I couldn't make sense of it, though I didn't have time before a woman shrieked, screaming a name that I knew, a name that haunted my blood.

"Father Dante Amorth, please!" A woman wailed, stumbling through the center of town. People moved and looked on, unsure of how to assist. I followed her, shoving past people and trying not to lose her in the bustle. I'd never seen the town so busy, so full of life, yet so new and unworn by age. It was as if I'd fallen through time...

The crowd parted, and an impossibly tall and broad hooded figure in black walked through, following after her, not looking at any of the townspeople. The woman stumbled at his feet, begging, "Please, please, I need an exorcist for my daughter."

"The Grimm Reaper," two men whispered in awe next to me before kissing their prayer beads.

I knew the tilt of his head, the ominous presence of the shadowed, nearly invisible face. Grimm Reaper was accurate... Dante was here. By the time I broke through the crowd, he was following the small woman into a small dwelling, and thankfully, I made it in without anyone noticing me or shutting me out.

The tiny space held only a bed, where the small adolescent body of a teenage girl lay, her hands and ankles strapped to her sides while a small oil lamp flickered on a nightstand.

Dante was too large for the room, and he seemed to suck the light, the air, and everything straight out of it. The mother sniffled as he gave her daughter a cursory glance. "I am an exorcist, not a healer," he rumbled plainly, his voice the deep timbre I'd grown to crave. Rain fell like bullets against the tin roof, and the room grew frigid.

Dante straightened, stopping at the door and looking around the room. I opened my mouth as he stared at me, ready to explain... that I had no explanation for why I was there, but he didn't acknowledge me— no— he didn't *see* me.

No one did.

"There is evil here," Dante mused to himself, though the mother nodded her head, clutching her prayer beads and pleading for her sleeping daughter.

The rain pounded overhead, and the room fell silent again as Dante stood by the bed— when suddenly it began to shake.

The girl violently vibrated as if a small earthquake was fighting to swallow her whole. Her eyes shot open, fully black, and she smiled a horrible smile.

"What is your name?" Dante asked, no change in his tone, seemingly unaffected by the horrific display of darkness that had overtaken the room.

The mother backed into the corner of the area next to me. Shaking, she answered. "Her name is Penny."

I could only see Dante lean forward, and being that I was essentially invisible or dreaming, I moved forward to the foot of the bed to watch in morbid fascination. "That isn't *your* name, though, is it?" he whispered.

The girl gave an exaggerated frown, so childlike yet not of this world, her mouth contorting in ways one shouldn't be able to move the muscles without assistance. My chest tightened. What was happening?

"Are you afraid of her? Our mother is here," Penny cackled in an echoey voice that didn't suit her small frame, and I startled as deep crimson blood trickled from the sides of her lips.

Dante reached forward a long finger. "Leave this place, demon. This body is of no use to you. This girl and her mother are of no use to you."

Sliding his finger down her forehead, a scream wretched from Penny's mouth, and she shook. At the sound, my head began burning, like a horrible, soul-wrenching headache. I held my head, watching as he drew a small horizontal line at the bottom of the long line on her forehead... the lines glowing black. Had he had ink on his fingers?

The bed shook violently as Penny screeched, her body contorting in painful, unnatural ways as she screamed for her mother. My head pounded, and I needed to leave, had to get out of this room. Fire burned in my chest, and the air grew thin. I was going to pass out. I was going to die. Falling to my knees, I crawled toward the door, but as I did, the sound of snapping jolted behind me, and thunder crashed.

The girl's mother screamed, and when I turned to look, the girl had attacked Dante, her elbows jutting out as she tried to strangle him. Darkness shot out around them, and he pulled back his hood, and I saw... I caught the faintest glimpse of a man's chiseled, broad face and bright blue eyes. Black hair combed back and a downward piercing gaze.

He met my eyes for a moment as I grasped the door handle. It was as if a tornado were blowing through the room. Darkness and shards of black whipped around us alongside the wretched screams. Soul piercing, head pounding screams, and I was losing oxygen, but he saw me then, he saw me, and his mouth opened to speak before—

Blood slashed across his perfect face. A cut so deep, jagged, and terrible accompanied it across his forehead, and he fell, the claws continuing.

"No!" I screamed with any air left within me, but I was fading fast. I needed to save him. I had to help. Dante was being attacked, mutilated before my very eyes, all because I had distracted him, and the voices of a million echoes laughed and screeched as his blood sprayed. But I had to get air before I could help. Twisting the knob, I fell onto the rainy street, gasping and grabbing my throat. "No, no, no!" I turned, twisting the door handle with any strength I had, but it wouldn't turn.

"Help!" I cried out, though it was a weak whine in the night as horses splashed puddles past me. Though, something stranger remained as the carriage passed. A man sat with his elbows on his knees, face toward the cobblestone he sat contented in the rain. His dark green eyes shot up and looked straight at me. I crawled for him, and he didn't move, his face growing stern and contemplative as I did. He looked like Dante; all except... except his temples, forehead, and jaw were marked with black tattoos. Small shapes and lines that made no sense. Though he was stunning and strong to behold,

He tilted his head in the same way Dante did, and then I remembered. It clicked. This must have been... "Nikolai," I rasped.

Leaning forward and narrowing his eyes like I was a rat on the sidewalk he was scrutinizing, he asked in pointed shock. "*What are you*?"

I gulped at the air, struggling through my pounding head. It felt as if I'd been struck and beaten by a thousand lashes of a whip. "Dante... needs... you..."

The man scoffed and pressed two fingers to my forehead. "Tell my *brother*..." he hissed softly in my ear, his scent like burning coals, making my headache worse. "To burn in hell." He pushed against my forehead, and I fell backward, engulfed in black.

Falling, falling down a pit of nothingness.

My back collided with something soft. When I opened my eyes, my headache was gone, and I was under clean sheets that smelled of lavender. White morning light poured through the sheer curtains of my room as I sat up, kicking off the blankets. "No," I said to myself. "This... this isn't happening again."

On cue, Sister Grace gave a short knock before breezing into my room, holding a tray of steaming oatmeal and her satchel of hair supplies. "Beautiful morning, isn't it?"

"No," I argued, crossing my arms. "I'm not falling for this again. You won't trick me. I know what I saw," I pointed out the window. "That was you and the other sisters, wasn't it? And—and how did you make me go..." I searched my mind, connecting the dots. "Back in time?"

Sister Grace paused with her hands still on the bowl as she sat it on my table. "Sounds like another vivid dream, darling—"

"Stop!" I shouted. "Tell me what is going on. What is this?" Tears pricked my eyes. "I won't tell anyone, I'm not mad, I don't care if you— if you—"

Sister Grace met my gaze then with a challenging stare. "I think..." she answered slowly, choosing her words carefully. "I think you should confess what you believe you saw to Father Amorth. He can guide you, Selah."

"Where is he?" I sat defeatedly on my bed. "It's been days since I've seen any of you."

I noticed then that I was in pajama pants and a soft T-shirt I'd had no memory of dressing in. "Father Amorth was gone, but he is back now. Your confessions can continue this evening," she smiled, nearing the door. "One of the ladies of sorrow is able to communicate a little. Is it true you were caged each night?"

Remembrance of my protection bars weighed against my shoulders. My protection. No, it *was* a cage. "Yes," I nodded.

The nun shook her head and turned to leave before I stopped her.

"Nikolai," I said plainly, quick to watch her reaction. She froze, and even her breathing stopped. "Wherever you sent me... I saw him. I spoke to him."

The room grew cold, and Sister Grace responded with a hoarse whisper. "Perhaps *don't*... confess that part to Father Amorth."

With that, she was gone.

That night, I pulled out my white robes and freshly pressed veil. I thought of the goat women's horns. I wondered what happened to the bleeding priest... I hoped the sisters were safe, that they were hidden, that the man was dead, and that the sisters were fed.

What I'd witnessed was undoubtedly the evils of the world I'd always been warned of. And then what I saw of Father Amorth... the distinct and shuddering knowledge that I'd scarcely allowed myself to believe was ever present and clawing at my mind.

It was real.

It was the past.

Images of his face without his hood had imprinted on my mind. His brothers were handsome in the same ethereal way that he was, though he commanded their beauty like marble carved so expertly it looked like linen. Dante was perfect, strong, and unsettling, and he'd looked right at me somehow before his attack.

My chest ached, remembering the blood, the shades of red I hated so much. He'd been mutilated. Is that why he now covered his features? It didn't matter to me if that perfect glance was scarred or even gone forever. I needed him, and he needed me. I was sure of it.

The knowledge that his past and his family ties were complicated... Silas had told me Dante had killed their mother. And Nikolai, if that had in fact been Nikolai, promptly instructed me to tell his brother to go to hell. Everyone feared him, resented him, spoke badly of him... and while he was fearsome, he was something else with me... he was gentle, he was patient, he was kind.

A breath of air left my lips as the fruits of the spirit entered my mind as a way to describe my exorcist. My collar was straight, and my black hair tucked neatly behind my veil. The Holy Virgin Daughter once more... in sight, at least. Because on the inside, I was none of those things anymore.

I was a naked woman, drinking the blood of a holy man under my goat horns. Lady of Sorrow Church would have me sacrificed upon their altar, wouldn't they? I would be going home to die.

And I was okay with that.

And I was okay with stepping into Dante's cathedral as a whore. My heart raged, jumping into my throat, as hundreds of candles dripped and flickered in the dim church. The small door to the confessional creaked open as if of its own accord, and I knew he waited on the other side.

It was time to confess my sins.

One last time.

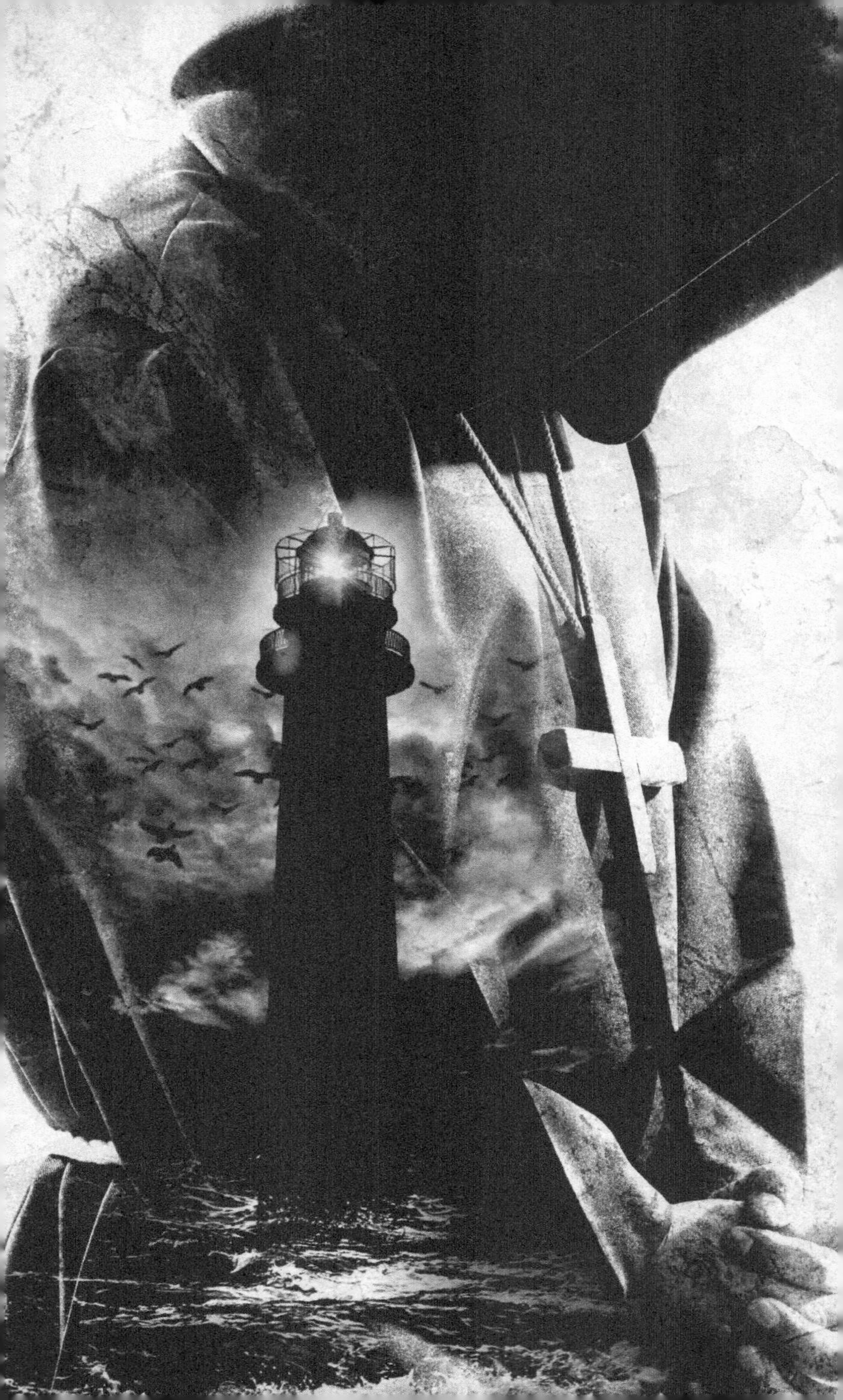

CHAPTER TWENTY-FIVE

Did she notice the offering I left her on the altar? Did The Holy Virgin Daughter know just how deep and twisted I'd sunk my roots into her and how, after this confession, she'd never escape me? The initial shock and rage of learning she'd witnessed the ritual had quickly waned when paired with the knowledge that she didn't flee. No, sweet Selah joined in the dance of blood, and my empty hole for a soul sprouted something like hope. Hope that she could love me back. Could she love me back? If she saw what I truly was, would she run in terror? I hoped she wouldn't because I knew I couldn't let her go. If Selah ran, I would chase her. I would chase her down and fuck her into submission; her blood, my offering. My cum would be the only holy spirit dancing inside her.

Silas was right. I was losing my grip. Yet, to little Selah's soon-to-be terror, I'd realized it entirely too late. God had always hidden his face from me, covering his ears, sitting in still silence as I pleaded and begged for sanctification and freedom from my curse. Now... I prayed he'd continue his disregard.

Truly, I was the most foul and sinful of all of god's creation. There would be no redemption found for me at the foot of the lord's holy throne. No forgiveness awaited me. No, I was no prodigal son returning home after his sin. Selah was my sin, and she was my home, and I would remain the bastard wretched sinner that I was, all in search of her virtue I sought to devour like altar wine.

The dam had burst forth.

The demons were back.

All hell was rumbling in the clouds above, just waiting to be unleashed.

As an ordained exorcist priest, the body and blood of christ had sustained me— but it was no longer satiating my desire. Now, I was starving for the holy virgin. To feast upon her flesh and drink in her nectar and blood.

She stepped into my confessional like a rabbit into a trap laid by a skilled and careful hunter, like the holy lamb settling down next to the ravenous lion. My prey was caught in my snare and surely wouldn't escape me now.

Sitting down, I made out her delicate features, soaking in the sight of her small jaw and her clutched hands atop a lap of too-heavy fabric. Gowns of a holy virgin servant, not a dark little demon priest's princess that she was or that I wanted her to be.

Selah was mine.

Mine.

Her breathing was hurried, her hair hidden from me beneath her veil, and her body shrouded in white robes. The sight of it now an insult. Did she not want me to see her for the glory she revealed in the woods amongst the ritual? I'd borne witness to it from the shadows, not wanting to interrupt the women's sacred dance and their feeding songs and offerings. To see her join in... my cock rose at attention at mere remembrance. Her supple ass, her small breasts, the curve of her hips as she spun and swayed as if the chant of the sisters was alive inside her bones.

Could it be she was one of us all along?

I sat in silence, hidden by my shadows, knowing she would let me. She would let me be quiet. She always did. There was never need for hurried words between us. Like she understood, like I understood, a familiarity I scarcely wanted to acknowledge... but somehow, seeing her embrace the darkness in the woods had led me to a spring of hope. My thoughts gathered like a pool of blood seeping into grass. I wanted to rip her apart... and then I wanted to sew her back together. Each thread a piece of my filthy soul. God rejected my offerings... but would she?

"Forgive me, father, for I have sinned," she said, breath already half a wanting pant that twitched my cock as if her voice was tied to me by an invisible string.

"Confess your sins, Selah," I growled, unable to hide the dark desire in my tone. "For I know they are many. Aren't they?"

Her lilac lips parted slightly as she looked up through dark lashes. "Kids are dying and then some... not dying. The nuns are in the woods torturing men and dancing naked, wearing goats' heads... what is this place?"

"Is that why you came to confession this night? To ask me that?"

She swallowed. "No, it's not." She unclipped her veil with practiced precision and dropped it to the confessional floor before smoothing out her two long black braids. Standing, she unbuttoned her collar, and my cock throbbed so hard it hurt beneath my robes.

"Selah—" I gruffly warned.

"Who was the dying man in the middle of the woods? In the middle of the star of fire?" Like a shy but bold minx, she revealed a bare shoulder as if she didn't care what my answer was. Such a thing was nothing to common folk, but we were clergy. We were vowed and ordained, set apart by a holy god. And Selah had already compromised her purity on the beach with me. Each step toward me was certain doom for us both. And that bare fucking shoulder... almost set me wild.

"Don't."

"Don't what?" She asked with small innocence. "You want to see my depravity? You want my sin, Father Amorth? My sin is that I would give up my body, my godforsaken purity, my soul's spot in Heaven, just to have sex with you one time."

"As your priest, I should advise you against that..." I said, standing, peering down at her through the bars that separated us. So close yet so caged, a grim metaphor. "The man in the woods is a portrait of hundreds, thousands, before him. Men who protect each other. It's how the evil survives. They're sent away to me expecting their exorcist to be mean, yes, perhaps throw a few lashes. But ultimately, they expect I'll protect them as a fellow man. Yes, they expect a man, a fellow priest, an exorcist. But what they get is the demon. The Grimm Reaper. A different kind of exorcism. And they don't make it back. The ones who deserve to die, *die*. Painfully." I stepped closer, judging her response. But she only stood nearer. "As *your* exorcist, I should send you far away right now." I unhooked the rope from my garb. "As a holy man, I should ask that you confess your sins before it's too late."

"You're more than all of that, Dante," Selah whispered softly, stepping forward and lacing her tiny fingers through the iron bars. "I saw it. I don't know how I saw you... I *see* you."

The implications of her words, the way they opened the door to more questions than answers, should have stopped me in my tracks. But it only tossed raw meat in front of the drooling monster. "Turn around," I instructed.

"Don't make me leave—"

"Do as I say."

Obeying, her back turned to me, and I took her hands, causing her to gasp as I wrapped them around the bars. "Lean forward and hold on."

"Why?" Her voice a breath of hesitation and willing intrigue.

I pulled her gown over her hips and yanked down her white panties.

"White, so much white," I mused, surveying her bare ass as it pressed up and spread naked against the confessional bars. "I want more pink... more red..." Pulling out my cock I rested it on the crack of her ass.

Selah inhaled a sharp breath, weighing the girth, the thick and heaviness of me without being able to see me. Again, a tragic metaphor for her and I. She'd weighed the cost of me without ever seeing my face, she'd taken on the heaviness of what I was without comprehending it fully... and now... she'd be fucked— in every sense of the word.

"You can," her voice wavered. "I want it."

"As if I need your permission, as if I'm a good man who'd wait for you to say yes. No, Selah, Holy Virgin Girl, you should know that I am not a gentle being. This will hurt. It will hurt a lot before it begins to feel good. And I will drink every delicious moment of your pain. If you'd like to leave, the door to the confessional and the church are open. Though... I cannot promise I won't chase you. Not with my cock now dripping its precum down the crease of your ass."

She sucked in a breath and looked to the side, still holding the bars of the confessional. Arching her back in quiet, indecent invitation, she shook her head. "I'm not running anymore."

I moved the head of my cock down her, letting the precum leave a trail of me that glistened in the dim lamplight. The bars were for her benefit, to keep me somewhat contained, though what I warned rang true. Virgin or not, I would never be a gentle creature. Lining my rounded head up with her slit, she let out a small whimper as my skin met with her wet pussy lips.

A low growl echoed from my throat. "I wonder how much you'll bleed on my cock, Holy Virgin Daughter? Will you coat me from shaft to tip? Will you drip blood down the backs of your thighs?"

"Dante," she pleaded, already breathing heavily, her ass exposed and pussy at my mercy. Her plea was my leash snapping. With a swift and hard thrust, I slammed into her tight little cunt. She cried out in pain but didn't let go of the confessional bars. I pulled out roughly and slammed back in, over and over, until I could feel the blood and cum mixing and pushing out the sides of her.

Groaning, I praised. "Oh, not the Holy Virgin anymore, now. Are you, Selah?"

"No," she panted, pushing her ass backward. "More, please, more."

My teeth gritted together as I took her, as I wrecked her virginity, as I blackened her standing as this pure and golden calf being led to the slaughter. She wouldn't be anyone's wife but *mine*. No one's virgin but *mine*. Certainly, not god's anything. Selah belonged to me now. Did she realize it yet? Was my full length buried inside her not obvious enough that she would never escape me? She moaned and bucked as I pummeled her, finally spilling into her with a roar of wicked breadth. Did hell shudder in anticipation for me as I pulled out of her tight cunt and remained hard as a rock because the blood-soaked cum was only the beginning of the damnable offenses I'd commit against her?

I hoped so.

Fuck hell.

Fuck god.

All that existed was me and her in my little cathedral of blood and sin. She stood, shaking and unsure, rubbing her palms where the bars had left their imprint on her skin. "Take off your gown," I commanded.

Turning to me, her cheeks were flushed with a rosy tint as she obeyed, sliding her robes off her shoulders and kicking off the underwear that gripped her ankles. She stood for me there, naked, with soft skin and every curve highlighted by flickering candle flame. Her breasts pointed, hips round, and thighs full.

Her tone was a husky quiver of fear and desire. "I'm bleeding." She looked down to the streaks of red painting her knees and reached for her gown.

"No," I stopped her. "Don't clean up. Leave it." I gestured to the door, and she followed me, barefoot and naked, into the sanctuary. We stood before a wooden cross above an old and splintered altar. The hooded exorcist priest of death, and the mauled virgin girl. I imagined it would make a macabre painting if ever an artist was struck with the vision of us in that moment.

"I'm—I'm a mess," she whispered, looking down at the horror I'd marked her with.

With a sadistic chuckle, I answered. "I want you dripping on the church floor, Holy Virgin Daughter."

"Won't god be mad at us? Won't he punish us both greatly for this, for what we're doing, Father?"

The leash snapped again, and I grabbed her chin, thrusting two fingers into her mouth. "If god chooses now of all times to spare us a glance... may his ears bleed with the sounds of our moans within his hollow walls. For he's as sadistic as I am if he looks upon you in such a torn and cum filled state and thinks he's gazing upon a child of god. You don't belong to god anymore, Selah. After this, after today, you are *mine*. You belong to *me*."

Her eyes rolled back as she sucked my fingers for a moment before taking my wrist and pulling my hand down. "God is a jealous and vindictive god, the holy book says. You touched me on the beach, we've compromised my purity, and someone died. What if he truly is punishing us for our sins."

"If that's true, Selah, is that a god you wish to serve? A god who would leave your prayers unanswered, a god who would watch you sleep in a cage each night, knowing not a day of peace and turn from your cries as you were hit and abused... yet would see your moment of pleasure, of your acceptance of your body and your bliss, to see that and decide to rain sorrow upon you? I ask again, is that the god you wish to serve?"

"No," she whispered. "That is a god I wish to... I wish..."

"Say it, go on."

"That is a god I wish to anger."

She couldn't see it behind my hood of darkness, but I hoped she knew I was smiling. "We're in his house, let's give him one hell of a show."

Selah

CHAPTER TWENTY-SIX

My life was over. Dante didn't take my virginity. I gave it to him wretchedly in a holy confessional. My confession that I loved him, and wanted him, that I would be destroyed for him. We would go down in flames for what we had done... and I didn't want to stop. No, to the contrary, I wanted to keep going in every way possible. More, I wanted more sex. I wanted more of the pain and blood. I wanted it to drip all over the church floor like a bastardized offering to god.

More, I wanted more knowledge of who and what Dante was, and what this place was. Because it wasn't normal or natural, it was wild, dark, and some sort of gothic abyss full of secrets. Secrets I wanted in on, secrets I wanted to uphold, whatever they were.

It went against everything I'd been raised to believe. Every word of sacred text and rules I'd been spoon-fed behind golden gates since infancy had been abandoned now. By Lady of Sorrow Church, I was now as good as dead. I wondered if they'd kill me for my sins. If I were to die for my unfaithfulness to god, like Dante said, I was going to put on a hell of a show of it. I was going to wring as much pleasure as possible from what little life awaited me between now and my judgment day.

If hell awaited me, at least I would burn as someone properly fucked.

Like Mrs. Paramour.

Like the women in the romance novels.

I would take one fleeting moment of their lives as free, sultry lovers over a lifetime as a set apart, secluded, virgin princess—a life I didn't choose. A religion not made for me but made against me. No, I wanted this... I wanted my unholy exorcist priest dripping his cum mixed with my blood down my legs. I wanted it over and over again. The pain still burned against my center, and a dull ache grew in my lower belly. Something like pain mixed with an insatiable need for more. I needed his dick, his touch, and oh, how I wished to see his face.

Leaving me naked in the center aisle of his cathedral, he knelt at the altar before the looming cross and motioned me forward. When I did, something placed at the base of the priest's throne caught my gaze amongst the hundred flickering prayer candles that cast a warm, dim hue around the church. Dante waved two long and calloused fingers, indicating that I take a seat on the holy throne. A throne only for men, for ordained males, for priests of high stature and standing with god.

To the world, it would look as if he'd completely debased me, and he had.

But to have me sit in his seat said the opposite.

He didn't see me as a whore, did he?

He hadn't suddenly lost interest in me now that I'd given up my purity. My sex life wasn't a piece of rotten fruit... it was mine... and I was still worthy of love and respect, virgin or not.

The Holy Virgin would have argued that I didn't belong... but Selah... she did as instructed and sat naked, sexed, and wet upon the holy seat. Still kneeling before me, his hood shrouding his features in darkness, my very own grim reaper. The clergy of Lady of Sorrow had sent me for an exorcism, and I had met my reaper instead.

Pulling my gaze from the shadow of power that he exuded, I finally examined what lay at my feet. Shock and unease hit against my chest as I clutched the arm handles of the dark wooden throne. Dried, veined, and blood-browned with decay, two eyes that I knew stared up at me. I'd recognize their hue of hazel anywhere. I brought a shaking hand to my mouth.

"Those are— my father— did you kill him?"

Father Amorth picked the two eyeballs up by their long red strings. "You have a new father now. He's not your father anymore, I am. I'm your father, your daddy, your everything, and you belong to *me*."

Something dark and cold trickled down my spine as I looked at the disembodied eyes with horror and fascination. The eyes that had watched me cry at his hand, the eyes that watched as I was beaten, starved, and tortured. Father Amorth continued. "He's not dead... yet. But his eyes will sit right here and watch what I'm about to do to his Holy Virgin Daughter." He sat them in the elevated communion dish, irises facing me. It was sinister and so wicked... and I clenched my thighs together because I *liked* it.

Cocking his head to the side, Dante grabbed my knees, making me yelp. "You don't close your legs to me. I want your juices pouring down the priest's throne. Let him," he nodded towards the eyeballs. "And him," he jerked his chin to the cross hanging above me. "Watch your possession."

I sucked in a shaking breath, feeling my cheeks heat and the moisture flow from my center onto the cold chair. "Are you a demon?" I asked.

"Much worse," he answered lowly. "And you are my prey, a bloody lamb, a wretched, darling unholy thing." With slow precision, he lowered his face between my thighs and licked at the sensitive skin there. A small moan escaped me at feeling the face I'd only seen in a dark vision and never in person. He was right here, and my father's dead eyes stared on as a cross hung above me, my life and purity gone— and all I could think about was how I wished to pull back his hood and look at him. To see his eyes staring at me, to imprint his features into my soul once more.

"I want to look at you," I whispered, feeling his tongue move up my inner thigh.

"Lay back, church bells, and let me clean you up. It would be sacrilegious to have you on your knees praying to god with me dripping from your claimed cunt."

Before I could respond or maybe beg that he remove his hood, his mouth found me, and I cried out at the feel of it. Warmth and wetness enveloped my sore center as his tongue licked me from where my ass made contact with the throne, to my clit, where he focused in more and more with each pass up and down. While being taken in the confessional hurt and led to a burst of pleasure, this was slow and soft and an agonizing buildup of intensity. My hips writhed of their own accord; the pants and whimpers coming from my throat weren't words, but feelings given sound. Dante hummed and groaned into me, holding my knees apart so hard it hurt before inching two fingers at my opening.

"That's it, Selah. Take it in front of god and your dad. Tell them I'm your Father, I'm your god. Tell them with your prayerful moans, Selah."

My body quivered, and I moaned an echo into the church as his two fingers thrust into my sore opening. He pumped them in and out as his mouth worked around my clit. This was surely my ticket to Hell. Cumming on my exorcist priest's tongue on the priest's throne, before god, before my father's limp and lifeless eyes... This was sacrilegious to the most extreme degree, and I half expected that at any moment, god himself would strike me dead.

But instead of feeling fear, the only sensation that flourished within me was Dante's knuckles. When he sharply pushed in a third finger, and his teeth closed around my clit, I shattered like stained glass. My ornate picture etched on sacred walls now a heap of broken and jagged shards along the church floor.

My scream clawed at my throat, and when he wouldn't stop thrusting, wouldn't remove his fingers or his mouth even when I tried to buck him away, I came again and again as he growled against me like a beast determined to have his fill of his meal. My demon collecting his pound of flesh over and over again.

When he finally stopped, he stood, towering over me, and took me by the jaw, pulling me forward and sliding me to my knees before him. With agile hands, he reached into his robes and pulled out his cock. My eyes widened. "No wonder that hurt so bad. You're enormous," I awed as it bobbed in front of me. "All of that was inside me?"

He chuckled darkly. "And it's about to be down your throat before it's in your cunt again. Take this as your brief reprieve and suck on me, Selah."

I'd never seen a man up close like this before, but I took the length of him in both of my hands, feeling his girth between my fingers, and they didn't touch while wrapped around him. "I'm-I'm not sure I know what to do," I confessed with no small measure of embarrassment. "I probably won't be any good." Every cell in my body wanted to please him, wanted to bring forth the pleasure he'd just done for me, but I didn't know the first thing about pleasing a man, especially not with my mouth. The women in books just sort of did it.

He grabbed my chin and yanked my gaze up to him. "Don't ever disparage yourself again, especially not in front of me. Now, take my cock between those sweet lilac lips, and suck." He pinched my cheeks and pulled my face down, palming his cock with his other hand and pushing the tip between my lips. I opened my mouth and let him inside, letting my tongue explore the salty flavor. A groan vibrated from me as I realized he tasted like the ocean itself, and he felt so nice in my mouth.

His voice was husky as he praised, "That's it. Look at you, you hungry, thirsty little child of god."

Though I didn't know exactly what I was doing, I sucked on him, hallowing my cheeks, and his heavy breathing and hard grip on my hair told me I was doing something right. It felt so good and so wrong.

"Oh god," I gargled against him.

"Yes," Dante growled. "God hears you moaning on my cock. He's so, so disappointed." His hold moved to my mouth, and he pinched my dimples together roughly, massaging the insides of my cheeks against his girth before pushing in with a vengeance. I gagged, choking on him, but forced my tongue to roam his ridges. Saliva pooled out the sides of my mouth, and I knew I must have looked horrible, but that shadowy figure only looked down at me and groaned in heavy satisfaction before hitting the back of my throat over and over as I choked around him.

And then he stilled, and warm liquid flowed down my throat, and what didn't, collected in my mouth. Dante pulled out and pressed my jaw, making me open my mouth. "That's it, let me see my cum on your tongue, Selah." I stuck out my tongue proudly, letting what was left of his release drip down my chin. Without thinking, I wiped my face with the back of my hand, and when I noticed the black smear, I looked at him in shock. "You're... it's black?"

Only extending his hand, he helped me to stand and led me down the altar.

"The church is still standing... we haven't been struck by lightning," I mused.

"Yet," Dante added with a sinister and teasing edge. "Perhaps we haven't pissed him off enough."

Holding his hands, I pushed my hips nearer to his. "There's still time," I cooed, not recognizing my own voice. These dark desires hadn't sated me. They hadn't tampered with my lust, and the guilt of premarital sex didn't silence my demons. On the contrary... I felt as if I were awakening. "Please, can I look at you while we..." I trailed off.

Father Amorth stood solemn, and I was sure he would ignore me or say no, but he gently reached for my face and tugged off my glasses. "To look upon me, Selah, is to accept sure death of mind or body, often both. However... you cannot see well, and I wonder if it is enough to spare you."

Hope sprang in my chest. "I don't want to be spared, Father. If looking at you kills me... it is worth it to me."

"Don't be so flippant with your life," he chastised. "No one is worthy of you, especially not a corrupt thing like me."

I opened my mouth to argue, but he dropped my hands and took a long step backward, clutching his hood. "Don't look too closely, understood?"

My heart raced, and my pulse quickened. Even the damp and cold air of the grim little church didn't chill my sensitive skin. I was about to finally see him. Though my vision blurred without my glasses, I could see better than he thought I could, but I wouldn't tell him that, and I would indeed be looking closely, as close as I could.

Turning his back to me, he flipped back his hood and began untying his robes. They dropped into the ground in a black puddle of heavy fabric, his prayer beads clattering with an echo. The back of his head, his strong, wide, and muscular back, was that of any exceptionally large man. I took in every inch of him, from his torso, his ass, to the back of his legs.

"Are you ready?" His tone was laced with hesitation.

"I'm ready."

I can't say what I expected when he turned around. I thought he may have been being dramatic, that nothing could be so forbidden as to hide one's face forever, that nothing could be so bad. Though... it was worse than I could have ever imagined. My bones felt shocked by electricity, my knees weakened, and the air caught in my throat.

Looking upon him, I had the urge to cry, to claw my eyes out and put them in the dish next to my father's, to beg for god to forgive me... and those unsettling feelings mixed with something else... something stirred within me like a cat awakening from a sleep. Dante stood, steel jawed, unmoved, and allowed me to survey him. I knew in that moment it was likely the most vulnerable he'd ever been for someone.

That he hadn't just taken my vulnerability, but he'd given me his own, too. My glance surveyed his face... it looked as if it had been cut and slashed a thousand times by whips with embedded nails. There were hardly any spaces between the deep red indents like the scribbles of red ink by a madman on a page, and they covered his strong features. Only eyes of milky black, no irises, no whites, sat between them. And the most horrific of all... a black, upside-down cross etched into the middle of his forehead.

"Wh-what— are you?" I managed.

He inhaled, and I watched with rapt attention as his face moved, finally something to hold onto besides shadow. He stepped forward, noting my reaction, and I was careful to steel my knees. I wouldn't run, though everything in my body told me to flee, to scream, to weep.

When he was a foot in front of me, he stopped. "I am... a guard dog. That is all."

Carefully, I reached my palm up to his chiseled jaw. Somehow, the wounds looked fresh, though they couldn't have been. It had to be magic of some sort that kept them that way. "Does it hurt?" I asked, resting my hand on his face.

He leaned into my embrace and let out a guttural sound. "Terribly so. My affliction is a pain like none other and one I deserve every ounce of."

"Dante," his name a whisper of a prayer on my tongue as I held his face tenderly with both of my hands, pressing our naked bodies together. "Kiss me?"

No sooner were the words spoken had his lips collided against mine. He kissed me with passion and fervor, and I closed my eyes, moaning into his embrace. His tongue parted my lips and danced with mine, flicking in and out of my mouth. His taste was more intoxicating than altar wine, the heat of our bodies like two prayer candle flames sparking upwards to eternity.

We were two instantly ignited prayer candles, him and I, and I would gladly burn beside him until the wick met glass, and we were nothing but forgotten smoke in an empty cathedral. Maybe our pleas for some almighty god to acknowledge us would always go unanswered. Maybe there was nothing greater awaiting us beyond this one life, and what a liberating and terribly wonderful thought that was. Because right there, right then, I had my exorcist priest's cock pressed against my stomach, his teeth scraping against my black cum-stained lips, and the only thing I wanted was to feel him inside me again.

As if reading my mind, he cupped the back of my head and leaned me gently onto the hard church floor. My toes idly fidgeted with a pew as he leveled me with a smoldering, shadowed stare. He was something from a nightmare, the shades of red violently slashed across his face, his fully black eyes swirling like a night storm on the open sea. The upside-down cross a black symbol on his forehead. Yet despite the fear he instinctually erupted within me, a small voice purred its approval at our union. Sex with Father Dante Amorth, my exorcist, was wrong— but somehow, it was the most *right* I'd ever felt.

This didn't feel like sin. It didn't feel like an obligation to a husband, didn't feel like pain accepting my burden of opening my womb to potential blessings from god in the form of children. When Dante's bare skin, so warm and all-encompassing, pressed against my middle, my breasts, it felt like wholeness. If I could step back, even just a few feet, and stand in my nakedness like Lady Vanessa had, I would have undoubtedly felt shame in my body in the blasphemous act of fornication on the sacred floors of god's church.

But then again, here our combined passion dripped to the floor, evidence of life and pleasure and bliss— while back at Lady of Sorrow church, red blood of pain, of sacrifice, of death stained the ground. Which would a loving god prefer in his house? Which offering was more pleasing to an all-knowing entity? Sinners painting the altar with love, or saints marring it with hate? I didn't know the answer. And though I'd been taught of god my entire life, I realized I knew nothing of the being that supposedly guided my every step and ordained my every purpose. What I did know in that moment was that Dante's teeth scratching across my jaw was the most divine sensation imaginable. That was until his hands slowly inched up my ribs and cupped my breasts.

Dante covered me like a storm on the beach, and I felt so small and gloriously insignificant underneath him. "Can you shield me from god's wrath?" I asked as his kiss travelled down my neck, filling my body with warmth and unearthly desire.

He looked at me then, every bit the evil force he'd warned me that he was, sending a shiver down my spine. "God would need to hide from *my* wrath if anything ever befell you, Selah. I am a lowly animal, but I am your dog now if you'll have me."

"Yes," I whispered. "Yes." This time, our kiss was slow and deep, and his fingers gently slid down my lower abdomen to my wanting and aching center. He teased the pool of wetness there, softly coaxing more forward, sparking more moans from my throat as my hips writhed. "Please," I breathlessly pleaded.

“Please, what?” He grumbled into my mouth. “Beg me to possess you like the demons you fled. Ask for me to fuck you while god watches, Selah.”

The words were no more wretched and sinful than what I had already partaken in, but they made the acts more real. I obeyed, screaming as the tip of his cock nudged at my opening, spreading me with agonizing slowness. “Please fuck me, Dante. I need you.”

His growl was something from another world as he sank into me, pulling me apart and wrecking me from the inside out. I was sure my screams shook the stained glass that cast us in red light, red that wasn’t so horrible now as it matched Dante’s markings. My hips moved with his, and I felt I was getting the hang of sex, or maybe our bodies were just made for each other because the deep and explosive feeling of ecstasy kept rising, higher and higher, and he hit someplace deep within me.

Toying with my breasts, he bit at my jaw and my neck, wringing every drop of pleasure from my core until I couldn’t take it anymore. Like fighting an oncoming tidal wave, I gave in and let Father Amorth consume me. Crying out, his groan married with mine, and as my pussy clenched and fluttered wildly around his thick cock, the warmth of him emptied into me. And then, as I panted, breathless beneath him, feeling cum drip to the church floor as he remained seated inside me…

the center of my forehead began to burn.

CHAPTER TWENTY-SEVEN

It was identical to mine, the upside-down cross that burned into her forehead in branded black. Had god finally taken notice and decided to punish me? Or was it a sign of the acts we'd committed in the holy church that night? It could be true that even looking upon me, touching me, in the way that Selah had, could come with consequences no one else had lived long enough to endure. Reasoning and theorizing aside, the fact remained, I had branded her with my unholy mark, the mark of the kindred, and now Selah was officially damned.

Cradling her naked body in my lap, I rocked her like a small child, checking periodically as the symbol sank into her skin. Hidden from human sight but not gone, never gone. When she awoke, rubbing her head, she was wrapped in blankets upon the altar. "What happened?"

"You said you saw me, saw me before this," I waved a hand over my grotesque face as I collected bowls and laid them near her. "Tell me about that."

"It was after the dance in the forest with the women and the... dying man. I sort of disappeared. And reappeared in Grimm, but from a time long ago. You were there, and a woman came to you sobbing, asking you to exorcise her daughter. I followed you into that room and... and everything went wrong." The terror in her voice, the details I'd never shared with a soul... Selah had indeed gone back to that place. But how? The dark power it would take to do such a thing was unheard of aside from the likes of... Oh, fuck. My brother.

"Did anyone speak to you while you were there?" I asked, willing my tone to be calm. I didn't want to scare her or give her a reason to be afraid. Because if she'd been noticed by Nikolai... she would have great reason to be fearful.

Her grey gaze flicked away from me when she answered, fighting to tame her hair that had grown tangled in our passion. "No, I tried to speak to you, but you didn't notice or hear me. No one did... it was like watching an old, vintage movie. It was very strange."

"Strange indeed," I mused, kneeling before her and dipping a cloth in warm water. "Stretch out your legs."

Doing as she was told, I began bathing her, scrubbing away my black seed and her blood. "Is this holy water?" Selah asked in a small voice.

"It is. And next are holy anointing oils."

"You shouldn't waste these on me... I am now so incredibly far from holy."

I stopped with my hands on her knees and leveled her with my stare, getting close so she could for once see my horrible eyes and my wretched face. If any point needed to be shocked through her, it was this one. "You are *sacred*, you are *worthy*, you are *beautiful*, you are *whole*. You are not changed because you've had a man inside you.

Men's cocks have no power over you. They do not change your virtue in the least. You *don't* deserve pain. You were *not* born wicked. You *are* and always have been *whole*. Understood?"

Only a small sniffle answered me as she nodded. Maybe I was too harsh, my face and presence too scary, but goddamn, if I was going to let her believe that she was born a wicked and sinful thing. The sacred text of Lady of Sorrows was wrong. The bastardization of the old text was wrong. If even they got it right for everyone else, they were wrong about her. She was perfect… the standard of holiness and worth.

"I apologize if I am too rough," I remarked after cleaning her and moving on to holy oils. I rubbed them in my palms to warm first before massaging into her feet and calves.

Drying her eyes with her wrist, she shook her head. "You speak words I've never heard, and they pierce the deepest parts of my soul, Dante. Why do you remain a priest if you believe such things?"

I shrugged slightly. "I do not believe love and my priesthood are so far removed from each other. There are things beyond the sacred texts, beyond the veil, that ring true. Men have fucked it up, muddied the waters, but that doesn't mean there isn't some good in there. More importantly, there are people within these systems who have been forgotten. They are worth fighting for, worth staying for. I do all that I do for them."

"For people like me? For... the kids who go to school here. They're all refugees from abusive clergy, aren't they?" She asked as if it had just dawned on her.

"I'd thought you'd pieced that together already. But yes, some find us, others we find ourselves. Mainly, Silas does the pruning. Finding the ones who need us most, spinning whatever lies, convince the clergy the deepest. Oftentimes, the need for an exorcist aids the process, as the clergy will deem a strong-willed person possessed by demons. We offer them shelter, schooling, and a life close enough to their old that they are familiar but far enough removed that they are safe. We teach them about subjects far beyond what was allowed under their cult rule of Lady of Sorrow. We allow them freedom of expression. Their families believe they are away at a prestigious religious university, which is true, but they cannot reach them here. If the student chooses to leave... well, let's say that's difficult to achieve."

"But you are a real exorcist, right?"

"That I am, though, the need for exorcisms is few and far between after... after the portion of what you witnessed when you went to that long ago place. Soon after that... happened... the town was overrun with demon possessions. My brothers and I— let's just say things changed forever. It hasn't been since you came here that there has been much need for exorcisms... but since you arrived, there have been several possessions."

"Why do you think that is?" Her voice hitched as I rubbed oil up her thighs and lower belly.

I tilted my head, looking up at her long dark lashes, wild black hair, and pale skin in the stained-glass moonlight. "Because you're pretty."

She laughed then, a glorious sound that reminded me of—

Selah startled, wrapping her arms around me as the room vibrated. And then I laughed. "It's the church bells. They really do like you."

Through her giggling, she buried her face in my neck. Emotion clouded my throat, realizing she'd been frightened and had jumped toward me and not away. That she'd kissed my lips and made love to me, having seen what I am, the disgusting creature that a failed exorcism had left me. A relic of hell. A sheepdog to guard this island and its inhabitants. Selah sought safety in my strength, and I would die defending her. I would give my last breath, my heart from my chest, to keep her safe. To remind her every day that she was worthy would be my most holy of callings.

"I guess my exorcism failed, huh?" She kissed my jaw, and my cock hardened.

A small growl grumbled from my throat. "You are very much possessed, my dear, and I will never free the demons within you, for I am far too fond of them."

Her kiss giggled against my lips, and I laid her back, using the remainder of the holy oils to pour over her pussy. There was hardly a moment's time for her gasp before my kiss devoured her, and I'd pinned her down once more. Feeling her legs wrap around me, her touch over my scars, licking up the taste of her and us on her tongue—everything that was Selah was exquisite.

A lamb locked away, but now she could flourish. With me, she could continue to learn. She could grow and pursue a life of her choosing... always within my watchful guard. Because whatever path Selah took, I would be there, following behind, her faithful protector. The grim reaper of death always on my lady's trail, ready and willing to do her bidding.

Soft sighs whispered from her lilac parted lips, and it went against my very nature not to swallow her whole if only to keep her safe within the cage of my ribs. With every moan I coaxed forth from sliding my holy oil-doused hand down her center, up to her nipples, along her neck, and back down on a descent to the sacred parts of her, my soul opened and made only enough room for her to abide.

An act of worship was my cock piercing her to the cross of my commitment. There would be no unhooking from my bloody nails, not as I thrusted so hard and so sure within her. Her arms wrapped around my neck, and her cunt bled for me again as the spike drove deeper, killing her, crucifying her for the sin of loving me.

The world forever changed by our act of wicked sacrifice. A virgin handed over to a ravenous beast on a bloody altar. Like the sacrificial lambs of old, her blood trickled down the altar, mixed with anointing oils, burned with my black seed, the indents of upside-down crosses on our foreheads burning with ire from a jealous and aloof god.

CHAPTER TWENTY-EIGHT

The pain eased with each new confession of desire. With each prayer on our knees, either Dante licking me clean from what we'd just done or me tasting the combination of us on his length, the pain eased. The throbbing ache between my thighs and in my lower abdomen was only the mounting tension of a symphony chorus, a hymn that would keep playing on and on.

My exorcist had let me see his face. He'd taken my offerings again and again and had worshipped me in return. I'd grown up in church, but my time with Father Amorth was the closest I'd ever felt to the divine. Was this what the songs and stories in the sacred text had tried to capture? We'd written our own proverbs that night until dawn's carmine and violet light peppered through the prayer candle smoke, washing the old cathedral in light.

Dante had washed me clean with holy water and anointed me with oils several times, only to hurry away his work with another prayer of passion on the church floor. But finally, as the morning hours came, he finished the ritual and helped me into my robes and fiddled with my braids before he dressed himself.

My body hidden again by garbs of white, and his face shadowed again by the cloak of his robes. Our masks, I realized. The knowledge that he'd seen under my white garments and that I'd viewed his hidden face filled me with pride and assurance. We were something, *this* was something, and together, maybe we really could do anything.

"I'm going to go shower and check on Luci—"

"And then you're going to be in our lighthouse waiting for me," Dante finished, securing his prayer beads around his neck. My cheeks flushed pink as he lowered and left me with a kiss.

Our lighthouse.

I'd stayed awake all night, yet I wasn't tired. My feet seemed to be floating as I walked. It was as if heavy chains had perpetually been dragging behind me my entire life, and they'd just been lifted. I found my glasses on a dusty pew and took a deep, hopeful breath before stepping outside into the sea air. As I made my way down the overgrown and brushy path back to the school, I called for Luci. He usually pranced around this area in the early morning, eating briars and trampling dandelions.

The bitter aroma of smoke invaded my senses and pricked the hair on the back of my neck. Even the sea began to quiet as I turned to look back at Dante's cathedral. Plumes of black smoke poured from the steeple. A scream racked through my throat, and I made to run but tripped, falling face-first into a mound of rocky sand. Something clutched around my ankles and pulled me backward. When I rolled over, a large, white mass stood over me, glowing with a bright milky hue against the burnt orange and grey of the sky and sea.

"Silas," I screamed. "Dante is in the church. You have to—"

He knelt, and with a sad look etched into his angelic features, he touched two fingers to my forehead, and pain shot through me like a hundred bolts of lightning. Through my screaming, the white faded, and everything went as black as the ocean floor.

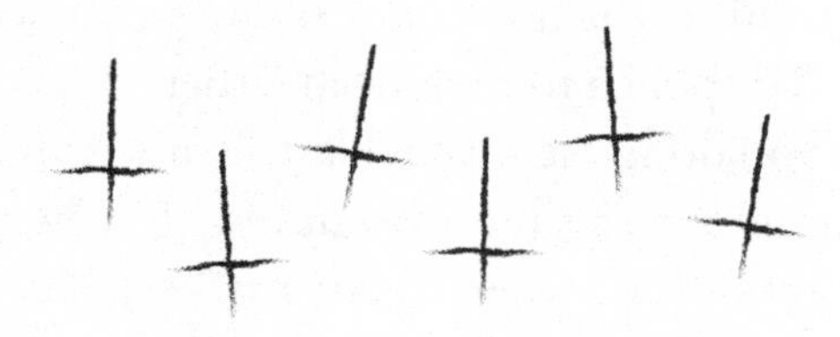

Something knocked against me, jolting me awake and causing me to be keenly aware that I was sitting in an inch of cold water. My hands were bound behind my back, my ankles tied together, and my head pounding. Dark grey, overcast skies hung above me, and the static sound of waves knocked me against the edge of the wooden structure again.

"Sorry, here you go," a deep voice casually hummed. The glowing white man paused his rowing and slipped my glasses onto my face. "Though I don't suppose you'll use them for long."

Silas came into view and resumed rowing, his cream priest's collar damp with sweat and his long white hair whipping wildly in the sea breeze. "What are you doing?

Is Dante okay?" I asked, panicked as I strained to look over the side of the tiny boat, only to take in miles of dark ocean.

"Everyone prefers the motorized boats now," he mused to himself, looking over his shoulder before flicking me a glance. "Our father was a fisherman. You know, the man you met on the dock? He's long dead, of course. That was his ghost you encountered."

Panic seized my chest. I was in the middle of the ocean with a seemingly unhinged Silas. The last I'd seen of Dante was him in his cathedral under plumes of smoke... and somehow, I'd spoken to their dead father. "Please, I don't care what you do to me. Just tell me Dante is alive."

Disregarding me again, he went on. "I knew there was something about you when you first arrived, but of course, my arrogant, self-centered brother wouldn't let me near to confirm. Though, he eventually came around, I suppose, as evidence by this."

A different kind of panic gripped my chest as I fought against my binds. "What do you mean?"

"What happened to Dante during the exorcism of little Penny Lockheart... it changed him. Altered the core of what a man is. And then the punishment inflicted by god afterward... Selah, Dante is a dark creature whose cravings are for even darker things. You should have heeded my warnings. He's drawn to sin like sharks to blood. And unfortunately, he is drawn to you, so you must be the blood in the water. I do not know what lurks within you or how or why my brother Dante, the most powerful exorcist known to humanity, cannot or will not see it.

Demons have infiltrated our paradise; they seek you out in particular, and Dante is no longer under the delusion that he can save you. He's risked too much, what with harming your father now, too. Lady of Sorrow will not soon forgive or forget his actions. This is for his sake, and most importantly, the sake of those we shelter here, that you be gone. He recognizes that and agrees to it, and thus, he gave you to me. In a dramatic fit, which he's so often prone to, he burnt his cathedral to the ground."

My mouth grew dry, and tears burnt the sides of my eyes. "That can't be true. You're lying..." I looked around at the desolate sea. "Are you going to feed me to your sharks now?"

Silas put a hand to his chest. "I am not the liar of the brothers, the Priests of Grimm, young lady. And well, you can't deny that feeding you to the sharks is an excellent idea..." He paused his rowing and rested his elbows on his knees, finally regarding me with a faraway look. "Father Amorth has agreed that your exorcism is complete. You should not speak to anyone of what you've borne witness to here, or I will personally find you, and I will kill you. That is not a threat, Selah. Understand it is a vital faction of the vows we entered."

Tears streaked my salt-stained face. "Stop, please, let me stay. Let me speak to him. I haven't had an exorcism." A motor buzzed faintly in the distance as our tiny boat rocked against the waves. A small *bahhh* sounded from a large sack at my feet, and Luci stuck out his head. "At least spare my baby goat," I cried.

Silas only spared me a steely gaze laced with judgment. "You spent extensive time with Dante in his cathedral, did you not? That was your exorcism, child. He has dealt with your demons, and now he wishes you well at Lady of Sorrows. It was always going to end like this, I'm afraid. I am sorry you were caught in my brother's inappropriate crossfires."

The buzzing stopped next to us, and the voices of two clergy called over and hit their vessel next to ours. Silas stood, picking me up with ease and tossing Luci in my lap. "I do wish you well, Selah. Understand this is for the protection of many."

The next moment, I was thrust into Bishop Terrance's hold as I screamed and thrashed. When the boat engine roared back to life, I kicked, hoping to throw myself overboard, to drown— because dying would be a better fate than what would await me. A life as the ruined Holy Daughter, a life marred with the absence and betrayal of Father Amorth. As I struggled, a hand covered my mouth, and something sharp stabbed into my thigh. As if time stood still, my eyelids grew heavy, my bones weighed down, and I fell into a fitful unconsciousness once more.

Selah

CHAPTER TWENTY-NINE

Sermons trilled through my head as I swayed in and out of lucidity. Thousands of hours of men speaking on the sacred texts. They explained in vague detail why the expansions to the vintage texts, formerly called the Bible, were necessary. They took out all the women's names, but the names I recalled bounced through my mind for some reason: Bathsheba, Delilah, Susanna. All such pretty names. I wondered if those women ever felt helpless, too. If they ever knew they were faceless side characters in the great scheme of holy men and lofty gods.

Men in the sacred texts had names, multiple names, first and last. They were even bestowed brand-new names sometimes. But women's were so unimportant that they were never given them. More recently, their names were taken away by Lady of Sorrows Church.

Glory to god in the highest, hallowed be thy name.

Hallowed be thy name.

My brain was coming back online, but my eyes wouldn't open, no wait, they were open... but the room was pitch black. I made to stand, and my head clanked against thin metal bars. Reaching all around, I realized I knew exactly what contained me, my protection— no, my *cage*. A dog cage. A dog cage I'd been raised to believe was protecting me from sin.

"Bullshit," I whispered into the dark, musty air. "Bullshit!" I screamed, hoping some old clergy or Lady of Sorrow would hear me and come to scold me. Reaching for my face, I confirmed my glasses were gone. Of course, they were. They'd strip me of any ill-fated freedom or independence Grimm had granted me. Dante had given me... and it was Dante, Father Amorth, who sent me away. Was it all just a part of my exorcism, like Silas had said? Had I truly been lured into the very process I had raged against... was the touching, the sex... was it all just him exposing my sin so thoroughly to send me back wretched and broken once more?

I rested my forehead against the cold bars and sobbed, letting my pain shudder through me. It couldn't be true. The love I'd felt with Father Amorth... he wouldn't just abandon me... yet here I was. Locked up, caged, alone. He'd done what he'd intended; he'd left me ruined, and now I was alone once more. Only worse, now I'd had a taste of freedom, felt the warm touch of passion... and now I'd never be the same again.

Something clattered near me, and I stilled, hushing my sobs to quiet sniffles. Something clattered again, like bars shaking. "Hello?" I called out into the stark black. "Is someone else here?"

The clattering continued, but now it was numerous and all around me. I shook my own bars to confirm the sounds were identical. "Are there others here... in cages too?"

The cages all over the room shook furiously, confirming there were more caged people around me in the darkness. This room was large and likely one of the locked rooms underneath the church that I was never permitted to go to. I could only wonder as a child what these rooms held... and now I shuddered at the knowledge that was dawning on me. "Can you speak?" I called out and was met with silence.

Maybe they were gagged, or maybe... oh, god. "Are you ladies of sorrow? Have—have you taken vows of silence?"

The cages rattled an unspoken yes.

"You can talk to me," I said in a hurried tone. "I won't tell anyone. Maybe— maybe, if we work together, we can get out of here."

There was silence again, and I searched the darkness to no avail. Why wouldn't they speak? Surely their vows didn't matter down here, caged for god knows how long. What more could their god punish them with than this?

And then I remembered the sisters of Grimm. How they'd hurried to take in the ladies of sorrow that accompanied Lady Vanessa. One lady had remained devote in her silence... the other... Sister Grace had said it was more than a vow that kept her silent. The way she'd looked at me...

"You *can't* speak... can you?"

Metal vibrated around me in a prolonged and eerie response. Something inside me rattled against a different kind of cage as an emotion I'd scarcely allowed myself to experience slowly surfaced— *anger*. This entire time, I'd believed what I was told that women aspired to take their vows of silence, when in reality, did any of them have a choice?

Their voices were taken somehow, and I'd never thought to question it. The thought that unholy, possibly magical, or paranormal means were involved in the process or workings of Lady of Sorrow. How could I have never looked at my surroundings more critically? While women were having their voices taken, my act of rebellion was reading smutty blogs off the internet, sneaking television use... I could have been doing so much more if I'd only opened my eyes.

The stark truth was that regardless of whether or not Father Amorth had cast me aside and exorcised me in a horribly intimate and heart-shattering way— he and the Isle of Grimm had given me sight. My glasses were gone and missing, but my vision and ability to perceive were sharpened now. That was a gift that Grimm and its inhabitants had left me. Silas could have been right. Maybe my presence there *was* a great threat. If demons were prowling, that was one thing. If Lady of Sorrow were focused on Grimm... Silas was right— it was better to get me as far away as possible.

Though now, here I was, locked in a cage in a basement with numerous ladies of sorrow. How was I going to save us? I opened my mouth to talk to the nameless, voiceless women around me when a door creaking open snapped my jaw shut. If I were going to get away, I had to be smart. I had to find a way out for all of us somehow. A small, singular bulb clicked to life on a narrow stairwell and illuminated the space just enough that I could make out the horrific sight. Dozens and dozens, oh god, maybe fifty to one hundred dog cages filled the concrete room. Veiled women all shuddered, looking around until their gazes found me. They held their hands to their hearts as if communicating something. Love, maybe? Hope? The thought that they'd feel anything of the sort for me made me want to break down into sobs again.

"I'm so sorry," I whispered to their gaunt and haunted faces. "I won't leave any of you behind."

The clip-clip of a woman's footsteps rounded the corner, followed by the heavy footfalls of a stout man. The woman I vaguely recognized was an older Lady of Sorrow, tall and thin with the same scathing expression as Lady Vanessa. I guessed she was her replacement, the new head lady. Bishop Terence followed behind her, neither of them sparing a glance at the women confined to dog cages around us as if it was a commonplace sight for them. Again, the demon of wrath reared its fire within me... only this time... I was finding myself less and less afraid of demons and more and more indignant toward the existence of Lady of Sorrow.

The head lady and bishop stopped at my cage, and I sat back and crossed my arms. I was sure they were more than ready to take me to my dad— no, Reverend Benedict, he was no dad to me— for my punishment. What would the sisters of Grimm do in this situation? Mrs. Paramour? The women from the romance novels? I didn't know, but I had to figure it out fast. In that moment, the only thing I could do was glare daggers as they unlatched my prison. "Come," the lady ordered.

I crawled out and stood, realizing my knees were weak, and standing made me dizzy, the humbling realization that if I tried to run, I wouldn't make it far. "You're disgusting," I spat at the woman.

No sooner did my spit land across her cheek did pain radiate against the side of my face as Bishop Terrance struck me with a backhanded hit. I cupped my jaw, feeling my lip burn with blood. "So are you," I sneered at him through bloody teeth. I wished in that moment, he'd someday be in the middle of one of the Sisters of Grimm's burning pentagrams.

"I can see our worst suspicions are confirmed, and your exorcism was futile. But you will show respect to the men, the high clergy of Lady of Sorrow, and our property." He grabbed my face with his stupid sausage fingers, his breath rancid within my nose. "And we'll cut your tongue if we must, if that is the only way to silence you."

"Please, do not touch her. We are never supposed to touch her," the head lady warned with a small, clipped tremor in her voice. Was she afraid? What did the new head lady fear most, I wondered?

"They'll never know, and by the time she could tell them, she'll be dealt with," he barked, grabbing my arm harshly and pulling me up the stairs. A worried lady of sorrow clutched her palms and trailed behind us.

She was right. No one had ever been allowed to touch me. Only with a rod or a roller slap, even caging me at night. The worshippers who washed my feet were only permitted to touch my feet with a rag separating them from my skin. Was that for my benefit or... for theirs? The events of Grimm played through my mind like a shuffling deck of cards. The tang of blood flitted against my tongue as Bishop Terrance flung me into a small room. "We're to watch you bathe before we inspect your purity."

I snorted, standing shakily, trying to force myself into some form of bravery. "You want to see me naked? Fine," I said, slipping a shoulder out of my heavy robes. "You're so dirty, Bishop. I bet you read the naughty stories I printed on your computer, didn't you?"

Terrance was wide and tall but not nearly as big as Dante. No matter his size, I'd never been fearful of Father Amorth. He never would have hit me. The look in the bishop's eye at my revealed shoulder told me that this man was *not* the same as Dante. A glance at the Lady in the doorway and her pensive and concerned expression confirmed that Terrance could, and would, do me harm before he handed me over to Benedict and the rest of the clergy. If this is what I had to endure to find a way out... then so be it.

I slipped off my robes and stood naked, sea salt still stinging my skin and reminding me of Grimm— of home— and of him. I gritted my teeth together to keep from crying. Not at the bishop's hungry and hateful assessment of my body, but in missing my exorcist, my sisters, my school, and my true church.

"Maybe I'll go ahead and perform her examination right now," the man said hatefully, taking a step closer. I couldn't run, and the lady brought a hand to her mouth. She couldn't help her position, couldn't help me, and what's to say the same... exams... hadn't been inflicted on them as well. We were all rabbits in enclosures with wolves.

Then the wolf grabbed me by the hair and all I could do was whisper Dante's name as I awaited what would happen next.

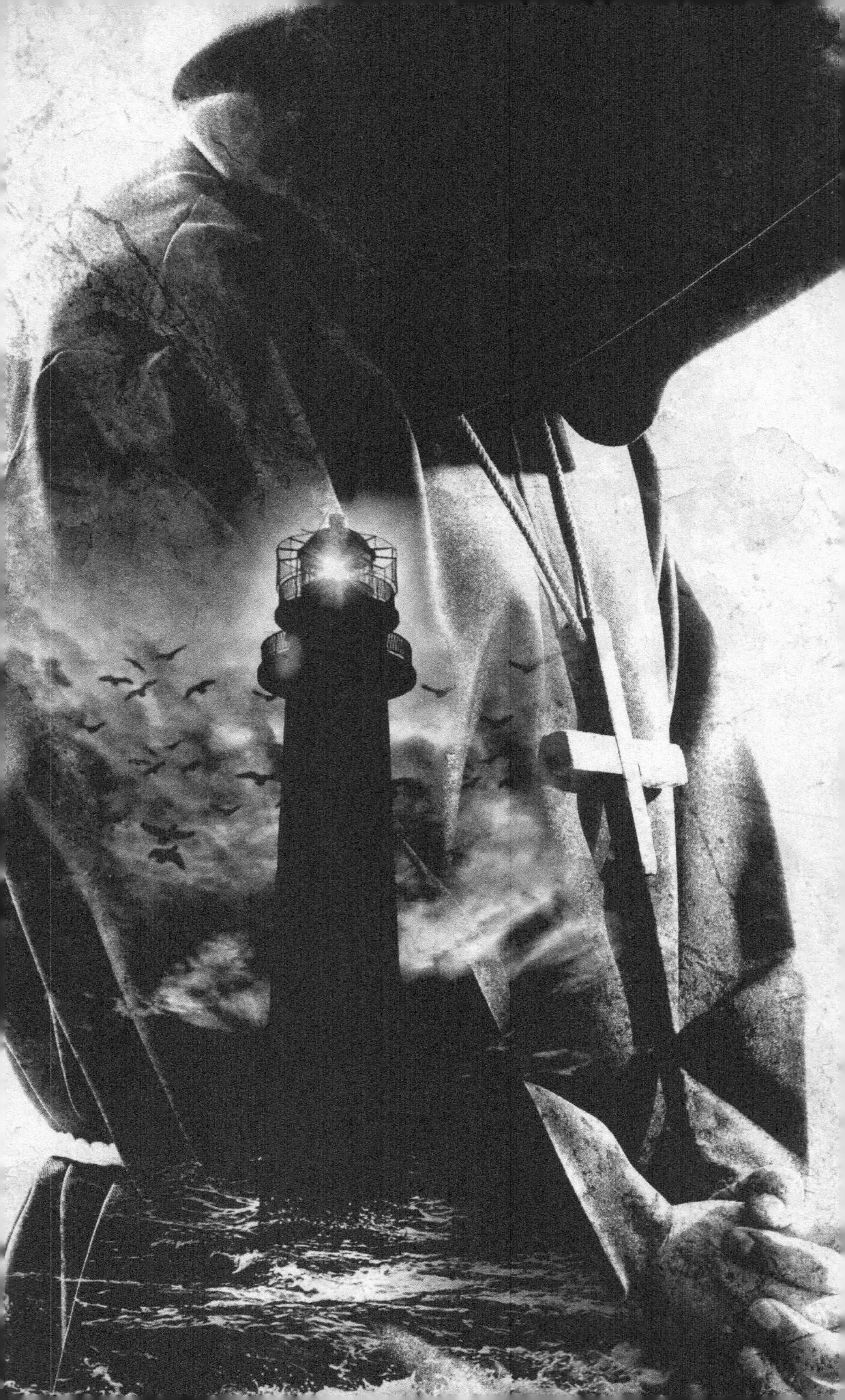

Dante

CHAPTER THIRTY

You could go to any resident of Grimm, any of my brothers, any of my church of present or past, and ask them the same question: What is Dante Amorth's greatest mistake? They'd each give you a different answer. My sins were more numerous than the grains of sand upon the cursed beach where my lighthouse stood. Why did a priest sleep in a lighthouse and not his parish? Not my cathedral? Because I didn't deserve to rest amongst the holy. Though that night, and really every night since her arrival, I'd taken what I hadn't deserved from Selah. I didn't deserve her trust or her adoration, and I certainly wasn't worthy of her body.

I'd taken it all anyway.

When the cathedral doors shut behind her, I made to chase after her, to not let her go—but my step was frozen in place. The room blasted itself in white light, and I fell to my knees. For a moment, I thought god himself was smiting me for my sins. The old bastard finally caught up with me. But then, a pentagram of flame erupted, trapping me in its center. The image of my brother surrounded by angelic light came into view through the burning and flickering flames.

Fuck.

"I'm going to *slaughter* you," I threatened, yanking off my hood.

Silas shook his head, sharing the same look my father so often gave me. "You've taken this too far. You've put us all at risk."

I fought against the flames, my scars burning fresh once more as blood poured into my eyes. "Don't touch her. I will crawl from hell to gut you in your sleep if you lay one finger upon Selah."

"Goodbye, brother. How I wish I could have saved you." His farewell echoed around me, and white light blinded me as I raged like a beast snared by a trap. A trap he'd laid. He'd known this would happen; he'd probably drawn the pentagram weeks ago, waiting for it to activate with blood. I should have foreseen it. I shouldn't have compromised Selah in this way. I was a fool. Tumbling backward the light became night and finally a muddy shade of sepia brown as my spine cracked and I landed upon solid ground.

If she got hurt, if he got to her before I could— I would send myself to hell after I ripped Silas apart limb to limb. Then god, I would find god next and kill him, too, if he didn't give her back to me. Nothing, no force of this world or any other, would stop me from reaching her. Seagulls cawed above me, and I sat up, knowing where I was from the smell, the sights of horse carriages trotting by, and townspeople milling about. Clarence passed out day-old muffins to people as they passed by; women donned petticoats, and men wore top hats.

"Not hell," I murmured, standing. "Worse than hell."

I marched through the street, calling out his name with frantic rage. The last motherfucker I wanted to see or deal with, but here I was. He was watching me; I knew he was. This was his lair, his pit.

"Nikolai!" I growled over and over, stomping through the phantoms of the past. My brothers were as crafty and depraved as I was. Silas would know that there would be no escape for me here, not without begging Nikolai for aid— fuck.

Something slammed into the side of my head, almost knocking my hood off, and I growled, searching for the source of the godforsaken rock on the ground. Then another hit me, its launch coming from above. Then I saw him crouched on the side of a rooftop like a goddamn gargoyle. My youngest brother threw another rock, and I dodged it. "Vulture trash hiding on the side of a roof like when we were kids, huh? Nice to see the rumors are true, and you've descended into madness, Nikolai."

Yes, perhaps antagonizing wasn't the wisest way to buy my freedom, but I couldn't help it. If he were going to hide on shingles like a rat, I'd treat him as such. "Oh, the good priest doesn't recognize a stoning when he sees it? Your vows fail you, Dante," he spat, his voice mocking and unhinged in a way only a madman's tenor could reach. My traitorous oldest brother Silas would warn not to anger Nikolai, to tread lightly, to be strategic. But Silas was the bastard who betrayed me— and he wasn't here.

I picked up the rock and threw it back at him, and another, and another. Before approaching the window frame, ready to climb the shop in front of a fabric store and beat the shit out of the dark crow perched upon the roof. His face was etched in runes, the whites of his eyes black, and the irises clear. He didn't look too different from many demons I'd exorcised, and I suspected their chaos had infected him. I guessed he'd accepted it willingly as he stewed below us in his hate.

He landed next to me with a thud, so close a lesser man would have fallen backward. Nikolai stood at almost my height and build, but just like when we were boys— I could still put him in the fucking ground. I swung with all my might and spun off balance as my fist met only air. All light was sucked from the town as if lights had gone out at a theater performance, and the curtain closed. Silence rang like a bell in my ears as I bellowed for the little freak to show himself, to fight, to something. It was long past time for his petty games.

He appeared again, perched on the side of the roof like the vulture he was, resting his elbows on his knees. The space around us black except for his outline and the implied town. Dark magic was all around him, demonic and ruthless. I'd pondered his spiral into insanity over the years, how being down here, isolated, would drive anyone mad. Though... I'd never considered he'd be spending this time to grow his strength considerably. The realization was ghastly as his gaze attempted to pierce through me, the runes on his face almost dancing with some emotion I didn't care to examine.

Pointing my finger, I shouted, "If I have to beat you to a pulp and exorcise every demon from your blood, one by one, to get back to her, I will. Don't fuck with me, Nikolai."

He smiled then, baring his teeth. "*Her*, you say?" He chuckled darkly. "You know, I could send you to hell now or later, for now, I'm enjoying the show— Wait," he held up a hand. "Wait, wait... is *she* the girl I met? Foggy-eyed, naive, blabbering idiot of a girl? Ringing any *church bells*?"

Fury threatened to turn me into a bonfire of flame. "You couldn't have," I said through gritted teeth.

"She didn't tell you? So, she's a liar, just like you? Perfect pair. Too bad you'll never see her again."

Selah had gone here through the ritual, and she had seen this fool... why hadn't she told me?

"Nikolai," I trained my voice into some sort of calm. "I vowed myself to Grimm, to her. I have to—"

Cutting me off was my brother's laugh as he tilted his head back and clapped. God, I wanted to kill him. "Oh, the sweet little girl with the misty eyes should get used to you breaking promises, now, shouldn't she? Is she doomed now, like mother was, by loving you?"

His words were a stone thrown against my black heart. "I didn't mean to— for what happened to mother—"

"You didn't *mean to*," he smiled again. "You didn't *mean to* possess our mother with a legion of demons. Oh, you didn't *mean to* shatter her body into a million puppeteered pieces, undead, unholy, eventually hunted and scattered across the dark abyss. God, Dante, if I'd known you didn't *mean to*—"

"Fuck you, Nikolai. Where have you been as I suffer for my sins? Dwelling like a lunatic in this—"

"Pit of despair, right? That's what you and Silas call it. Catchy, I like it. I'm going to like keeping you here, too. Maybe for a few hundred years until I drive you mad." He jumped down from the roof again. "Maybe I'll make you watch the moment you killed our mother. How about that? Make you replay it and watch it over and over like I have— until you hate yourself as much as I hate you."

My throat vibrated as I reached out. My brother flinched, ready for me to grab his throat or jerk him by the collar. Instead, I only cupped his tattooed jaw. "Do it. It's no less than what I deserve, but I can assure you, little brother, you are wrong about one thing. No one can hate me more than I hate myself, and the depths of which my hatred reaches go far beyond the hell that hungrily awaits me." Nikolai didn't answer, instead cocked his head in a way that reminded me of both our mother and a house cat assessing a field mouse. "So go ahead, do your worst, but I ask, brother, that you allow me to save one girl first."

"Only one person?" he challenged, "And leave Grimm to burn in your absence? All those school kids you and Silas have collected like haunted dolls? The mad women and their magic and bloodlust? You'd let them all perish for this one girl?"

"I would let all of Grimm burn for her. I would break my every vow for her. I would watch our mother die at my hand one thousand times for the undeserved peace of knowing that Selah lived."

"You are no better than me."

"Much, *much* worse, we both know that."

The darkness faded like mist around us, and we were in the old cobblestone streets of vintage Grimm again—a town long dead by my hand.

"I cannot send you back," he said finally, examining me with snakelike eyes.

A heavy breath left my lungs as I put my hands on my head in exasperation. I opened my mouth to speak, but he shocked me with his interruption. "But... I can accompany you back. For a price."

Selah

CHAPTER THIRTY-ONE

The new head lady pressed her forehead against the doorframe and muffled her sobs at what she was witnessing. Strange that I was the one nearing rape, but I wanted to comfort her. Bishop Terrance groped my breasts and held my throat, pushing me against the wall as he hastily yanked up his robes. He was sweaty, and his touch was rough and painful. It dawned on me then that weak men's touch was cruel and painful, while strong men's touches were gentle and kind.

I could barely stand, much less fight back, so I decided to conserve my energy, and I squinted my eyes closed, feeling tears fall once more. The tears angered me. I didn't want this disgusting man to see me cry, but what did it matter? There was no one coming to save me.

There was nothing I could do.

It began to rain outside–a huge thunderstorm. Silently, I was grateful for the storm. It was something to listen to, to pretend I was wrapped in the clouds instead of feeling rough fingers paw around my thighs, searching for my entrance so he could tear it down, abuse it.

The lady of sorrow screamed, and the bishop paused his actions. I opened my eyes and saw his face turn as he yelled at her to shut up. But then... what I saw next... my mind could hardly compute. A large, horned figure lurked in the doorway. It had the head of a massive goat but the furry, black-furred body of a muscular, hoofed man. A standing man-goat? I'd seen this monster before in my room at Grimm. The woman dropped to her knees, sobbing and shaking, and the creature strode past her.

Bishop Terrance let me go, and I fell to the floor as he shakily clutched his prayer beads. "Be gone, creature of Satan!" he squealed, trembling in terror.

The goat-headed creature tilted its head to look at me... it was... it was asking me something. How did I know that? Not knowing what to do, I nodded. "Yes, yes," I scratched out.

Blood splattered across the room like red spray paint. Red dotted and drenched my cheeks, my naked body, and my white robes. Something fell to the ground with a thud. I pulled on my robes and shook in the corner, only the sounds of the lady of sorrow weeping, her face still pressed to the ground, breaking my trance. The creature's hooves creaked the flooring as it stepped over the heap of a dead Bishop Terrance and stood before me and... bowed. Reaching out an unsteady hand, I petted its coarse fur and long, rough horns. I knew the feeling of this fur, the ridges of the horns.

"Luci? Lucifer?" I asked softly.

He nodded.

Maybe I should have pieced it together sooner... maybe I'd been blind to a whole world of demons and darkness beyond my wildest nightmares... and maybe I was a part of that terror now. The thought rumbled like waves of hope within me as I crawled through the blood to the head lady. Pulling her up, I held her shoulders as I shushed her. "I need you to go unlatch all the cages in the basement."

She mumbled frightfully, and then she saw the creature behind me. "Baphomet!" she screeched in horror, her face blanching white. I covered her mouth with my palm, begging her to be quiet. Who knew how many clergy were lurking around and ready to finish what the bishop had started?

"Listen, please," I begged, forcing her to focus on my eyes. "I don't know how to be brave either— I'm— I'm faking my way through this. But we have to be brave, okay? There are more of us women than there are men. We can end this and be free, but I need your help."

"They'll kill me, they'll take my voice, and they'll do to me what they did to your mother."

It was as if a bucket of cold water had been dumped over my head. I quickly strained a look down the hall before asking, "What did they do to my mother?"

She swallowed, her eyes flicking from the baphomet to me before becoming laced with sadness. "You are the daughter of many... and your mother had no choice. What they did to her... chained to the bed for your conception, for your pregnancy and birth."

The wind rushed from my lungs, and I felt I would faint. "So, my dad is not... he isn't my real father?"

"Any of the clergy could be." She rose onto her knees. "But there are stories, and once we learn of the story, our voices are taken— it is like some curse. I've feigned ignorance for a chance I might tell you someday."

"What is your name?" I asked, realizing I didn't know, and it felt important. It felt so fucking important that we all had names.

Her wrinkled eyes grew watery. "I was her friend, and I have waited in hate, waited for Lady Vanessa to die. I have strived so hard to be the one to take her place."

A plan had been in motion before I'd even fathomed what was happening. I was wrong... the ladies of sorrow did know how to be brave.

"In your mother's anger, she prayed to other gods—not the gods above but the ones below. And unlike the ones in the sky, the ones beneath the ground spoke back. *They answered her.*" She flicked a small glance to the baphomet behind me.

There was a commotion down the hall, and I stood, feeling sick. "You have to go, and you have to go now. I'm sending Luci with you," I gestured towards the baphomet and he nodded in understanding. "Go," I shakily hurried them out the door and down the hall. As they disappeared around the corner, I stood watching after them for a moment.

My nameless mother had cursed me, hadn't she?

I could only hope that was true.

I could only hope that what I was about to do would work.

I could only hope that the gods below would answer me, too.

And so, I gathered my bloodied robes, using my feet as my sight, and padded down the cold marble hallway toward the holy sanctuary.

Selah

CHAPTER THIRTY-TWO

My nameless mother had walked these dreary church halls. What horrors had she been through to birth me? I cut through the less traveled pathways, knowing the route by heart. Even at Grimm, I'd walked these halls in my nightmares. The blood splattered on my white robes reminded me that I had at least one nightmare on my side, though, through Luci— which now seemed a ridiculous nickname for a whole, scary baphomet. The memories of the ritual I witnessed in the woods at Grimm peppered my hysteria like sharp rain on the beach. The sisters had chanted about such a creature... how had it gone? My time naked in the woods had spit me out to a different time and place entirely, and the song they sang had settled to the bottom of my dusty consciousness.

Hurry the goats to keep her.

Let every baphomet find and guard her.

Could Luci be the manifestation of my mother's prayer, no— her song, her *spell*? Though, what was really the difference between a prayer pleaded to god and a spell whispered into the ethers? It was a question I wished I could ask Dante, or the nuns, and their absence made my heart ache with loss. It was very likely I'd die before ever setting foot outside these white, marbled, and gold walls. However, it would be a worthy death if I could manage to distract the clergy long enough for the ladies of sorrow to escape. The most my life could offer anyone here, the price of my ignorance, my debt paid. Luci would help keep them safe— at least, I hoped Luci was enough.

Frozen, I looked up at the outrageously high sanctuary doors. No one had stopped me, no ladies were in the halls cleaning, and no sounds of clergy echoed.

My garb was bloodied from the dead bishop, and I wished I'd thought to stop by a dressing room and clean up first. Walking in like this would mark an obvious change and distress. But I had no choice—

Something behind me groaned, and heavy footfalls sounded. I turned, pressing my shoulder blades to the doors. Another monster? A priest? Which would be worse?

A groan, a footfall, the sound of sliding, and then repeated, echoing rhythmically in my direction. As he rounded the corner, I gasped, feeling my bones weaken with fear. Bishop Terrance stepped slowly as he made his way toward me, holding something in his arms. His face bland, and it seemed it was an effort for him to stand— but his clothes were clean, there was no blood on his body, and no recognition of past events on his face. He neared, and I flinched before he shoved white fabric into my hands. His head fell backward at an uncomfortable angle and then lolled back forward... it reminded me of the contortions that Oliver had made when he was... he was demon-possessed.

Taking the robes, I looked into the bishop's hollow eyes. "Are you... are you Bishop Terrance?"

His mouth opened too far and wide and snapped shut after a gargled noise. It was thoroughly creepy, but he wasn't attacking me. In fact, he'd brought me clean clothes so as not to blow my cover. Though I had the eerie and unnerving feeling this was not the Bishop Terrance from my childhood or even from an hour ago...

"Try to speak first, then your mouth will open on its own," I explained softly to whatever was inhabiting the bishop's form.

He took a moment, as if every joint and movement was foreign, until straightening and speaking in a voice that was not the bishop's, a voice that was not of this earth, one that rose the hair on my arms. "*You will bleed*," he said evenly as I shrugged off my bloodied robes, not caring if the demon inhabiting the bishop saw me naked. Despite his ominous words, it felt as if he was on my side.

"Will you help me in there?" I asked, pulling on the clean gown and fastening a white veil over my hair. The bishop's head knocked forward like a doll, and I took it as a nod. "Good." I was conspiring with demons who were possessing men's bodies, sending a baphomet to save ladies of sorrow, and desperately missing my exorcist priest. This all felt like a horror movie I couldn't hit pause on.

But it also felt like power, something I'd never had before.

Taking a steadying breath, I grabbed the knobs and pulled them outward. My counterfeit father and two dozen clergy were seated at the priest's throne. More men sat in pews, robed, and collared... more priests. I walked down the long aisle, feeling the large expanse of the sanctuary making me small. It had always seemed huger with each time I entered. Like a dragon that was constantly being fed its meals. Every furnishing glittering gold, every surface buffed white. I noticed the white ribbon tied around his eyes as Benedict stood, and I smiled. He couldn't see me, couldn't look at me ever again— because of Dante.

I remembered when we were on the priest's throne in his cathedral, my father's dead eyes staring at us from a communion plate. My throat tightened, and I knelt at the altar.

There were whispers above me before a man's voice ordered me to stand.

My father addressed the bishop, not me, and asked. "Is The Holy Daughter Pure?"

The body of the bishop stepped next to me, and I looked at my feet. "She meets every holy standard of purity. The Holy Virgin is intact, and her purity remains. We did a thorough examination, careful not to touch her."

My eyes widened as I looked over, the demon within the man giving me the smallest of smirks, like, *hey, you didn't think I could do that, could you?*

No, but I guessed evil forces were fast learners. Clearly, he either had access to the bishop's brain and memories, or the demon was already aware of the purity standards from Lady of Sorrow. Either way, my confidence in this unlikely alliance was growing.

Benedict raised his eyebrows above his blindfold as if he were surprised by that answer. My heart pounded in my chest that they all had supernatural powers and could smell the sex on me.

But instead of scolding or blasting me with verses from the sacred texts, Benedict motioned that I join him at the altar.

"Lay on the sacrificial stone," he ordered, and my blood went cold again. "Soon, you will watch as we give the priests and nuns of Grimm back to god, for they have fallen off the path. Though, praises that one amongst them stood with us and sent you back pure." It was the same place where I'd witnessed the shades of red that haunted me. The death and torment... of course, they would want to play sacrifice with me and threaten the home and people I'd come to love. I did as I was told, making unsure glances at the bishop's dark and faraway eyes. The body of the man who'd tried to rape me. The spirit of a demon trying to help me. The combination of the two wildly unsettling.

I laid back on the white stone, and Benedict spoke. "The Holy Daughter has returned, free of demons, exorcised by The Holy Father Dante Amorth."

Hearing his name made me want to sob, but I bit my lip and tried to think of what I'd do next if they tried to kill me. "Bring in the new Holy Daughters."

I sat up on my elbows, "What?"

"Are you not going to ask after my eyes?" Benedict cut a rough tone.

"No," I answered, letting a hint of my anger shine through before it was drowned with horror as all the ladies from the cages were herded into the sanctuary. They walked with their heads down, like I always had, and stood at the base of the altar. "What is this? I'm the only Holy Daughter."

Benedict snarled. "And god spoke to us in your absence about what a problem that was. We relied too heavily upon you, and you were too weak and sinful to bear such a high calling from the almighty. In your leave, god has blessed us with sixty Holy Daughters. They have taken vows of silence, and they will be beacons to the world of how women should behave until they are given to their husbands when the time comes."

"Sold like cattle, no voices, nameless, sounds a lot like what you did to my mother. Do you plan to create more girls like me? Is that what you want?"

The clergy gasped as Benedict grabbed my throat. "You were the last thing we wanted. You are a plague we can't rid ourselves of. If anyone touched you, they would be possessed— you were born evil— you remain evil." I squirmed as he squeezed my neck. "We tried to invoke your silence; it wouldn't work. We prayed to keep you nameless, but only *Selah* hissed in our minds until we named you. Your mother was a wolf in sheep's clothing, a tempting songstress who fooled us all. You are the fruits of a wicked woman's bargain with Satan."

"So, kill me then," I breathed out, fighting the emotion in my chest. My mother had protected me. I imagined her chained to a bed, and instead of giving up upon her impending death, she sought out beings in the shadows. She saved me with her curses and her songs, like the song from the full moon night in the woods on Grimm... her gifts were the only things that had likely spared my life up until this point.

Benedict let out an angered breath. "If we could manage that, we would have the moment you were born. Your wretched, wicked mother, a woman of the moon, a mistress of satan, cursed you. So rather than remove you from the light of Lady of Sorrow and risk worshippers wondering where you went and why you never lived up to your promised potential, you shall be married."

"Married?" I scoffed. "To whom?"

"Today, you shall be married— to me."

"This is insanity— are you outright admitting you aren't my father now?"

Benedict rounded the sacrifice table. "You could be any of the clergy's child. Though we suspect you could be the very daughter of Satan himself. But you are *not* my child by blood. You were simply put under my charge for a time. But now, as a sin I must reap, I shall take you as my own. Through you, we will create a new Holy Child. You will be the first to carry on and simultaneously destroy your mother's legacy. What darkness has intended for evil, Lady of Sorrow shall use for good."

I swallowed, my blood running cold. Death would have been a much, much better fate. "You're going to chain me to a bed and rape me until I am pregnant. Until I have a child, and then kill me?"

"This is a Holy calling, Holy Virgin Daughter. You will give me a child that I can use as a testament to bring many to the church. The new Holy Daughters will grow into the same fate until we have populated our clergy with worthy worshippers, teachers, and guides for the sinful world."

"I will make you bleed," I threatened, not even recognizing the tone of my voice as I threatened. Priests and men surrounded me; I couldn't overpower them.

"Bishop, come and marry us. I will bed her here, in front of all of you, so you can witness her presenting her purity to her husband. What a glorious act of god I am performing this day. And soon, every Lady of Sorrow Priest will be given a Holy Wife of his own to perform this same offering."

The clergy clapped and agreed as Bishop Terrance climbed the altar steps and stood before Benedict and me. Who I thought my whole life to be my father— and he wasn't— and now he'd be my husband... and he wanted to make that stance, the taking of my purity, very clear.

What an absolute sicko.

The congregation sat and gawked, priests from Lady of Sorrow churches all over the world here to make sure this horrific event took place. I wondered how many of them were the fathers or clergy of students sent to Grimm and how many of my friends' abusers were watching me then.

The girls just stood, terrified, likely knowing their predators were sizing them up. Future husbands picking out their breeding stock as I sat on the sacrificial stone.

"Father Benedict, do you take The Holy Virgin Daughter to be your bride?" Bishop Terrance spoke so smoothly; I wondered if I'd imagined what had happened. Had it been a cruel trick? A dream? Had he never fallen in his own blood at the hands of a baphomet? And where was Luci now?

Horror tightened my throat. This was happening. My fate worse than death. And as I would soon be tied to a table or bed and raped, impregnated, the world would watch. And I would watch for nine months as other Holy Daughters suffered the same fate.

"I do," Benedict said.

The bishop didn't ask me. I didn't get a part in this; there was no *I do,* or *I don't* to be asked from me or from any of the women of sorrow after me. We were nameless, titles at best, servants, walking, and silent wombs to be used.

When I looked up, the bishop was staring at me intently as if waiting for me to say or do something. His eyes were swirling with darkness, and something vibrated silently between us.

"*Mother*?" he asked.

The clergy looked at him. Benedict lowered his eyebrows below his covered eyelids.

"Mother?" I repeated. "Am I mother?" I asked, frantically trying to make sense of what was happening. I felt my own mother around me, and the mothers before her. A host of nameless women stomped out by men... The demon was trying to help me, and I just had to... my forehead began burning, and someone from the clergy gasped. "Say my name," I whispered back.

"She wears the mark of the devil," a priest shouted.

"The mark of the beast!" another man cried.

My upside-down cross was back and burning... no, no, no, I couldn't pass out right now. I had to— I had to—-mother.

"*Selah*," the demon within the bishop hissed like an echoing and deep teakettle. The sound resounding in my bones, and I knew the church felt it too as men started to stand and scream.

Benedict stumbled backward into the priest's chair, holding up his cross attached to his prayer beads at me.

At me.

He was *afraid* of me.

The mark on my forehead must have been something they feared greatly then. I slid off the side of the stone, ripping off my veil, and looked into the eyes of the demon. "Come out, come out, all of you. Possess them, torment the men, but do not touch the women."

The pain in my forehead... eased... it not only eased, but it began to glow with black light. My body felt euphoric, and suddenly, when I turned to see the bishop, it wasn't the bishop but a tall, dark, horrifying creature—a demon. The light in the cathedral turned a pale purple, and I was seeing things others couldn't. A large, black-bodied demon radiated outward from the bishop and regarded me. He gracefully moved his pointed hands, summoning more darkness, as demons sprouted from the altar's steps.

Screams of men began shattering around the sanctuary. The demon gestured a long arm to where my supposed father cowered on the priest's throne.

"You will die today," I said confidently as more shrieks echoed around me. "But first, you will hear their screams, and you will say my name." My voice echoed and my body felt electrified, glowing black.

And then suddenly, the doors to the sanctuary burst open, and when I turned, my exorcist priest strode forward, hooded and dark, with another man beside him. He found me immediately, ignoring the men on their knees screaming, their bodies contorting at odd angles. When he made it up the altar, he cupped my face. I opened my mouth to speak, but before I could, his mouth was on mine, kissing me passionately.

"You didn't send me away?" I asked, gasping into his embrace.

"Never," he answered. He looked over his shoulder. "Doesn't look like you need my rescuing though."

I cupped his scarred jaw in my hands, pulling his forehead to mine. "But I do, Father Amorth. You see... demons have possessed every man in this church. I believe we are in need of an exorcist."

Behind Dante came the sisters, standing proud in their black robes. "We could help with that as well," Sister Elodie smiled, flashing her fangs.

"Feed, bleed them, but leave Benedict for last. Let him listen to every moment of me slaughtering his congregation," I said with authority that was mine.

The man beside Dante raised his eyebrows. "Not so shy and scared now, are you? Nice mark of the kindred," he said casually as if blood wasn't pooling on the marble floor around us. I recognized him then as Dante's brother Nikolai. "No— I'm not afraid of the dark anymore. I am the dark. Let them bleed. Let the walls bleed."

Nikolai smirked, tapping his own upside-down cross that appeared on his forehead, matching the other tattoos scrawled across his mysterious face. The ground rumbled beneath us as men screamed. The nuns ascended, biting priests' necks and drinking their blood as demons ravaged the clergy from the inside out. Other priests spasmed and shrieked as the demons inhabited their bodies, tormenting them.

Dante prowled among them slowly, like a professor overlooking students' homework, deciding who he would exorcise, to kill, and when. Letting the demons have their fill. Demons and exorcist at peace, working together to destroy the main church of Lady of Sorrow and bring down the leaders of the others.

Sister Grace smiled with bloody teeth up at me. "The rituals, the chants, the song of your mother, were all for you. We should have seen it sooner." She lightly brushed the upside-down cross on my forehead. "Evil suits you, Selah."

"Thank you," I grinned back at her. And then the sisters began their chants, and a hymn echoed through the bloodied marble and screams of suffering holy men. Tears pricked my eyes, and I felt my mother's dark spirit in the room that tried to kill her— but she lived on through me. Through her songs of protection.

May Satan love her and, in the darkness, find her.

May every sin empower, and may she partake in every fruit from every forbidden tree.

Send the snakes to tempt her, hurry the goats to keep her, let every baphomet find and guard her.

May she be the greatest of evil to burn the holy, mar the mighty, and bring the men of power to ash.

For every soul damned to heaven.

For every child taught they were dirty.

For every woman cursed to serve as a rib from his chest.

Use the rib, stab his heart, and drink his blood.

May it be.

May the devil guide her.

May the reaper find her.

Dante was squeezing the life from a priest, working in tandem with the demon inside the man, and when I approached, he dropped the body to the ground—taking me into his arms.

"I guess the ritual came true— I found my reaper. My mother's wish... though it appears I am quite evil."

Dante lightly ran a finger over my forehead mark. "Then you are my counterpart, my goddess, and the greatest failed exorcism of my life. I will serve as your guard dog for eternity."

The sound of rain or rushing water radiated around us, and my baphomet was soon behind me. Before Dante could remark, I pointed behind him over the men being strangled to death by demon possession. "Look, the walls are bleeding."

And they were. The walls of Lady of Sorrow Church poured with blood. It puddled on the ground like rainwater, washing all the white in red. Leaving my exorcist, I rejoined my father as he shook from his throne.

"Get up," I ordered. "That's my seat now."

Dante was by my side instantly, grabbing the back of Benedict's head and throwing him to the ground while I took my seat.

"I want you to hear and feel what comes next," I said as Dante placed a loving hand on my shoulder. I looked at him and asked, "Get the nuns and women out? I will be right there."

"I'm not leaving you," he answered but motioned to Sister Grace, who seemed to understand his instruction as she wiped the blood from her chin and began gathering the women and ushering them out. The ladies of sorrows' robes were drenched in blood, but not their blood.

Never again would it be their blood.

I closed my eyes and focused on the dark energy inside me. No longer running from it, feeling guilt or shame, I'd made peace with my legion of demons. I loved my demons, and they loved me back. Thoughts flowed through my mind, and the space warmed to an uncomfortable heat as fire sprang from pews.

Wood cracked and white marble moaned as flames licked up every surface of the pristine sanctuary. I burnt it, I burnt it all. I burnt the church that tried to burn me but failed. The sacrificial stone broke in half and demons hissed their approval, like tea kettles, between their tormenting of their chosen holy men. The righteous had failed, they had failed miserably. The inferno raged more holy than the sacred fires told in all the sermons from the sacred text. These flames rivaled hell and were a hell of my own creation.

Nikolai chuckled before leisurely stepping over a writhing, possessed priest. "I guess now we know what you are. Nice to have met you, Mother Selah." He gave a small wave before disappearing into the flames.

I spat at Benedict as he cowered on the ground,"Mother Selah is fitting, and you will die here with your church."

"There are more sorrow churches, and they will come for you. The Lady of Sorrow will not be stopped by your evil," he warned shakily.

"Say. Her. Name." Dante growled, kneeling by his head.

"Selah," Benedict cried, shaking and hugging his knees in terror. Dante had taken his eyes and I would take his life.

"But *you* will be stopped," I retorted to the pathetic man's curse before my name was the last word he'd ever utter. I stood, taking my exorcist's hand as a lash of fire pounced like a fox upon my father. He screamed and screamed as the flame-seared him, coiling around him like a snake that had found me, just as my mother wanted, and it slowly seared his body before it burnt his beautiful church.

Once we were outside, beneath the plumes of black smoke, Dante squeezed my hand. "Let's go home."

I swallowed, my heart full. The dark mark etched thickly and not leaving my forehead, now was a sign of my transformation, a sign of who and what I truly was. It was protection left over from my mother and so many women before me.

Voiceless, nameless, *until me.*

"Yes, let's go *home.*"

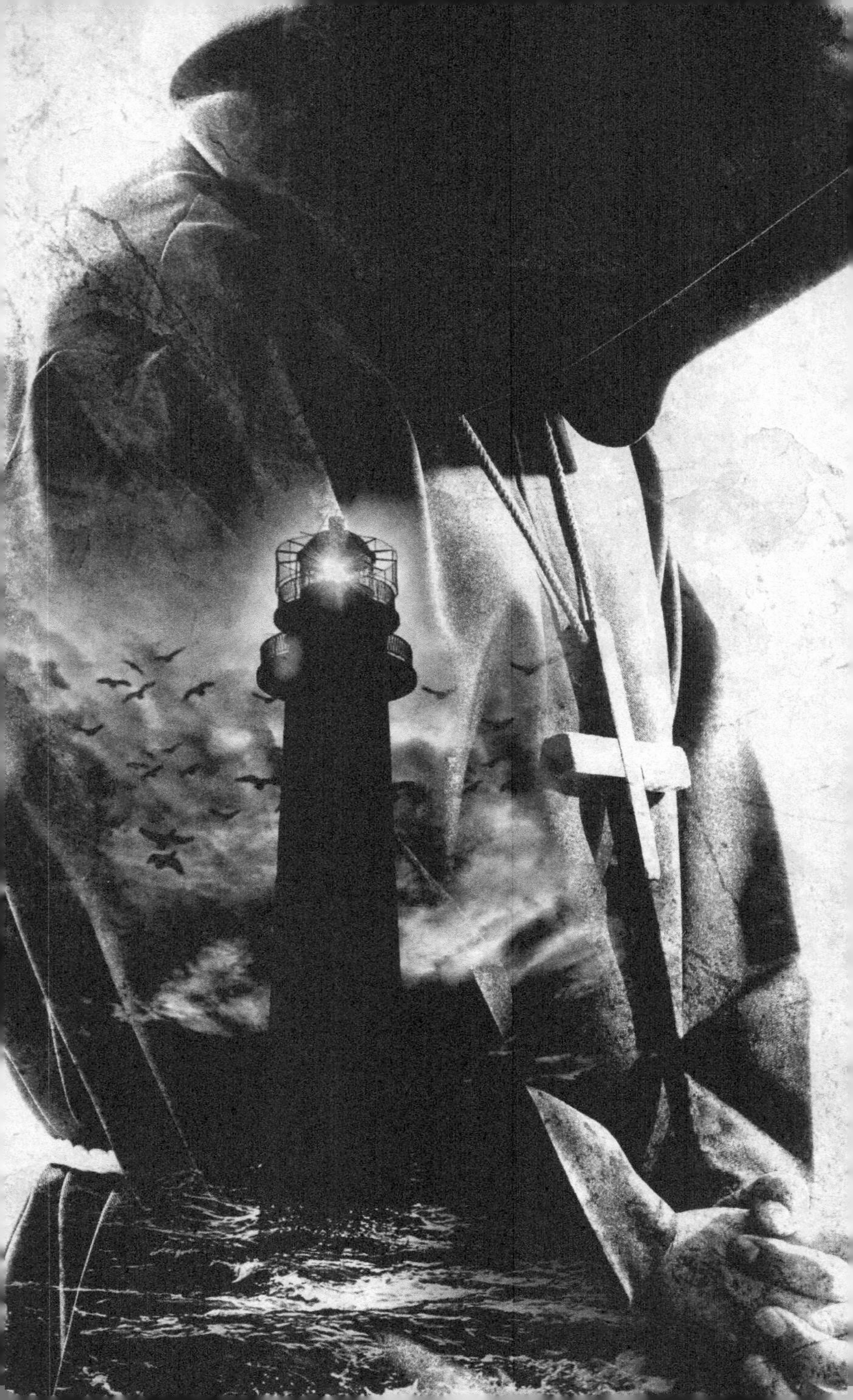

CHAPTER THIRTY-THREE

"I will kill you now or at a later date. Your fate is whatever she allows." I wouldn't keep Selah from any of these conversations, and she was eager to be involved. She had taken an active role in everything from transporting the ladies of sorrow to Grimm, to making sure classes at the university were still on schedule and nothing was amiss. To say I was proud of her would be an understatement. Perhaps most had underestimated her in her life, I felt that I had always known this strength and power existed within her. To see it shine was a blessing I didn't deserve, one my other brother would surely come to collect payment for.

Silas offered me a small glare before leaning on his office desk and turning to Selah. "I cannot convey my deepest regrets in what I did to you, Selah. It was my only choice in that moment, and had I known what horrors I was sending you into... I would have protected you— I would have sheltered you here. Please, please accept my deepest apologies."

"Not good enough," I growled. Selah put a silencing hand on my arm.

"I understand why you did what you did with the information you had. You're right that Lady of Sorrows has operated in secrecy for far too long. Secrets I hadn't even uncovered, and I lived within their mission my entire life. And there are more churches like it. Though, I did just burn the main one to the ground."

"The sanctuary was burnt. The rest of the building is mainly intact," Silas mused, stroking his white stubble. "I am concerned for what the brother churches will do when they piece together what happened. If they ever learned the real reason why the priests were sent to a wedding never returned home."

I huffed in annoyance. "What are you angling at?"

Silas's stare remained fixed on Selah, who was no longer wearing white robes but black trousers and a black lace shirt. Her long dark hair cascaded over her shoulders, and her eyes shone bright beneath her thick-rimmed glasses. God, she was a dark vision, an evil temptress, and she was mine.

He tilted his head slightly, examining her. "You are... an antichrist of sorts. The demons call you mother. Your touch, your essence, calls to the darkness and demons like some sort of beacon. They obey you, too, much like children. You're a sort of guardian, I believe, just as we are." He motioned to me and the cathedral beyond. "We have never been able to infiltrate Lady of Sorrows. There are more priests like us, more sisters like the ones here, and our vow and calling are to protect those Lady of Sorrow have forgotten and abused. Though I'm afraid their walls are high, and clearly from what you all have told me, and we just witnessed of them, what they did to your mother...

there is a great magic working with them. With you... we have an in."

"No," I snarled. Selah's hand tightened on my bicep, and she stood, crossing her arms.

"I'm not letting Dante kill you... *today*.... But I think I know what I want to do." She turned to me and raised her eyebrows in a challenge that I shut the hell up. I was glad my hood concealed my smile. "You will go to Lady of Sorrows... as the new Reverend and head priest." She held up a finger at my objection as I stood. "Dante and I will stay here and run the school with the sisters. But I will check in a few times a month and make appearances as the Holy Daughter. Would that be enough to get you the intel you needed? Would it be enough to bring them down?"

Silas's mouth dropped, and a soft white glow enveloped him. "It would be more than enough— Selah, we could rescue thousands and destroy their entire operation from the inside... as long as they bought it."

"I'm sure you can convince them the fire was an accident or act of vandalism against the clergy."

Silas countered, "I could build a new clergy of folks like us while I'm at it... it would be a long game. I would have to preach the same sermons and go through the same motions as Benedict had. There would be much groundwork to lay with the other Lady of Sorrow churches but... the access it would grant us... is astronomical."

Selah turned to me then and patted my chest. "Good boy for not killing him right away."

"This is ludicrous," I murmured to my brother's smug face. "You won't be able to pull it off. Their roots are too deep, and their mission is more sinister than we ever imagined. There is dark magic protecting them."

Silas shrugged. "Maybe you're just worried about running the university without me now. Perhaps Father Joseph would visit from Ash Grove and lend you a hand. You know, I've heard stories that he communes with the devil himself now."

I rolled my eyes. "We'll manage."

Selah interjected. "And I don't want to lie to the students here anymore. They're curious, and they know something is going on that you're not telling them. We should trust them with the truth. No more hiding things."

Silas chuckled as I stared down at her. I wanted to argue, but I also found myself turned on by her sense of authority.

"This is going to be fun," my brother said.

Selah smiled. "So much fun."

CHAPTER THIRTY-FOUR

One year later

The new school year brought two dozen new students. With Silas's inside involvement, we were able to rescue more people, and swifter now. These eighteen-year-olds were fresh from Lady of Sorrow Churches from all over the world. And Lady of Sorrow still regarded me as their Holy Daughter. When I made my appearances, I wore white, and I played my role, only now I was even more revered, exponentially more precious now that god had spared me during a vicious attack from the devil that wiped out the entire clergy and all ladies of sorrow in the main, Father Church of the religion.

The rescued ladies of sorrow, of course, were safe at Grimm. Learning, healing, and working with the sisters and me, to break their curses, regain their voices and remember their names.

Silas was a natural in his role and played the part well. Dante would argue *too* well.

My attire at Grimm was black gowns with no veil, only my two long braids and glasses. I'd joined the sisters in their teachings and full moon rituals, with Dante watching on as the faithful guardian he was.

A student raised her hand. "Excuse me, Mother Selah. The bananas at our desks... will this be a lesson on purity?"

I smiled, "There's no such thing as pure or impure, dear. These are just snacks. We just got a shipment of fresh fruit in, and I thought I'd share. Welcome to Grimm, I can't wait to be your professor this year."

They'd whisper about the upside down cross etched in black on the middle of my forehead. And when they were ready to hear the tale, I'd tell them. I'd tell them as unabashedly as Mrs. Paramour had shared her lust-filled journeys.

In the end, I wasn't a virtuous woman. I wasn't a Proverbs 31 wife. No psalms would be written about me and my virtue. But I began my journey toward my exorcism as a nameless title, as The Holy Daughter, a piece of fruit that dare not be bruised so as to offer my virginity to a man with fewer rules and more freedom than me.

Even the name I was given meant *the end*—a period to a song, the ending of something beautiful. Until I met my demons, and they taught me that in fact the mystery of my name was so much more. That it meant what I wanted it to mean, that *Selah* could, in fact, mean a new beginning, the start of a new song entered.

I was no longer a holy daughter, or a spotless virgin. There was nothing about me that would tempt a man down an aisle of matrimony. My old church was right in that I was riddled with sin, filled with demons, and that the outside world had sunk its claws into me so deep I'd never be saved from the fires of hell.

But in the end, unlike the virtuous woman, the Proverbs 31 wife, the holy daughter, lady of sorrow, the sacred virgin—

I had a name.

And they'd remember it now.

This is the book inspired by my *own* word, my own testimony, my very own holy text of which to live my life by.

This book, this life, I wrote for me.

I'd always lived two lives. Arriving in Grimm, I was a lost sheep. In being banished by my dad, I'd found my Father. My entire life, I hid who I was under the cover of something righteous. But somehow, in meeting my exorcist, I didn't have to hide anymore, not from him at least. Now, I'd pretend to be a nun, using holy robes and prayer beads to cover up my naked and unyielding desire for my Father...

Buried with *darkness* in baptism... resurrected to live a brand new life.

My name is mine.

I am Selah Gothic.

You are forgiven

Acknowledgements

ALWAYS THANKFUL TO MY FRIENDS WHO BECAME FAMILY. THE ONES I COULDN'T WRITE WITHOUT. I WOULD NAME YOU, BUT NO ONE DESERVES TO BE ASSOCIATED WITH THIS BLASPHEMOUS SACRED TEXT.

TO THE READERS THAT WILL CONNECT WITH THIS. I'M SORRY THAT YOU DO, BUT I HOPE IN SOME SMALL MEASURE, SELAH, DANTE, AND GRIMM SHINED A LIGHTHOUSE OF COMFORT INTO YOUR SOUL.

TO THE PEOPLE WHO SHOVED BANANAS IN MY HANDS AND MADE ME FEEL UNWORTHY... THANKS FOR THE INSPIRATION. I CREATED THIS MONSTER FROM THE PRAYERS OF YOURS THAT DIDN'T WORK.

UNTIL NEXT TIME...

Kat Blackthorne

-HAUNTING ROMANCE-

ABOUT THE AUTHOR

KAT BLACKTHORNE IS A BESTSELLING AUTHOR OF HAUNTING ROMANCE. SHE WRITES PASSION, CHARACTERS, AND WORLDS THAT SHAKE THE CHAINS IN THE ATTIC OF YOUR MIND. HER TALES EMBRACE COZY DARKNESS WITH MAGICAL AND SPOOKY TWISTS. CATNIP FOR KAT IS BANTER, BEGGING, CHALLENGING NORMS, AND MEN WHO WORSHIP THEIR WOMEN.

KAT BELIEVES IN CELEBRATING THE BEAUTY INSIDE THE DARKNESS OF OCCULT AND DARK THEMES. DEMONS, HELL, THE UNDERWORLD, AND EVERYTHING SPOOKY CALLS TO HER AND BRINGS HER COMFORT. POLYAMOROUS AND QUEER ROMANCE ARE HER FAVORITE TO WRITE, AND SHE'S PASSIONATE ABOUT SHOWCASING CHARACTERS THE MORTAL WORLD TOO OFTEN OVERLOOKS. ALL SIZES, ABILITIES, AND ADULT AGES.

IN 2022 KAT FOUNDED HER LLC, DARK HEARTS PRESS FOR PUBLISHING EVERYTHING HER SPOOKY HEART DESIRES.

IN HER FREE TIME, SHE'S DISASSOCIATING WITH SOME OTHER ART FORM AND ENABLING HER STARBUCKS ADDICTION.

ALSO BY

Kat Blackthorne

- HAUNTING ROMANCE -

THE HALLOWEEN BOYS SERIES

GHOST

DRAGON

WOLF

DEVIL

LADY VENOM TAKES A MISTRESS

Made in the USA
Las Vegas, NV
01 April 2024